EVERYTHING WE ARE

Cover Design by Melissa Williams Design

Cello by Gstudio Group, Adobe Stock

Microphone by grimgram, Adobe Stock

Speaker by ilia, Adobe Stock

Lights by tartumedia, Adobe Stock

Fame Star by Eduard Radu, Shutterstock

Janci's author photo by Michelle D. Argyle

Megan's author photo by Heather Cavill

Published by Garden Ninja Books

ExtraSeriesBooks.com

First Edition: June 2019

0 9 8 7 6 5 4 3 2 1

EVERYTHING WE ARE

THE EXTRA SERIES *Book 3*

MEGAN WALKER & JANCI PATTERSON

For Andy Patterson

ONE

Felix

'm sitting on Hollywood Boulevard, a few feet from Johnny Cash's star on the Walk of Fame, playing my cello rendition of "Ghost Riders in the Sky," when I spot the drug deal going down across the street. My bow hand starts to shake, resulting in some skating on the strings. I'm probably the only one who can hear it, but it still makes me grit my teeth. I've always prided myself on my steady hands.

But I guess six weeks of heroin detox will do that to you.

A kid wearing skinny jeans and a fedora skates by and drops a condom into my cello case. There are six others in there—the peril, I suppose, of busking two blocks down from a Planned Parenthood.

I look down at my strings, even though I don't need to. This song isn't exactly a Haydn Concerto, but I need somewhere to look besides at the two guys leaning against the wall of The Vine, exchanging something from hand to hand.

I pick up the pace of the song to cover for the shaking, gradually, so no one else will notice the shift in time. Honestly, my audience right now consists of a lesbian couple making out with their hands in each other's hair and the homeless guy camped out by Humphrey Bogart's star with a wrinkled cardboard sign that reads "My wife had a better lawyer," so I'm pretty sure I could switch keys mid-song and no one would bat an eye.

When I look up at the front of the theater again, one of the men is gone, walking casually down the street, a hand in his pocket, no doubt comforting himself that his newly-acquired gear is still there.

It might not be heroin. It could be something else. But somewhere at the back of my brain a shrill pitch like the elusive F6 sharp—the highest note I've produced on my cello—vibrates through my bones.

If the dealer doesn't have any H, he'll know where I can get some, and it won't be far. I close my eyes and repeat the refrain of the song, adding in my mind a mantra. I'm not going to walk over there. I'm not. I'm not. But my brain is already calculating how much change, how many small bills have been discarded into my case this afternoon.

It's enough to buy at least a quarter gram, which is lower than what I used to take, but probably enough after six weeks sober.

I finish the song and look up to see a man walking his border collie pausing in front of my case, throwing in a dollar. I smile at him, but I know it looks weak. I lower my bow, just for a moment.

And then I lift it again and start playing "Walk the Line." I play it fast, and with far more vibrato than necessary, because it requires more movement. While I play, I glance up at the dealer, still leaning against the wall of The Vine, no doubt waiting for his next customer.

It's not going to be me. It's not. I look down at Johnny's star, and try not to remember, as I play his song about sobriety and fidelity, that he relapsed again and again.

But I close my eyes again. I stay on my stool. My cello's name is June, and like Johnny, I try to stick with her. I think about the thirty-day chip buried in my pocket. I keep my hands moving. I don't go across the street to look for drugs.

When I finish the song, someone claps. I look up and find a kid standing in front of me with sandy blond hair and a sweater-vest—an odd choice for the late-July heat. I look around, but I don't see an adult with him, even though he can't be more than six or so. Definitely not old enough to be wandering the slummy neighborhoods of Hollywood alone, looking like some all-boys prep-school escapee.

"You're good!" he announces.

I smile. "Thanks, kid."

"My mom's a musician," he says. "Her friend Mason plays the cello, but Mason is a douche."

My laugh sounds natural. "Is that right?"

"Yeah. It's okay if I say that word to you. You aren't a nana, or the pope." He squints at me. "Are you?"

I laugh again, and put down my bow, pulling out a set of wipes and cleaning the sweat off my hands. "Am I the pope?"

"I don't think you are," he says, studying me carefully. "My mom says the pope wears a funny hat, and drives a popemobile, which sounds like a superhero, but he's not."

"No, I'm not the pope." I look around again, but still no parent. "Where did you come from, kid?"

"My mom," he says, like I'm a bit slow on the uptake. "And my biological father. That's like a dad who isn't there for you." He scuffs the tip of his black loafer against the sidewalk.

I have no idea how to respond to that, so I toss my wipe into the end of my cello case where someone else has donated a used Kleenex, and backtrack. "So what did Mason do to you?"

"Nothing," the kid says. "But he did drugs and stole money from my mom."

I stare at him for a moment, and out of the corner of my eye, I see the dealer check his watch and then mosey down the block, probably headed to his next appointment.

"Well," I say. "That does make him a douche." I'm hoping a parent is going to show up soon, because I'm fairly certain Planned Parenthood doesn't provide missing child drop-off services, and I really don't love the idea of him wandering out here alone.

God knows I'm hardly fit to be responsible for myself, let alone him.

Jenna

'm standing at the counter of a game store down on Hollywood Boulevard, waiting for the cashier to ring up *The Game of Life*, which my eight-year-old son has just selected for family game night after much deliberation. Ty has shuffled off behind a rack of board games, which makes me wonder if he's going to change his mind immediately after the game has been rung up.

If he does, I suppose I can buy a second one, too. Games go fast on family night with only the two of us playing. Not that we don't have a mountain of other games to choose from at home.

My phone beeps and I look down at it, just as the cashier takes my credit card. It's a message from our manager, Phil.

I sent you another list of potential cellists, it says.

I sigh. My band is about to go on tour in a month, and last week I discovered, while going over some accounts, that our cellist—not to mention our *friend*—Mason, had been stealing money from us to support his drug habit.

Thanks, I text back.

I can practically hear Phil opening his jar of antacids and chewing them by the handful. Alec and I are super hands-on with band management, and all decisions go through us.

Sometimes, though, I think Phil would rather we just let him get things done, especially with tour so close. Finding a cellist who's good enough to play our stuff, has zero prior commitments, can take off on tour with us with only a few weeks' notice, gels with the band, *and* is someone I'm comfortable having around my son?

That's not something either Alec or I are willing to leave to

Phil. Especially after what happened with Mason.

The cashier at the game store grips my credit card in her hand, and her eyes flick down to my name, then widen. "Jenna Rollins. From Alec and Jenna?"

"Yep," I tell her. Getting recognized still feels new to me, even though it's been happening increasingly often over the last year and a half. I try to take my card before she asks any uncomfortable questions I'll have to lie to answer.

She pulls it back, pressing it over her chest like it's something near and dear to her heart.

"I'm a huge fan. I mean, your music is so—" She closes her eyes, as if she's too overcome to finish the sentence. "It's just so inspiring, your love story. It makes me believe that—"

Somewhere in the middle of this utterance, I realize I haven't heard Ty moving around behind the game racks in a while, and he's not one to hold still unless he's found someplace very small to hole up.

If he gets stuck behind some game store rack and requires the fire department to extract him again—

"Ty!" I call. I stand on my toes to try to peer over the racks of board games and dangling novelty keychains. No Ty.

"—that love like that is just around the corner, you know?" she continues, as if I haven't said a word. "That I could just meet some guy and we'll fall madly in love like you two, that kind of love that can weather anything and—"

I take a step back to peer around the racks. I don't see Ty, but I also don't see any small spaces he might have climbed into. He hasn't done that in a while, so he's probably outgrown it. I dearly hope.

But the door to the store is wide open.

Shit.

"Ty!" I call again, hoping he's just outside the door, jumping from star to star on the sidewalk. I reach for my card, but the cashier is still clutching it to her.

"I'm so sorry," I say, and I mostly am, but my nerves are

spiking because Ty's eight, and though he's not about to run out into the street or anything, no amount of discussion about not talking to strangers has ever done any good. "I need to hurry, my son is—"

"—and I mean, really, if he was as hot as Alec, I wouldn't care much if he could sing, you know what I—"

"I really need my card, please," I say, taking a few steps toward the door. I can't see Ty on the stoop out front. Shit shit shit.

I don't have time for this. I stomp back to the counter and lean across it enough to rip my credit card away from her chest. Then I grab the plastic-wrapped game I just bought and hurry out onto the sidewalk, avoiding seeing the look of shock or betrayal on her face.

It'll be one of those five-minute twitter storms I hate. She'll tweet about how awful I am—tweeting it right @ me, no doubt, so I don't miss it—and lots of fans will jump to my defense and others will say how they always knew I was a bitch and Alec could do so much better.

You're welcome to him, I wish I could say.

"Ty!" I call again, looking both directions. To the left, a long stretch of street has a few tourists taking pictures of the Hollywood stars, and a homeless man sitting cross-legged and appearing for all the world like he's meditating. No sign of Ty. To the right, there's a liquor store, and then the street intersects with Hollywood Boulevard proper. I hope with everything in me that he's just around that corner.

It's a short jog to the corner—would be shorter, I suppose, if I was wearing something more practical than my three-inch-heeled black boots—but my mom brain has already summoned every nightmare scenario that could come to my child because of my neglect.

"Ty!" I yell as I turn the corner. And there I see him down the street, my little boy in the sweater vest and button-down he insists on wearing even during the summer, his mop of golden hair picking up rays of sunshine. He's standing in front of a busker with a cello. He turns and waves.

"Hi, Mom!" he calls brightly. Like he didn't nearly just give me a heart attack.

My relief is immediate and near-overwhelming. I let out a breath, my pounding heart starting to slow.

Still, for him to just run off like that, in this part of town . . .

"Ty!" I say, in the voice that usually precedes him losing video game privileges. "You can't just run off like that." As soon as I get close to him, though, I give him a hug—more for me than for him, since clearly he wasn't the least bit afraid.

"I didn't run off. I was listening to the music."

And that's when I really see the guy holding the cello.

The *incredibly good-looking* guy holding the cello.

He looks about my age, and has a kind of casual but preppy vibe, with a blue button-down open over a plain gray t-shirt and nice, dark-wash jeans. The blue in his shirt heightens the clear blue of his eyes, and his blond hair falls just over his ears. He's giving me The Look—the one that says he recognizes me but doesn't know where from. I'm really used to that look, especially when I'm not with Alec.

He's also giving me another kind of look I'm not totally unfamiliar with—the one where his gaze drifts down and back up. Where his lips twitch in a kind of stunned smile.

I know I should be thinking about filling that position in our band, but maybe not with a guy this sexy.

I don't think Alec would appreciate *that*.

Felix

This kid's mom looks up at me, her pale gray eyes taking me in. She tugs down the hem of her short black lace dress, which hugs her figure and ends mid-thigh—and rode up higher when she bent to hug the kid. She looks familiar, but I'm sure I don't know her, because I would definitely remember a woman this gorgeous. With her long black hair streaked with bright red highlights, she has a sort of punk-rock beauty that's intimidating as hell, but in a good way. She looks about my age—way too young to have a six-year-old. But he did call her mom.

"He's good like Mason," Ty says. "You should hear him play."

The woman smiles, and I see her check me out and like what she sees. "Is that right?"

Now my hands are sweating for an entirely different reason. I've never exactly had trouble with women, but it's been years since I've hit on anyone while sober.

"Yeah, well," I say. "I hear Mason is a douche."

She looks sharply down at Ty, and he grins up at her. "Mason is a douche," she says. "But you don't have to tell that to every-body."

"It's okay, Mom," Ty says. "He says he's not the pope."

She laughs, a clear, good-natured sound that makes her even more beautiful.

"I get asked that a lot," I tell her.

Her eyes crinkle as she smiles at me.

I gesture to the box she's carrying. "That game is terrible,"

I say. "Have you played it lately? It's all bankruptcy and dead-end jobs."

"Like real life," she says, and I smile.

"Yeah. Way too real."

"I'm going to win," Ty says. "I always win."

She shakes her head at him. "I might beat you at this one."

"No way," he says. "I'm going to be a doctor and have all the kids."

"We'll see," she says. I expect her to herd the kid away, but instead she looks me over again, her eyes lingering on my cello.

"I hear you're a musician," I say. If she's wanting to stick around longer, I'm more than happy to keep the conversation rolling.

She shrugs. "I play piano a little. But you definitely look like you know how to straddle that thing."

I grin at her, and she smiles back, the suggestion passing back and forth between us, and apparently over the head of the kid, who is eyeing the condoms in my cello case. "Can I have one of your candies?" he asks.

"No," I say, too quickly. "They're . . . not very good."

"What do they taste like?" he asks.

I open my mouth, but no words come out. I look up at the kid's mom, waiting for her to bail me out, but her eyes dance instead, and for a moment I can't look away.

"Rubber," I say.

She laughs again and the little boy squints up at her. I run my hand down the neck of my cello, unable to stop smiling.

"Well," she says, and she's got this mischievous quirk to her lips that kills me. "Why don't you play for me? I'd like to see your fingering."

Ty looks back and forth between the two of us, and I sure as hell hope he isn't understanding.

"Happy to please," I say, picking up my bow.

I've been playing Johnny Cash all afternoon—I made up my own covers of his songs back in high school as a way to warm up and wind down from more difficult practice.

But for this girl, I want to play something different.

I choose an Apocalyptica cover of "Enter Sandman." It's complex and beautiful and interesting—all the things I'm imagining she is after only a few moments of meeting her. I look up at her while I play, and her expression has gone from amused to impressed. She likes what she hears, and she's paying enough attention to what I'm doing that I'm wondering if she may know a thing or two herself.

When I finish, her face is serious. "I'm going to give you my number," she says, reaching into her purse.

My mouth falls open a little, and I smile. "I won't argue with that."

"I want you to come audition for my band," she says.

I blink. "Your band."

"Yes," she says, holding a card out to me. "I'm Jenna Rollins, from Alec and Jenna. We're going on tour in a few weeks and we just lost our cellist—"

I lose track of what she's saying as my brain stutters over the first part. That's why she looked familiar. She's *Jenna*. From Alec and Jenna. I've heard stuff from their new album playing on the radio, noticed the cello pieces, but that's not what stops me.

Alec and Jenna are in love, like dramatic-movie "kiss-in-the-rain, roll-end-credits" kind of love—most of their songs are duets about their relationship. She was a teen mom and Alec stepped in and parents her kid—*this* kid. Their perfect couplehood practically *is* the band. If they're going on tour then there hasn't been some breakup I didn't hear about.

But there is no way in hell she wasn't just hitting on me.

Shit, I think, and then realize she's waiting for me to respond. "Your cellist is Mason Brenner," I say. "He's good. I've heard him play."

"He's also a douche," she says. "So we're in the market." She's still holding out the business card, and I take it. It's done in sleek grays and black, and behind her name and phone number is the

Alec and Jenna "AJ" logo.

"Let me give you my number, too," I say, because I'm not sure how I'm going to convince myself to call up Jenna Rollins and ask to audition for her and her boyfriend. Especially because she's even more beautiful in person.

"Sure." She pulls out her phone. "And you are?"

"Felix," I say. "Felix Mays."

She smiles at me, and I get the sense that she knows exactly how confused I am. I'm beginning to wonder if she and Alec have some kind of open relationship they somehow manage to keep secret.

I give her my number, though I have to fish it out of my phone. It's a new one, on my dad's phone plan, so my dealer can't reach me and my old friends can't call. Which means the contacts list on this thing is embarrassingly bare, but I'm not about to show her that.

Jenna fidgets with the clasp on her purse, still smiling. "I really hope you'll audition for us. I'd love to work with you."

I can't imagine why that would be, but I also know I can't turn it down. "What do you want me to play for the audition?"

"Anything," she says. "But preferably something you love." And then she puts a hand on her son's shoulder and he waves at me, and they walk off down Hollywood Boulevard along the row of stars.

I grip my bow, stare after them, and wonder what the hell just happened.

TWO

Felix

My sister Gabby calls while I'm packing up. When I answer, she sounds nervous, which for Gabby means overly enthusiastic, like a cheerleader on uppers.

"Hey, Felix! How're you doing!"

I know exactly what she means to ask. "Hey, Gabs," I say. "Still clean."

She lets out a tiny relieved sigh and her voice dips to a more natural pitch. "That's good, Felix. Really good."

"Agreed." Now, with that out of the way, we can have a conversation without her trying to discern the state of my sobriety from unrelated news. Any less direct answer would only serve to increase her anxiety. I don't fault her for it. She loves me, and I put her through hell. Any response she deems "dodgy," and she'll be peppering me with questions designed to divine the truth without having to outright ask.

Probably because she's learned from experience that if I'm back on drugs, I'm not going to answer honestly.

"You will never believe what happened to me today," I say.

"You still coming over for dinner?" she asks. "You can tell me all about it. Will has his critique group tonight and I'm just getting off my shift now, so I can grab us some take out."

"We're still on," I say. Before I got out of rehab this last time,

16

I'd only spoken to my sister once in six months, when she came to visit me in treatment and stared at me like I'd been diagnosed with a terminal brain tumor. When I got out, I begged her to give me my cello back so I could make money doing something other than cashiering at the gas station, where not only would half the clientele be high, but the meniality of the job made it a constant fight not to put a needle in my arm.

She'd cautiously agreed, getting it from where she'd had it stashed in a climate-controlled storage unit to which only her boyfriend had the key. I'd known when I started using again that she was the only one I could trust to keep me from pawning it, even if I begged her or broke into her apartment. Both of which I did.

God, she has every right to hate me. I'm beyond thankful she doesn't. And more, that she actually seems to want me back in her life.

"I'm feeling Chinese," Gabby says, and I know she's talking about this crazy place she loves.

"Get me the Mountain Dew Chicken," I say. "And a couple of those breakfast egg rolls. The ones with the sausage."

"Done. See you at my place in an hour?"

"Give me an hour and a half," I say. "I've got to run by the clinic first."

Gabby pauses and takes a deep breath. I've told her that the medication is prescribed, and I can only take it under supervision of the clinic at least for another week or two, but I know it still makes her nervous. I don't blame her. Suboxone is an opiate, and I'm in recovery. I didn't want to stay on the stuff myself, but my therapist sat me down with the numbers and convinced me I had a much better chance of staying clean if I let the maintenance drugs block some of the cravings, probably for a couple of years.

"Okay," Gabby says. "See you in a few."

I hang up, empty my cello case of today's earnings, and put my cello away. I'm not loving the dirt left behind by leaving her case open, so I'm thinking if I want to keep doing this I might need to get my backup case from my dad's place for money collection.

If I don't get a job with Alec and Jenna, which seems so far-fetched I'm beginning to wonder if I imagined it.

Except there's her card tucked in my pocket, next to my chip.

I load my cello into my dad's spare car and drive halfway back to Valencia to the clinic. It's at the facility where I did rehab— my dad read an article while I was still doing inpatient about people finding drug dealers out of corner Methadone clinics and insisted I do all my outpatient treatment at an upscale facility. I was fairly certain this was because he cared about me staying sober and not because he wanted to brag to his friends about how much my treatment cost. It doesn't make the treatment easier, but it does keep me out of sketchy neighborhoods where I would be more likely to find a dealer, so I didn't argue. After peeing in a cup (to ensure I'm not on heroin, and that I *am* on Suboxone) and swallowing my pill in front of the nurse, I head back to West Hollywood to Gabby's apartment.

Gabby opens her door and throws her arms around me, and already I can smell the delicious scents of Fong's, creators of all things that don't belong together and yet somehow do. I squeeze her back, and she holds on way longer than she used to. We were close before I went to New York, and I wish I could put things back the way they were.

I wish a lot of things I can't make happen.

Gabby lets me into her new apartment—I still think of it as her new place, though she's been here almost a year—which is a mismatched mess of mod furniture and stuff she bought on Craigslist.

"Still working on the exorcism of Sarah?" I ask. Last time I was here, all the furniture had been purchased by Will's ex-fiancée. Now Gabby's footprint is starting to contend with hers, at least.

Gabby rolls her eyes. "Getting closer. But until we sell that couch—" she points at a high-backed, sharp-angled purple

18

couch that dominates the living room—"we can't afford to buy another one."

"I'd buy it from you, but I don't have a room to put it in."

She raises an eyebrow at me. "There are only two kinds of people in this world. Those who can afford to buy our couch, and those who want it. I'm guessing you're in category B."

I smile. "Yeah. And I owe Dad enough money to buy a house in a lot of places." I pause. "Not in LA, though."

Gabby gives me a look that screams pity, and I wish I hadn't said that. It's my fault I've been in rehab three times. It's my fault I didn't stay clean the first time. Or the second.

"Are you going to pay him back for rehab?" she asks. "You know he doesn't expect it."

I shrug. "I know. And it'll probably take me the rest of my life, but I want to try. I want to pay back all of it—even though Dad said I should just pay him back for the two times I screwed it up."

"Ha," Gabby says. "That sounds like him."

Gabby dumps food on plates and we eat it on the purple couch, which is more comfortable than it looks. "Okay, so tell me about this incredible thing that happened to you today. Did you get thrown a fiver by Angelina Jolie?"

I smile, glad she finally asked. I've been dying to tell this to someone. To even say it out loud. "Better," I say. "I got hit on by Jenna Rollins."

Gabby scrunches up her face. "Whaaaat?" A piece of sauce-covered broccoli slides off her fork and onto her jeans, and she frowns at it. "There's no way."

"I'm serious. You know, from Alec and Jenna?"

"I know AJ," Gabby says. "They're Anna-Marie's favorite. She played their first album on a loop for three months."

Ah. Anna-Marie is Gabby's best friend. They were roommates before Anna-Marie moved in with her fiancé and Gabby moved in with Will.

"But she definitely did not hit on you," Gabby continues. "Jenna and Alec are like soul mates."

I stab my fork into a chunk of bright yellow chicken. "Well she was definitely hitting on me. She talked about my straddling and my fingering. It was crazy."

Gabby rolls her eyes, and wipes at the stain on her knee with one of the paper towels we're using as napkins. "That's just music talk."

I glare at her over a bite of chicken. "That is *not* how musicians talk. We don't sit around the cello section complimenting each other on our *straddling*."

Gabby still looks skeptical, which is a little insulting, but whatever.

"She asked me to audition for her band," I say.

Her eyes widen. This she seems to believe, at least. "Her *band*. She wants you to audition to play with AJ."

"That's what she said." I toss her Jenna's card, and her jaw drops. "Jenna Rollins gave you her card."

I smile. "And hit on me."

Gabby throws the card back at me. "She did *not* hit on you. You're just desperate. And you'd better remember that or you'll blow your audition." She grins, though, and squeals a little. "My brother could play with Alec and Jenna! Anna-Marie will die."

I give her a wry smile. "Anna-Marie doesn't know me as anything but a junkie."

Gabby wrinkles her nose. "She does remember you as the guy who broke into her apartment, but if you get to play with AJ, she just might forgive you."

I groan and flop back on the couch. I don't love being thought of—even rightfully—as that guy, but that's not what's consuming my mind right now. I just keep seeing Jenna's gray eyes, and the dress riding up her thigh. And god, that laugh ...

"You should have seen how hot this girl was," I say, shaking my head. "It's been a month and a half. I need to get laid."

Gabby eyes me over her broccoli beef soft taco. "Try twenty-three years."

I groan again. "Where's the sympathy? You have to know

someone you could hook me up with."

I both do and don't mean it. Since all of my friends have either left the area for college or are off getting high without me, I have quite literally no one to spend time with besides my immediate family, and since my other sister Dana won't let me see my nephew Ephraim for "a reasonable waiting period" out of rehab, not even all of them. I'm dying for some human connection, but I don't exactly want to hook up with random girls anymore. I'm trying to move past that, and besides, I didn't enjoy it that much, even before the drugs.

Jenna, on the other hand, didn't feel random.

Gabby points her fork at me. "I don't feel the need to know the girls you're hooking up with. And no, I don't have any available single friends."

"Come on," I say. "You have to know somebody."

"Anna-Marie is engaged. I've been hanging out with her fiancé's best friends, but they're both gay and married."

"Do your gay friends have any female friends? Come on, Gabby. I'm desperate."

Gabby rolls her eyes again. "Felix, I really don't want to know how horny you get after just a month and a half. You're barely out of rehab."

She's right, but I'm on a roll now, and I can't stop until I've garnered at least some pity. "Plus," I say, "sex on drugs kind of sucks, so it feels like a lot longer."

Now she looks interested. I figured that would do it. "Really?"

"Yeah," I say. "Half the time you're too high to get it up, and the other half you can't finish."

She cringes. "I did not need to know that about my brother."

She looks a little sorry for me, though, so I take that as a win and bite into my breakfast roll, which tastes like a cross between a pot-sticker and an Egg McMuffin. From what I heard in rehab from some of the veterans, being on Suboxone can be just as bad for your sex life, so I hope I'm one of the lucky ones whose symptoms get better and don't drag on for years, even off the H.

"Ooh!" Gabby said. "I could set you up with Sheena from work! But you'd have to be nice to her because she's the RN in charge of the whole shift schedule, so I really want to stay on her good side."

Gabby hasn't gotten fired from a job since she started nursing two years ago, but apparently she still worries about it. "I'm nice," I say. "And even Jenna Rollins thinks I'm hot."

"She does not," Gabby says. "You're cute, but Alec is a million times hotter."

I pretend to be offended, and maybe I mean it a little bit. When I was waiting for my pill at the clinic, I Googled Jenna and Alec, and scrolled through all their couple photos like a Facebook-stalking ex.

They do look cute together, and I hate him for it.

"I have to warn you, though," Gabby says. "Sheena is really fond of her hamsters. She's given them all personalities and matching little felt hats."

"The hats match the hamsters?" I ask. "Or—"

"The personalities. Like one is Napoleon, and another is wearing a fedora—"

I at once want to see these hamsters and am very afraid.

"They run in tubes through her house," Gabby says, "so they have access to all of the rooms. She drilled the holes and installed the whole thing herself, like one of those ball machines where the balls roll all over and then get lifted up to the bottom to go again." She pauses. "Except with hamsters."

I grimace. "Do the tubes run through the bedroom? Is this a sex thing?"

Gabby shakes her head. "Jeez, I hope not. But given the things I've seen come out of people's asses at work, I can't say I would be surprised."

It's my turn to point my fork at her. "Find out."

"Done," Gabby says.

"If it's not, you can set me up with her." This Jenna thing is not happening. I know it isn't. Even if she's in an open relationship, I really do not want to get in the middle of that—especially not with a girl with a laugh like hers.

Gabby's right. In a pissing match between me and Alec, I'm not going to win.

"I'll try," Gabby says. "But if you screw her over I'll be working graves for the rest of my life."

I'm doing Gabby's dishes—the least I can do since she bought dinner—when my phone rings next to the sink, and my heart climbs into my throat.

Every time the phone rings, I'm afraid my dealer or one of my old drug buddies has somehow found my number. I called them all before I left rehab and told them I was done, and most of them were cool with it. A couple of them swore at me over the phone, which actually helped, but if any of them get my number, they're bound to start inviting me back to parties, trying to get me to hang out, even if I don't use.

I can't do that. I'll never be able to do that, even if it means resigning myself to the company of Sheena the hamster-hat lady for the rest of my life.

I dry my hands and turn my phone over. It's a number I don't recognize—not my dealer, then, unless he got a new phone. I take a deep breath, and answer.

"Hey, Felix?"

I recognize Jenna's voice instantly. And now my heart's in my throat for an entirely different reason. "Yeah," I say. "Is this Jenna?"

Gabby looks up from the couch, where she's thumbing through the *Writer's Digest* website on her phone, trying to find markets for Will's novel. "Really?" she mouths.

I nod.

"Yeah, hey!" Jenna says. "I know this is kind of last minute, but the band's getting together tomorrow and I wondered if you wanted to come to the studio to audition."

"Sure," I say, before I can think about it. "I mean, I'll have to check with Johnny, of course. He schedules me pretty tight."

She pauses. "Oh, is Johnny your agent?"

"No," I say. "Johnny Cash. I'm booked for his star for the rest of the week."

"Ah," Jenna says, getting it now. "Well, if Johnny can spare you, we'd love to see you around three o'clock. I'll text you the address."

"I'll be there," I say. And I expect her to say bye and hang up, but she hesitates. Gabby's leaning toward me, as if she's torn between giving me space and coming over to press her ear to the phone.

"So how'd you get into busking?" Jenna asks.

"Oh, you know. Between tours with Springsteen and returning Clapton's calls—"

She laughs. "All right, fair enough. If that's my competition, maybe we'd better audition for you."

"I don't know," I say. "I think I can squeeze you in."

Gabby stares at me wide-eyed. I've been unconsciously smiling while I'm talking and I turn around so she won't see.

"Good," Jenna says. "Can I ask where your last job was?"

"You mean in music? It's been a little while, but I've played Carnegie Hall and with the LA opera—" I cringe. Not exactly the most exciting credits for an audition with a pop band.

"That's awesome. Don't worry if you haven't worked in music lately. I used to work as a roller-skating waitress. And I was horrible at it."

I smile, picturing her wobbling around on roller-skates in one of those god-awful diner uniforms. And looking cute as hell doing so. "But I bet you got a lot of tips."

She laughs. "Mostly from people who felt sorry for me, though there was the occasional guy I spilled on and had to help wipe down."

"No," I say.

"Ha. Sadly, yes."

I wait for her to gracefully make her exit, but she pauses again. I turn around and find Gabby leaning against the counter, her curiosity apparently overcoming her good manners.

"I'm really looking forward to playing for you," I say.

"Me too, Felix," she says, and the sound of my name from her mouth gives me chills. "See you tomorrow."

I hang up and try to shake off the goosebumps, but Gabby is staring at me.

"You're going to audition for AJ," she says.

"Yes," I say. "Tomorrow."

She lets out a squeal higher-pitched than any note ever played on a cello, and throws her arms around me again.

I need this job. I know I do.

But what makes my heart hammer is the thought of seeing Jenna Rollins again.

THREE

Felix

Alec and Jenna's practice space is in a flat-topped building in West Los Angeles, across the street from a Sprouts and a yoga place. I recognize the neighborhood—my last dealer liked it for its many small alleys, and I force myself not to look for his car.

Somewhere around two AM last night, when I was lying awake trying not to think about using, it occurred to me that joining a band might be hell on my sobriety. Not the music or the job, both of which I need, but the associations. So many people in music use that it's better than even odds *someone* playing for AJ is an addict—bonus points because their last cellist left them when his own addiction took him off the rails.

The idea of playing, traveling, staying at hotels with someone who's using was enough to break me out in a cold sweat. The long nights on the road or catching red-eye flights, the backstage parties, the appearances at clubs with people using in the corners—

I couldn't do this. I knew that I couldn't. Give me a week and I'd be flying high again, and I knew exactly where that led.

God only knew who I'd get killed this time.

It was only thoughts of Jenna that got me out of bed this

morning—or, more accurately, hauled my ass off of my dad's fold-out couch. I'd showered and dressed and driven out here—listening to Kurt Cobain's rendition of the Vaselines' "Jesus Doesn't Want Me for a Sunbeam" and humming along to Lori Goldstein's cello part—all the while telling myself it isn't hopeless. I'm not trapped in a world with dealers on every corner. I can stay safe and stay clean.

Even if I feel like I can't.

When I knock on the studio door, my palms are sweating. I'm greeted by a woman with cotton-candy pink hair, shaved on one side, wearing Converse sneakers and a little girl's jumpsuit-style dress made entirely of shiny black leather. I can't tell if the look is missing a whip or a Hello Kitty backpack. "Hey," she says. "Judging by the size of your instrument, I'm guessing you're Felix."

"Um, yeah," I say. The size of my instrument? God, maybe Gabby was right. Maybe pop musicians do just talk that way. But the way Jenna said it . . . I force myself back to the present. "And you're . . . Roxie?" I don't mean to sound unsure. I Googled the band last night to learn about all of them. Roxie is the drummer, and she signed on with the band right before they recorded their second album, less than a year ago, when their original drummer quit to spend more time with his family.

Roxie doesn't notice my hesitation. She's already turned around and beckons me to follow her. We head downstairs and through a set of sound-proof doors, into the basement studio. It's a fully-equipped, professional setup with what looks to be all the latest gear—not that I know a ton about sound equipment. There's a black leather couch and a couple matching chairs on one side of the room. Roxie's drums are set up in the corner, and a guy with spiky blond hair and a tall pair of cowboy boots bends over an amp next to it.

Leo. The bassist.

"Hey!" he says. "Help yourself to some jerky." He straightens and yells through a doorway to the back. "Jenna! Your boy's here!"

I lean my cello against the wall and rub my hands on my jeans, trying not to react to being called Jenna's *boy*. The jerky he's referring to is sitting on top of a speaker, long strips of pale meat, almost like bacon.

"You might want to pass," Roxie says. "It's home-cured alligator. No telling what you might catch."

Leo shakes his head. "Just because you're a vegan doesn't mean you have to ruin it for the rest of us."

"Vegetarian," Roxie says. "It's different."

Leo picks up a strip of alligator jerky and takes a big bite. "Either way, you're missing out." He holds out a piece to me, and I'm trying to figure out how to politely decline—drug-laced alligator jerky might be a stretch, but it still puts me on edge—when Jenna breezes through the door. She's wearing more makeup than yesterday, and a skirt that shows off her legs. Her t-shirt fits tight around her waist and I can't help but stare.

"Hey," I say.

"Hey," she says back.

She's watching me as intently as I'm watching her, and I look away, sure Leo and Roxie have noticed. But Leo is sitting in the corner next to his bass guitar, tugging off his cowboy boots. He's not wearing socks underneath.

"Ew, Leo!" Roxie says. "Put your boots back on. We don't need to smell your feet."

Leo shakes his head. "I can't play with my shoes on."

Roxie's brow furrows. "Since when?"

"Since I realized it ruins my acoustics."

There's a pause, in which Roxie just stares at him. "Dude," she finally says. "That's insane. Besides, you're not playing. You're listening to an audition."

"Still. Got to get in the right frame of mind."

Roxie groans. "I apologize for him," she says to me. "He's the weird one."

"Keep LA weird, man." Leo leans back against the wall.

Roxie closes her eyes and shakes her head. "I've told you a

thousand times, that is not a thing."

"How do you know?" Leo asked. "Ever been there?"

Jenna turns to me with a small smile. "According to Leo, LA is Louisiana."

"It's not just me," Leo insists. "Ask the post office."

Roxie groans. "Just put your damn boots back on."

Leo wiggles his toes in her direction. "Hey, if you'd air out your toes once in a while you wouldn't have foot fungus."

Roxie looks offended. "I do *not* have foot fungus!"

"You do," Leo says. "I saw it last week when you were wearing those strappy shoes. You know how your left big toenail's lifting up? Foot fungus."

"Ew. No." But Roxie eyes her sneakers warily.

I realize I'm still standing there like an idiot. I turn back to Jenna and catch her checking me out again.

I'm wearing jeans that are just tight enough without being trendy, and a t-shirt with a fit to match. I almost always wear slacks and collared shirts to audition—I'm a big believer in dressing for the job you want. But when that job is with a pop band, I figure dressing down is the look, and Leo's t-shirt and jeans tell me I'm not wrong.

Still, it's nice to be appreciated.

"Sorry," Jenna says. "We're a little scattered today. And Alec is late. This is . . . pretty much normal for us."

I smile. "No problem. Mind if I tune up?"

She smiles back. "Of course," she says. "Have a seat."

She gestures to a chair against the wall that I'm guessing used to be Mason's. It's covered in stickers, most of them from metal bands. I pull June out of her case and get her ready to play. Jenna sits on the couch across the room, her legs folded to the side, and I feel her watching me as I play a few notes, my nerves vibrating like the strings.

Fingering.

Focus, I tell myself. I am going to jack up this audition before it even gets started.

29

That's when Alec walks in.

I've seen pictures of him online, of course—I stayed up past midnight again last night torturing myself with every image of him and Jenna the internet had to offer. Gabby was right. They *looked* like soul mates.

Meeting him in person is something else. Alec is tall, a good six inches taller than me. His dark hair is slicked back into a low ponytail, and he looks up from his phone and fixes his blue eyes on me.

"Hey," he says.

"Alec!" Jenna says, sounding like Gabby's cheerleader twin. "This is Felix, the cellist I told you about."

"Yeah, I guessed that," Alec says. "What with the cello."

I give him a half-wave. "Hi," I say, when what I want to say is closer to "I swear I wasn't hitting on your girlfriend except I really was please don't hit me."

"He was playing Hollywood Boulevard when I was out with Ty," Jenna says. "Ty ran off and I found him telling Felix here all about Mason and his douchery."

I smile. "He's a cute kid. Did you guys try out *Life* yet?"

Jenna laughs. "Yes, and you were right. I was a childless mortuary assistant. And you *make money* for having kids. What the hell is that?"

"Right?" I say. "So did Ty win?"

"Of course," she says. "He was an accountant with four kids who became a musician after a mid-life crisis and this somehow all worked to his benefit financially."

I laugh. "I warned you."

"Yeah," Jenna says. "*After* I bought it."

Alec is looking between the two of us with a concerned expression, and I wipe my hands on my jeans again.

There it is. I've blown the audition before I even played. Jenna and I haven't exactly devolved into *straddling* and *fingering* yet, but the chemistry is obvious.

I hope he sticks with just nixing me for the job and doesn't feel the need to kick my ass.

"Seriously, Leo," Roxie says, folding her arms across her chest. "Put. On. Your. Shoes."

"Seriously, Roxie," Leo responds. "You need to get some cream for that fungus."

Roxie huffs, grabs her stool from behind the drums, and settles on it in the corner. Leo drags over a folding chair and sets it up so close he's practically on top of her.

Alec sighs. "Welcome," he says to me. "Let's hear you play."

He settles next to Jenna on the couch, and Alec extends his arm along the backrest, but I'm grateful Jenna doesn't lean in. My goal now is to get out of this as quickly as possible without burning bridges.

"Jenna asked me to play something I love," I say. "So I've got a couple pieces for you."

I stand June up on her peg and raise my bow. I never get nervous when I audition—I can play, and I put in the time to be prepared. But playing for these guys is different, first because I've never auditioned outside of classical, second because playing for Jenna feels like a hell of a lot more pressure than anyone I've auditioned for before.

And third because I can feel Alec's eyes on me, and he clearly knows why I'm really here. I don't dare look up at any of them while I play. There's too much tension in the room, too much happening out there, and the music has to be just me and June.

I start with "Head" by The Meat Puppets. It was a change in sound for them—slow and moody—and has a surprising range for a cello part in a rock song. It's one of the only rock songs I ever performed—outside of Hollywood Boulevard, anyway—in a duet with my friend Ryan playing the piano part. As I play, the notes drown out the tension, and it's just me, June, and the music. The vibrations calm my nerves, and I'm glad I'm here, sharing this with them, even if it's only this once.

It feels good to play for someone who's here to listen to me, and not just pass by on the street.

Toward the end of the song I steal one glance up at Jenna. She's watching me with a smile on her face and a faraway look in her eye—

And Alec is watching *her*.

Next I play a cover of Red Hot Chili Peppers' "Under the Bridge" that I arranged my second time out of rehab, the week before I went back to the drugs. Anthony Kiedis wrote the song about trying to stay sober in Los Angeles, and it has this melancholy feel of a guy who's trying to be clean, but it lands him utterly alone.

I relate.

I finish with a selection from Shostakovich's "Cello Concerto Number Two," which is straight up classical, but it's dark and beautiful and crazy demanding. I love it. The sounds June and I produce during that concerto—both bright and dark—are what I'm proudest of as a cellist.

When I finish, I find them all staring at me. Which is what they're supposed to do while I audition for them, but still.

Jenna speaks first. "That was beautiful. Are you sure you'd want to play with *us*?"

"Come on, Jen," Leo says. "We could play that kind of stuff if we wanted to."

Roxie gives a doubtful grunt.

I clear my throat and put away my bow. I've probably shot too high. I should have gone with more Cash songs, or at least something a little more lowbrow than Shostakovich, who nobody outside of classical can even spell.

Jenna leans forward, those gray eyes studying me. "Why did you pick that last piece?" she asks.

I'm not sure how to answer. She told me to pick things that I love, so what other reason would I have? But the truth is I love a lot of music, and I've played hundreds of pieces.

"Because that one sounds like I feel lately," I say, and her face softens, like she understands something I'm not sure even I do.

"You're amazing," she says, and my heart flutters a little. Then

32

I look at Alec and see him watching us both with sharp eyes.

Yes, he definitely understands, probably better than I do. He gives an exaggerated sigh, and I wait for him to politely tell me they'll get back to me and dismiss me so he can tell the others there's no way in hell.

"Can we just hire him already?" Alec says. "He's more than good enough to play our stuff, and you've obviously already made up your mind."

I stare at him. He can't have just said that.

Jenna's whole face lights up, and she turns to the others. "Leo? Roxie?"

"I'm cool," Roxie says.

"Works for me," Leo says. "If he can handle Roxie's foot fungus."

"Shut up!" Roxie kicks at him, but he dodges back as if afraid to even be touched by her shoe.

"It's okay, Rox," Leo adds. "I'll get you a tube of cream. It'll clear right up."

"If you do that," Alec says, "will you shut the hell up about Roxie's feet?"

"Sure," Leo says. "I'm just looking out for her hygiene."

"Band vote," Alec says. "Leo buys anti-fungal cream. All in favor?"

Alec, Jenna, and Leo all put their hands in the air. I sit absolutely still, reeling from their previous decision.

All of them just said they want me to join their band. For the first time, I actually consider playing on stage with Alec and Jenna.

"I'm not using his stupid cream," Roxie says.

"You're outvoted," Alec says. "You use the cream. Leo shuts up. That's the deal."

Roxie folds her arms and slumps on her stool, while Leo looks thoroughly proud of himself.

"Anyway," Jenna says, looking at me apologetically. "Are you sure you want to join us?"

Join a band. Based in LA. Playing new music and traveling. With *Jenna*. All worries fly out of my mind.

"Okay," I say. "Yeah, sure. I'm in."

Jenna smiles. "Do you have any questions for us?"

About a million, first of which being what in the hell I'm signing on for. Alec is staring at me with this look of resignation on his face, like he's not especially happy I'm joining the band, and I can't say I blame him.

Can we just hire him already?

What did *that* mean?

"Yeah," I say. "What's the time commitment? You're looking for someone to fill in for the tour?"

For a second, Jenna looks worried. "No," she says. "I mean, yes, we do need someone immediately, but we're looking for a full band member. You'd be on salary, travel with us on tour, and then have about a month off before we start putting together our next album. Do you write?"

"I'm not a composer," I say, but immediately realize writing music doesn't work the same in pop as it does in classical, where composers need to play a little of everything in order to write, but they almost never master any one instrument. "But I can work out cello parts to the songs on your first album, if you want me to play those, too."

Jenna looks at Alec, and he looks more impressed than irritated, which is probably the best I'm going to get.

"That would be great," Jenna says. "Mason was going to sit out the old stuff, but if you want to play, that would be fantastic."

I smile at her. She sounds way too eager about this, and Alec is glaring at her. I have no idea what kind of stroke he had that inspired him to suggest I join them, but I'm still riding the high. I'll take it.

"One last thing," Jenna says. "I'm sure by now you've read why Mason left us."

I nod. "He stole money from you."

"For drugs," she says. "It turns out Mason had this whole other life he wasn't telling us about. None of us are saints, but we're serious musicians and we work hard to keep this about the music."

"No problem," I say.

But Jenna isn't done. "For that reason, we've started undergoing random drug testing. Alec and I do it, too, so it's fair. Our manager Phil handles the whole thing, and even Alec and I don't know when it's coming. But if anyone fails—no matter who— they're out. That's the rule. Do you think you can handle that?"

I stare at her. "None of you do drugs."

"No," she says. "Not anymore."

This is the best news I've heard today—which is really saying something—and I start to wonder if I'm still back on my dad's couch, dreaming. "Yeah, okay. That's no problem. I can pass a drug test." Even the Suboxone won't show up on a screening unless they test for it specifically.

She stares at me, and for that instant, I feel like she can see right through me. She knows how hard it is for me to stay clean every day. She sees the struggle, the siren call of the needle that wakes me every morning, sings in my ears until I fall asleep at night.

"Are you sure?" she asks.

"Yes. I'll pee in a cup today, if you want. I can pass anytime." Hell, I've been tested every day since I left rehab, just to get my maintenance pill. If I fail, I have much bigger problems than getting kicked out of a band.

Jenna smiles. "Excellent. Phil will have the first test for you tomorrow, along with the paperwork. Want to meet Alec and me back here in the morning, and we'll get you signed?"

"Yeah," I say. "Sure. I'll be here."

Jenna grins like this is the best news she's ever had, and all I care about is continuing to see that smile.

FOUR

Felix

When I get to the studio the next morning, I've got more on my mind than just Jenna. I'm signing a contract for a job. A real job that isn't selling cigarettes or teaching cello to whiny kids who hate the lessons and never practice. Sure, I've had paying gigs before, but never anything consistent, without an end date.

Whatever is going on with Alec and Jenna, the longer I think about it, the more certain I am.

I cannot let it mess this up.

Alec comes to the door when I knock. "After this you'll have your own key," he says, "so come on in." He walks me down to the studio where Jenna sits on the couch. Her black hair is pulled back into a braid, the streaks of red threaded through like ribbon. She's wearing another short skirt, this one in a shimmery silver, with a tight black t-shirt. The cellist's chair sits empty right in front of her. My pulse, which has apparently missed the message about not screwing this up, races at the sight of her. I pull the chair back to take a seat, while Jenna grins at me and hands me a contract.

"You can take a few minutes to look it over," she says. "It's pretty standard. You won't earn royalties on this album, but your salary is right there at the top. You could negotiate for more next time, but this is what Mason was making, so it's set in the budget at least until the end of the tour."

I'm staring at the number at the top of the page, right under their names and mine. I'd say it's more than I've ever made, but that's not exactly impressive, given I've never had a full-time job. Even my gig at the Kum-N-Go—which was amazingly a gas station and not an actual brothel—had only been part time, and nearly every dime I'd earned there went to drugs.

This, while far from millions, is enough to get both a decent apartment and a head start on paying back my dad. Two things that just days ago seemed desperately out of reach.

"Does it look all right?" Jenna asks.

She sounds nervous, and I nod. "Yeah, it's great. That'll be fine."

Alec sits down next to her, closer than yesterday, and I notice too late that my knees are almost touching hers. I clear my throat and push back my chair, reading through the first page of the contract to avoid meeting his eyes.

"Some things to note," Jenna says. "There's a tour schedule attached. If you have any conflicts, let us know, but we really need you there for every performance."

I glance at the schedule, but I already know it's fine. For me, every day has only one task in it, and that's to stay clean. I can't think past the next hour sometimes, so I sure as hell haven't planned weeks in advance.

"No problem," I say. "I'm in."

Alec gives Jenna a look. "There's one more thing," he says. I spot the plastic cup inside a ziploc bag on the arm of the couch.

"Yeah," I say. "Like I said, you can test me anytime."

"Not that," Jenna says. "On the last page, you'll find a non-disclosure agreement. After you sign that and the contract, you'll receive some information. If you reveal it to anyone, you'll be fired. We're just as serious about that as the drug test. And even if you leave us for any reason, if word gets out because of you, we'll sue."

I look up at her. "Like, your new songs, things like that."

Now she and Alec exchange a look. There's definitely something I'm missing.

"Among other things," Jenna says.

I look down at the line where I'm supposed to sign. "You should know that I've been staying with family. Is it okay if people overhear when I practice? I guess I could make sure I always come here, but my dad and my sister won't—"

"No," Jenna cuts in. "That's no problem. I mean, when you're working on new material, make sure they don't record you, but even if something like that got out, it would probably just be good for publicity, especially since it's just the cello part."

I stare at her. She seems even more nervous than before, her fingers toying with the end of her braid. "That's pretty much the opposite of what you just said," I say.

Her smile is forced this time. "Ready to sign, or should we give you a few minutes?"

"No," I say. "I'm ready." Alec hands me a pen and I scrawl my signature at the bottom of the contract, and then again on the NDA. "Okay, so what's the big secret? Do we work for the Russians? Are we spies for the DEA?"

"No," Jenna says. "We're not dating."

I choke on my own spit. I'm well aware that she and I aren't dating, but I'm not sure how to respond to this statement of the obvious.

"Alec and I," Jenna says quickly. "We're not together."

I catch Alec giving me a knowing look, and I try to play my stumbling off as surprise.

Damn it, Gabby. I *knew* she was hitting on me.

"We *were*," Jenna says. "We broke up about a year ago. But we'd already built the band around being a couple, and our first album had so much success that we didn't want to just abandon the whole thing and start over. So, for now, we're living together, but not *living* together, you know? And no one outside of the band can know."

I'm sure I should be thinking about what this means professionally, but my mind keeps stuttering over this one thought. Jenna isn't with Alec. They aren't together.

God, is she *available*?

"Okay, yeah," I say. "I see why that would be a big deal. I won't tell anyone."

"No one," Alec says. "Even Mason hasn't talked, because he knows damn well we will sue his ass, and we'd do the same to you."

"You won't have to," I say. "I swear."

Jenna looks between the two of us and smiles, sincerely this time. "All right. So that's settled. Felix just needs to pee in this cup and then we'll get all the paperwork to Phil and get you copies of the music. The LA kickoff concert is in a week, and then tour just over two weeks after that. First practice is the day after tomorrow. Think you can get up to speed by then?"

"I'll try," I say, but my mind isn't on the work.

Jenna hands me the cup, and Alec leans back on the couch, crossing his arms, his eyes boring into me. While I'm now sure he has everything figured out, I get why he allowed Jenna to hire me.

And I'm flying so high I don't even know what to say.

FIVE

Jenna

Alec waits about thirty seconds after Felix leaves the studio before turning to me, and I'm all too conscious of the way my heart is still pounding, of the warm, happy flush I feel all over at being near Felix. At knowing he's joining the band.

"Oh my *god*, Jenna." Alec shakes his head. "What the hell was *that*?"

"What?" I say, convincing exactly no one.

Alec leans back into the couch. "Never mind. I know exactly what that was. You need to get laid. Bad."

I give him a withering look, but as much as I don't love getting sex advice from my ex-boyfriend, he probably has a point. It has been a long time. At least, that's what started running through my mind shortly after I first met Felix.

I'd blamed my nearly-a-year of self-imposed celibacy, and Felix's general gorgeousness—oh my god, that smile—for my shamelessly-forward flirting, something I haven't done in a very long time. And definitely not in front of my son like that, though I know he's too young to get what I was really talking about. But the truth is, I've met lots of hot guys since Alec and I broke up, and I doubt I'm suddenly so much more desperate for action now than I was, say, last week.

No, there's something more to this attraction I have to Felix.

Something stronger, this indefinable pull, there from that very first meeting. I feel it still, my eyes wanting to drift to the door he just walked out through.

"And clearly," Alec continues, because knowing when to drop something isn't exactly his strong suit, "he'd be up for it."

"Because you know him so well." Really, though, I'm pretty sure this intense attraction is a mutual thing, even if I'm not as quick as Alec to assume he's ready to jump me. For all I know, he's super religious and saving himself for marriage or something.

"He could have a girlfriend," I point out. I really don't love this thought, but I don't actually think it's true. I saw the look in those incredible blue eyes of his when we told him Alec and I weren't dating—there was the expected surprise, of course, but I could swear there was something else.

Something like hope.

My heart both flutters and aches at the same time.

Alec makes a dismissive sound. "If he does, he's not all that into her." Alec reaches over and picks up one of his guitars, an acoustic lying against the armrest of the couch. "I know the look of a guy dying to bang a girl. And the look of you dying to bang him back."

"Always such a way with words." I roll my eyes. "This is why *I* write our songs. I'm not sure 'Bang a Girl' would appeal to our core audience."

Alec grins at me, and plays a quick chord progression, like he's making that song up right now, and I can't help but smile. We were always better as friends than as anything more, and I'm happy we've been able to keep that part of our relationship intact.

Even if it means enduring conversations like this. With Alec.

"Besides," I say, slumping back into the couch, the ache getting stronger. "He's in the band now. So . . ."

"Exactly. So this thing you two have going on"—here Alec gestures with his pick between me and the empty folding chair, like the sexual tension is still hovering in the air—"you need to get it on, and get it over with. For the good of the band."

"So I'm supposed to just sleep with him once, and then . . . be over it?"

"The rules say one-night stand. They don't specify how many times in one night," Alec says, with a sly smile. "But yeah. Spend the night with him. Get it out of your system. And then tomorrow after practice, he's in the band and it's over." He gives me a look like he's being magnanimous, making an exception to the rules just this once.

And I understand why. It will be ridiculously difficult to be in the band with a guy I'm that attracted to and not do anything about it—if indeed Alec is right that Felix returns the inclination. But the rules we've set up give us the best possible chance of keeping our secret from the public. And though they seem to work better at meeting Alec's relationship needs than mine, I agreed to them because they're smart. They keep this incredible career we have going strong. We're too new to weather a major scandal, and neither of us wants to move back to Ann Arbor and give up everything we've worked so hard for.

Most importantly, the rules allow me, a single former-teen mom who came damn close to not even graduating high school, to provide a great life for my son, all while doing what I love— performing and writing music. And I know Alec dreads the idea of losing everything and ending up back home with his big Greek family and his old job selling appliances on commission, scribbling songs on receipt paper just to keep from losing his mind.

People love our music. We shouldn't have to lose all this just because we didn't end up being the dream couple the fans want us to be.

I chew on my lip, actually considering his suggestion, despite myself.

When I'd first met Felix, I'd thought that maybe discreet one-night stands *could* be a good thing. Maybe this guy would just be fun and satisfying and wouldn't leave me feeling sick and lost and a little afraid. Like all those years ago when I'd wake up in some guy's dorm room and only vaguely remember how I got there.

But then I'd heard him play, and we'd needed a cellist, and more than anything, I'd just wanted to have an excuse to see him and talk to him more. To get to know him, and find out if the incredible, haunting depth I could hear in his music matches who he really is.

And I'd known then I was giving up my chance to sleep with him. Because I can't imagine having a one-night stand with him and then working so closely together.

I was already pretty sure I'd want more.

"One-night stands aren't my style," I say with a sigh, and Alec groans.

"Well, okay, but you've got to do *something* to get over it, because *that*"—again he gestures at the empty air between me and where Felix sat; has he developed pheromone-cloud vision or something?—"won't play well with the story. I mean, if you really just need to get laid to take the edge off, I'd be happy to help."

"Oh my god, Alec." I toss one of the couch's small throw pillows at his face.

"What? Just as like a favor for a friend," he says, as if that makes it better. I think in his mind it actually does.

"Well, thanks for your *incredibly generous* offer of pity sex," I say, "but I'm going to pass."

"Your call. All I'm saying is—"

"I know what you're saying, Alec. So you can stop saying it now."

Alec shrugs, and starts playing the bridge to "You're Reading My Mind," the third song on our new album. It's clearly pointed—all about the desperate longing at the beginning of a relationship—but I can almost hear the cello part to that, and see Felix playing it.

43

Like he's playing it for me.

My body feels all warm again, all light like when he smiles at me.

"He's really good, isn't he?" I ask, because despite my body's reactions, Felix's cello-playing seems a safer topic than any one-night stands I may or may not have with him. "Maybe even better than Mason."

"Maybe." Whenever Mason's name gets mentioned now, Alec gets this same hard look on his face. I think he'd rather just forget Mason ever existed than have to talk about him.

I get why. The whole thing hurts me, too. He didn't start out in our band, but like Roxie, he seemed to fit in almost instantly. He and I would hang out at the studio after practice sometimes, or back at my house, and he'd gush about the latest hot guy he'd met at Pinkberry or TCBY (frozen yogurt places being a surprising gold mine for Mason's dating life) and I'd tell him about the latest fight Alec and I'd had.

I'm not going to say we were BFFs or anything, but I'd thought we were fairly close.

Apparently not enough that I had any idea of what was really going on in his life.

Apparently not enough that he didn't mind constantly lying to me—to all of us—and stealing money from us and generally treating us like shit when we called him on it all.

And now, instead of picturing Felix in that chair, I'm seeing Mason, with the thick-rimmed glasses that Leo always teased him about and his cello that, like the folding chair, was also covered in stickers from random bands he liked.

I blink and look away.

"But yeah," Alec says, and I think he was lost in thought about Mason for a minute there, too. "Felix is great. Good find, especially so close to tour." He stands up and stretches, then sets the guitar on the couch where he was sitting. "Just take my advice and—"

"Please don't say the word 'bang' again. Seriously, does

anyone even say that anymore?"

Alec grins. "I'm a hot rock star. I can get away with it."

I shake my head at him but smile back. Confidence *is* Alec's strong suit.

Alec holds his hand up in goodbye and leaves the studio. I pull my phone out of my purse to do some work before I head out, too—I need to send Felix our music, and then answer some questions about color preference from our costumer, Allison—and I see I've got a message from my mom.

No, not from my mom. From Ty, using my mom's phone.

Hi Mom! Is Felix in the band!

I smile. Ty has been even more excited these past couple days about Felix possibly joining our band than he was back when Roxie first joined—and I heard him talk about her "hair that's pink like bubblegum!" for weeks.

Yep, I text back, adding a smiley face for good measure.

Ty texts a bunch of celebration emojis, and then some random animal ones, because anytime he gets his hands on a phone, he feels the need to text a whole zoo at me.

God, I love this kid.

I text a bunch of animals back and lean against the armrest of the couch.

I'm happy Ty likes Felix so much. Band members being good with Ty is important to me—Ty comes to practices occasionally, and he always comes on tour with me, so they all end up spending some time with him. And Felix and Ty seemed to hit it off pretty well—at least Ty sure thinks so.

Is Ty *too* excited about this, though, what with Felix being some guy he just barely met?

Am I?

I think I know the answer to that second question, unfortunately.

I let out a shaky breath and focus on sending the files of music to Felix. I've finished that, and gotten halfway through my email to Allison, when my phone rings.

It's Felix, calling me.

My heart slams against my ribs as I answer.

"Hey," I say, hoping he doesn't hear how breathless I sound. "I just sent over the music. Did you get it?"

"Just got it," he says. "But I had some questions. I'm not used to performing with a band, you know? Would you be willing to meet me for lunch?"

It's not a date, I tell myself. Not really. A business lunch.

I try to ignore the fact that we could probably talk about any questions he had over the phone, or text. Because really, I'm just so happy to get to see him again, even though it's probably been twenty minutes since he left.

And I think maybe he feels the same way.

"Sure," I find myself saying. "Name the place."

"There's this sushi place on Wilshire," he says. "Sound okay?"

Getting some time to talk with Felix over sushi, just him and me? It sounds way better than okay.

"Great," I say, not able to wipe the smile from my face. "Send me the address and I'll head over there."

It's after I hang up that the pit in my stomach forms, somewhere underneath all the butterflies going haywire at the thought of time alone with Felix.

I'm going to have to tell him about the rules. If he's as interested in me as I think he is, I don't want to lead him on.

I'm going to have to decide—well, *we're* going to have to decide—if the one-night stand thing is an option. If that would help us, as Alec says, "get it out of our system" and just be able to be band mates. Friends, maybe.

But for right now, I can't help but let myself feel the butterflies, that excitement of the possibility—even if it's not real—that we could actually be something more.

SIX

Felix

I grin all the way to the restaurant to meet Jenna. Sure, I lasted less than thirty minutes before I called her, but I'm desperate to talk to her. And it's not as if there's anyone *else* I can tell about what's going on.

When I get there, Jenna's waiting for me, and Alec is nowhere in sight. I've never been so happy to *not* see someone in my life.

Jenna's whole face lights up when she sees me, and she throws her arms around me like we're old friends. I squeeze her back, careful not to hold on too long, but long enough to learn that her hair smells like coconut.

When she steps away, my whole body aches.

Jenna asks for a table away from the main room, and the waitress either recognizes her or sees enough celebrities to honor these requests, because she shows us to a booth that's tucked in a side room. This must be an overflow area because all the other tables are empty.

Jenna smiles and thanks her, and the waitress takes our drink orders and disappears. And for the first time ever, I'm alone with Jenna Rollins and I'm trying like hell not to look like an idiot.

"So," I say. "That was some bomb you guys dropped on me."

Jenna cringes. "I know, right? It's pretty intense. If you don't think you can handle it, we can't make you stay—"

"No, I'm good. It must be hard, though, yeah? Living with your ex?"

Jenna wobbles her head. "It's not so bad. Alec's gone a lot, so he leaves the house mostly for just me and Ty. And he sleeps in a room off mine. It used to be a huge closet, actually, so no one sees it, and we can look like we go to bed together if there's anyone over, just for appearances."

I nod. "But you're not sleeping with him."

"No, not since we broke up." She winces again. "And maybe for a little while before that, too."

The waitress brings our sodas, and I take a sip of mine. I'm glad she ordered one, too, if only so I don't seem out of place not ordering alcohol. I've never been an alcoholic, but I hear enough stories at twelve-step about people trading one addiction for another to keep the clinic rules for sobriety.

When the waitress leaves us again, I flip open my menu, but I don't look at it. Jenna does the same. "Was it a bad breakup?" I ask.

"Not really," Jenna says. "We'd been unhappy for a while. Fighting all the time. One night we were bickering about what to get for dinner, and I was in the middle of saying something huffy when Alec asked me, 'Jenna, are you *happy*?'" She rolls her eyes. "And I was like, 'No. Your dinner selection does not make me happy.'"

"But he meant for real."

"Yeah. And once we both admitted how miserable we were, I think we were just relieved to discover we weren't breaking each other's hearts."

"So you weren't in love with him."

Jenna meets my eyes, and my cheeks burn when I realize what a personal question that is. But they've spent the last two and a half years plastering their love all over the internet, parading their relationship around as the pinnacle of true love.

And besides that, I need to know.

"I thought I was," she says. "And we care about each other.

But no. I wasn't in love with him. At least not in a forever way."

"Is it hard to lie about it?"

"Sometimes. But it doesn't all feel like a lie. We're performers, and we're telling a story. I believe in the story, even if it isn't ours."

My shoe rests against hers under the table. I've been a flirt all my life, but never a romantic. Listening to her talk about the story like that, though—

It makes me want to believe in it too.

"That's a nice way to look at it," I say.

She eyes me cautiously. "You don't approve?"

I shrug. "It's just a lot to keep straight."

Jenna shakes her head. "I'm with Alec. That's all you need to remember."

"Is that what you want me to remember?" I ask.

I hold my breath, my pulse pounding in my ears, and her eyes meet mine. For a moment, we stare at each other, and the current between us is so strong I'm surprised the air doesn't crackle.

Then Jenna gives me a coy smile and looks down at her menu. "Have you been here before?" She studiously avoids my eyes, but the smile keeps playing at her lips.

I take a long drag of my Coke. "Yeah, once," I say. "But it's been a while." I notice she hasn't asked me what my questions are about the band, which is a good thing, because I can't think of any. I just needed to see her, and she sure as hell doesn't seem to mind. I wonder if this secret she's carrying has left her as isolated as sobriety has left me. It can't be easy to have friends outside the band when you have to carry on the facade of a relationship even for them.

And with her ex-boyfriend so involved with the band—it's probably hard even to talk to them about how she really feels.

The waitress comes back, and we both order. I get the salmon sashimi, because last time I had a tuna roll, and I hate to order the same thing twice. Jenna gets the sushi sampler, and when the waitress leaves again, I shake my head at her. "You know samplers are for people who can't make up their minds."

"I made up my mind that I want to try everything."

"All right," I say. "I can't argue with that."

Jenna's shoe taps against mine, and I know she's aware it's there. She doesn't move hers away.

"So does Ty know about you and Alec?" I ask.

"Yes. The band knows, Ty knows, Phil knows, and my parents know. And that's it."

"Alec's parents think you're together?"

"Alec's parents are still in Michigan," Jenna says. "That's where we're from. And he barely talks to them. So they get the news about our relationship along with the rest of the world."

"But your parents are out here?"

"Yeah," she says. "They followed Ty and me. We're kind of all they have, so they wanted to be close. My dad found a job here and we all moved together."

"You get along with your family?"

She nods, and then shakes her head. "We do, now. It wasn't always that way, but it's nice to have them around for Ty."

I'm aware I'm peppering her with questions, but I can't help it—I want to know everything about her. And she doesn't seem to have any hesitation in telling me. "And Ty's dad? Is he still in the picture?"

"No," Jenna says. "The public story is that he was a guy I dated in high school."

I've read as much. I was right about her age when I first met her—she's only twenty-three, just a year older than me. And her kid is eight, not six.

"The public story," I say. I'm not sure if she's going to tell me the rest of it, but we're in this strange place now. I know these intimate details about her life, things hardly anyone else knows, but I'm missing the basic facts. It's a bizarre way to get to know someone.

She takes a deep breath. "Yeah. The truth is I don't know

who Ty's father is."

Her hand is resting on the table, and I want to reach across and take it, but I don't dare. The waitress could be back any time. I move my ankle closer under the table.

Her knee brushes against mine. "Ty's father," she says, "was one of a number of guys at various frat parties at the U of M. I have no idea which one, and even if I did, I never really knew any of their names."

My throat constricts. I've had my share of one-night stands, especially when I first started using, before the drugs messed my body up. I don't remember most of their names. Except the last one.

But. "You were a kid," I say.

She gives me a sad smile. "Fourteen."

The idea of Jenna as a fourteen-year-old girl at a party like that makes me want to punch all frat boys in the face. "They must have known you were underage."

She laughs, but it's humorless. "Oh, they knew. They might not have known *how* underage I was, but they definitely knew what they were doing."

I tighten my fists. "I'm so sorry that happened to you."

Jenna fiddles with a napkin, like she's suddenly aware of how much she's told me. I expect her to change the subject, but instead she sighs. "It didn't happen *to* me. I knew what I was doing, going to those kinds of parties. If I hadn't done that, it never would have happened."

I stare at her, but she won't meet my eyes. There are so many things wrong with what she's saying that I don't know where to start. "You were a kid," I say. "That isn't your fault."

"Yeah, well," she says, "I knew better. But I don't regret having Ty. Just the way I had him, I guess."

I want to circle back around to how very much she's not at fault for a bunch of guys who think statutory rape is a good way to spend a Saturday night, but this is our first real conversation. I don't want to argue with her, to shut her down.

All I want in the world is for her to keep talking.

"Ty seems like a cool kid," I say. "Even if his taste in board games is questionable."

She smiles, clearly more at ease on this topic. "He is. He likes you, you know. He was thrilled when I told him you're joining the band."

It surprises me the kid remembers me enough to care, but I smile anyway. Her knee brushes mine again, sending a thrill through me, and I have to ask. "So, are you seeing anyone?"

Her face falls, and for a second I'm terrified she's going to confess some passionate love affair with her bassist.

"I can't," she says. "We have . . . rules."

My tongue seems to swell in my mouth. "Rules?" I manage.

"Yeah." She gives me an apologetic look that tells me she knows exactly where I was going with this. Her foot moves away from mine under the table. "When Alec and I broke up, we agreed we couldn't get serious with anyone. Too much chance someone would find out."

I'm aware I must look crestfallen, but the ache is too powerful to cover. "So, what? You're going to be celibate for the rest of your life?"

She laughs. "Oh, no. Alec was worried about that, so there are some loopholes. We can't date anyone, but we can have sex. As long as it's never more than once with the same person. There are other rules, too. No fans. The other person has to be clear that this is just a one-night thing, no strings. And of course we have to be crazy discreet."

Jenna is back to not meeting my eyes. I lean my elbows on the table. I wonder if that's why she agreed to meet me, if I'm about to become a notch in her bedpost.

I'm startled to find I don't like the idea.

"How's that going for you?" I ask.

"It's been ten and a half months," she says. "So there's that."

"Ouch," I say.

She lets out a little sigh. "I'm just not all that into one-night stands, as it turns out. Too much like the old days, I guess. I'm more of a relationship person." I must look like I pity her, because she shrugs. "It's not forever. When we broke up, we made a five-year plan. We figure in that much time the band will have peaked—we'll have gotten the mileage we need to launch our solo careers. So then we'll script a breakup that lets us both get out of this with our dignity intact and hopefully a good chunk of our fan base as well." Her forced smile is back. "One year down, four to go."

"Damn. You must be lonely." I wince. "That sounded like a line."

Jenna laughs, and it's genuine this time. "It did. Are *you* seeing anyone?"

Ha. I should have thought that was painfully obvious. "No," I say. I'm trying to figure out how to tell her I meant that line about being lonely exactly the way it sounded, but the waitress comes back with our sushi, and instead I mix some wasabi and soy sauce and fill my mouth with raw fish.

"So your family's here in LA?" Jenna asks. "You said you're living with your dad?"

"Yeah," I say. "My dad is down in Valencia and my mom's in Orange County."

"They're divorced."

"Just over a year."

"Is that hard?" she asks.

"Yes and no." It's sure made it easier to play them off each other, both for money and a couch to surf on. The former I'm making a point not to take advantage of since rehab. The latter, not so much. "It's not like it affects me all that much, so it's fine. But all they want to talk about is what the other one is doing. They either need to move on or get back together and get it over with."

"Do you think they will?"

"No," I say. "So I think I have many years ahead of me of telling them to call each other if they need so badly to know what the other one is doing, or buying, or saying."

"That sounds super fun." Jenna scrunches her nose. It's ridiculous how adorable that expression looks on her. "Are you their only child?"

"No," I say. "I have two sisters. Gabby and Dana. You?"

"I had a sister," she says quietly.

I remember too late she said that she and Ty were all her parents had.

"She died." Jenna swishes her chopsticks around in her soy sauce.

"I'm sorry."

She hesitates. "It was a long time ago," she says after a moment. "A car accident. I was nineteen. She was only seventeen."

I wonder why I didn't read about this online. It must not be something she talks about. I get the feeling I'm hearing a lot of things she doesn't talk about, and I wonder what it is we're doing here. She's been flirting with me for days, but now I know she's available, she says we can't date. But here we are, out to lunch, in a booth so secluded we might as well have our own private room.

We are, as far as I can tell, on a date.

"You miss her," I say, mostly because it's written all over her face.

"Yeah. She was always the good one, you know? Like I was still running around partying, and she was at home with my parents, taking care of my kid."

"Why did you have him?" I ask. I realize too late that's a more deeply personal question than the others. "You don't have to answer that," I add quickly.

"No, it's fine." She doesn't even look surprised that I've asked, as if we're old friends who are reconnecting instead of total strangers who now happen to be in a band. And somehow, I feel the same way. "The short answer is that my parents pressured me into it," she says. "But really, I wouldn't have told them if, deep down, I didn't want to have him. I knew what they'd say, so I told them because I trusted them to get me to do it, even though I was scared."

That sounds like a pretty messed-up situation, but I don't know how to say so without sounding like I'm judging her. And I am honestly the last person who should be judging anyone.

"I'm glad, now," she says, grabbing a piece of yellowtail with her chopsticks, but just staring at it. "But at the time I was a mess. I wasn't ready to be a mother. My sister, Rachel, she was more of a mother to Ty than I was. He still remembers her. Aunt Rachel. He was inconsolable when she died. He called me Mom, but I'm not even sure he knew what that meant."

"He knows now," I say. She looks so sad, and I realize how true it was, what I said about her being lonely. And god, I get it. I know what it's like not to be able to connect with people—not really—both because of circumstances, and because of things you've done.

Jenna smiles. "Yeah. That's because of Rachel, too. After she died, I could barely function. I couldn't sleep, couldn't eat. I was in the car, too. I was the one *driving*. And I just didn't get why she died and I was barely touched. Like, it should have been me, you know?" Her voice cracks a little, and my heart along with it. "And ultimately I decided I had to get my life together. For her."

There's a lump in my throat the size of a sushi roll, and I can't swallow it. I know exactly what that's like, changing your life because of something terrible, something you can't change or take back.

Katy had a sister too, I remember.

I want to tell Jenna the story, but I know I can't. I need this job, for the opportunity, and because even if I can't be with her, there's something in me that longs to at least stay close to her. I have to. If I tell her about the drugs before she even knows me, I'm afraid of what will happen. I've just promised I can pass a drug test, but I haven't even been out of rehab three weeks.

But I can't just let her tell me these things and give her nothing back.

"I understand a little of how that feels," I say. "The loneliness, and the regret."

She looks up at me. "Yeah?"

"Yeah. Did I tell you I used to go to Juilliard?"

"No, but it doesn't surprise me. You're too good for this band, you know that?"

I laugh. "I don't know about that. Anyway, I got mixed up with some stuff out in New York. Partying, you know. Bad crowd and all that."

She nods. "I know how that is."

I'm not sure she does. "And I left school and came back here and did more or less the same thing. So now here I am, trying to figure my life out again, and I've got no one to talk to except my messed-up parents and my sister Gabby. One day I'm playing on the street and the next I'm a band member in this hugely popular rock band."

"We're pop. But thanks."

"I got kicked out of Juilliard," I say, "but it wasn't by accident. I wanted out."

Jenna looks confused. "Why?"

It's the question I want her to ask, the one I was leading up to. It's something I haven't told anyone, not the real answer, because I know how terrible it sounds.

But I want to tell Jenna, and not just because of everything she's said to me. I get now why she flirted with me, why she agreed to meet me here. She's starving for something, for someone to talk to, to be with, and deep down, so am I. I'd told Gabby I need to get laid, but the truth is, what I need is for someone to see me, and I can see in her eyes, Jenna needs that, too.

It's more than just convenience, though, more than just needing *someone*. I feel like I've been missing something, all the while never knowing it was *her*.

"I messed up at Juilliard," I say, "because I was bored."

Jenna looks surprised. "Really."

"Sounds cocky, right? I'd worked all my life to go to that

56

school. I'd always wanted it. It was the obvious next step. And all my teachers warned me about how it was going to be, small fish, big pond and all that. And I got there, and I wasn't the best, but I was damn close." I shrug. "And I found that clawing my way up half a percent to be the best of the best—it didn't matter to me like I thought it would."

I look at Jenna, waiting to see the judgment in her eyes. Poor rich kid who has everything but doesn't appreciate it, and all that. But instead, she's listening closely, trying to understand. And I desperately want her to.

"It was like I climbed to the top of a mountain and realized there was nothing there," I say. "Nothing I wanted, anyway. It was supposed to be this exciting experience, but nothing was as good as I imagined it would be. So I distracted myself. I started partying."

What I can't bring myself to say is that I started doing heroin, and lasted another eight months at school besides. I take a deep breath before continuing. "I didn't want to admit—to myself or my family—that I'd done all that work and gotten exactly what I wanted only to find out I didn't want it at all."

"But you still want to play," Jenna says.

"I *only* want to play. I don't want to compete for best. I don't want to play the games of who's this teacher's favorite or who plays that concerto a hair better than everyone else. I love the *music*. I just want to play." I smile. "So a couple of days ago that meant sitting in the heat down at Johnny's, and then suddenly this beautiful girl walks up and hands me a salaried position. So I guess you could say I'm feeling pretty good."

Jenna smiles. "You should be feeling good. You earned it."

And while I don't think that's even a little bit true, I'll take it. Her knee bumps mine again, and all I want is to talk about what's going on between us, but I'm afraid to break the spell.

"So ten and a half months, huh?" I say. "There must be at least someone you're interested in."

Her eyes narrow slightly. "Mmm, maybe. But I don't think

I'm going to tell you about that."

"No? Why's that?"

She tugs her lower lip between her teeth. "It's personal."

I laugh. "After everything you've said to me, *that's* too personal?"

Jenna shrugs again, and something passes between us. I know that she knows that I know and so on and so forth and the air buzzes and I can't stand it anymore.

"If this were a normal situation," I say, "this is about the time I'd ask you to dinner."

She holds my gaze. "If this were a normal situation, this is about the time I'd accept."

We stare into each other's eyes, and I can't look away. There it is. This thing that's been going on, this half-spoken attraction, laid bare.

"But it isn't," she says, and I feel my heart break into a dozen pieces. She pokes at the fish with her chopsticks, her eyes narrowed. "You should have heard Alec after you left. 'Oh my *god, Jenna*. What the hell is with you? Jeez, just bang him and get it over with.'" She rolls her eyes. "Thank you, Alec, for your industrious suggestion."

"He said that?"

"Oh, yes. And then he offered to sleep with me himself, if I was so desperate. Like, as a favor for a friend."

Her voice is bitter. I want to punch Alec in the face, for her and for me.

"Are you going to?" I ask.

"Which? You or him?"

I rub my forehead. This conversation is getting away from me, and I don't know what to make of it. "Either."

Jenna's leg rubs against mine under the table and my whole body lights on fire.

I want her. God, I want her, in a way I've never wanted anyone. I had sex with girlfriends in high school, which was okay, I guess, but not the revelation everyone else seemed to think it was. I figured it was because, you know, *high school*, but college wasn't much better, and then there were the drugs, which were their own thing.

I can see in her eyes that she wants me, too, and I can't help but hope things would be different with her.

"Are we allowed to?" I ask.

I wait for her to tell me she doesn't want a one-night stand with me. I try to remember I don't want that with her. But all I can feel is her leg against mine, and damn it, I don't want to make the smart choice.

"I don't think it's a good idea," she says. "Because I'd want more."

My heart swells and aches to hear her say that. I put my hand on her knee under the table. She's right. I would, too. God, I already do. I look up at the ceiling, and her hand rests on top of mine and squeezes.

"Four years, huh?" I say.

Her face shifts in surprise. "Yeah. But don't think I expect you to wait."

I'm shocked to find I'm considering it. "If we're still in the band together, I'm not sure what will have changed."

She closes her eyes. "And I suppose I won't be seeing anyone else. But really, a lot will change in four years. You'll find some-one else. You *should*."

She sounds almost scared, and I turn my hand and take hers in mine beneath the table. I'm not sure how it is we're talking like this, but like all the personal stuff, it feels so right.

"I wouldn't be so sure," I say. "I haven't felt like this . . ." I realize too late that there are no more words to follow that. I haven't felt like this. About anyone. Ever. Jenna's looking at me, waiting for me to finish.

"That's it," I say. "That was the end of the sentence."

Her eyes widen, and her mouth opens, and I'm sure I've lost her. It's too much, in too short a time, and I know it and I'm sorry, but I can't help it. I fish around for something to say, anything to soften what I've done—

But then her hand squeezes mine, and it doesn't let go.

I run my other hand through my hair, and groan. "Not to play devil's advocate, but do you really think being together once will make this any worse?"

She opens her mouth and then shuts it again. Her eyes crinkle. "That's a really good point."

I smile at her. "I don't think that's what you were supposed to say."

"Mmm," she says. "Wasn't it?"

We both sit there for a moment over our half-eaten fish, our hands linked under the table, the tension tight between us.

"Are we doing this?" Jenna asks.

"I think I'm supposed to say no, but I can't convince myself why. You?"

She laughs. "Same."

"We don't have to if you don't want to."

"What I want is a dangerous proposition. We'd have to meet out of town. Drive separately and all that."

And while having to sneak around with her is the last thing I want, I know if I let her go now, I'm going to regret it.

"If we keep sitting here," I say, "I'm going to kiss you."

"The Ramada in Santa Ana," she says. "One hour."

"One hour," I repeat.

And when the waitress comes with the check, we let our hands go under the table.

But her ankle still rubs against mine.

SEVEN

Jenna

By the time I get to the Ramada, I'm a bundle of nerves and conflicting emotions, and no amount of telling myself "It's not a big deal. I want this guy and he wants me and it's okay to go get some" has made it any better.

I do want Felix. Everything in me wants him, and no matter what I tell myself, sleeping with him feels like a very big deal.

It's not like I haven't had plenty of sex before, and with guys I'd known for far less time than Felix. And as much as I feel sick at the thought of going back to that life, I doubt one random afternoon in a Ramada would push me into that pit any more than that one night with that Finnish guy last summer about a month after Alec and I broke up—the one and only one-night stand I've had since I was nineteen.

The sex had been okay, the guy nice enough, but the morning after, I'd just felt empty. Lost. A reminder of the way things used to be, and painful enough that I hadn't even considered another one.

Until Felix, that is. But talking with him today felt like talking with someone I've known all my life, someone I could tell anything to, but laced with the giddy thrill of discovering this new, fascinating person I want to learn everything about.

Not exactly a prelude to getting this out of my system.

I grab the bobby pins I keep in the glove compartment, and flip down the mirror above the driver's seat. Then I undo my braid and start pinning the red streaks up, where they can be hidden under a hat. Fortunately, I'm not so famous that people instantly know who I am everywhere I go, especially when I'm not with Alec.

With my hair pinned up, I grab a straw sun hat from the backseat, left there from a beach trip with Ty the day before we met Felix. Three days ago, only. It's kind of hard to believe.

The hat looks like it would go way better with a flowy bohemian sundress than with the shiny metallic skirt and black shirt I've got on now, but whatever. I don't need fashion approval from the hotel receptionist. Just enough distance from my public persona that even if they think they know me from somewhere, they aren't likely to connect the dots.

Meeting at the Ramada will help with that. Celebrities having clandestine hotel meetings isn't exactly uncommon, but from what I've heard—and I've heard a lot—most still do so at the fancy luxury hotels, like they just can't imagine a rendezvous that isn't followed by room service prepared by a Michelin-starred chef. Supposedly the staff is more discreet at places like that, but you can always find someone willing to talk to the paparazzi for the right amount.

Not that I trust the discretion of the staff here any more than anywhere else, but the truth is, no one expects to see a celebrity walking into a budget-friendly hotel chain for a nooner.

Or so my theory goes. I don't exactly do this often. Or ever.

I already had a fake name, complete with credit card, for times when Alec and I didn't want to be recognized, so it was easy to call ahead and pre-book the room, and when I check in at the front desk, they have the key card ready for me.

"The other room key has already been picked up," the receptionist says, giving me a pleasant smile. And no trace of recognition.

My heart speeds up. Felix is here, in the room, waiting for me. And even though we've only been separated for an hour, I just want to be with him again. I'm like a moth diving straight for the flame.

God, is that what I'm doing? It took me six months to say yes to dating Alec, after he saw me singing karaoke one night and asked me to join his band. I'd been so afraid of slipping back into my old life, so I hadn't made a single decision impulsively, or out of passion. I'd waited until I was sure that being with Alec made sense.

Was that the smarter way to handle it, or was it the reason Alec and I turned out to be such a bad idea?

I take the elevator up to the fourth floor. Then I head down the hallway and find room 415. I take off my sunhat and pull the bobby pins out so my red streaks join the rest of my hair, which after being in a braid hopefully has a nice wavy quality to it now. I put the pins in my purse and stare at the door.

Then I stand there for a moment, toying with the key card.

Are we really going to do this?

I want to; god, I do. But I can't help feeling unsettled in a way I didn't when we were at the sushi restaurant, the connection between us so strong, so tangible, like I could see it if I squint hard enough. I felt comfortable talking about things in my life I rarely talk about with anyone—and never, never so quickly. I'd been friends with Alec, and part of his band, for weeks before I told him about the frat parties and my part in what happened to Rachel. And even then, I think I mainly told him because while Ann Arbor is a big city, it's not *that* big. I knew he'd hear rumors eventually. Besides which, I had to give him some sort of reason why I kept turning him down for dates, even though I'd as much as admitted I liked him. Leo, Roxie, Mason—none of them know as much about me as Felix already does.

I slip the card into the door and open it. And there's Felix, lying on his back on the bed with his hands behind his head. He's still in his dark-wash jeans and a fitted t-shirt, and his blond hair has that perfect slightly mussed quality to it. He smiles, but there's something nervous about it.

The door clicks closed behind me, and I set my hat and purse down on a table by the door. The hotel room is predictably nice, in a generic hotel sort of way, with an impressionistic forest painting on one wall and a sizeable TV on the other. On the nightstand, staring right at me, is a brochure with some All-American Family—forgettably attractive parents and two kids, a boy and a girl—splashing around in the Ramada's Luxury Pool and enjoying the hotel's "low rates and family-friendly accommodations."

Not exactly a place that screams secret afternoon sex romp. But probably a hell of a lot more hygienic than the type of place that would, so there's that.

Felix smiles, like he knows what I'm thinking. "I can turn the brochure around if you want. So that family isn't silently judging us."

I laugh, but it sounds nervous, and Felix wipes his hands on his jeans.

"Hey," I say, still fiddling with the key card.

"Hey," he says back. "Are you having second thoughts?"

I guess it's obvious. Probably because I'm still standing by the door. "I'm having all the thoughts," I admit. "You?"

He groans and covers his eyes. "Yeah."

I'm not sure if his thoughts are the same as mine, but there's something comforting to not being the only one conflicted about this. The aching parts of my body aren't nearly as comforted, though. Because if he's also conflicted, then it's probably best, and most responsible, if this doesn't happen.

I sigh and sit down at the edge of the bed, though I wish I could be much, much closer to him. I'm not sure if that's what's best for him, for me, for us.

How can I be thinking of an *us* already?

We smile weakly at each other. "Have you seen *Jerry Maguire?*" he asks.

That pretty much leads the list of conversation topics I wasn't expecting. "Um, once. A *long* time ago."

Felix sighs. "There's something Cuba Gooding Junior's character says to Jerry, and I can't stop thinking about it."

Now I'm really confused. "Show me the money?"

He laughs, and my heart thrills a bit, because god, he's got a great laugh. He holds out an arm to me. "No. Not that. Hey, no one can see us in here. You want to come closer?"

Do I ever. I want to climb on top of him and muss his hair up even more. I want to feel his hands running up the back of my short skirt. I want him to kiss me and kiss me until I can't remember my own name.

I settle for scooting in next to him so I'm lying up against his side, my head on his shoulder. I close my eyes, letting myself soak in the warmth of his body against mine. And more than the sexual desires—though there's definitely that—I feel . . . content. Blissfully so.

"So the girl Jerry's dating is a single mother, you know?" he says. "And the Cuba Gooding Junior character, I can't remember his name, but his mom was a single mother, too."

The contented feeling becomes a hard pit in my stomach so fast I'm not sure how I manage to take a breath.

So that's what he's conflicted about. Of course.

"Oh," I say. "You don't want to get mixed up with someone with a kid."

He looks a little stunned. "No, that's not—that's not what I'm getting at. That's not what he says."

I pause. Maybe I jumped to that assumption too quickly. "Okay. What does he say?"

"He says you don't shoplift the pooty from a single mother."

I can't help but laugh. "Shoplift the *what*? How do I not remember this?"

"The pooty," he says, with that gorgeous grin of his. "And I do not know."

I may not know what the hell a pooty is, but I can—kind

of—see where he's going with this now, and I'm relieved Felix isn't averse to being with me because of Ty, who is, of course, a non-negotiable part of my life and always will be.

That relief is great enough that I giggle, putting my head back on his shoulder. "So is that what we're doing? Shoplifting?"

He groans. "That's how it feels. Tell me that's stupid."

"Mmm. I'm not sure that it is." But stupid or not, I've never wanted to shoplift so badly in my life.

"I told you I'm not proud of my past, right?" he says.

I nod. He did, in vague terms, though I sure know what it's like not to want to think about the details of past indiscretions.

"One of the things I've been working on," he says, "is paying attention when my gut tells me something doesn't feel right. Making sure I'm doing what I need to stay out of trouble, even if it interferes with what I want."

"And this doesn't feel right," I say. I both agree and disagree with that, and apparently so does he, because he shakes his head.

"It does," he says. "Too right to happen only once."

What he's saying is true, and I know it. I close my eyes.

"I think I knew that before you showed up," he says. "I was lying here checking my phone waiting for the text that would say you'd changed your mind. Sometimes when I'm stressed, I have this habit of sitting still and not moving, because if I don't move, I can't make a mistake. But I think in this case, I could have picked a better location."

Something about that stings, the way he's describing me as a mistake he has the potential of making. And even though he just said this feels right—too right—I can't help but wonder. "Do you want me to leave?"

He shakes his head. "I really don't."

I relax against him, under the warmth of his arm, even though I'm not sure what it is we're doing here.

"How is it possible," he says, rubbing his forehead, "that I'm lying here next to you, in a bed, in a secret hotel room in the middle of the afternoon, and I'm somehow suggesting we *not* have sex?"

I laugh. "I don't know. You do seem torn up about it."

"I really don't know who I am right now."

I put my arm around his chest, feeling the muscles through his t-shirt, and lean in close enough that my nose presses into his cheek. "You're cute, whoever you are."

I'm so intensely aware of how close his lips are to mine that I'm finding it hard to breathe. He pulls me in even closer, which doesn't help my breathing any. It does, however, feel *so* good. My body fits perfectly tucked up against his like this.

I can only imagine how perfectly it fits with his in other ways.

His fingers trail along my bare arm, raising goosebumps along my skin. "This isn't how I want it to go," he says, and I know I'm not the only one imagining us fitting together with less clothes in the way.

"How do you want it to go?"

"In another situation, I would have asked you to dinner. And then maybe to coffee after. And then breakfast the next day. You wouldn't have been able to get rid of me, I'd be so clingy."

My heart flutters happily, thinking of Felix and me on long romantic dates, talking about anything and everything—like lunch at the sushi restaurant, only without the restraints of all the rules. "You do seem the high-maintenance type," I say with a laugh. "But somehow, I think I wouldn't mind."

And I wouldn't. Something about talking with him, being with him—I never want it to end. I think of how it was even talking with him on the phone to tell him about the audition, frantically trying to think of something to say to keep from hanging up. I wasn't even aware before today of how much I needed someone to talk to, someone who cares about me for me, and not as part of a band, or as a member of their family who they depend on. Alec and I lost that—the easy way we used to talk—long before our relationship ended.

And even then, it was never like *this*.

"Maybe we'd sleep together," he continues. "And maybe we

wouldn't yet. But I'd treat you with respect, and whenever that did happen, I'd sure as hell still be there in the morning."

My throat goes dry and my heart pounds faster. He would be; I know that. He wouldn't be like those other guys, the ones I let use me. The ones who only wanted me for sex, the ones who never saw me.

He would be there in the morning, and he would look at me like he's looking at me now, like there's no world outside of this room, outside of us.

And I know, sadly, what I need to do. Or not do, I suppose. "I have an answer to your question now. It would make things worse if we slept together."

He covers his face with his hand. "This is the worst," he groans.

I laugh, knowing all too well how he feels. "Tell me about it." I move to sit up, but again his arm around me tightens.

"Do you need to go?" he asks.

I look back at him, surprised.

"You can if you want," he says quickly. "But we've got a couple hours, right? You could stay and talk. Fair warning, though. I'll probably kiss you."

I at once feel flushed with desire and completely confused. "You want to kiss me, even if we're not going to have sex." I'm not sure what to do with this. It goes beyond my experience with guys—even the good ones, like Alec.

But Felix responds like the answer to this is obvious. "Yeah. What about you?"

I do. More than that, I just want to be with him longer, even if all we can do is hold each other and talk. I settle back in next to him, and it's like my whole body relaxes—like it had tensed up in that brief moment we'd been apart, and I hadn't even realized it until I was back in his arms.

He wants to kiss me, even if we aren't going to have sex. The girl I was four years ago would have found this laughable, impossible even. Which may be why I feel the need to sort out what, exactly, we're doing. "So you'll kiss me today. And after this we'll just be friends."

It hurts to say that last part, but it's what's necessary. Isn't it?

He shakes his head. "I can't do that. I can't pretend to be just your friend."

My throat closes. "Are you going to leave the band?"

"No," he says, and I let out a breath of relief. "But it's something I'm working on—trying to be authentic. True to myself, I guess." He pauses. "That probably sounds stupid."

"No. You're talking to a professional liar. I get it. It sucks to put on an act." I didn't think it would, or at least not so badly, when Alec and I agreed to keep doing this for the sake of our careers.

But even in the worst parts of my past, I was never much of a liar. Except, maybe, to myself.

Felix brushes the hair back from where it's falling over my face, and I close my eyes against the touch of his fingers, soft and yet I can feel the callouses of years of cello playing, which is somehow crazy sexy. Or maybe just on him. "Exactly," he says. "I can pretend for the world, but I can't put on an act with you. I can keep the rules. We don't have to date, and we don't have to touch. But I also don't want to pretend this is anything other than what it is."

"And, what is that, exactly?"

He gapes a little, like it didn't occur to him to define it. "I don't know. If you have a clue, you're welcome to fill me in."

I press in tighter against him. "Whatever it is, I like it."

There's this moment where we're silent, just breathing each other in. I can feel his heartbeat under the palm of my hand. I find myself wishing this was my life. Only this, and no rules about what we can and can't do.

But this is just a perfect, stolen afternoon, and I need to know what follows. Partly because as amazing as it feels to be more to him than just a sexy encounter and a friendship after, I can't put my finger on what more we could be. "So if we're not together and we won't touch, what's the difference between that and being friends?"

His lips twist as he considers. "You have close guy friends, yeah?"

"Yeah. I was close to Mason." A stab of hurt follows those words. I'd *thought* I was close to him. "And there's Leo."

"And you talk to Leo like this?"

I laugh. "Ha. No."

"Well. There you go."

I roll off him enough to prop myself up on my elbows. I should let it go, should just be satisfied that there's this thing between us, and we both feel it, even if we can't put a name to it. But part of me needs some kind of label, as if that makes it more likely to be real and still exist the moment I leave this hotel room. "I'm still not entirely sure what it is we're doing here."

Felix's blue eyes study mine. "I can't pretend to be your friend because I'm past there. It's like, there's friendship, and there's sex, and then there's like this third thing . . ." He cringes. "I can't believe I'm about to say these words. I can assure you I have never uttered them in my entire life."

My heartbeat picks up. Friendship. Sex. A third thing. "Go on."

He bites his lip. "I guess it's like, emotional . . . intimacy?" Then he closes his eyes. "Oh god, what is wrong with me?"

I laugh, because Felix said those words like they're a foreign language, and also because it's less scary than the word I was thinking.

I lie back down on his chest, my arms around his neck. His heart is racing, and mine's keeping pace. "Emotional intimacy," I say. "I like it. I could get behind that."

He sighs. "So does that put us on the four year plan?"

Ugh, four years. But that he would even consider it . . . "I'm still not sure you actually remember I have a kid. And a past. And a hell of a lot of baggage."

"I have baggage, too. I'm not ready to tell you all of it yet, but I will."

This stings a bit more than is reasonable. I mean, I was open with him at the restaurant—far more so than I've ever been with someone I've known for so little time—but it's not like I went into all the details of my past over sushi.

I wonder, though, if someday I could tell him everything.

I wonder if he would still feel the same about me, after knowing all the things I've done.

"It's okay," I say, because I believe him when he says he will tell me. Maybe I'm being stupid and naive, but I find I trust him. I trust he's not playing with me or using me. I trust that this thing between us—this emotional intimacy—is as real for him as it is for me.

And then something occurs to me. "You know I'm still going to have to pretend to be with Alec, right?"

"I know. I get it."

I'm not sure he does, not really. "That means we have to go out. Like scheduled appearances. Phil makes us appointments, gives us places to go. Like . . . on dates."

"Yeah," he says. "I get that you have to keep up appearances."

But I'm realizing how unfair it is, if he has feelings for me, to have to see me with Alec. Being a couple with Alec, which isn't the same thing as watching us at band practice. "And sometimes we have to like, kiss and stuff. Only in public, and it's not like we full-on make out or anything."

His arms wrap around me. "Jenna, I get it. I know."

And even though everything in me is begging me not to say this, I do anyway. "So you should date other people."

His hand runs through my hair, his fingers gently separating the strands. "We're not in a committed relationship. We can't be. So I'm absolutely allowed to date other people."

I told him he should, but my heart feels like it's splintering apart.

"And you're going to want to," I say quickly, as if saying it out loud will help. "Of course you are. Why wouldn't you?"

His fingers graze the curve of my ear, then cup my chin. I

71

meet his eyes.

"I don't exactly want to spend my time leading girls on," he say. "Unless you plan to hire me a fake girlfriend to throw off suspicion."

But four years is a long time. And if my world can have changed so quickly, so thoroughly, in two days . . .

"You might find someone," I say, the words barely more than a whisper.

His thumb caresses my cheek, and his lips quirking up into a smile. "Because in my experience, something like this is *so* easy to come by."

His words from before echo in my head: *I haven't felt like this.*

Neither have I, I want to say. But words fail me, because I can see the look in his eyes as he cradles my face in his hands, and my breath catches and my blood rushes and then his lips are on mine.

And in the heat that consumes me, it's like everything shifts—my life, the world, everything.

Or maybe I finally realize how much it already shifted, before I even knew it. Back when I first met eyes with a gorgeous guy playing his cello and sitting in the bright sun on Hollywood Boulevard.

It's more than wanting him; it's needing him. We're kissing, and his hands are running over my back, my waist, down my thighs, and mine are doing the same to him, and we may be clothed now, but I can feel in a very definite way how much he also wants more than this, and I know it's only a matter of time before we abandon our good sense.

I break off from the kiss and bury my face in his neck. I feel the fever-heat of his skin against my cheek and hear the hammering of his heart against my chest.

"Four *years*," I say, my body aching. My heart pounding. "Are we really talking about that?"

He presses his forehead against mine. "I'm going to go out on a limb and say we probably won't make it four years before we start breaking rules. But I do think we can make it more than four *days*. How about you?"

I can't help but laugh. "I can't believe we're talking about this. This isn't normal."

"Not normal at all," he says, his breathing still a little ragged. "I think that was the point I was making before." But he's smiling, and I'm smiling back, because while I'm scared, I'm also giddy and a dozen kinds of wound up right now.

"Ahhhh. What are we doing?"

He kisses my forehead, and it takes everything in me not to start making out with him again.

"Taking Alec up on his one-night offer," he says, grinning against my skin. "At least somewhat."

I groan. Alec would be disappointed in me that I'm not doing more than making out. But if kissing Felix feels like this, I can't imagine how hard it would be to go back if we did more. "I think it's having the opposite effect," I say. "It's more like free sample day at the grocery store."

He smiles. "Ha. So we're trying this out with the intention to buy."

The intention to buy. For good. His smile slips after he says this, and I think I know why.

Because it sounds insane, but it feels exactly the opposite.

"You're right," I say, slowly. "It doesn't have to be four years. If things stay this way, I might be ready to get out sooner."

Oh, god. I should not be considering that. After everything Alec has done for me, after this freak success he and I have had—I have a *kid*, for god's sake. I can't throw all that away, just because I'm terrified Felix is going to rightly decide I'm not worth all of this.

Felix must sense what I'm thinking, because he shakes his head. "It's okay if you're not ready to destroy your career trajectory for a guy you just met. Let's just see how it goes, okay?"

I let out a breath, closing my eyes. I'm not going to be able to be with him, not like this. Not after today. We'll be able to talk, to be emotionally intimate, as he said, but to not even be able to touch him? To not feel his arms around me like this?

"Okay," I say, reluctantly. "But I already know it's going to suck."

"Yeah," he murmurs, holding me close. "It will." He pauses. "I need to ask you something."

There's enough hesitation in his tone that I pull back a bit. "What?"

"I signed that piece of paper, saying I wouldn't tell anyone."

"Yeah. And it's really important you don't." Alec would kill me if he said anything.

Felix's brow furrows. "If things keep going like this, I'm going to need someone to talk to about it."

He sounds apologetic, so I think he gets the magnitude of what he's asking for. But he did just tell me he's trying to be more authentic, and I'm the one who saddled him with an enormous lie he wasn't prepared to deal with.

"If I just told my sister Gabby," he continues. "She wouldn't tell a soul. I swear. When she understands how important it is, she'd never do anything that could hurt me like that. It would really help have someone to talk to about what's going on."

I pause, thinking it through. I want to give him this, when he's being so patient with me, but I also don't want the secret to get out. Alec and I have worked so hard. He doesn't deserve to lose everything just because I'm having the world's worst-timed emotional intimacy with our cellist. "She won't tell anyone. Not a soul."

"No one," he says. "If I impress upon her how much depends on that, she wouldn't."

"Don't tell Alec. Or anyone else in the band."

"Not a word. No one will know but her."

I know Alec would be so pissed at me for agreeing to this, but I have to. Felix deserves this, and so much more. "Okay. With everything you're putting up with for me, I can't deny you that." I pause, thinking of him telling his sister all about me.

Imagining how a sister might react to all of this. "Tell me how she takes it, though? Otherwise I'll worry."

He grins. "Talking isn't against the rules, right? So I intend to tell you everything."

Everything.

Warmth fills me, all the way to my toes, and I'm grinning back at him. It won't be physical intimacy, but maybe the emotional will be enough. Until we decide it isn't anymore, and we make our plans—and my exit strategy—accordingly.

His lips are so close to mine, and I can't resist leaning in close and kissing him, slow and soft, and then deeper, until all my thoughts are scattered at his touch. I don't know when I'll be able to kiss him like this again—maybe not for years—and I'm not wasting a single, perfect moment. We kiss and kiss and kiss, just lost in each other.

And I don't ever want to be found.

EIGHT

Felix

By the time Jenna leaves the hotel to pick up Ty, I feel warm and safe in a way I haven't in a long time. I've never felt this way, not with any of the other girls I've been with, not even close. And that makes my heart ache because I'm finally feeling something deep and real for someone and I want to see it all the way through.

I already feel empty without her. It's only been a few minutes since she left my arms, and somehow, I've agreed to do this for something like four years.

I'm not sure what I could have been thinking, except that when I go over my options again, I know this is the only tolerable one. I can't leave the band. Not only do I need the money and the steady job, but the idea of not seeing Jenna at all is excruciating. And it's not that I don't want to be friends, but I already know I'm physically incapable of it. This pull between us is too strong to hide. I need to be able to talk to her about how I feel, to make sure she knows how much I want her, even if we can't act on it. Telling her the truth about what I'm thinking—it's like finding my way again, after I thought I'd permanently lost it.

The part I can't get over is the fact that she wants this. She wants *me*. Maybe as badly as I want her.

I was right to ask her if I could talk to Gabby about this, because if I don't tell someone, I'm going to go insane. I leave the hotel a safe amount of time after Jenna, so we aren't seen walking out together, and call Gabby from my car. "Hey. Please tell me you aren't working right now."

"If I were," Gabby says, "I wouldn't answer the phone. Are you okay?"

"Still clean. But I have some news I have to tell you in person. Can I meet you at your place?"

"Sure. But you didn't answer my question." Concern is growing in her voice, despite my assurance about the drugs.

"I'm okay," I say quickly. I really don't want her worrying about me any more than she undoubtedly already does. "Better than okay. Mostly. I'll be there in an hour." I look at the time. I'm going to hit the mid-afternoon rush. "Make it two."

As I drive to Hollywood the latest Accidental Erotica single comes on the radio. Every song from Shane Beckstrom's last album makes me laugh, even though Gabby assures me it's not even a little funny that he titled the thing "I Still Love You" and wrote every song about how much he wants to reunite with Anna-Marie. Apparently it's all for show—which makes me wonder if there are bands that *aren't* faking their narratives. It seems to be working for Shane almost as well as it did for AJ.

More power to him, I guess.

As I sit in traffic, I realize I haven't been to a meeting today. This is the first day I've skipped since I left rehab, but I don't really want to go vomit some vague story at a room full of miserable addicts. I've seen twelve-step veterans and newbies alike jump all over some poor guy who dares to say he's looking at a relationship sooner out of rehab than they think he should be, and I don't want to be the reason the facilitator has to crack down on the cross talk. I just want to talk to my sister.

But since I'm not stupid, I drop by the clinic on my way to her apartment for my Suboxone, and get the good news: my fine behavior and passed drug tests have granted me the privilege of a two-day maintenance prescription, meaning I only have to come in every three days from now on.

I smile all the way to Gabby's apartment, reliving the memory of Jenna's lips on mine, of the feel of her tucked up against my side. When Gabby opens her door, I smell hot tomato sauce and cheese, and my stomach rumbles. "Pizza," I say. "Please tell me you saved me some."

"There's some left," Gabby says. "But I have to warn you, it's made of cauliflower."

I stare at her. Gabby is many things, but she's not a health nut. "Cauliflower pizza?"

"Yeah. They make the crust out of cauliflower, actually. It's Will's favorite."

I make a face, and she rolls her eyes. "He made some to take over to Josh and Ben's guys' night thing. I bet they're making the same face."

I realize I have no idea what guys do at a guys' night thing if they aren't playing music or doing drugs. "So Will isn't here?"

Gabby shakes her head. "No, is that a problem?"

Actually, it makes things easier. "Not at all."

Gabby's still looking at me nervously as she dishes up some of the pizza Will left us. It's thinner and flatter than regular pizza, but other than that it looks the same.

She hands me a fork. "So? What's the news?"

"Well," I say, "I signed with the band this morning."

Gabby's eyes open wide. "With AJ. You signed with *AJ*."

"Yeah. As a full band member. Not just for the tour."

Gabby squeals and leaves the plates on the counter to give me an enormous hug. "That is *crazy*. I mean, not that they would sign you because obviously you're amazing, but that it happened so fast! So you're going on tour?" She pauses. "Is that going to be okay? What about your medication? Will you be able to get it when you're traveling?" She looks down at the pizza and I can tell she's having all the worries I had before my audition.

"No one in the band does drugs," I say. "They even drug test, to make sure, after how they lost their last cellist."

Gabby perks up, and hands me a plate of pizza. "Seriously? That's *great*."

"And for the medication, I'll figure it out. Trust me, they're going to have Methadone clinics wherever we go. And I just got cleared for a two-day prescription." Methadone gets sold on the street in two seconds after being prescribed, but the Suboxone I'm on instead has Naloxone in it, which is the drug they give people to stop overdoses. You can't get high off the stuff, which makes me way more functional than a Methadone patient, and also means the clinic is keeping tabs on me because I agreed to that as part of my outpatient to increase my accountability. I'm pretty sure if there's a reason, they'll make an exception.

Gabby brings her pizza over to the purple couch, seeming mollified. "Okay, so Alec and Jenna. Are they as cute in real life?" She looks ready for some gossip, and boy, do I have that.

I take a deep breath. "So, I'm going to offer you a choice. And I want you to really think about it, okay?"

Gabby pauses with her fork over her pizza. "*Okay.*"

"There are two versions of this story. One you can tell anyone, and one that I can tell you, but you cannot repeat to another soul. Not to Will, not to Anna-Marie, not to anyone. I don't have to tell you, but I want to, and if I do and it gets out, it'll destroy me, personally and professionally, so I need you to be sure you can handle it."

Gabby stares at me, and I make a show of taking a big bite of pizza while she considers. Eating pizza with a fork seems pretentious as hell, but I immediately see why it's necessary. The crust doesn't hold together as well as normal. "Hey," I say with my mouth full. "This isn't bad."

"Felix," Gabby says. "Are they working for the mob?"

I laugh and swallow my pizza. "No. I promise, I'm not doing anything dangerous or illegal."

She narrows her eyes. "And no drugs."

I hold up my hands, one still holding the fork. "No drugs. I swear."

"And I can't tell *Will?* You know I suck at that, right?"

I smile. "I don't have to tell you."

She tosses a throw pillow at me, and it lands in my pizza. Gabby doesn't seem to notice. "Obviously I have to know now! You can't just lay that on me and not tell me."

"Honestly, I don't think Will is going to care that much about this secret. Anna-Marie on the other hand . . ."

Gabby squeezes her eyes closed, like she's bracing herself. "Okay. Tell me."

"And you won't breathe a word of it."

"I won't."

"Not to anyone."

"No one."

"Not to Will or Anna-Marie."

"Not to a damned goldfish—Felix, will you tell me already?"

I cut another bite of pizza with my fork and Gabby stares at it like she's going to snatch it out of my hand. I have to admit, I'm enjoying this a little too much.

"Okay," I say, "Alec and Jenna broke up a year ago."

Gabby stares at me. "Whaaaaat?"

"They were dating, but they weren't happy. So they broke up but they didn't want to split up the band. So now they're faking it."

Gabby puts her hand over her mouth. "No. No, they are *so* cute! That can't be fake."

I nod. "It is. And there's more."

Gabby's pizza lies forgotten in her lap. "More."

"I may have spent the afternoon in a hotel room making out with Jenna Rollins."

Gabby lets out a little yelp. "No way."

I settle back on the couch, giving her a smug look. "I told you she was hitting on me."

She tosses her remaining throw pillow at me, but this one

flies by my head. "You made out with her in a hotel room . . . and that's it?"

I nod. "Yeah. Because I suggested we weren't ready to have sex yet. Because we can't, like, be in a relationship yet."

Now she looks confused. "Weren't you just sitting in that very spot telling me how much you need to get laid?"

"Well, that's what I thought was going to happen. But then we got there, and we were only allowed that one time, because Jenna and Alec agreed they shouldn't be in relationships with other people, because it's bound to get out. And I didn't want just a one-night stand with her, you know? I wanted more than that." The ache sweeps over me again, how very much I want more than that with her.

Gabby is back to looking at me warily. "More than that."

"Yeah. So we talked about how there's friendship, and sex, and then, like, this third thing, and if we want more than friendship, that's what we're allowed to have."

Gabby stares at me, deadpan. "Yes, Felix. There *is* a third thing."

I swallow a bite of pizza, and nearly choke. I know what she means, but I'm not even the slightest bit ready to admit I'm thinking it. "Right. But I can't be with her because she has to pretend to be with Alec for another four years."

Gabby's brows draw together. "Four *years?*"

"Yeah. Something about by then the band will have peaked and they'll be ready to launch their solo careers."

Gabby points her fork at me. The tines are covered in tomato sauce, and some flicks onto the couch. That's not going to help her sell it.

"And you're not allowed to sleep with her," Gabby says.

I nod. "Or touch her at all, really."

"For four years."

"Or until she's sick of the situation," I say, closing my eyes briefly.

Gabby bites her lip. "Are you sure this is a good idea? That sounds like a mess."

"What else am I going to do?"

"I don't know," Gabby says. "*Not* get involved with her?"

"It's kind of too late. Besides, I'd have to leave the band. And it's a really good job. They're paying me on salary. To play cello."

Gabby nods. "Okay, yeah. That's hard to pass up."

That's not even close to the most important part. "What would you do if it was Will in this situation? Would you just walk away?"

Gabby seems to honestly consider it. "I love Will. But I don't think I could wait four years, watching him pretend to be in love with someone else. That would tear me up. I'd constantly be worried he was going to rekindle things with her."

I could see that. It seems like the sort of thing I should be worried about, but I'm not. "I'm not going to walk away. I need this job, and I really care about her."

"Okay," Gabby says. "But say this works out. She has a kid, and you are like the opposite of a kid person."

She's not wrong.

I fold my pizza, pick it up and stuff it in my mouth. "I like her kid," I say. "He's kind of hilarious."

Gabby grabs a cloth and cleans up her cushion and pillow of the pizza sauce. "I hate this couch, but I do want to sell it."

I'm still planning to buy it, and to pay Gabby back for the cello storage with interest, but I need to get paid first. And now I'm stressing about Ty, because yeah, I'm not a kid person, and Jenna doesn't know how much she shouldn't trust me to start. A pit is forming in my stomach that has nothing to do with the cauliflower pizza. "She doesn't know about the drug stuff yet," I say. "After she does, you're right. She won't want me around her kid."

Gabby shakes her head. "That's not what I meant. Do *you* want a kid? Because I thought that wasn't something you were into."

I shrug. "It's not like I hate children. I'm twenty-two. It hasn't

82

really been on my mind."

"And in four years, you'll be twenty-six. Will you be ready for kids then?"

The truth is, I don't know. Right now, I know I'm not even half as responsible as I'd need to be to take care of a kid. I don't have an apartment; I just barely got a job. I've done pretty much nothing with my adult life besides irrevocably fuck it up.

But I care about Jenna, a lot. People do crazy things for people they care about.

Though I'm the first person to admit that they hurt them, too. "I don't know," I say.

Gabby looks sympathetic. "I'd say you should spend more time with Ephraim, but Dana won't let anyone watch him but Mom. I got to babysit him exactly one time, and she yelled at me for an hour because I put in the wrong Neil deGrasse Tyson DVD."

I roll my eyes. "Did she really?"

"Apparently I ruined his 'education plan' by showing him the same video twice."

That sounds like Dana. I stare at the pizza on my plate, not really seeing it. "You really think I'd be a bad father?"

"No!" Gabby says quickly. "That's not what I meant at all. I just didn't think you'd *want* to jump into parenthood like that."

She was probably right the first time, and I'm pretty sure Jenna's going to agree with her. "I like Ty. I could see having a relationship with him, playing games and helping with homework and stuff. He's cute and smart. And kind of a troublemaker, but in a good way."

Gabby smiles. "Sounds like you as a kid."

I shrug. "Maybe I haven't changed that much."

"Hey," Gabby says. "Since I'm keeping this epic secret for you, do you think you can do me a favor?"

I owe Gabby about a million favors after the last few years, so I'm glad she's starting to cash them in. "Sure. What?"

"Do you think you could get AJ to play Anna-Marie's

wedding?"

I pause. "When is it?"

"Two weeks."

That's right between the LA performance and the tour, so it's not out of the question. "I'll ask," I say. "I might be able to talk Jenna into it, because she'll clearly want to impress you."

Gabby laughs. "Jenna Rollins. Will want to impress *me*."

"Of course. You're my favorite sister, after all."

"And I have such fierce competition."

"Yeah, well," I say. "Out of every sister, you're pretty much the best."

"You're buttering me up for when Jenna says no. But if you can pull it off, Anna-Marie will die." Gabby pauses and then laughs again. "How did this happen to you, anyway? I mean, you're good looking, but you're not *that* good looking."

I raise an eyebrow. "If you tell me Alec is hotter than me again, you're getting a slice of pizza to the face."

"No, really," she says, "are you exuding some kind of strange pheromone you should be aware of? Because that could be good for business if you're playing on the street, but it could become a problem in a rock band."

"It's my new cologne. Busk, for men."

"Yes," she says, with a mock eye-roll. "I'm sure that's it. And this is totally not self-serving and definitely because I'm an overprotective big sister, but I will need to meet Jenna at some point."

"You can probably come to band practice. But you'll have to pretend not to know anything, because only Jenna knows I've told you."

"I can keep my mouth shut."

I smile. "I'll text Jenna and let her know."

Gabby pauses. "Should you be doing that? Texting her a lot, I mean?"

"Sure," I say. And then I realize what she means. "Shit. Celebrity phones get hacked all the time."

"Just something to be aware of."

I groan. "We're not going to be able to go out, and Alec is going to be there during band practice. If I can't text or call, then when *am* I going to talk to her?" We could always sneak around, but I don't love the idea. Too much chance of getting caught, and besides, she'll have to be home a lot, since she has a kid.

It scares me how much this bothers me. I've never been high maintenance before. If anything, I've been chewed out—even dumped—by a number of girls who said I didn't pay enough attention to them, that I wasn't open enough, that I didn't spend enough time with them. Wouldn't talk on the phone with them for hours, or text them all the time.

But this—the way I'm feeling right now—it changes everything. And I know I'm hoping for something better with her, something that might resemble the holy grail that everyone else is always talking about, the thing I play along as if I understand. Because yeah, sex feels good. But, like the drugs, the aftermath always felt . . . empty.

This afternoon in the hotel, though, even just talking and kissing and holding each other . . . There was nothing empty about that. Only about not being with her anymore.

Gabby smiles. "You could get some of those pay-as-you-go phones. Like they use in movies."

"You sound like you're joking, but that's actually a really good idea."

"See? I am the best sister ever. Totally worth getting your band to play at my best friend's wedding as a surprise so I can also be the best maid of honor."

I finish my pizza and take our plates to the sink. "Agreed," I say. "Let me see what I can do."

NINE

Felix

I spend most of the next couple days practicing the cello parts to the songs on the most recent AJ album. *Everything We Are* is more musically complex than their first album, but it still isn't Bach. Playing the notes isn't a problem, though there are places I want to play differently than Mason. I text Jenna, and she says that's fine.

I hope it's still fine when she hears me play.

Alec is the first person to show up to practice besides me. I've already been there for hours, as evidenced by my three empty coffee cups. I haven't eaten much and I'm jittery, but I have all the songs down, and tentative cello parts for several of the songs Mason didn't play.

Alec walks in and surveys the damage. I've got the sheet music to just about everything printed and spread all over, and I'm halfway through track six of *Everything We Are*, a ballad called "Imperfect Perfection" about finally finding the person who will accept and love you for your faults as much as your strengths.

This part of the story, I'm still not sure I believe.

"You've been playing with the recording?" Alec asks. He leans against the wall, his thumbs jammed into the pockets of his fitted jeans.

"Yeah," I say. "I know it's not the same as live, but it's something."

Alec nods. "You don't have to be a carbon copy of Mason, you know."

"And I'm not. But it's not a bad place to start. It's what your fans will be looking for, anyway."

"*Our* fans," Alec says. "They'll accept you if you do something different, as long as you don't suck."

"Thanks, man. No pressure."

Alec laughs. "Dude. You're jumping in with a week to performance. Pressure is definitely on."

"Yeah, well," I say. "Bring it."

Alec smiles, but then his face grows serious. "I heard you and Jenna didn't take me up on my offer."

My mouth opens a little, and I try not to gape at him. Are we seriously going to have a conversation right here in the studio about how I didn't sleep with Jenna?

How much does he know, anyway?

"You heard right," I say.

Alec shakes his head, like he's disappointed in us. "Jenna's gorgeous, but don't let her get to you."

Now I actually do gape at him. "Are you suggesting I can't control where I put my penis when there's a beautiful woman around?"

"I'm suggesting she's *hot*," Alec says. "I was all over that, remember?"

I remember. I'm surrounded by reminders, right down to the very music I'm playing. Which suddenly seems a whole lot less theoretical with Alec standing in front of me. I have no idea how much of the stuff in their music is made up, and how much is based on how they used to be together.

I at once want to ask her, and am afraid to know.

"I don't blame you for being into her," Alec says. "I still think you guys should have done it and gotten it over with.

87

But if that's *not your style*, hands off. That's all I'm saying." He scratches at the dark beard scruff he seems to keep in a constant five o' clock shadow.

He seems to be judging me for *not* wanting to have a one-night stand. "Thanks for the advice." I sound more pissed about this than I want to on my first day on the job, but far less than is warranted by Alec's remarks.

Alec doesn't seem fazed by any of it. "No problem," he says, as if I'd meant to thank him earnestly. Then he starts turning on and checking the sound equipment.

Thankfully Jenna and Ty arrive before Alec thinks of any other warnings to issue me, and before I decide to tell him off for suggesting I'm not into Jenna for anything but her body.

Ty bounds in, waving his iPad. "Hey, Felix! Look how far I am in *Angry Birds*!" Just like the first time I saw him, he's wearing a sweater vest—a dark green one this time—over a collared shirt, with dress pants and loafers. Private school uniform, maybe? I realize that for all I know about Jenna, which is a considerable amount after so few days, there's a lot I still don't know when it comes to the day-to-day—both for her and Ty.

Jenna strides down the stairs, looking over his shoulder. "Wait," she says. "How far are you? You haven't passed me, have you?"

She smiles at me and I smile back, and have a hard time keeping it from lingering. I feel better just being in the same room as her. She's wearing a gray tank top over dark jeans today. Her black bra straps peek out from under the tank top, and a dainty silver necklace with a small medallion dangles just below her collarbone. It's a simple look, more so than I've previously seen on her, but she looks no less amazing in it.

"I'm on 4-16." Ty's bright voice tears me away from staring too long at his mom. He shows me a screen with a pile of pigs in a hole, with a bunch of stone blocks holding them in.

"Oh, no," Jenna says. "If you get to 4-18 during practice, let me know right away, okay? You are not allowed to pass me up.

It's the only thing I can beat you at."

"That's not fair," Ty says. "I could beat you if you let me."

Jenna shakes her head. "This is my one remaining strand of pride, and I'm holding on to the bitter end."

Ty scowls at me. "If I get ahead of her, she'll take my iPad away."

Jenna nods. "Damn straight."

Ty settles down at my feet, almost sitting on my bow. "Here! You can watch!"

And I do, as he sends a bird sailing right into the pig defenses and knocking a bunch of them out.

"Nice," I tell him.

Ty grins.

Out of her bag, Jenna produces two big pastry boxes, and presents one to me. "I made you a pie," she says. "To welcome you to the band."

Alec rolls his eyes, and Ty gives me a sly smile. I feel like they know something about this pie that I don't. Also, she *bakes*? It's not something I would have suspected, but somehow I can see it—Jenna rolling out the dough, accidentally getting flour in her jet-black hair. "Thanks," I say. When she hands me the box, our fingers brush, and we both smile.

Again, I have to remember to stop.

Roxie arrives, and is adjusting the height of her stool for her platform boots when Leo comes in, waving a tube around in his hand.

"All right, Rox!" he calls. "Take off your boots."

Alec swears. "After practice, Leo."

"No way," Leo says. "And let her toe fungus continue to grow in those contaminated wedges?"

Roxie looks surprised that Leo calls her shoes that, though I don't know whether it's because he's correct or making stuff up again.

She recovers quickly. "Leo," she says, wielding a drum stick like a hammer. "If you come near me with that stuff, so help me—"

"Enough!" Alec says. "Roxie, just put on the cream. You lost the vote. The sooner you get it over with, the sooner we can play already."

"Do you have toe fungus, Roxie?" Ty asks. "Maybe you should keep your feet in the refrigerator so they don't mold. That's what Mom does."

We all look at Jenna.

"With *food*," she says. "Not my feet."

"Right," Ty says, frowning. "That's what I said."

Leo, at this point, notices the pastry box in my lap. "Jenna made pie? Sweet! Dish up, man."

Jenna shakes her head. "That's for Felix."

"All for him?" Leo whines. "Come on, Jenna. Don't hold out on us."

"Let her be," Alec says. "She just needs to give him the pie and get it over with."

Both Jenna and I glare at him, and now the kid looks confused.

"I brought *two* pies," Jenna says. "One to share with the band, and one for Felix. To *welcome* him. One of us has to be a decent person."

"I'm decent," Leo says. "And I have an indecent appetite for your pie."

Alec looks at Leo like he's just said something utterly disgusting, but he does take the slice of what looks like kiwi-lime pie Leo hands him as he digs into the second box.

I set mine aside, too nervous about the upcoming practice to eat. "Mind if I save it until after?"

"Sure," Jenna says. "It's your pie."

Ty looks at me like I'm crazy. "I want a piece *now*." Jenna arches an eyebrow at him, and Ty grumbles out an abashed, "Please."

Leo offers him one, and Ty sets about destroying it.

I start warming up, even though technically I've been playing for hours. Mostly I just want to look like I'm doing something while Leo puts down his pie, pulls Roxie's boots off her feet, removes her socks, and proceeds to give her a foot massage.

I've never had foot fungus, but I'm pretty sure he's exceeding the amount of caressing that is medically necessary. I look at Jenna, and Jenna looks back at me, and we both have the same wide-eyed look.

Are they? I mouth at her.

She shrugs, and shakes her head.

Roxie has her head tilted back now, and her eyes half-closed, her mouth emitting sounds that remind me of yesterday afternoon with Jenna at the hotel. I try not to think about the way my body felt when I kissed her, the way her fingers teased the back of my neck, spreading goosebumps all over my body. I go back to playing, but now I'm not even hitting the right notes. They all look at me in surprise, and I lower my bow.

"Sorry," I say, and I cast around for an excuse that doesn't involve me getting lost in fantasies or not knowing how to play my own damn instrument, and fail to find one.

"All right," Alec says. "Can we get started?"

Jenna sits down at the keyboard, which I notice used to be positioned across the room, but is now next to my spot. Alec gives Jenna a look that tells me he notices, too, but he doesn't say anything else.

And then we play.

The first song is a crashing, fast-paced number in which Jenna and Alec take turns singing about all their many exes and how they don't compare to what they have now. The cello part is simple, and I watch Jenna as I play. Her fingers are light on the keys, and she sings like she means it. Her voice is husky and gorgeous and I find myself getting lost in it.

It's not like I haven't heard her voice plenty by now, given how many times I've heard their albums over the last couple days, and I already knew she's seriously talented. But listening to her sing live like this—damn, she's *good*. And this shouldn't affect the way I feel about her, but it does. I know it's probably my imagination, but as we play, her voice and the notes from my cello seem to vibrate together with this intensity that echoes the attraction I felt for her yesterday, and always.

I smile as I think of Alec being one of the exes in the song, like Jenna is singing it all for me.

Next we play one of the slower numbers. Alec is calling the shots, and I wonder if he realized when he picked this song that it would be more difficult for me than the last. The cello part for this one is complicated, because it ticks up into counterpoint, adding a second melody during the bridge. I'm actually impressed with Mason for having tried it—it's daring for pop music, and while I don't think this one is going to be a hit single, the effect is both beautiful and fun. It also requires me to blend like hell.

When we hit the bridge, I don't blend. I'm not even listening to Jenna anymore as I try to get the tone right. I'm playing the notes, but the tempo is off. For the recording, they played the song more straight up, but now everyone is following Roxie's lead, when I'm used to either following a conductor or making it up as I go. Roxie doesn't stand in front and signal me when she's going to speed up or slow down. In the part where I've been practicing a rubato, slowing down to emphasize the melody, she speeds up, and so do Jenna and Alec on the keyboard and lead guitar.

The result is disastrous. I try to correct, but it's too late. We all careen in different directions and Alec stops playing and waves for everyone to stop.

I want to walk out right there. I cannot be so bad at this.

"All right," Alec says. "You okay, Felix?"

I feel like disappearing. "Yeah, sorry."

"No big," Alec says. "This is why we practice. You want to do the bridge again, or take it from the top?"

"From the top." And this time I listen to Roxie, focusing on following her. I've come up with a set of bowings, but I can already see where I need to make corrections to fix my sound. I can't fix the sheet music fast enough while we play, but I also know that a week from now, I'll be up on a stage without music in hand, because that's how they roll in rock music.

The idea is terrifying.

The second go through of the song is better, but not great. We move on to a couple easier pieces—for me anyway—and then Alec wants to do a song that has no cello part.

"You want to sit this one out, Felix?" he asks.

"No. Let me try what I've come up with and see what you think."

Alec nods, and Roxie counts off.

This one goes better. When I hear it all together, I quickly realize the music I've composed is too complicated—it sounds like I'm trying to compete for attention. So I simplify a bit on the fly, and by the end of the song, it's actually blending.

Alec looks at the others when we finish, and everybody nods.

"That was great," Jenna says to me, and Alec agrees.

"Almost as good as Mason," Ty says, and Jenna gives him a look.

I'm not sure I would call it great, but at least now I'm bordering on passable. "I'll catch up to Mason eventually."

"Sure," Alec says. "Let's try another one."

Alec tirelessly grinds me through every song in their repertoire, listening to everything I've written to go along with the songs. Some are better than others, and Leo offers me some notes about how I can change to better complement his guitar line, which frankly is doing the same job my cello wants to do in most of the songs. He doesn't seem to think I'm trying to step on his toes, though, barefoot or otherwise.

By the end of practice, I'm doing better, but still not great. I can't even remember the last time I came out of a practice having performed so badly. I even played better when I was high.

My hands are shaking again, and I hope no one notices.

Jenna pulls her stool over to sit next to me. "What do you think?"

I grumble under my breath. "I think I have a lot of work to do."

She smiles, and I don't love the hint of pity I see in it. "You're a brilliant cellist. But this is a lot of new material really fast."

It's not the material. I can play the music. "I guess I underestimated how different it would be to play with a band. Orchestras are more . . . organized. I have to get used to not being conducted."

"I don't know," Jenna says. "We could make Alec wear tails and stand in front of us and wave his arms."

Alec ignores this suggestion. "You did fine," he says to me. "It's not as bad as you think."

I've been told that a million times in my life. I'm not any more inclined to believe it now. "Thanks."

Jenna looks down at Ty and gasps, seizing his iPad so fast I'm afraid he's been watching snuff porn right at my feet.

"No!" she says. "That's 4-18. My turn."

"You said I couldn't *beat* 4-18. I was just going to try a few birds."

Jenna clutches the iPad like it's her precious and sits down next to me.

"You're on my bow," I say, and I put my hand on her shoulder to move her over.

When she moves, I don't want to let go.

"Good to have you with us, man," Leo says. He lifts his bare foot onto one of the amps and fishes something out from between his toes.

Roxie makes a face. "Tell me you're not going barefoot on stage." She appeals to Alec. "Tell him he can't do that. I don't care about his acoustics."

"I care about his sound," Jenna says. "But I'm not sure the bare feet actually improve it."

"All band members will continue to wear shoes," Alec says. "All in favor?"

Everyone's hand goes up but mine, not because I oppose footwear, but because I'm not getting in the middle of this. Though I do reluctantly remember to move my hand off Jenna's shoulder. Not that she protested it being there.

Even Leo votes yes.

"There we go," Alec says. "No longer an issue."

Roxie looks at Leo suspiciously. "You want to wear shoes?"

"Heck, yes," Leo says. "I just got the tracking number for my alligator boots. I shot the gator myself, and now the boots are all ready, right in time for the show."

Roxie's eyes bug so large she's practically an anime character. "You're going to wear alligator boots on stage? What if PETA shows up? We'll get paint thrown on us."

"Roxie, baby," Leo says, "you wear enough leather to have killed a whole ranch by now. I think if PETA were coming after us, they'd already be here."

"Ha! 4-18! Reigning Rollins champion." Jenna hands her iPad back to Ty and then turns to Roxie. "Leo will be wearing long pants," she says. "No one will even notice the boots."

"True," Leo says. "My matching alligator vest, on the other hand—"

Roxie makes a sound that's a cross between a roar and a groan, and Leo grins. Roxie looks at Alec, presumably hoping he'll object to the vest, but Alec just shrugs. "No one goes barefoot, you use the cream, and Leo shuts up about your foot fungus. Problems solved. Leo can wear his vest as long as Allison approves it."

"Allison is our costumer," Jenna tells me. "We'll want to run your outfit by her, as well. Do you know what you want to wear?"

"I wear what I'm told. Allison can have free rein."

"I wouldn't give her that much freedom," Jenna says. "She'll turn you into David Bowie."

I must look afraid, because Jenna laughs. "We'll give her some guidance. Something like your normal look would be good. T-shirt and jeans—nice ones, like the ones you're wearing. Maybe a little tighter, with some nice black boots."

"Tighter?" I give Jenna a look. A small smile plays across

her lips.

And then I notice Alec glaring at us.

Right. Whatever we are to each other in private, we're not supposed to be doing that in front of anyone else.

I clear my throat. "If that's what you want."

Jenna's eyes flash, and I see her bite back a comment about what exactly she wants.

It's mutual.

I fish for a change of subject, and remember what I promised to Gabby. "Hey, by the way," I say, "my sister's best friend is getting married in a couple weeks. Her friend is an actress on that soap, *Southern Heat*? And her fiancé is this big deal Hollywood agent. Anyway, my sister was wondering if we'd play the wedding, like, as a maid of honor gift. I know it's kind of last-minute and you guys probably don't play small stuff like that, but it's going to be this huge thing with lots of people from the industry. I mean, the wrong industry, right? But still it might be good for—"

I stop talking when I realize I'm rambling and everyone else is staring.

"Did you rehearse all of that?" Jenna asks with a grin. "Because you're in the band. You can just say, hey, can we play this wedding, and we would say, yeah, if we're in town, why not?"

"Except Alec," Leo says. "Alec will want to know what's in it for him."

"Hollywood connections," Roxie says. "What do you say, Alec?"

Alec shrugs. "Sure. It's before we leave on tour?"

"Yeah," I say. "Between the LA concert and when we fly out."

Alec points to a calendar on the wall. "Write it down." I grab a marker and while I start writing, I notice that three weeks ago, they played an event someone wrote down as "Roxie's mom's garden party."

Okay, yeah. I may have oversold.

"My sister," I say, "is going to die."

"I hope not," Leo says. "We don't do funerals."

Everyone digs in to Jenna's pie again, and I eat mine right out of the tin. It's apple, and straight-up delicious, but it isn't warm. Jenna smiles at me, and I wonder if that joke is intentional.

I'm pretty sure it is.

"How is it?" she asks.

"The best," I say. I hope she gets that I'm talking about more than just the pie.

When everyone packs up to leave, I wave for Jenna to hold up. Ty is already outside bouncing up and down, but Jenna calls for him to wait a second. She turns to me.

I pull a phone out of my pocket. "My sister pointed out that I probably shouldn't be texting you much on your regular phone. So I got you a burner."

Jenna looks delighted. "Do you have one, too?"

I pull out a second, identical phone. "My number's already in there."

Jenna grins. "So I can call you anytime."

"Day or night," I say, and her eyes dance.

We both look away, and I'm pretty sure she's thinking exactly what I'm thinking.

"Call me tonight?" I ask.

She gives me a smile that makes me want to pull her in my arms and kiss her right there. It's a good thing I have all that practice not doing drugs, because I manage to stay still. If I don't move, I can't kiss her.

But god, I want her.

"Absolutely," she says. And then she floats up the stairs, and is gone.

TEN

Felix

Jenna calls around ten o'clock, after my dad has already gone to bed, but before I stop hearing the moaning from his porn. I'm thinking of buying him some headphones for his birthday.

"Hey," I say. I settle into the pull-out couch. It's a piece of furniture Dad clearly bought for looks over comfort—the mattress is way too thin and the metal bar jams into my back while I sleep. But considering he fronted three stints of rehab and still offered me a place to stay, I'm not inclined to complain about his furniture choices.

"Hey, yourself," she says back. "Just so you know, at some point in this conversation, I may need to shout, *we've been had!* and flush the phone down the toilet."

I smile. "I'll keep that in mind. Especially while I worry that Alec is listening to our every word through the door."

"I can put you on speaker. You could ask him yourself."

An intense wave of jealousy rushes over me. I don't want it to—it won't help anything—but it tears me up that he gets to be there with her and I don't.

"I'm kidding," Jenna says. "He and Ty are both in bed, so I'm hiding out downstairs. The steps creak, so I'll have plenty of warning if one of them is coming."

I bite back a comment about the warning I'll give her myself. Even though I'm pretty sure she was thinking the same thing as me back at the studio, I'm nervous as hell I'm going to mess this all up somehow.

Things are complicated enough as it is.

"So," she says. "What did you think about practice?"

I groan. "I thought I sucked."

"You didn't. You're a brilliant musician. We just need to practice."

"It's the sound, I think. I'm fine playing the songs by myself, but when I try to blend with you guys—it's like I'm an orchestral cellist trying to play with a rock band or something."

"Yeah," Jenna says. "There's a shock."

I've played rock songs on my cello almost all my life, but rarely with other people, and when I did, it was always other classical musicians. I close my eyes. "I hate it when I'm not perfect."

"And are you usually?"

Yes, I want to say. And once, years ago, it was true. "You really don't want to hear this," I say.

"As it turns out, I want to hear everything about you," she says. And while there's a hint of teasing in her voice, I can tell she means it.

My heart flutters. I can't argue with that.

"Yes," I say. "I've never auditioned for a part I didn't get."

"*Really?*"

"Yeah. Everybody warned me about it when I went off to Juilliard. I had to fail sometime, you know? Things would be a lot more competitive in New York. And they were."

"But you were still the best."

"No," I say. "But I never auditioned for anything I wasn't confident I could get. I would practice for hours and hours, stuff I knew, stuff I could do in my sleep. And not just at Juilliard. Before that, too. Because I had to be the best."

"Did you do that for your audition with us?"

"No. It was different. You asked for music that I loved."

"Ah," she says. "So you're not a fan of classical? Because that's odd, for a cellist. Even Mason started in orchestra."

"I didn't say that. The third piece I played for you—the Shostakovich? That was classical."

"I thought it was, but I didn't recognize it." She pauses. "To be fair, I didn't recognize the first song, either."

"The Meat Puppets," I say. " 'Head.' "

"Right. That."

"At least you got 'Under the Bridge.' "

She makes a little sound like a verbal wince. "It sounded familiar."

I bury myself under the crocheted afghan on Dad's couch. "You're a pop star. You cannot tell me you don't listen to music."

"I *do*," she says. "I just don't like classical. And I don't know the Meat Puppets."

I pull the blanket up over my head and pretend I'm mortally wounded. If Dad hears my death throes, he'll probably just assume I'm doing the same thing he is.

"Um, Felix?" Jenna says. "Did I just murder you?"

"Close. But I might pull through."

"Because I don't like classical? Or classic rock?"

"Yep." I make my voice sound hoarse. "That was the death blow."

"Oh, shut up," she says with a laugh.

I drop the act. "The Meat Puppets, for your edification, played with Kurt Cobain for his *MTV Unplugged in New York* album. He sang their song 'Plateau,' which should be required listening for anyone with a career in music. Probably a career at all."

"Wow, you're serious about this."

I'm aware I'm ranting, and probably giving her serious second thoughts about ever having kissed me. But I can't stop. "And if you don't like classical, it's because you haven't heard enough of it."

"Maybe," Jenna says.

"You sound doubtful. No, you sound like a mom, like, *maybe* we'll buy candy while we're at the store, but really you're just hoping they forget."

"I *am* that mom."

"Well, I'm not going to forget."

"Neither does Ty," she says. "Classical music is just—it's like those books I had to read in high school."

"Okay, sure, some of them. But didn't you read even one book in high school you liked?"

Jenna pauses.

I'm incredulous. "I can name several offhand, the top of the list being Tim O'Brien's *The Things They Carried*."

"I didn't read that," Jenna says. "Come to think of it, I don't think I ever actually read any of the books I was supposed to read in high school. I wasn't exactly a model student."

I make another noise like I've just been murdered. "You are comparing classical music, my first love, to books you *didn't* read in high school? That's it. Challenge accepted. I'm going to teach you to love it."

"Yeah, all right," Jenna says, probably mostly to appease me. "I'm sure I could learn to appreciate it."

I groan again. "People say that about music they think they ought to like but don't. You're not supposed to appreciate music. When you love it, it appreciates *you*."

Jenna laughs. "That sounded like it was supposed to be deep. But I don't think it made sense."

"Yeah, well," I say. "I'm the guy who suggested that we should have emotional intimacy instead of sex, so you get what you paid for."

"Ha, yes," Jenna says. "And what does that make us again? We're not dating. We're emotional . . . intimators?"

I laugh. "That has an interesting ring to it." Then the words settle in my mind, the words for what I hope we are, and I can barely breathe.

"You're quiet all of a sudden," she says.

She's right. It's a heavy quiet. One pressed down with things I'm afraid to say, afraid to even think. I change the subject. "So are you worried I'm going to mess up the performance?"

"No," she says. "Are you?"

"I'm nervous. That's also new."

"You never get nervous before a performance?"

"I never used to," I say. "I'm a cocky bastard. What can I say?"

"Yes, well. I noticed that."

"The scariest gig I've ever had is the first day I played the street. In a concert hall, you know what's expected of you. The culture is rigid. Everyone knows exactly when to clap, when to bow, when to stand, when to sit. People are there because they've bought tickets and they want to hear you play, excellently, exactly what's in the program. It's all very . . . structured."

"Okay, yeah," Jenna says. "More so than our concerts, even."

"Definitely. On the street, people are there for a lot of reasons, but you can bet it isn't to listen to you. You're hoping to give them something they aren't expecting, something that makes them want to give back to you. But I had no idea if anyone would pay me to play, and even less idea of whose territory I might be stepping on, which norms I might be breaking."

"Why'd you do it?"

I hesitate. I want to tell her the truth, not just what I want to believe is true.

"Because I did the structured, good, and expected things until I was nineteen years old. And it took me places I never want to be again." I pause. "And because when I stopped, everything got scary, so what was one more thing, you know?"

"And look where it got you," Jenna says.

I smile. "Feels pretty good. But it'd be a lot better if you were here." I feel that deep ache again of wanting to hold her close to me—to be back at that Ramada with her tucked under my arm, her head on my shoulder and her body pressed alongside mine. "Crashing with your family."

I laugh. "Okay, less that. But hiding out on your couch hoping Alec and your kid don't catch us doesn't seem like a picnic either."

"Maybe not," she says. "Though Ty would be happy I'm talking to you. He likes you."

"And I like him," I say. She's quiet for a moment, and I wonder if that was the wrong thing to say. I don't want to insert myself into her life in ways I'm not welcome. "Does that bother you?"

"No," she says quickly. "I guess I'm just nervous about giving him false expectations. With things being so . . . uncertain."

"That's fair. Do you want me to discourage him? I don't like the idea of ignoring him, but I could if you—"

"No, nothing like that. I'm just overprotective, I guess. He and Mason were friends. I even left Ty with him a couple of times, but then I found out later that Mason was high when he watched him. I'm pretty sure he even did drugs at our house."

I sink down into the couch cushions. The gaping pit in my stomach is back. I want to tell her the truth, but this isn't the moment. Besides which, I'm terrified. It seems like my opportunity to say, "Hey Jenna, by the way, I'm about five minutes out of rehab" passed me by long ago, but at the same time, I'm not sure when that could have been because it's only been a few days.

"You don't have to worry about that with me," I manage. "Like I said, you can test me anytime."

"I know," Jenna's voice is quiet. "Sorry, I don't mean to put that stuff on you. And it's not like I'm asking you to watch Ty. I'm sure that's the last thing you want to be doing."

She sounds sad, and I think back to us talking about *Jerry Maguire*, how she'd been so sure I wouldn't want to date someone with a kid.

"I wouldn't mind," I say. "I mean, I'm sure you have plenty of people more qualified to do so, but—"

"Ha," Jenna says. "I was a mom at fifteen. Sometimes I'm not sure *I'm* qualified."

"That's not true. You're a good mom."

"Who leaves her kid with her drug-addict friend."

"Who trusted someone who it turned out was lying. Welcome to the world, Jenna. That happens to everybody."

She doesn't speak for a moment, and I realize how much I mean it. She is a good mother. I can tell by how much she worries about being a bad one.

"Four years ago my son barely knew me," she says. "My parents were raising him—them and Rachel, who was only seventeen at the time. Mostly I wasn't even living with them."

There's a harshness to her voice, a judgment she's passing on herself. And while I do that, too, I still hate hearing it from her. "Where were you living?" I ask.

"With guys, mostly. Boyfriends, sometimes. I was a mom with a four-year-old son, and I was out partying and drinking and—"

She takes a sharp breath, like there's more. I can tell there's something she's deeply ashamed of, and I'm afraid to ask. I'm still not telling her everything about my past. I have no right to ask for everything about hers.

But I can't help but wonder. "Was it drugs?"

Jenna sighs. "That was part of it. I did a lot of pills at parties. I prided myself on being up for anything, so half the time I didn't even know what I was taking. I don't remember a lot of that."

My breath catches. "You don't remember because guys drugged you."

"Yeah," she says. "I mean, I knew what was happening. I took the drugs. It's not like they made me. But sometimes I'd wake up and not know who I was with." Her voice grows quiet. "Or how many."

This sick feeling settles over me. Sometimes when I was high, days would pass and I wouldn't really be able to account for them, but nothing ever happened to me like *that*. But I know how much worse it is for women—I got drugs from a lot of girls who were looking for a partner to get high with, someone they knew who would be by their side, making them that much less vulnerable to asshole guys taking advantage of them.

She told me before about the frat guys, about the statutory rape. I want to use that word now to describe this, but if she isn't ready to hear it, I'm afraid it will just shut her down. I take too long to figure out what I should say, and she continues. "I get it if that changes your mind about me."

"What?" I say. "No, no way. And I still think you're a good mom. God, to have gone from places like that to having the relationship you guys have now—it's really impressive, you know?"

"I don't know about that. The way I let them treat me—I wish I could just go back to the girl I was and shake her, you know? She had this amazing kid who needed her and a family who loved her and everything in the world going for her."

"I was that person once, too," I say. "Minus the kid. And I hate myself for it."

"Really? I mean, you said you partied, but you were in college, right? Practically everyone does that."

The part of me that wants to rationalize screams that she doesn't need to know. I'm not on drugs, and I'm not going to be on drugs. It's the same part of me that wants to rationalize going by the houses of some of my old friends, just to see how they're doing.

I know how that will end up, and it's not pretty.

"I'm going to tell you something," I say. "I'm not ready to get into all the details yet."

"Okay." Jenna sounds nervous, and the longer it takes me to get this out, the worse that's going to get.

"I used to do drugs."

She's silent, and my mind reels. After what happened to her with Mason, this is the end. It has to be.

"Is that it?" she says. "Because yeah. I used to do drugs, too."

"No. I mean, yes, that's it, but you don't understand." I take a deep breath. "I did heroin."

"I've heard that's intense."

"It was. And I did things on drugs I'm not proud of. I got kicked out of school, and I gave my family hell."

"I know what that feels like," Jenna says.

She doesn't. She can't. But it feels so good to hear her empathizing with me instead of rejecting me that I tell myself it's enough for now.

"You're sure that's not a deal breaker?" I ask. "I'm not on drugs now, and I'm not going to be. You can test me every week if you want to."

"No. I'd be a total hypocrite to judge you for that, after everything I've done."

A wave of relief crashes over me. I can let the story come out slowly. I don't have to bare my soul overnight, and I don't have to lie to her, either.

For the first time, I let myself think about telling her everything. If I could be sure she wouldn't hate me, I'd do it right now.

"So you're sure my stuff isn't a deal breaker for you?" she asks.

"Of course not," I say. "We've both done stuff we're not proud of, but . . . god, no. Not a deal breaker. Not even close."

There's a pause, and I wonder if I should say it again, say it stronger somehow so she gets that I wouldn't judge her for any of that. Not like I do the guys who did that to her.

"The worst part is, I don't really know why I did it," she says, softly. "Any of it. It's like there's some part of me that's so broken I just needed someone to need me, but god, I shouldn't have wanted anyone to show it like . . . like they did."

There's even more behind those words, more darkness she's not telling me, and it makes me furious to contemplate the kinds of things she might have been subjected to. But I don't think telling her that will help her any.

There is, however, something that just might.

"I need you," I say. The simple truth of those words stun

me. I've spent so much of my life not ever thinking I needed *anyone*, not really.

Her breath catches, but then, as if she can't let herself believe my words, she scoffs. "Yeah, I'm so sure you need all of this dumped on you by some crazy girl who makes your life more difficult."

"Yeah," I say. "I do. And I think you need it, too."

She's quiet for a moment, but then her voice is softer. "I do," she says. "So, my emotional intimator. What the hell are we going to do?"

I know she's talking about the future, but for now, that's a question without an answer. "For starters," I say, "I'm going to keep you on the phone for at least another hour. Maybe two. And at some point in there, you're going to tell me how you got insanely good at pie-making."

"Mmmm, okay," she says, the smile evident in her tone. "I think I can live with that."

I curl up, hugging my pillow. Wishing it was her. "Me, too."

ELEVEN

Felix

When I wake up the next morning all I want to do is get high. There's no trigger; there's no reason. Talking to Jenna last night was incredible, but that feeling somehow abandoned me in my sleep. Maybe my brain was sorting through old boxes and found the snapshots of the first time I smoked H, and the easy, laid-back way it made me feel, combined with the brightest, sunniest, best-day-of-your-life happy that was everything I didn't know how to be in my real life. Everything I was chasing when I went out to New York, but could never seem to catch. One of the reasons heroin is so dangerous is there's no hangover after, no shitty feeling when you come down.

You just feel normal. And after a while, heroin is the only thing that makes you happy, and real life is the hangover.

Like a binge-drinker the night after a keg party, I don't want to open my eyes. I already know what I'm going to feel—the nerves and confusion and frustration and loneliness, all things my therapist says I repressed before I started doing drugs, all things I could wipe away now if I'd just shell out for a gram and some new equipment. It wouldn't be like before. I'd do just enough to get by. The needles would be clean and the doses low and no one would have to know.

Ultimately, it's this thought that forces me to squint at the light sliding between the blinds in my dad's picture window.

Those lies will lead me right into relapse. A part of me wants to focus on Jenna, but that's not right either. I can't stay clean for her, or for my family, or for anyone, really.

In the end, if I'm not doing it for me, I'm going to fail.

I get up and shower, walking the mile like I learned in rehab, instead of just trying to push the craving away. If I bought a gram, I'd be throwing away six weeks of sobriety. I'd lose my job with the band and any chance with Jenna. Gabby would know, and my parents. It would change the way I acted, from my interests to my ability to be honest. I'd go back to being that guy, and maybe I'd wake up one morning next to someone else who was cold and dead because of something I gave her.

Or maybe karma would finally stop doing its wicked dance, and this time, it would be me.

I'm not shooting up. Not today. Not tomorrow. Not ever, ever again.

My hands are shaking when I leave Dad's house, but it's okay because I'm confident I'm not just finding excuses to leave so I can use. Just last week I felt like I had too much time on my hands, and now I don't have nearly enough. Even though I don't have to go into the clinic every day, there's still practice, and meetings, and my weekly visit to my therapist, which I'm dreading. Addicts aren't supposed to make any major changes in their lives for the first year of recovery, and I've had enough happen in the last week for a whole year of upheaval.

I'm a few minutes early for my therapy appointment, and well-dressed, because the last thing I want to look like today is an addict. The waiting room is empty except for a kid who looks about twelve or so playing a game on a tablet. He looks nothing like Ty—he's black, for one, and older, and not dressed like he's a senior partner at an accounting firm. Still, there's a hollowness in my chest as I watch him swipe on the tablet. I want to ask him if he's playing *Angry Birds*, but I also don't want to be the creepy guy who chats up random kids, so I settle for drumming my fingers on my knees while I wait.

What I really don't want to be is the guy who has to be here in the first place, but it's years too late for that.

The kid's mom comes out of the office and they leave. My therapist, Cecily—who is big on punctuality—shows up in the waiting room to retrieve me right after, not three seconds past our appointment time. Cecily's probably around thirty, tall and slim and always wearing these drab, old-style pantsuits that look like they came from the wardrobe on *Law and Order*. Still, she's got a nice smile, and a kind of girl-next-door attractiveness. And way more importantly to me, she's damn good at her job and tough to bullshit.

"So?" she asks as we sit down in her office. Behind her desk on the windowsill sits a potted plant that appears to always be in the same state of wiltedness and a row of Simpsons bobbleheads. "How was your week?"

I don't lead with how much I wish I was high. "Well, I got a job."

"Really? No more playing on the street?"

Cecily was not fond of this method of making money, and had suggested I either teach music lessons or try to find employment that didn't involve my cello, due to the "entanglement of music with the origins of my addiction."

She had it all wrong. Music never made me want to do drugs. It was everything *else*.

"Yeah," I say. "I joined a band."

Cecily looks substantially less pleased. "A band."

"Yeah. But it's a real job. I'm on salary and everything. They're a pop group who are going on tour in a couple of weeks, and they just lost their cellist. It's an incredible opportunity, really."

"So you're excited about this."

"Yes," I say. "Employment, music, travel, awesome people—this job pretty much has it all."

She nods. "You don't *sound* excited."

"Well, the cravings are making me their bitch today."

"If they were," Cecily says, "you'd be out getting high instead of sitting here."

I want to snark and say maybe I should get on that, but I don't. That joke will never be funny.

"Was there a particular trigger?" Cecily asks.

"No. Just living."

"That's one trigger you should never avoid. What about the other musicians in your band? Are they addicts?"

I smile. I like this about Cecily. She doesn't beat around the bush when she thinks I might be doing something stupid. "No," I say. "Actually, their manager does random drug testing, and if anyone in the band fails, they're out."

Cecily raises her eyebrows. "You sound excited about that. You're not worried about the pressure?"

"No. It means I can play music with a rock band without having to worry about my band mates doing lines off a mirror on the way to the concert. If I relapse, I'll lose more than just my *job*."

Cecily smiles. "Well, that's great, then. If they're so specific about testing, are some of them in recovery?"

I should have known this was coming. Cecily has this thing about me needing to make friends with people who are recovered addicts, when to me that seems like a really stupid thing to be doing. "I don't know," I say, "but I doubt it." Jenna made it sound like they've all done some drugs in the past, but I hadn't gotten the sense that any of them had needed a program to recover.

Cecily looks down at her notes. She has this list of things she's trying to get me to do, and I know which one is coming next.

"Any progress on finding a sponsor?"

"I'm still going to meetings. But I'm not really looking, no."

Cecily taps a pen on her paper. "You've decided against it entirely?"

"Not necessarily," I say. "I just haven't met anyone I'm close to yet. It takes me a while to get to know people."

Usually, anyway. I think of Jenna's ankle against mine as we talked over sushi. Of telling her things within days of meeting her that I've never told anyone in my life.

"Are you still hopping meetings, going to a different one every day?" she asks.

"Whatever's convenient, you know? Especially now that I have to practice."

"Different programs, even."

"Sure," I say. "AA, NA, there's a couple of churches with their own programs. It's all twelve step, and it's all the same stuff. Just different locations and times, is all."

"And different people," she says.

"Yeah. I mean, new people like me I'll see again every once in a while, because they're going to a lot of meetings, too. And I see the veterans at this meeting or that meeting again when I go back. Especially to the ones with the best coffee."

I smile at Cecily, and she gives me a look. She doesn't call me out this time for joking about not taking recovery seriously, but it's implied.

"How are you going to get to know anyone well enough to be comfortable asking them to sponsor you if you're seeing different people all the time?"

"Maybe I'm not," I say. "Look, I know it says in your little handbook that these people at meetings are supposed to magically be my BFFs now. But I know that sixty percent of addicts relapse, a lot of them again and again. It seems like the last thing I need is a group of friends, more than half of which are going to be getting high again within the year." My hands are gripping the armrests of the chair too tightly, and I force myself to ease up.

"So you're afraid of losing your friends again."

"I'm thinking that sounds a lot like this life upheaval I'm supposed to avoid."

Cecily narrows her eyes.

"So no, I don't have a sponsor, and I feel like hell today. But I'm still clean. So take that, statistics."

Cecily wisely decides to move on, though I know we'll revisit this. "Any major triggers this week? Besides the cravings today, I mean."

I take a deep breath. "The other day I was busking down on Hollywood Boulevard, and there was this drug deal going down across the street."

Cecily turns fully toward me. "How did you know?"

I shrug. "Guys leaning against the wall, trying to look casual, stuff changing hands. Plus, the look of them. They were probably meth heads."

"You can tell just by looking at them?"

"A lot of the time I can."

"That must make it hard to avoid making contact."

"Well, I did avoid it," I say. "I sat and played and didn't get up until I didn't want to go over there and ask if the guy had heroin."

"And then you did get up?"

"Then I didn't have to think about it. I just went back about my day, like, not high, and not worrying about getting high. Mostly."

"That's good," Cecily says. "So you recognized the trigger and you coped with it effectively."

"I guess so. I've been doing what you said, you know? Trying to pay attention to how I feel and listen to myself instead of just shoving it away."

Cecily nods. "Good. How's that going?"

I hesitate. My impulse is not to tell her about Jenna. I can hide it, and I won't have to hear about how I'm violating that life changes rule I was just using as an excuse for sponsor avoidance. But if I rationalize keeping this secret, my secrets will inevitably eventually be about drugs. All I need is to believe the lie that no one needs to know and I'll be right back to the needle.

"Well," I say. "I met this girl."

113

Cecily looks surprised. "Really."

I roll my eyes. "Thanks for the confidence."

She laughs. "I'm sure you're fully capable of finding women who are interested in you. You've made that quite clear."

I sit back on the couch. In our first session back when I was in rehab, I had been mostly interested in hitting on Cecily, which she quickly pointed out was a deflection of treatment. When I got over wanting to avoid the work, it occurred to me that Cecily is simultaneously too old for me and way too serious. She's good for me as a therapist, even though I don't always like the things she says. But as a girlfriend? No, thanks.

"Tell me about this girl," she says.

I can't tell her the details. She's ethically required not to repeat them, of course, unless she thinks my life or someone else's is in immediate danger. But I can give her enough of the situation without those details to be honest about what's going on.

"She's in the band," I say.

"Ah," Cecily says. "So you had an ulterior motive in joining."

"I'd have done it anyway. It's a legitimately fantastic opportunity. But yeah, she's the one who invited me to join."

"So you've known her for a while."

"No," I say. "She heard me play the other day, and they were kind of in a bind."

Cecily sits back in her chair, playing it cool, but I can already tell she thinks this is bad news.

"I know, I know," I say. "No big life changes for at least a year. Of course, I'm supposed to turn my whole life upside down for clinic visits, therapy appointments, and daily meetings, all the while cutting out all my old friends and places that might make me nostalgic for my junkie days, become best buddies with a bunch of recovered addicts, plus the tiny detail of not, you know, shooting heroin. So I'm not sure how I'm supposed to manage all that without adding *anything* to my life without driving myself insane."

Cecily sidesteps my rant, when really I wish she'd wade into it with me, because I'd rather talk about the abstract merits of consistency than hear a lecture about Jenna.

"This girl. Does she have a name?"

"Jenna," I say. If Cecily followed music, she'd be more likely to put the pieces together, but I know from past conversations that she only listens to show tunes, which lately means *Hamilton* on endless repeat.

If she does put it together, joke's on her, because she can't say a word to anyone.

"And is Jenna aware of your interest?"

"Yeah," I say. "She feels the same way, but she's not really ready for a relationship right now. And, you know, neither am I. What with the recovery stuff and all."

Cecily smiles. "That's mature of you to realize that."

Somehow, if I tell her I was making out with Jenna in a hotel room mere days ago, I think she'd find me less mature.

"Do you think her unavailability for a relationship is something you like about her?"

"I'm really not sure what the hell that's supposed to mean. But no. I'm not *that* mature. I'd date her if I could."

"And you don't think that might put your recovery in jeopardy?"

"Look," I say. "Walking down the street puts my recovery in jeopardy. Living anywhere outside of a locked-down facility. Having friends. Being alone. Being overwhelmed. Getting bored. Living my *life*. I'm doing the best I can to avoid old friends and old habits. Back doors locked and all that. But I can't avoid *everything* that might cause me to slip."

This rant, too, Cecily sidesteps. "Have you ever heard the term limerance?"

"Is it the state of speaking in limericks?"

That earns me a tiny smile, but no comment. "It's that feeling you get when you're in a new relationship, or when you have a crush on someone. The elated, obsessive, can't-think-about-anything-else feeling. You know what that feels like?"

Um, yeah. "I'm familiar."

"So one reason you're advised not to jump into new relationships is because that feeling—limerence—can be addictive, especially while you're looking to form new patterns of behavior. You can become dependent on those feelings, so much so that you chase that high the same way you did with the drugs."

I soak that in for a minute. I can see what she means. The feelings of happiness that come with being near Jenna are intense and euphoric, not unlike the happiness of being on drugs.

"This morning when I woke up and decided not to get high, it wasn't because I was thinking of her. I did it for me."

"That's good," Cecily says. "But it's still something to keep an eye on."

"But it's not wrong to like someone. It's if I'm skipping from person to person chasing the high, that's the problem."

She nods. "Or if you become dependent on attention from one person who is unavailable enough never to give you what you need."

Okay, so that sounds a little more like what's happening.

"It's not like she doesn't like me," I say.

"Is she in a relationship?"

She is, but not like Cecily means. "No, it's a work commitment thing. Like she's not supposed to be with me because we're in the band together, and it makes things complicated."

Cecily seems to think that sounds reasonable, even though it probably isn't without the rest of the circumstances. "So if you weren't in the band, she could date you."

Not really. "I see the predicament you're in here," I say. "You don't think I should be in the band, and you don't think I should be in a relationship. If they're mutually exclusive, which are you going to pick?"

Cecily folds her arms. "It doesn't matter what I'd pick. It's about what you'd pick."

"I'm in the band," I say. "I signed a contract. And Jenna and I can be close, we just can't be physical. So that's good, right?"

"Maybe," Cecily says. "Unless that just lets you stay in the place of intense feelings you can never requite, and you become dependent on her for that."

I see her point. "I had an opportunity to sleep with her. One of the other guys in the band, he said we should just do it and get it out of our system, so that it could be over with. And we were going to, but I was paying attention to how I feel, and it just felt *wrong*. So I didn't. I told her how I felt about her, but I didn't have sex with her, even though I had the chance. Does that sound awful? Like I'm doing something that will damage my sobriety?"

"It sounds like a lot at once," Cecily says. "But also like a solid decision. Do you think you can keep making it?"

I take a deep breath. "Honestly? I don't know. I'm just taking it one day at a time."

She narrows her eyes at me again, like she does when I use program language to dodge her questions. Which I'm good at.

"You could still consider a sponsor," she says. "Someone who can help you sort this out, in addition to talking to me."

"Ah. Sick of me already?"

"You're deflecting," Cecily says.

"So I am."

"You could also consider if you're really ready for such a tumultuous career, and you could think about what we talked about before, about pursuing a career outside of music. Or going back to school, perhaps with a new major."

"I'm not going back to school," I say. "I just got a fantastic job. Aren't you supposed to be happy about that?"

Cecily nods. "I think it's great you've found something to give you purpose, and to support yourself."

"And it'll be enough to start paying my dad back for rehab."

"Which is important to you."

"Yes," I say. "Damn right it's important to me. You forgot to ask me how things are going with my family. Isn't that on your list?"

She ignores the sarcasm in my tone. "How are things going

117

with your family?"

"Great. My dad's letting me crash at his place, but he asks me about meetings and stuff every day, to check up on me. And I've been hanging out with Gabby again. It's really great to talk to her, almost like old times. But not the old times that I'm supposed to avoid, so you can check the box off there." My tone is getting more and more angry the longer I talk, and Cecily shifts defensively, even if her response is calculated.

"You seem upset," Cecily says.

"I *am* upset. See? Look at me being more in touch with my emotions. That's a good thing, isn't it?"

"Yes," Cecily says. "Does it feel like it's being a trigger for your addiction?"

I think about that, and she waits for my answer. As much as I hate to admit it, it's an important question.

I'm surprised to find I actually want to use *less* than I did when I walked in the door. The craving is still there, but it's weak now. Like a dull ache that isn't even worth popping a Tylenol for.

"No," I say. "At this moment it feels like more of an annoyance. Like my body wants to use, but I know I don't, because I have too much to lose."

Cecily looks happy about that, at least. "And what happens if you do lose those things? Relationships fail, especially early ones, and most especially ones with complications. Bands break up. Tours fall apart. Jobs end."

"Then I'm no worse off than I was before," I say. "And I don't have to start using again. It's my choice, right? No one can make me."

"That's true. I'm glad you think of it that way."

We stare at each other, at an impasse. And I get where she's coming from. My life seems crazy right now, even to me.

"I'm keeping the job," I say. "And I'm going to take things with Jenna as they come, and see how it goes. It's not like we're jumping into a committed relationship right away."

"No one can make those decisions but you, either," Cecily says. "But I hope you'll continue to keep our appointments, and attend your meetings."

"I will. I'm not stupid."

"I know," she says. "You're very smart. But I've seen very smart people do stupid things in the face of their addictions. Even good swimmers get pulled under by the riptide."

I nod. She's right. I know she's right.

But I can't—I won't—dismiss the feeling I have when I'm with Jenna. Not the elation or the infatuation—although there's certainly plenty of that—or even the sexual attraction, but the way it feels to just *talk* to her, like I'm saying crazy things and being perfectly understood.

"I'm not going back to the drugs," I say. "That's what matters."

"Yes," Cecily says. "I can help you figure out how to maximize your chances of success, but in the end, everything comes down to that."

Sometimes, that one thing seems impossible, and it has to be broken down to the decisions I'm making each hour, each minute, each second at a time.

But at this moment, it feels easier than before.

"I'm going to do it. I'm going to stay clean."

"Excellent," Cecily says. "I'll see you again next week."

TWELVE

Felix

Later that day, I'm at the studio with Roxie when Jenna calls me. Roxie is playing her heart out, and I'm trying to follow her lead no matter what she does. She's getting into the game of Mother May I, slowing up and speeding down like she's shot a cocktail of uppers and downers that are taking turns controlling her before they kill her.

She's loving it, and I'm sweating trying to keep up, but I think it's helping. Still, when my secret phone rings, I jump at the chance to answer it.

"Hang on," I say to Roxie, though she nods and keeps on drumming, so I have to plug one ear and go upstairs before I can hear a thing.

"Is there a practice I don't know about?" Jenna asks.

"It's just me and Roxie. I wanted to practice the way you guys play, but I didn't want to bother everyone."

"Should I be jealous?" she asks, a teasing note in her voice.

I laugh. "Only if you're into Leo."

She giggles, and I lean back against the wall, glad for the soundproof studio door now closed behind me.

"But hey," she says, "I need to ask you something. And you can totally say no if you want to. Like, really. Don't feel like you have to."

"I do have some practice saying no to you."

"Hmm," she says. "So you do. All right, were you serious about being willing to watch Ty for me?"

This is the last place I thought this conversation was going. "Of course. Why? Is everything okay?"

"Yeah," Jenna says. "I mean, it is for me. My dad got food poisoning from some bad tuna salad and my mom has this ladies Bunco night she's obsessed with and Alec and I have this scheduled date thing tonight at this big private party at a club, and Phil really wants us to be there for some press before the show—"

"Jenna," I say. "Did you rehearse that? Because all you have to say is, hey, would you come over and watch Ty tonight? And I'll say, yeah, sure. No problem."

She takes a deep breath. "I just feel horrible asking you to do this."

"I offered."

"You didn't offer to watch my son while I go out dancing with the guy I'm pretending to be in love with."

I press my lips together. "I knew the score when I got into this. You're not doing anything wrong."

She's quiet for a second. "I know. But it doesn't feel that way."

I want to put my arms around her, to hold her and tell her it's going to be okay. But I can't. "This sucks," I tell her. "But I can watch your kid and not be a jealous asshole, all right?"

"Okay," she says.

"Though I make no promises about your lead in *Angry Birds*."

"I passed him up by a wide margin. And I won't give you the password to the iPad."

I smile. "As long as you've secured the important things."

"Be aware," she says, "that Ty wants to play a concert for you on the piano. So you may be hearing a lot of 'Merrily We Roll Along.'"

121

"I'll bring my cello. We can jam together. I happen to know that one."

We arrange a time, and Jenna texts me her address. I'm feeling giddy when I go back downstairs, mostly that Jenna would trust me with Ty. The distraction seems to help more than it hurts, or else Roxie and I are starting to gel. Possibly both.

When I arrive at Jenna's house, I'm struck by how normal it looks. It's in a nice neighborhood in Orange, and has a wide driveway and a row of tiny palm trees lining the fence. It looks like the kind of house where a single mom and her boyfriend might live if they both have good jobs—but not so much if they're pop sensations. I know their success is recent, but I'm pretty sure Jenna could afford better than this.

The fact that her first priority wasn't to move them all to a place like Brentwood to live in ostentation makes me happy.

I knock on the front door and Jenna answers wearing a tight black dress with knee-high boots and fishnet stockings. Her hair is pulled back in this funky silver clip and she's got a silver chain around her neck with large, thick links.

My mouth falls open a little, and I'm glad Alec isn't there to see. "Hey," I say. "You look amazing."

Jenna winces. "Thanks. And sorry."

I smile. I understand what she means. We both wish she was dressed up to go out with me, but I get it. It's a performance. I don't begrudge her looking the part. I have a hard time imagining Jenna looking less than beautiful, no matter what she's wearing.

Ty comes around the corner. He's actually in regular kid clothes today; a t-shirt with Squirtle on the front and jeans. "Felix! You're here!"

"I am." I step in and set June down in the entryway. Ty grabs me by the arm and pulls me into the house. Jenna gives me an apologetic look, but I follow Ty into the living room. He lets go and launches himself into a belly-flop on the couch.

Opposite the door is a tall bookshelf, atop which sits a set of light-up marquee letters. Two of them.

AJ.

I look at Jenna.

"*Yeah*," she says. "Alec and I disagree about decorating, so we take turns bringing home things to annoy each other. Those are my fault."

I shake my head. "I guess now I can't say I'm living in Alec's shadow. More like his limelight."

Jenna smiles, but her eyes look sad. And she's right. It isn't funny. Her hands hang by her sides, and I want to reach out and take one. Technically, the only one who could catch us here is Alec.

But it doesn't matter if we're alone. I'm not allowed to touch her. Those are the rules. I realize we're both standing there looking at each other, neither of us saying anything. But it's not awkward. More like intense. Which I'm pretty sure is that limerick thing Cecily was talking about.

I believe her that it can be addictive, but it doesn't feel anything like heroin.

"*So*," Alec says, and we both startle, looking up to see him at the bottom of the stairs. He eyes Jenna. "You ready?"

"Yes," she says. "Let me just show Felix around."

She sweeps through the house, showing me the emergency numbers, snacks, bathrooms, and fire extinguisher. "Ty's bedtime is eight-thirty, but he'll want to stay up late, because you're here. You can keep him up as late as you can stand him." She waves her phone at me. "And you can call if you need anything, but I probably won't hear my phone at the club. Text is better. I'll check it periodically."

I nod and Jenna looks at me sadly again. "I wish I could stay," she says quietly. "Believe me, I'd rather be here with you."

I smile, though I know it looks forced. "We'll be fine. Have fun."

She takes a deep breath. "I'll try. But I promise nothing. Thank you again." Then she breezes over and joins Alec at the door. He barely glances at me, and they're gone. I notice her long black sweater hanging on a hook behind the door next to Alec's leather jacket.

I was good with them living together when it was an abstract concept, like the idea of a picnic on a beach. It seems fine in theory, but in reality your paper plates blow away and there's sand in your teeth.

I look down at Ty. "So," I say. "What do you want do?"

He doesn't answer my question. "My mom likes you," he says.

I blink at him for a second. "I like her, too."

"Do you want to kiss her?"

God, do I. "Yes. But I can't. You know the rules, right? She's not allowed to date anyone until she and Alec are ready to break up the band."

"In four years."

Jenna has clearly already explained this to him, and I'm grateful for that. "Right."

He rolls his eyes. "Four years is forever. Mom says I can't have a dad for at least four years. Katelyn from school says we're not a real family because I only have a mom and not a dad."

Ouch. I think for a second that kids are mean, but it's not like we really improve when we get older. "Well, Katelyn is wrong," I say. "And also judgmental. Do you know what that means?"

"Yes. That's what Mom says about the people on the news."

I laugh. "Exactly."

"Katelyn doesn't have a dad either. But she has a real family because she has two moms."

"Seriously?"

"Yes," Ty says, very seriously indeed. "But I don't want two moms. I have one mom and she's great."

"She *is* great. And Katelyn needs to learn about irony."

"What's irony?" Ty asks.

I think about that, but I'm not sure how to explain it. "In this case, it's when someone ought to understand something, but they don't."

"Katelyn doesn't understand," he says. "And Mom says no matter how mean she is, I'm not allowed to explain to her that Mom isn't allowed to get married for four years. But sometimes my mom calls her moms and has a chat."

I bet she does. "Good for her."

"But I'm allowed to tell you because you already know. Do you know how old I'll be in four years?" Ty's clearly not giving up on this four years thing.

"Tell me."

"I'll be twelve. I won't even need a dad anymore."

"Nah," I say. "That's not true. Do you know how old I am?"

Ty shakes his head solemnly.

"I'm twenty-two," I say. "And I still need my dad."

Ty's eyes widen. "Really?"

I'm not sure if this is a reaction to how ancient I am, or to the dad thing. "Really."

Ty grimaces. "Four years is still stupid."

"Yeah, well. Your mom promised Alec. You wouldn't want her to break a promise, would you?"

He shrugs. "We should tell Alec to change the rules."

I sit down on the fluffy white couch behind the triangular coffee table, and lean back against the cushions. "Yeah, maybe. But if your mom was with someone else, Alec wouldn't live here anymore. Wouldn't you miss him?"

Ty thinks about this. "We wouldn't see him anymore?"

"You probably would. But he'd be like a friend who comes by, not someone who lives with you."

"That would be fine," Ty says. "Alec doesn't really spend much time with me anyway."

My heart squeezes a little. The public face is all about how much Alec loves Ty, how he's a real part of their family. "Does that bother you?"

Ty shrugs again. "No. He's not really my dad. It's just for show, like a play. And sometimes he and Mom fight, but not like with Mason. Alec isn't a douche."

125

"I appreciate the distinction," I say. I expect Ty to be confused at that, but he's not even paying attention.

"Oh!" he says. "I need to show you something. But you can't tell my mom about it because it's a surprise for her birthday." He narrows his eyes at me. "Are you good at keeping secrets?"

I laugh. "Yes. I'm good at keeping secrets."

Ty takes off at a run up the stairs, and I spot a picture hanging above the banister. At first I think it's Ty and Jenna. Her hair is lighter—a chestnut color—but Jenna's is obviously dyed.

But this girl has a rounder face, and a different smile. On second look, I know it's Rachel. Ty's young in the picture, probably Ephraim's age, which would mean it was taken not long before she died. Rachel has her arms around Ty, and neither is looking at the camera, but she's squishing him up against her and they're both laughing. I look up the stairs, but I only see pictures of Ty, not Jenna and her sister.

Ty returns with a stack of papers crookedly stapled together on one side, like the books Gabby and I used to make when we were little. Across the front, in uneven letters, Ty has written, *The Adventures of Superpope*. Below it he's drawn a picture of what I can only assume is the popemobile, surrounded by tiny dots with lines shooting off them.

"Ah," I say. "Are those bullets?"

"Yes. But they can't hurt Superpope, especially when he's in his flying popemobile. Here. Read it. You'll see."

He thrusts the book into my hands, and I turn the pages.

"See," he says. "Here is the pope fighting crime. And here he's saving a nana who's crossing the street."

On the next page, a man with an uncomfortably-square crotch is shouting at Superpope. In bright, menacing letters, Ty has written, *Doosh*.

I laugh. "You aren't supposed to say that in front of popes!"

"I know," Ty says. "It's because it makes him lose his powers."

Sure enough, on the facing page, the flying popemobile has crashed.

"I only have one more page so far," Ty says. "I'm not sure what happens next." His face brightens. "Maybe you can help me with it."

"Sure. Though you have to do all the pictures. You're a much better artist than I am."

He looks suspicious again. "And you won't tell Mom, right?"

"No," I say. "Though I want to hear what she says when you give it to her. When's her birthday?"

"August twenty-fifth. That's at the end."

"It is." I commit that to memory. I want to ask Ty to let her open it when I'm around, but I can't be sure we'd be able to arrange it. There's no question in my mind she's going to love it.

I turn to the last page, and find Superpope standing between a large TV and what I assume from the polka-dotted dress and the frizzy hair is a nana.

"What's he doing here?" I ask.

"He's saving the nana from the angry people on the news. Next he's going to lose his powers when one of the angry people calls someone a douche."

I laugh. "Does your nana like to watch the news?"

"Yes," Ty says. "And my mom says not to believe anything they say on there, because it's not good to be mean and angry like Donald Trump."

"Hey, he should be Superpope's nemesis. Do you know what that means?"

"No," Ty says.

"It's like the main villain that you're always trying to beat. Like the Joker is Batman's nemesis."

"Like Team Rocket," Ty says. "They're Ash's nesmisis."

"Nemesis. Exactly. And Donald Trump would be the perfect nemesis for Superpope, because he says bad words in front of nanas *and* popes."

Ty's eyes widen. "For real?"

To be fair, I don't know that Trump has ever used the word douche in front of the pope, but I'm confident that if the mood

127

struck him, he would.

"For real," I say.

Ty scrunches up his face. "What if he's too powerful for Superpope?"

"Nah," I say. "Superpope is awesome. He needs a formidable foe. Do you know what that means?"

Ty shakes his head.

"Like a powerful enemy."

"A nesmesis."

I nod. "Exactly."

Ty takes the book back from me. "I better go hide this, in case Mom comes home." He races back up to his room, and when he returns, he jumps onto the piano bench. "Mom said you wanted to jam with me. She says you know 'Merrily We Roll Along.'"

I get my cello and have to fiddle with the latch for a second to get it open. The little pin that holds it closed is bent, and I really should retrieve my spare from my dad's basement even if I'm not playing on the street.

I pull June and my bow out of her case and sit down on the couch. "Do you want me to play melody with you? Or the accompaniment?"

He pauses for a moment, and I think maybe he doesn't know what that is. "It's the fancy part that goes with the melody," I say.

He gives me a look. "I know that," he says. "Play the melody first, just to make sure you know it. And then I'll play it again, and you can accompany me."

He over-enunciates the last part, and I smile. "Will do."

We play through the song twice, and I improvise a part to go with it. When we finish, Ty turns around and eyes my cello.

"You want to try?" I ask.

His face lights up. "Can I?"

I motion him over. My full-sized cello is miles too big for him, but I don't think he's in danger of actually running up against that limitation in the three seconds I expect him to be interested in playing it. I have him stand behind the instrument and I sit behind him, supporting June and helping him hold the bow.

"This thing is taller than you are," I say. "But I think you can handle it." I do the fingering, and show him how to run the bow across the strings, which he does with broad strokes, making an amount of screeching I haven't heard come out of my instrument since I was ten.

"Whoa," I say. "Are you trying to hit all the strings at once?"

"Yes. I think I missed one."

"Do you play the piano by smashing your arms down on the keys?"

He thinks about this. "Sometimes."

"When you hit the strings all together, does it make notes, or noise?"

Ty pauses. "I like it, but I think the answer is noise."

I laugh. "Fair enough."

Ty makes a few more screeching noises and then lets go of the bow. "Can I have a snack?"

He may have lasted a whole four seconds. "Sure," I say. "What do you want?"

"I don't know. What is there?"

He probably has a better idea than I do, but I lay June down carefully beside the couch and walk into the kitchen and start checking out what's available in the pantry. On the shelf above the snacks I see a row of cookbooks, with names like *Cookies for All Occasions* and *The Big Book of Pies*. Most of the books appear to be pie-related. I grin, remembering Jenna telling me how she got her love of baking from her grandfather, a grizzled Navy Captain who took up baking as a hobby after his retirement and spent Saturdays with her, making every pie imaginable. I can still hear her laugh as she talked about how excited she was when her parents finally got her an Easy-Bake Oven for Christmas, and how disappointed she was that very same day when she realized that baking by the heat of a single weak light bulb is the worst.

I could have listened to her talk about her life all night long.

I realize Ty's still waiting, and so I scan the shelves and start calling options to him. I expect him to follow me in, but he doesn't. He doesn't even respond.

"Ty?" I call.

I hear a loud thunk. I walk back into the living room, but he's gone. "Ty? Where'd you go?"

A muffled giggle arises from my cello case. June is still resting on the floor next to the couch, and the case lid is closed.

"Hmm," I say. "I wonder where Ty could have gone."

Ty giggles again, and I move over to the case, standing just above it. The latch has flipped closed when the case shut. He must not have supported it when he tipped it closed. I'm glad it didn't clock him on the head.

"Oh well," I say. "Guess I'll have to pack up and go home." I nudge the case, sliding it over on the carpet.

Ty squeaks, and I laugh. "Ah ha! I found you. Climb out of there."

I hear Ty pressing on the lid, but the latch holds it closed. "I'm stuck," he says.

"*Yeah* you are. Remember that next time you decide to close yourself in a box, okay? They don't always open again." I kneel beside the case and pull on the latch.

It doesn't move.

Ty knocks on the lid. "It's getting hot in here."

"Hang on. It'll just be a second." I jiggle the latch. I'm sure there's a trick to it, but it hasn't been broken long enough for me to know what it is. I slide my nails—which are trimmed too short for this task—up under the pin, trying to wiggle it free.

And that's when I notice the hem of Ty's Squirtle shirt jammed in the pin. I bend down, looking at it from beneath. The cloth is wedged up under the bent pin, and the latch is closed over it. I try to push it apart, but it won't budge.

"Shit," I say. I check the other latches and wiggle the lid up and down, but it doesn't move an inch.

"Felix?" Ty calls.

"I'm here, kid," I say. And I sit there, staring at my broken cello-case latch.

Ty is stuck tight.

THIRTEEN

Felix

"Okay, Ty," I say. "I need you to try to help me open the case, okay?"

"Did you forget how?" Ty asks.

"No. But your shirt is caught in the latch and it's stuck. Can you try to pull it out?"

"I can't see my shirt. It's dark in here."

"Okay," I say. "But you can feel it, right? Because you're wearing it?"

He squirms inside the case. "It's fuzzy in here."

"Okay. Find the fabric that's not fuzzy. That's your shirt."

"I feel my pants," he says, "but my arms are stuck to the sides."

He's weirdly calm about that, and I hope he stays that way, because if he starts crying inside there I might join him. Jenna trusted me with him, and I let this happen. "Slide one up a little and reach the bottom of your shirt, okay?"

There's a thump in the case. It isn't anywhere near the place where his shirt is caught in the latch.

I look around. These cases are built to withstand blows, but I could probably cut the latch off if I went at it hard enough. But then I'd risk gouging the child inside, and I really don't want to have to explain to Jenna why I stabbed her kid in the arm with a knife.

"Shit," I say again.

"That's not a nice word," Ty says.

"I'll watch out for Superpope. I wish I could call him to get you out of here." Who *would* I even call about this? A locksmith? They'd probably take forever and I have no idea how long it takes to suffocate in a cello case. "Ty, do you know where your mom keeps the screwdrivers?" If I can't cut the locks off, maybe I can get better leverage with a flathead than with my fingers.

"I don't know. Maybe the garage."

"Okay. You wait here." As if he can do anything else. "Don't be scared, okay?"

"I'm not scared," Ty says, as if the thought is ridiculous. "I like it in here." He pauses. "But my face is getting sweaty."

Shit. His isn't the only one.

I run out to the garage and search around until I find a Rubbermaid container marked *tools*, and I can't help but think that I definitely belong in that box. Jenna apparently isn't much more of a handyman than I am, because the container doesn't have much in it. I do find a screwdriver, though, and a utility knife, which I take just in case.

When I return, the cello case has moved a good foot from where it was. I hesitate, and inside the case Ty squirms, edging the thing another inch.

"Hey," I say. "I thought I told you not to go anywhere."

Another giggle.

I kneel beside the case again and work at the latch with the screwdriver, but it doesn't budge. I swear again. "Okay, Ty. I'm going to cut some holes so you can breathe, okay? I need you to cooperate, so that I don't hurt you."

"Okay," he says. I move to the wide end of the case. I know his feet are down there, because he's talking from the skinny side. His head must be wedged in there too tight to turn. I tap on the side of the case with the hinges. Those areas are reinforced, but the top isn't. I can probably cut through there, if I work at it. "I need you to move your feet over here," I say. "All the way over until they hit the side."

Ty squirms inside the case. "Okay," he says.

I wish I could see inside to be sure he's done it. I knock on the case again. "Your feet are on this side? Toward me?"

"I can't see you."

"But you can hear me, right?" I knock again. "Are your feet over here?"

"Yes!" Ty shouts. "I know what my feet are!"

Fair enough. At the far other side of the case, I gently cut through the top of the plastic with the utility knife. I get enough of the case cut away to stick all of my fingers through. Inside, I can see the hem of Ty's jeans, and the tops of his sneakers.

"Okay," I say. "You should get some air in there now."

Ty pauses. "My feet don't breathe," he says. "What about my face? That's where I breathe."

I sigh. He has a point, and I imagine two holes are better than one, but I *really* don't want to cut his face with a utility knife.

I eye the skinny end of the case. He *is* shorter than the cello, but I don't trust him to tell me how far down he's scooted. "All right, Ty," I say. "I'm going to stand you up, and I want you to let yourself slide until you're standing with your feet flat, okay?"

"Okay," he says, and I stand at the skinny end of the case and lift it with the flat side toward me until it's standing on end.

"Whee!" Ty shouts, and then the case rocks back and forth as he throws his weight from side to side.

"Stop rocking!"

He stops. "But it's fun!"

"It won't be fun if I drop you." Still, I shake the case a bit, as if to settle him down to the bottom. "Are your feet flat?"

"No. They have arches."

"I mean—Oh, never mind." I wrap my arm around the case to keep it still and then gouge a hole in the end only slightly smaller than the one at the bottom. "Okay. Now you should be able to breathe."

Ty heaves a few breaths inside the case. "I'm giving you a thumbs up," Ty says. "But I can't get my arm up that high, so you can't see it."

I sit on the floor. The holes help the immediate problem, but I'm not confident I can cut enough of the case to get him out without hurting him, especially because most of the structural parts are reinforced. I could still call the locksmith, but I'm pretty sure of what they would say.

"Okay, Ty," I say. "I'm going to carry you out to my car, and buckle you in. And then we're going to go to the emergency room and get you out of here, all right?"

Ty is quiet. "But that's for emergencies. This isn't an emergency."

I'm glad he's still thinking of it that way. "It's for when you need help right away. Which we definitely do."

I try to call Jenna, but she doesn't answer. They've probably reached the club by now, and it's loud. I really don't want to explain what's happened by text message, but she'll probably get back to me when she sees she's missed my call.

I go to lift the cello case, but Ty tells me to wait. "I never got a snack."

I stare at the hole in the top of the case. I can see Ty's blond hair poking up in tufts against the soft lining.

"Ty," I say. "How am I supposed to get you a snack when you're stuck in a cello case?"

"You could put something through the air hole. Like Cheetos."

I want to refuse, but I really don't want him getting scared or crying in there. It's all fine while it's fun, but at some point he's going to realize he's wedged inside a box from which there is no escape.

"Do you have any Cheetos?" I ask. I can't for the life of me remember all the snacks I called out before.

"Not in here."

I can't argue with that. I go back to the kitchen and in the pantry. Inside I find a half-full bag of jalapeno Cheetos.

I head back to the case. "Okay, I have Cheetos. But if I drop them in there, I think you're going to get dust in your eyes. Can you reach up by your face?"

A thump sounds from halfway up the case. "No," he says. "My hands are stuck."

I put my hands at my sides and try to figure out how to maneuver them above my head while keeping them against my body. "Can you move your hand up to your stomach?" I ask. "And then across to your hip?"

There's some rustling. "Yes."

"Okay, then up to your shoulder and onto your face. You got it?"

"This is a fun game," Ty says. "I'm touching myself in all the places."

I choke. "Don't tell your mom we played that game."

Immediately, I hate myself. Now he's going to tell her we played games about touching ourselves and then I told him not to tell her. Jenna's probably had a talk with him that he should always tell when some adult doesn't want him to.

"Or tell her," I say. "Just don't call it that."

"Why?"

I am not going to explain that to a kid in a cello case. "Never mind. Wiggle your fingers." I peer through the air hole and I can see his fingers wiggling. "Good. Stretch your arm up a little bit more and I can give you some Cheetos." He does and I take a handful and try to get them into his fingers. Most of them scatter, but he gets a few. His hand disappears, and a crunching rises from their air hole. "Thanks," he says. "Can I have some more?"

He eats for so long I feel like Jenna is going to come home and I'm still going to be here feeding Ty Cheetos through a slot, but he's finally happy, and before I've completely drained the bag.

"Felix?" Ty says.

"Yes?"

"I'm thirsty."

I squeeze my eyes shut. "I can't pour water on you. You'll drown."

"I can swim!"

"Not in a cello case. You can't even move your arms."

Ty thinks about that. "What about a juice box?"

I don't think a juice box will fit through the hole I've made, but back in the pantry, I find a package of Capri Suns. I have to put the straw into it before I ease it through the hole, because I know he can't do that while squished in the dark. Juice squirts from the straw as Ty grabs it, soaking his hair, but he manages to pull it down toward his face.

He slurps.

"All right," I say. "Are we ready?"

Silence. "I have to go to the bathroom."

"We are going," I say, bracing the case and lifting it again. "*Now*."

"But—"

"Pee yourself if you must, but we are not coordinating some kind of fluid removal." I hoist both case and boy out to my dad's spare car and flatten the passenger seat as low as it can go. Ty rocks minimally, and I manage to get the case in skinny-end up, so at least if he wets himself it won't run toward his face. I buckle the case in, even though I'm frankly not sure how much good that would do in a crash.

I set my GPS for the nearest ER. Jenna still hasn't called me back, so I send her a text telling her where we're going and why. The pit is my stomach is back and larger than ever.

After this, there's no way she's letting me watch her kid again.

FOURTEEN

Jenna

Alec and I take my car to the club, and I drive while Alec updates our social media accounts about the big party tonight and posts one of our standard "adorable couple" selfies he took before we got in the car, with him kissing my cheek and me all smiles.

We've put on the act for so long now it's as easy as slipping on a mask. But now I can't help but think of Felix having to see it.

I wish so much it could be him and me in that picture. It should be.

But I look over at Alec, dutifully tweeting and responding to messages and undoubtedly already working with Phil on setting up our next impromptu public appearance. He doesn't love keeping on top of all the gazillion social media requirements any more than I do, but he's got a head for the business—he always has—and the vision for where we could go, and the drive to do what needs to be done to get there.

We're talented musicians, both of us, and we've certainly caught a few lucky breaks. But it's this drive of Alec's, this vision he works his ass off to see through, that's the real reason we've been so successful so quickly. It's the reason I'm able to have this dream career I love and financial security for myself and Ty (and

138

my parents, who would never be able to afford living out here by us, otherwise). It's the reason I'm not still back in Michigan, working two minimum wage jobs just to raise my son, all while rarely being able to spend time with him.

I owe Alec, big time. Between that and my own fear of losing this dream career and all the security that comes with it—I've seen enough spectacular plummets from stardom to know what one ill-timed scandal can do—agreeing to the rules seemed a small price to pay a year ago.

Those rules seem like a staggering price now, but that doesn't mean I can just abandon them, or Alec, no matter how much my heart wants to.

But that pull between Felix and me is so strong, and I don't see it getting less so anytime soon. I think Felix was right back at the hotel; we're not going to be able to stick to these rules, to not really be together, for *four years*. Three *days* has been brutal. God, even just seeing him today, at my door, looking at me like that—I wanted to kiss him and kiss him and never stop.

But if we could make it even a good chunk of that time—

"So you're cool with Felix watching Ty?" Alec says suddenly, cutting into my thoughts. He's still typing away on the phone, but there's an edge to his voice that tells me his mind is elsewhere.

"Yeah," I say. "Is there some reason you think I shouldn't be?"

He shrugs. "I mean, you're usually super picky about baby-sitters, and you haven't known him that long. I was just surprised." Then he looks over at me with a grin. "But I suppose we've got both a clean drug test and background check on him. Not a bad way to vet a babysitter."

For a second, I think maybe Alec's making a dig about my having let Mason watch Ty. But no. The dig is more focused on how quickly I've let Felix into our lives, a decision he doesn't agree with, unlike our former mutual trust for Mason.

"Well, I trust him. And Ty was excited to have him over." That last bit's an understatement. When Mom called with the news that Dad had spent all day in tuna salad purge mode, Ty begged with all the tricks in his cute kid bag—widening those green eyes, offering to do extra chores, giving me un-asked-for hugs—to get me to ask Felix to watch him.

I didn't tell him there weren't many other options at this late notice, what with my mom's plans, and Leo and Roxie both out on dates tonight (though not with each other, sadly, despite all the weird-ass fungus cream massaging going on there lately). I also didn't tell him how much I loved the idea of him and Felix getting to know each other more, even as I was afraid to find out that when it comes down to it, Felix is more okay with Ty in theory than in reality.

I'm still nervous about that. Ty's the best kid in the world, but I'm under no illusions about what most guys—especially guys as young as Felix and I are—are equipped to realistically handle when it comes to dating a single mom. It's one thing to know I have a kid, and another thing to become part of that kid's life in a real way, to see him as more than just baggage that comes along with dating me.

Alec is frowning at his phone like he's already stopped paying attention to the conversation. And thankfully I'm saved from having to talk to Alec any more about Felix when we arrive at Club Fu. Paparazzi and groups of hopeful club-goers mill around out front. Valets trot over to us and Alec puts his phone smoothly in his pocket and gives me the "time for game face" look, as the valets open our doors.

And then we become Alec-and-Jenna again, at least as far as the public is concerned. When we get out of the car, and start heading into the club, Alec slings his arm around my waist, and we smile and wave at the cameras and laughingly oblige when a paparazzo yells "Aww, just kiss her, Alec!"

Kissing Alec has felt empty for a long time, but after kissing Felix, it now has the added effect of making me feel sick.

We're escorted by one of the valets—who have undoubtedly been trained to recognize the celebrity guests, even the lesser ones like us—through the crowd of people trying to flirt or bribe their way past the bouncers. I doubt many of them will have success. Tonight the club is invite only, a private anniversary party being thrown by Adam Levine of Maroon 5 for his model wife Behati, and honestly I'm surprised *we're* on the guest list for this one. Apparently Phil knows Adam's manager, and called in a favor.

So now we can pretend we're all buddy-buddy with Adam and Behati, even though our only interaction with either of them was the one time Alec was in the bathroom at the same time as Adam at last year's Grammys, and apparently Adam said "Hey," and Alec said "Hey," and that was it.

Not exactly a friendship for the ages, but the press from being invited to this party is pretty fantastic, especially so close to tour. So I'll play my part, and play it well, for the good of the band.

Even if I wish I could be here with Felix instead, with his arm around my waist.

Club Fu is fairly small and while it's new, I'm kind of glad to see it's not one of those overly trendy places that always seem like they're trying too hard, with aerialists or waitresses all dressed up like Marilyn Monroe. Strobe lights are strobing and house music is thumping and well-dressed people are dancing and drinking and probably snorting lines in the bathroom stalls—it's your basic club scene, even if this one has more recognizable faces and photographers from *People* with the exclusive right to shoot inside.

There's tons of people crammed in here, though, and I'm guessing we're not the only ones who made it in on a manager's favor.

"Time to make the rounds?" I ask Alec.

He grins. "Hell, yeah."

We do so, scoping out who's here and who we need to talk to, Alec taking the lead as usual. The networking, the making business connections, the being in the right place to be in the right picture—this is Alec's forte.

As we do all this, we dance and cuddle and get drinks. I don't drink much, not anymore. But it's a lot easier to do all this with a cocktail in hand, even if I wish I was back home to see what Felix and Ty are up to, and how they're getting along.

I try to focus on the conversation Alec is having (as much as he can, yelling over the music) with this pretentious guy with a soul patch and gin-soaked breath who is apparently a casting director. The guy goes on at some length about his latest coup—getting A-list actress Kim Watterson to play a dying young mom to child star Axel Dane in the film treatment of some weep-fest novel I've never read and probably never will.

We don't exactly want to be actors, Alec and I, but at a party like this, connections are connections, and you never know which ones will lead somewhere.

Still, I'm glad when we move on.

We dance a little more, though it all feels distant, like I'm an actor in a movie playing the part of myself. Alec is respectful, and doesn't dance any closer than necessary, which is already pretty damn close, but it still reminds me of the way I used to feel, detached and numb, pretending to be the girl who was up for anything and didn't care. I'm glad when we stop dancing and pose for a picture—thankfully not one where they shout at us to kiss—and Alec guides us closer to the end of the main bar, where Adam and Behati and several other members of Maroon 5 are holding court, and where the *People* photographers are snapping away.

"Hey," Alec says, squeezing my hand. I look back at him, and see him holding up a sign that was on the bar, advertising an upcoming karaoke night. "You could show off your 'Total Eclipse of the Heart.' Maybe mix it up, do some 'Holding Out for a Hero.'"

I laugh, and it's genuine. "I could. But my Bonnie Tyler karaoke game is strong. I don't want to risk some random dude trying to get me to join his band. It's happened before, you know."

"Sounds like a smart dude."

"Persistent, too."

Alec laughs. "Yeah, maybe. But hey, look where it got us."

I smile back. When Alec picked me up at that karaoke bar, I was just trying to get out with some friends, trying to feel like a normal person again after Rachel died. I couldn't have hope then that I'd ever be in a healthy relationship, which was most of the reason I joined the band but held out on dating Alec for the first six months. We may not have turned out to be meant for each other, but being with Alec gave me hope that the story we sang about was one I could actually have someday.

Now I wonder if it's the thing that's going to drive away the person I think I could actually star in that story with.

Alec tugs on my hand. "Come on, that's Adam's manager over there by Behati. Phil said he'd introduce us to them."

I try to figure out who Alec is pointing to, but the steady beat of the music is starting to feel like it's stabbing me in the back of my eye. Not that I'm any stranger to the club scene, but spending too long in places like this—especially when I'd rather be elsewhere—still reminds me of the parties I used to go to, of the press of dancing bodies and the hands on my skin from guys I don't know and don't want to. My pulse matching the music, spurring me on, desperate to be enough, to be numb, to forget, even though I knew it would only last for a minute, and all feel worse in the morning.

"Give me a second," I say.

Alec looks concerned—he's been at these things with me when I've felt the need to go home early before, but if I do it this time, I'm pretty sure he's going to blame it on Felix.

I told Felix I'd check for messages, but I haven't since we got here. I pull out my phone, and there's a text. From Felix, and not from the secret phone, either.

Ty's stuck in my cello case, the message says. *He's fine, but I can't open it, and I'm taking him to the hospital to get him out.*

He pinned the address of the hospital for me below that.

Shit.

The message was from nearly a half-hour ago, and I completely forgot to warn Felix about Ty's proclivity for very small spaces.

"We have to go," I say to Alec, ignoring his protests as I drag him toward the door.

FIFTEEN

Felix

I drive toward the hospital going ten over, hoping Ty doesn't get carsick.

"Felix?" he asks.

"Yes?"

"Would you want to be my dad?"

I open my mouth and then close it again. That question is so loaded it might as well be a handgun. "Kid," I say finally, "anyone who got to be your dad would be super lucky."

"So will you be my dad?"

I glance at the cello case, as if he can see me. "Definitely not for four years."

"But then?"

"Maybe then. It depends."

"On what?"

"On whether your mom still likes me." Which after this debacle I'm not thinking is likely.

"Do you think you'll still like her?"

Maybe it's the limerence, but I can't imagine ever not wanting to be with Jenna. "Yes."

"So when you're my dad, will you make me a little brother?"

I run a yellow light. "Do you know how that works?"

145

"You have the sex to make the baby. Do you want to have the sex with my mom?"

Oh, *god*. I can't exactly say *no*. "Yes, but I can't."

"Are you a dad?"

"No, I don't have any kids."

"So you've never had the sex."

Now I give the cello a look I wouldn't dare give Ty if he could see me. "It just—It doesn't—" I take a deep breath. "It doesn't always make babies. Just sometimes."

"So your penis doesn't work."

"Ahhhh," I say. "It works just fine, thank you very much."

"So you can make me a brother."

This kid. There is no dodging his questions, and I have to respect him for it. "Theoretically, I could make you a brother. I have the equipment, and it works."

"What does theoremically mean?"

"Theoretically." That's another hard one. "So, like, theoretically you could throw a baseball through a window, right? But you wouldn't."

"So you could make me a brother, but—"

"But your mom probably wouldn't want me to, and also it's against the rules." I desperately need to get him off this subject, even to something mostly adjacent. "You know parents don't get to choose if they have a boy or a girl, right?"

Silence. "Really?"

"Yeah. You just get what you get."

"But that's not fair."

"Yeah, kid," I say. "Tell me about it."

We reach the ER and I haul the case through the double doors as gently as I can. I walk up to the registration desk and put my case down in front of it. "There's a kid stuck in this cello case."

The nurse looks down at it. "Is he conscious?"

"Yes," I say. "Say hi, Ty."

"Hello!" Ty calls. "Felix took good care of me. He gave me

juice and Cheetos. But I have to pee."

The nurse gives me a withering look, no doubt weighing the quality of my parenting and finding me wanting. I don't point out that I'm not his parent. This could only complicate things further.

She hands me a stack of paperwork. "Fill these out. We'll call you back when we're ready for you."

I look down at the case. "But he's stuck—"

"I heard you," the nurse says. "Fill out the forms and we'll call you back."

The waiting room is crowded, and I see several people eyeing my now-battered cello case in confusion. I slide the case over to the nearest empty chair and sit down in it. "Hang on, kid," I say. "We're going to get you out of there." I check my phone, but there's no response from Jenna. I start to fill out the paperwork. "Ty, is your last name Rollins like your mom?"

"Yes," he says.

"Do you know if you have insurance?"

"I think so."

I check the appropriate boxes, though even if he's right about having insurance, I'm certain he doesn't know his insurance number. "What's your address?"

"You know my address. You came to my house."

He has a point. I pull out my phone again and copy it over from my text messages. "What about your phone number?"

"Didn't you call my mom and talk to her for a long time?"

I freeze. "Were you listening to that?" Especially at the end, things had gotten pretty . . . intense.

"No," he says. "But my mom was yawning this morning."

Ha. Good. "All right. Yes, I also have your phone number." But apparently not enough brain to remember that I do.

There's a long list of things that might be wrong with Ty ranging from obesity to glaucoma. "Ty," I say. "Do you have any health problems?"

"What are those?"

147

"Like, where you're sick. Like asthma, or . . ." I look over the list. "Brain trauma."

"My friend Declan has asthma."

"That would be helpful if I were filling out a form for Declan. What about you?"

"Sometimes I get colds. Or throw up. One time, I threw up in my mom's purse."

I bet Jenna loved that. "Great. No health problems. Are you allergic to any medication?" I stare at the form. "You don't need medication. You are *in a cello case.*" I walk back to the registration desk and slap the papers down on the table. "There. Can we please get the kid out of the case now?"

"We'll call you back when—"

"When you're ready," I say. "*Right.*"

I stalk back to the case and sit beside Ty with my head in my hands. I have a text message on my phone: *On our way!*

Jenna is definitely going to kill me.

We're waiting now, I respond.

Jenna doesn't answer.

It takes another fifteen minutes for the nurse to take us back. Ty amuses himself by regaling me with the similarities and differences of being inside a cello case and driving in a pope mobile. The nurse brings out a stretcher, onto which we load Ty, case and all. Twenty minutes later, the doctor is cutting Ty out of the case with a cast saw, and Jenna comes into the room.

She doesn't even look at me.

"Ty!" she says, as the doctor lifts the top of the case away.

Ty pops up, his hair sticky with juice and orange Cheeto dust. "Hi, Mom!"

I sit there in agony as Jenna lifts Ty out of the cello case and looks him over. Fragments of Cheeto fall to the floor.

"Jenna," I say. "I am so sorry. I didn't mean for this to happen, I swear."

I'm ready—as ready as I'll ever be—for her to glare at me. To yell at me, even, for endangering her kid like this. But instead

Jenna laughs, and dusts off Ty's shoulders. "I guess I should have told you about his affection for small spaces."

I stare at her. "He's done this before?"

"Oh, yes," Jenna says. "One time he got his arm stuck between a restaurant booth and the wall. They had to cover him in butter while I sat on the floor feeding him chicken fingers. Once at a movie, he decided to slide down the back of his seat, and it took a guy the size of the Hulk to pry the seat apart. And once my mom took him to the art museum, and he got his head stuck behind a statue. They had to remove it to get him out. We may have inspired them to put up signs and gently suggest we don't come back."

Huh. No wonder he wasn't scared—or even surprised—when he got stuck.

Ty grins like these are his proudest accomplishments, and Jenna hugs him. Orange dust sticks to the dark sequins of her dress. She cringes at me. "Sorry. He hasn't done this in a while or I would have warned you. I'll pay for your cello case."

I shake my head, shell-shocked with relief. "No, I'm sorry. Don't worry about the case. I have another one. And I should have been paying more attention."

"You were paying attention," Ty says. "You were getting me a snack."

Jenna runs her hand through his sticky hair. "I can see that."

I grimace. "He was hungry . . ."

"And now I need to pee *so much*," Ty says.

"All right," Jenna says. "Let's get you to the bathroom, and then I need to give them our insurance information and we'll get you home."

"When can Felix watch me again?" Ty asks.

"I'm pretty sure your mom isn't going to *want* me to watch you again."

"That's not the case," Jenna says. She gives Ty a look that tries to be stern, though her lips are quirking up at the edges. "But I'd understand if Felix didn't want to be responsible for

149

you after this."

"Why not?" Ty asks. "We had fun, didn't we Felix? And I need your help on my secret project."

"Yeah," I say. "We sure did. And I'd be happy to help you if your mom's okay with it." I look at Jenna. "I really am sorry."

Jenna smiles, and her hand half reaches toward me before it drops to her side. "Really. It's okay. But I'd better get this boy to a bathroom, and Alec's waiting outside. I'll call you after I get Ty to bed."

"Yes, please," I say.

Jenna ushers Ty off, leaving me alone with the remains of my cello case.

And I try not to desperately wish I was the one taking them home.

SIXTEEN

Felix

Since we have practice the next morning, I crash at Gabby's instead of driving all the way out to Valencia. Will's home, so my communication with Gabby is limited to her questioning looks when his back is turned, which I answer mostly with shrugs. I know she's going to interrogate me at her first opportunity, and it's not like I mind.

Gabby and Will have just gone to bed when Jenna calls. I curl up in the dark on Sarah's mod sofa, under Gabby's fuzzy throw. "Hey, beautiful," I say.

"Hey," she says, with a smile in her voice. "You know, you left a special someone here. I think she misses you already."

I chuckle. I'd realized about halfway to Gabby's that I'd left my cello behind when Ty and I fled for the hospital. I'd been seriously tempted to turn around right there and head back to Jenna's to get it, but I know that would have been way more about seeing Jenna again than any need to play some late-night Rachmaninoff.

"Yeah, well, I miss her already, too," I say, softly.

"I assured her I'd bring her with me to practice tomorrow and she could see you again then. She very reluctantly supposed she could live with that," Jenna says, the smile still teasing in her voice.

I smile back. "Yeah, I reluctantly suppose I can, too," I say. "So how's Ty?"

"He's fine. All the way home he couldn't stop talking about what a good time he had."

"I bet Alec loved that."

Jenna groans. "There was that."

Suddenly I remember Ty's touching game. "Um, so when he was stuck in there, I was trying to explain to him how to move his hand up to grab the Cheetos. We were basically playing Simon Says, you know? Move your hand up to your waist. Now to your shoulder. Now to your face. Right?"

"Okay." She doesn't sound like she's heard this before, which gives me hope I've gotten there first.

"So then Ty is like, 'This is a fun game! I'm touching myself in all the places!' "

Jenna laughs. Also a good sign.

"And without even thinking about it, I'm like, 'Don't tell your mom we played *that*.' And then I realize now he's going to tell you we played that game and I said not to tell you—"

"Yeah," Jenna says. "He's not supposed to keep secrets from me. It's a rule."

"I figured," I say. "I thought of that as soon as it came out of my mouth. Sorry."

"I'm just sad Ty didn't tell me this first."

"Yeah, well. I'm sure it's coming."

Jenna is silent, and I wonder if she's biting back the same joke I withheld last night.

"I think Ty wants to move into your cello case," she says. "In typical Ty fashion, he seems to have learned nothing from this experience."

I laugh. "They cut the latch off. It's of no use to me. But I'd still be afraid he'd find a way to get himself locked in it again." I have an idea. "Unless I could find some way to brace it open. Then he could squish in there to his heart's content."

"He would love that."

"I'll see what I can do." Frankly, I have no more idea how to permanently brace open a cello case than how to sail around the world. I'm pretty sure one involves brackets and the other boats, but that's the extent of my knowledge. "Though I hear he'd much rather have a popemobile."

Jenna laughs. "Ah, yes. I really need to show him pictures of the actual popemobile, but I don't want to crush his dreams."

I don't dare tell her about Superpope. I promised, and besides, I don't want to ruin the surprise. "So the pope thing. Are you Catholic?"

"Ooooh," Jenna says. "That's right. We haven't talked about politics or religion."

"Well, I know you don't like the news."

"I don't. But honestly, I'm not that political. Too much fighting and yelling. It stresses me out."

"I used to be conservative," I say. "I grew up in Brentwood."

"Wow," Jenna says. "Rich boy."

"Ha. Yes. That was before my parents went bankrupt and got divorced. But I grew up near a lot of people who have millions, and don't want the government moving around said millions. But then I moved to New York where people believe polar opposite things, and now I've landed somewhere in the middle." I pause. "But you didn't answer my question about being Catholic. I just wondered, what with the pope references and Ty's school uniform—"

Jenna's laugh cuts me off. "It's not a school uniform. He's not even *in* school right now, since it's summer break. He just has this thing where whenever he leaves the house, he likes to, as he puts it, 'look like a grown-up.' Even though it's not like any adult we know dresses that way. It's so weird."

I grin. Somehow I can totally see this about Ty. "And super cute."

"Definitely that, too," Jenna says. "Anyway, we're not Catholic. You?"

"Atheist. Or at least, I was."

"Really?" Jenna says. "Not anymore?"

I immediately regret bringing this up. The truth is, I was the staunchest atheist around until I started the program. The steps are all about putting your faith in God, giving up control over your own life and asking him to fix you. When I was in rehab the first time, I tried to get out of doing the work by saying I didn't believe in God, and one of the therapists gave me the version designed for atheists. It was all about believing the actual steps have power over your life, and yielding control over to them.

By the time I was ready to do the work, I'd come around to thinking maybe I didn't know everything about the way the universe worked, and I'd rather believe in God than believe that words some guy wrote down have magical powers to keep me sober.

"I guess I'm agnostic now," I say. "I've done things I'm not proud of, and maybe it's wishful thinking, but I'd like to believe there's such a thing as absolution and forgiveness."

"I get that," Jenna says quietly. "I grew up Mormon,"

"Really?" I say. "I had a Mormon friend in high school. He had a hard time even looking at girls." At the time I teased him that he'd promised himself to Jesus, but I think the truth might have been that he was just shy.

"I don't remember much about it. We stopped going and joined a Methodist church, and around the time I was in high school and started to rebel, my mom joined the Jehovah's Witnesses and decided my soul would be saved by not celebrating Christmas or my birthday."

"I take it that didn't go over well."

"Ha. No. But that didn't last long, either," she says. "As for me, I'm not sure exactly what I believe, but I definitely believe in God. I have to think Rachel still exists somewhere."

My whole body tenses. I know what she means, but I don't know how to explain without telling her everything. I need to tell her about the drugs. I know I do. But the idea of having to tell her about other things makes me want to put a needle in my arm.

Especially about Katy.

"I want that to be true," I say.

"I think it is. It has to be."

I try to shake off the dark memories. "These last few days have me thinking that, too. I've never believed in fate before. But then I met you, and well—here we are. So the universe can't be random. There's no way I'm that lucky, and I sure haven't earned the karma."

Jenna makes a soft humming noise that lets me know she likes this idea.

"If something like this can happen," I say, "who knows what else is out there."

Jenna is quiet for a moment. "What is it you want to be forgiven for?"

I close my eyes and draw the blanket up around my chin. There it is. A direct question. I can't lie to her, but I can't tell her the whole story, either. I don't know why, but I know it in my bones. I want to believe it isn't because I already know that'll be the end.

"I knew a girl who overdosed," I say. "I was there when it happened."

"Oh, god, I'm so sorry."

I'm not the one she should be sorry for. Katy is the one who's dead.

"So, yeah," I say. "I want to believe there's an afterlife, even though I never did before."

"That makes sense," Jenna says. She pauses for a moment. "Were you in love with her?"

There's the same hint of jealousy in her voice I must have had when I asked if she was in love with Alec. "No," I say. "It wasn't like that at all." I know I should tell her the rest of the story, but the idea of the way she might react—with silence, or with anger—it's too much. Maybe Cecily is right. Maybe I need this too much, maybe I'm putting my sobriety at risk by depending on her approval, and her affection and attention.

155

But I also can't hang up. I can't walk away. Jenna is too important to me. The stakes are too high.

And that's when I'm sure what that third thing is. The thing I couldn't bring myself to admit when I was telling Gabby about it after the hotel, even though it was already true then, and part of me knew it.

I'm in love with Jenna. I fell in love with her over sushi on our date-that-wasn't-a-date, or maybe I was somehow already there before I even walked into that restaurant. Either way, the situation scares the hell out of me.

I'm in love with a woman I may not be able to be with—to even touch—for four years. I'm in love with a woman who doesn't know the full truth about my past, and who might want nothing to do with me if she did.

I'm glad Jenna speaks next, because the full force of admitting this to myself robs me of any words of my own.

"I've thought that I'd like to give Ty the opportunity to be a part of a faith community," Jenna says, "but I don't know. It's a lot of work, trying to find one that fits."

I hold my breath, though I'm glad to be back on a slightly safer topic. "Here's another embarrassing truth. I've never actually been to church."

"Really? Never?"

"Nope." I've now attended an alarming number of meetings held in churches, but never a church service itself. "My parents aren't religious. They never took us, and I sure as hell wasn't going by myself. But I wouldn't mind trying it, now."

Jenna sighs. "I guess we can put that on the list of things we can do in four years."

I groan. "That is the worst."

There's a long pause, and then Jenna says quietly, "You talk about wanting to be forgiven—there's more, you know."

For a panicked moment, I think she's calling me on leaving out the rest of the story, but she continues speaking. "About my past. I was scared to say it last time, worried it might be too much . . ."

"You can tell me anything." I mean it.

"It wasn't just random guys at parties. I had boyfriends, too. I dated the last one for about six months. I finally ended it with him after Rachel died."

I'm guessing it's not the fact she had a previous relationship back in her wilder days that she expects me to be upset about, so I wait for her to finish.

"He—he wasn't a good guy," she says.

The picture in my head shifts, and suddenly I think I see what she's getting at. "He hurt you."

"I let him."

I dig my fingers into my hair and pull tight. "No," I say. "God, if some guy hurt you, that isn't your fault."

"Not like that, exactly," she says. "He was into . . . choking, you know? At first he just wanted me to do it to him, but then he wanted me to try it. I know some people are into that, but to me it was—I didn't like it. It hurt and I was so afraid, but I said yes anyway. Over and over again. And the awful things he used to say to me, that he would call me while he was—" She cuts off, and my gut twists. "I used to go home with these bruises on my neck," she continues, "and my dad would threaten to call the police, but Mom would talk him out of it, tell him that if he did, I wouldn't come home again, and they were right. And I kept going back, even though I knew my parents were worried sick about me. Even though I had a son at home. I kept going back to this guy."

I hold my breath. She's so much braver than I am, and I wish I had the guts to tell her everything about my own past, but I'm not going to interrupt this, not going to make it about me now. I get the sense she's testing me, seeing how I'll react, seeing if she can trust me. "Jenna," I say. "It doesn't change how I feel about you. Not even a little."

She's quiet for a moment. "How can it not?"

"Because I know what it's like to wish you could change the past."

157

"What would you change?" she asks. "Would you want to stay at Juilliard?"

"No," I say. "I'd drop out like a normal person, without getting mixed up with drugs. I'd go back home, and figure things out from there. Maybe I'd start auditioning, work my ass off and try to make it without doing school first. I don't know. But I wouldn't do drugs, and I wouldn't hurt my family. I'd face my problems instead of self-destructing."

"Wouldn't that have been nice," she says softly, and I know she's not talking about me.

A question occurs to me that I'm pretty sure I know the answer to, but need to ask anyway. "Alec," I say. "He . . . never hurt you like that, did he? Or made you do anything you were uncomfortable with?"

"No," she says quickly. "Alec's a good guy. He can be a jerk sometimes, but nothing like *that*. He always treated me really well, showed me I deserved way more than those other guys. It was my first actually functional relationship." She lets out a little breath like a laugh. "You know, until it stopped functioning."

I wonder if I should be jealous of Alec for being the one to show her a healthy relationship, but honestly, I'm not. I'm just glad he did.

"What's it like now?" I ask. "Pretending with Alec?"

"It doesn't bring the feelings back."

I'm grateful as hell for that, but that wasn't what I meant. "I mean, are you miserable? Is it still fun, because it's kissing?"

She thinks about that. "I imagine it's like being an actress. Your co-star is hot, but you don't feel anything for them."

"That makes sense." I wish I could get the image of them kissing out of my head, but sadly, Google is full of animated gifs.

"It bothers you."

"Yes," I say. "But really because I'm not even allowed to hold your hand. I just want to be with you, and I can't."

"Mmm," Jenna says. "And what would you do if you were here?"

My whole body sizzles, and it takes me a second to respond.

"What would you want me to do?"

I can hear her shifting, sense the way her body is stretching out. "Everything," she says.

My body catches fire. Last night we stayed on the phone until neither of us could put two words together. For the last hour or so, we'd barely been capable of more than murmurs, lost in fatigue and each other. We'd whispered each other's names, and though neither of us had admitted it, from the cadence of her breathing I was pretty sure she was doing the same thing I was. "You want me to tell you about it?"

Her voice goes husky. "Yes, please. In detail."

I settle in beneath the blanket. "Are we allowed to do this?"

Jenna hesitates. "It's not technically against the rules. And with the grief Alec's given me, I'm going with the strict interpretation." A sly edge creeps into her voice. "Besides, if we're not, what was last night?"

"Mmm," I say. "You did that, too, huh?"

She draws a deep breath. "You want to hear the details?"

"God, do I." I check to make sure Gabby's door is closed.

Jenna whispers to me the details of her hands running up and down her body, and I wish more than anything in the world I was there, that it was mine instead. I remember that moment in the hotel, when we kissed and kissed, and I thought, *this* is the moment I want to disappear into and never emerge. My body is reacting now in the same way it did then, and any doubts I had about the Suboxone keeping me from getting it up are long gone. Hell, all we're doing is talking, and I don't remember feeling anything close to this kind of elation ever before in my life. I've felt stupid, wanting more out of sex, wanting to feel this cataclysmic emotional shift when I crawl into bed with a woman. We're not even touching, now—not each other, anyway—and we haven't done anything more in real life than kiss, but I feel it with her, this connection I've always wanted, always needed, and felt incompetent to ever find.

And now, even if I can't be there with her, I know. Even after such a short time, I love her, and it's real.

SEVENTEEN

Felix

The next morning, I'm making coffee on this ancient coffeemaker Gabby has inexplicably named Bertrude. Bertrude is loud and always appears on the very brink of appliance death, and yet every morning she manages to keep sputtering out a substance just close enough to coffee to justify her continued existence. In Gabby's eyes, at least.

It's undoubtedly Bertrude's obnoxious squealing that drags Gabby out of bed. Her hair is half falling out of its ponytail, and she's wearing Cookie Monster pajamas. "Hey," she says. "How'd you sleep?"

There's a hint of suggestion in her tone that makes me look over at her. "Fine. Why?"

She stares at me with a look of horror on her face, and I know exactly why.

"No," I say.

She covers her face. "I got up to go to the bathroom—"

I step back against the counter. "No! What did you hear?"

She winces. "There was moaning—"

I cover my face and emit a guttural yell that spills over her next statement.

"—and narration."

"Oh *god.*" This feels far more violating than my sister hearing me having actual sex, because the auditory component is the only part Jenna could experience as well. It's like I was getting it on with a girl and accidentally stuck it in my sister.

Gabby cringes. "And I couldn't get it out of my head, so I woke up Will and told him about it, too."

"Ahhhhhhh!" I drop my hands and stare at her. "What? Why?"

"I had to tell someone! But don't worry. He doesn't think you're seeing anyone, so he assumed you were calling a hotline."

I choke. "Gah! Is that supposed to make it better? That your boyfriend thinks I'm some kind of perv?"

Gabby raises an eyebrow. "Well, it *was* pretty specific narration."

I shove a cup of coffee at her and it sloshes onto the counter. "This is what it feels like to die of mortification."

"*You're* mortified," Gabby says. "I'm the one who has to keep sitting on that couch after this."

It's my turn to cringe. "I'll wash the blanket."

"Thank you."

"I need to get an apartment. But if I keep couch surfing, I'll be able to pay Dad back . . ." I groan. "Would it make it up to you if I bought your couch?"

Gabby takes a long sip of her coffee, and perks up. "I won't turn that down."

"And maybe a new coffeemaker?"

"That I will turn down. Bertrude is great." Gabby looks offended on her coffeemaker's behalf, and I decide not to push it.

I run my hands through my hair, which needs to be washed. "Between the horror show that is my sister hearing anything from last night and the cello case debacle, I'm starting to feel like I've somehow taken over your ability to stumble into embarrassing situations."

"That's what Anna-Marie said when she fell in love with

Josh," Gabby says. "Though she got attacked by a moose, and a bat, and some Boy Scouts. So you're doing better than her."

"Boy Scouts?"

"Yeah, that ended in a video of her nude on the internet. At least there's not a recording of you ejaculating in my living room."

"Oh, god." I cover my eyes again. "I will definitely buy your couch."

"It was a lot like that music you used to play in high school to bother Mom. Where the orchestra is playing and the chorus is making all those ohs and ahs and basically having a collective orgasm?"

"*Daphnis and Chloe*. I did do that to bother Mom, but it's a legitimately good piece of music." I peek at her through my fingers. "You're never going to let this go, are you?"

"I'll let you off the hook," she says, "the day I forget the words my baby brother uses to describe his own climax."

"Ahhhh," I say.

"Yeah, that was part of it."

I chug my coffee in an effort to disappear. "On the internet or not, my humiliation is complete."

Gabby takes another sip of her coffee. "Does that make this a good time to ask if your band will play Anna-Marie's wedding?"

"Oh, yeah," I say, grateful as hell for the change in subject. "They said that's fine. I put it on the calendar and everything."

Gabby squeals. "I have officially won the wedding."

"Hopefully Anna-Marie wins the wedding."

Gabby rolls her eyes. "So?" she says. "I'm guessing things with Jenna are progressing?"

Um. You could say that. "We talked for hours."

"And somewhere in the middle of that she verbally jumped you?"

I have to laugh at that. "Something like that. There were some politics and religion in between. If this keeps up, I'm never going to sleep again."

162

Gabby gives me a look.

"And I'll be staying at Dad's."

"*Yeah*, you will," she says. "So she's okay with you being in recovery and all?"

My stomach drops. I tip back my coffee mug, even though there's only a little left, and the dregs of this coffee are even worse than the rest of it. "I told her I used to do drugs. And that I did heroin. But that's it."

Gabby raises her eyebrows. "She doesn't know you were in rehab? Or how recently?"

I don't know why I'm telling Gabby this. Maybe it's the embarrassment, but my relief from last night is gone and replaced with overwhelming guilt. "No," I say. "I'll tell her. I just—" I sit on Gabby's counter. "I want to tell her everything, but I'm scared."

"Felix," Gabby says. "If she can't handle it, don't you think it would be better to know sooner rather than later?"

I don't, but it takes me a minute to figure out why. "Did I ever tell you why I went back to rehab? The last time?"

Gabby shakes her head. I don't know why I phrased it that way—I already know she doesn't know about it. I haven't told anyone but my therapist outside of a meeting.

"I'd been couch surfing for a while," I say. "Staying with friends, mostly, after Mom and Dad each finally told me I couldn't crash with them anymore."

"I remember. Mom cried."

My chest aches. "At the time, I was pissed, but now I see they must have agonized over it. Dad caught me shooting up in his bathroom, and that was the last straw, but with Mom it was kind of out of the blue."

"She wanted to let you stay," Gabby says. "Just so she'd know you weren't lying dead somewhere. But she thought maybe if you didn't have anyone covering for you anymore, you'd be more likely to get help."

"I didn't get help," I say. "I burned out every last one of my friends, and then I started picking up girls and going home with them, just to have somewhere to stay." Gabby looks at me like I'm a wounded puppy, which is wrong. I'm the monster in this story, not the victim. "I didn't always have sex with them. Sometimes we just did drugs."

"Yes," Gabby says. "I remember the sad tale of your flaccid penis."

I close my eyes.

"Sorry," Gabby says. "That was funny in my head."

It would be funny. If it wasn't true.

"I did have sex with the last one. And then we shot up after. Neither was great—I thought I had enough for her to take some and still get a good high, but the dose I'd been taking was starting to ebb, and I needed more." I shake my head. "Or maybe I gave her more than I thought I did. I can't be sure."

Gabby holds still, like she senses what I'm going to tell her.

"When I woke up in the morning, she was dead."

Gabby looks like she's going to cry. "She overdosed."

I rub my hands together. "Yeah. So I called 911. I mean, she was cold. Stiff. But I didn't know what else to do, so I called, and they asked me for her name, and her address. I didn't know either, so I found some mail in the kitchen and I read it off to them." I can't look at her and tell her this last part. "It was her roommate's mail. I gave them her name, because I didn't know any better."

Gabby puts a hand on my arm. "Oh, Felix."

I still can't look at her. "So then I got to explain *that* to the police. And of course I hid the drugs, told them I didn't know she was high. They knew I was lying, but they didn't have cause to test me, so they let me go."

I swallow. "I went straight to Dad and begged him to send me back to rehab. I was shaking, crying. I didn't tell him what happened. I just told him I had to get clean and I didn't know how to do it without help. At first he refused. Something about the hundred grand he'd already sunk into my first two stints."

My voice breaks. "But eventually he agreed."

Gabby's hand slides down my arm, and she squeezes my fingers. "Because he loves you."

"I know." I take a deep breath. "Later, I looked her up online. I remembered her address, and her roommate's name. The girl who died—her name was Katy. She played tennis and rode horses. She was an economics major at UCLA, before she dropped out because of drugs."

"She was an addict," Gabby says.

"I killed her."

"*No.*" Gabby squeezes my hand so hard my fingers ache. "You didn't. You said she did drugs before you met her. It was just happenstance that you were there."

"I've asked myself a hundred times if that's true, but I don't know." I shake my head. "And you're right. I have to tell Jenna. But if I tell her that story and it's over, I will damn well go buy some heroin and shoot up into oblivion."

Gabby looks terrified, and I take a deep, steadying breath.

"And that's why I'm not going to tell her. Not until I'm sure I can handle the rejection without putting a needle in my vein."

Gabby is quiet for a moment, and I regret dumping this on her. I wonder if, deep down, I'm doing this as a kind of trial run. Gabby is my sister, and she's loved me through all the shit I've done.

I need to know if this is the thing that convinces her I'm not worthy of forgiveness.

"I love you," she says finally.

Tears creep into my eyes. "Am I doing the wrong thing?" Keeping this huge thing from the woman I love. The woman who trusts me. The guilt gnaws at me, and yet—

"No," Gabby says. "No, that actually makes sense. You have to put your sobriety first, right?"

"Yeah. But I'll tell her. I will," I say, assuring myself as much as Gabby. "I just need a little more time."

Gabby puts her arms around me, and I squeeze her back.

Somehow I know she's thinking the same thing I've thought so many times. It could have been me someone found lying cold and dead.

"I'm not going back to the drugs," I say.

"You better not."

"I won't." I take another deep breath. "I have practice today. Do you want to come and meet Jenna?"

Her face brightens. "Can I?"

"Sure. Just don't give away to the rest of the band that you know about us."

"I think I can handle that."

We both smile. I've done so much stupid, hurtful stuff in my life. I don't deserve to have a sister like her, but I'll take it.

EIGHTEEN

Felix

Gabby and I arrive at practice just as Roxie pulls up on her motorcycle. She takes off her helmet, her pink hair tumbling down on the unshaved side. Gabby's eyes are wide as she takes in Roxie's outfit, which today includes shiny leather pants with suspenders (that judging by the tightness of the pants are not serving any functional purpose) over what looks like a child-size Sailor Moon t-shirt. Roxie waves at me. "Hey, Felix."

"Hey Roxie. How are your feet?"

She glowers at me. "The damn cream worked."

I smile. "This is my sister Gabby. She came to watch practice."

Roxie nods at her and we all head into the studio. Leo must have heard us coming down the stairs, because he stands in front of Roxie's drum set with his chest puffed out, sporting his anticipated alligator boots and vest. He's not wearing a shirt under the vest, and his tattoo of the Louisiana state flag—which for some reason involves a bunch of pelicans—can be half-seen over his left pectoral.

I probably should have given Gabby some warning about these two, but it's kind of hilarious watching her eyes get increasingly larger.

"Good god," Roxie says to Leo. "You look like you should

be narrating the Jungle Cruise at Disneyland."

Leo grins as if this is a compliment. "Next time I go home I'll shoot one for you, and I'll name her Roxie."

Roxie looks incredulous. "Why would I want you to shoot an alligator named Roxie?"

Jenna comes down the stairs behind us, and the sound of her voice raises goosebumps on my neck. "Is he on about that again? He told me he was going to shoot an alligator named Jenna and I told him he sounded like a serial killer."

Jenna's wearing a short white cotton dress with a studded black belt and black motorcycle boots, and she's carrying June and my bow. I set down my broken cello case—which I decided to bring at the last minute, because until I pick up my spare case, it's better than nothing—and take my cello from her with a murmured, "Thanks."

I smile at her and she smiles coyly back at me. I don't have to read her mind to know she's thinking about last night.

"I told you I'd name her Jenn*ifer*," Leo says. "As payback to all the people who think that's your real name."

Jenna shrugs. "I do hate that." Her eyes land on Gabby.

"Gabby," I say. "This is Jenna Rollins. Jenna, my sister Gabby."

Leo raises an eyebrow. "What, you bring a hot girl to practice and I don't get an introduction?"

Roxie glares daggers at Leo, and Gabby looks shocked.

"Hey," I say. "Did you not hear the part where she's my *sister*?"

"And taken," Gabby adds.

Leo shrugs, like this matters not at all, which I imagine it doesn't, because I'd lay odds he's not actually interested in Gabby as much as in making Roxie jealous.

And it appears to be working.

"It's so good to meet you," Jenna says, just as Ty catapults down the stairs from behind her. He's back in his 'grown-up' attire today. I wonder how many sweater vests this kid has—the thought of his closet packed full of them makes me grin. "Felix!"

he shouts. "Look how far I am in *Angry Birds!*"

"Hey!" Jenna says. "Did you pass me up again?"

Ty hides behind me, clutching his iPad.

"Oh, no," I say. "I am not getting in the middle of this."

Alec comes down the stairs just as Ty ducks under my arm and starts showing me all of his *Angry Birds* accomplishments. "And in this next one," Ty says, pointing at the screen, "the pigs have built a boat, and it fills the entire lake they're in, which is kind of silly because they can't sail it anywhere. Unless it flies, too, like the—" Ty cuts off and looks up at me in alarm, and I know he's thinking about Superpope.

"I don't know anything about flying vehicles of any kind," I say.

Ty grins.

I look up to see both Gabby and Jenna smiling at me like I'm in one of those pictures of cats cuddling goats.

Alec clears his throat. "We ready to start?" He picks up his guitar from its stand and starts tuning without even looking at Gabby. I shrug at her. I told her she'd get to see what the band is like and, well, here it is.

Roxie is still glaring at Leo. She steps up behind him and begins grabbing at his vest.

"Whoa," Leo says. "Settle down, there." He swats at her hands, but she grabs him by the waist.

"Cut that out. I'm fixing your vest. It's askew."

"What are you talking about?" Leo says. "This vest is hand-tailored. It doesn't skew."

"*A*skew," Roxie says.

"Bless you," Leo says.

Roxie pulls on his vest so hard I think the buttons are going to pop. "Hold *still*."

"Oh. My. God," Alec says. "Can we please just play?"

His tone is even sharper than normal, and everyone turns to look at him. Gabby glances at me in alarm.

"Just have a seat on the couch," I tell her. "And welcome to practice."

Ty settles down right at my feet, and Gabby smiles like this is adorable. I wonder if this is what the goats feel like.

Roxie is still petting Leo's back in the name of straightening his vest.

"Roxie!" Alec says. "*Now*. It's like being in a damn limo on prom night in here. We're here to work, not play."

Everyone falls silent. "Jeez, Alec," Leo says, stepping away from Roxie. "What bug crawled up your butt?"

Ty looks appalled. "Did a bug crawl up your butt, Alec? Does it tickle?"

Both Jenna and I snicker. "I think Leo has a cream for that," Jenna says, and I laugh.

Alec glares at both of us, and Leo holds his arms out like he's going to hug Alec. "Whatever's bothering you, man, just let it all out."

"Ugh," Roxie says. "Please, not one of your group bonding sessions. I really don't want to hear about Alec's *feelings*."

"Not now," Alec says, and he turns to glare pointedly at Gabby.

"Hey," I say, but Gabby is already holding up her hands, starting to stand up from the couch.

"I can leave," she says.

"No," Jenna says quickly, then softens her tone. "We want you to stay, Gabby. And we're going to play." She turns to Alec. "Let's start with 'Together.' The bridge needed serious work."

Alec nods, and Roxie counts off.

As we play, I try to shut out everything but the music, which isn't easy since I'm playing a love song that the girl I want to be with is singing to another man. The song is about trying to align their lives so they still get to do the things they love, but now they're doing them in tandem. I watch her while I play and try to imagine she means it for me. As she sings, she looks over at me and smiles, and my heart skips a beat.

I love her, and while I haven't quite gotten the courage to say those words to her, I think she might feel the same about me.

So since I can't sing it back to her like Alec can, I try to play it for her so she'll know how much I mean it.

When we finish a set, Jenna grins at me. "That's sounding good!"

She's right. I'm blending better, and on the new cello parts, Leo and I are starting to adapt to each other. I'm changing the music like a rock parts a stream, and I can't help but be proud of that.

"All right," Alec says. "Anything else we need to practice before we quit?"

Jenna looks surprised. "We're just getting started. We need to get through everything at least once, and there's a couple that'll probably need work. Did you have someplace to be?"

"*No*," Alec says. "That's fine."

From the look on his face, it is definitely not fine. Clearly Alec needs to get stuff off his chest that he can't say in Gabby's presence, and I wonder if he wants to say in mine.

"Why don't Gabby and I go grab lunch?" I ask. "Since we're going to be here another couple hours at least."

Gabby jumps up. "I can drive," she says. Which she better, because I came with her.

"That would be great," Alec says.

"Can I come, too?" Ty asks.

"No, you stay," Jenna says, but she's glaring at Alec.

I give Ty a small smile, and Gabby and I head up to her car.

"Wow," she says. "Is it always like that?"

I climb in the passenger side. "It's been escalating. I think my joining might have something to do with it."

She smiles at me. "Ty's a cute kid."

"Yeah, he is. And don't think I didn't see you being all patronizingly happy that he and I are friends."

"You really are cool with it, though," she says. "The kid thing."

"Yeah, totally." And I realize it's true. "It's not just the idea of Ty I'm okay with—I genuinely like the kid. Even if he does think he's some kind of invertebrate who can squeeze into small places."

171

"And Alec?" she asks. "That's about you?"

"Probably. I'm sure I'll hear all about it sooner or later."

It turns out to be sooner rather than later. As we arrive back at the studio with bags full of deli sandwiches, Ty is sitting on the steps right outside the door, iPad in his hands.

"They're fighting," he says gravely. "And Superpope would *not* like the words they're saying."

Gabby looks worried, and I wave a hand at her. "Hey, Ty, you mind if Gabby stays here for a minute and watches you play?"

"Sure!" Ty says. "This level has a shark in it!"

"Oooh," she says, sitting down on the steps next to him. "I haven't gotten this far yet."

Gabby and I exchange worried looks, and then I step inside. I can hear Alec as soon as I open the door.

"I'm not trying to kick him out of the band. I just want to have a meeting."

"I told you," Jenna says. "We are not having a band meeting without Felix, because Felix is *part* of the band."

"We had band meetings without Mason," Alec says. "Mason was part of the band."

"Mason was high," Jenna says. "And also stealing from us. Felix is neither."

I pause at the top of the stairs, not sure if I should leave and let them finish, or go downstairs and let Alec say whatever he wants to say to my face.

"Look," Jenna says. "Felix and I are following your damn rules. And as long as that's true, you have no reason to get in my face about it, any more than I did with you and the dozens of girls you've slept with since we broke up."

"Burn," Leo says, and someone—I'm assuming Roxie—shushes him.

"Clearly we need new rules," Alec says. "No more flirting with members of the band."

I almost snort. Leo and Roxie would be the ones having the hardest time with that.

"That's ridiculous," Jenna says. "Who gets to decide what flirting means, anyway?"

"I'll decide for you," Alec says. "And you can decide for me."

"You don't want to flirt with anyone in the band!" Jenna shouts. "You just want to tell me I can't talk to Felix."

"Damn right, I do. In fact, here's a better rule: you don't talk to Felix. I'll be the cello manager."

"The *manager*?" Jenna says, her incredulity echoing exactly what I'm feeling. "We have *one cellist*!"

"You can manage Leo and Roxie," Alec says. "So it's fair."

"Hey," Leo and Roxie both say at once.

The idea that I'm going to let Alec be the *cello manager* is enough to propel me down the stairs. "Hey, guys," I say. "What's this about management? I thought Phil was the manager."

Jenna gives me an apologetic look, and then goes back to glaring at Alec. "He *is*. The *only* manager."

Alec raises his hands in the air. "*Fine*. Practice is over for today." He storms up the stairs and I hear the door slam behind him.

I hope Ty and Gabby got out of his way.

Leo and Roxie look at Jenna, who sighs. "Yeah, go home, guys. We've got a couple more days before the performance. We'll pick up where we left off tomorrow."

Leo and Roxie hurry up the stairs, leaving me alone with Jenna, whose arms drop helplessly at her sides.

"I'm sorry about that," she says.

"I want to hug you so bad right now," I say. "But that would kill our moral high ground about following Alec's rules."

Jenna yells wordlessly at the ceiling and collapses onto the couch, while I go back upstairs to let Ty and Gabby in. A part of me wonders if I shouldn't just step gracefully away from the band and let them get back to playing in peace.

But one look over my shoulder back at Jenna, her head in her hands, her dark hair hiding her face, and I know I can't.

NINETEEN

Felix

Ty, Gabby, and I join Jenna down in the studio, where Jenna is splayed out on the couch looking done with the world.

"Ahhh," I say. "You clearly need a hug. Gabby, hug her for me, please?"

"I'll hug her," Ty says, and catapults himself on top of his mom.

"Oof," Jenna says.

Gabby stands at the foot of the couch while I collapse into my chair next to June.

"Do you need another hug?" Gabby asks.

Jenna sighs. "Yeah, I think I could use one."

I was mostly joking, but it actually does help to watch Jenna and Gabby embrace on the couch, and then settle back next to each other like old friends. Almost like Jenna's allowed to be part of my life.

"I am so sorry about that," Jenna says to Gabby. "Alec isn't usually that bad."

"No, I'm sorry," Gabby says.

"You both need to stop apologizing," I say. "Knowing the two of you, you're going to get caught in some endless apology loop and we'll all be here until the end of time."

"Alec should apologize," Ty says, settling onto the floor next to the couch with *Angry Birds*.

"He should," Jenna says, and looks over at me. "He wants to make a rule against flirting between members of the band."

"I heard," I say. "I also heard he wants to be the cello manager."

"Just what you want, I'm sure."

I raise an eyebrow at her. "I am the first chair cello. I have always been the first chair cello. Whether there is one cello or twenty cellos, if there is a cello manager, it is me."

"And he's humble about it, too," Gabby says.

Jenna smiles. "Yes. Always underplaying his own skill."

They laugh, and I figure I should be bothered, but it's actually awesome to watch them bond over mocking me. Then I remember what Gabby heard last night, and my cheeks flush.

Hopefully Gabby herself is too embarrassed to bring that up, even in the name of humiliating me.

"It really is good to meet you," Jenna says. "Felix speaks highly of you. And of your ability to keep secrets."

"Oh, yeah," Gabby says. "I won't tell anyone. The last thing I want is to make trouble for you guys."

Jenna looks up the stairs, and I know what she's thinking. Trouble doesn't need to come at us from without. It's already brewing from within.

"Do you want me to talk to him?" I ask.

Jenna looks surprised. "You don't have to. I'm fully capable of yelling at Alec on my own. I do it often enough."

"She does," Ty says, not even looking up from his game.

"I don't mean yell at him," I say. "Maybe I could just tell him we're trying here, and ask him to cut us some slack."

Jenna considers this. "You would do that?"

"Of course. If you think it would help."

"Well," she says. "It can't hurt."

Gabby nods her agreement, and Jenna turns to her. "So, tell me all the embarrassing stories about Felix."

Gabby's eyes widen, and she looks at me. *Her* cheeks turn pink.

Jenna gives her a curious look, and I know I have to get ahead of this.

"My most embarrassing quality," I say, "is clearly my inability to speak quietly on the phone in the middle of the night, wouldn't you say, Gabby?"

Jenna's eyes widen, and Gabby looks horrified, like a trauma victim describing the origins of her deepest scars. "Yeah," she says. "There's definitely that."

"Seriously?" Jenna says.

I rub my forehead, and then Jenna starts to giggle. It grows more and more high pitched, and she hugs her stomach.

"Ty?" I ask. "Is your mom having a breakdown?"

"That's her tired laugh." He looks down at his iPad. "But it's only two in the afternoon. You guys must have talked really late."

Jenna giggles even harder, and Gabby gives me an alarmed look. But from Ty's general disinterest in the conversation, I'm sure he doesn't have a clue what we're talking about.

At last, Jenna gasps for breath. "Yeah. I think I need a nap." She smiles at me, and I smile at her, and I wish we could curl up right there on the couch and fall asleep in each other's arms. Something. Anything. When I agreed to this, I had no idea how starved I'd feel for little things like that.

But if I had, I know I'd have made the same decisions. The idea of cutting her out of my life now is like thinking of removing my own hand.

"We should let you get home," I say.

Jenna eyes me. "Do you have to?"

"No," I say. "But you probably should get a nap in, if you're going to call me tonight."

"Mmm," she says, her gray eyes gleaming. "This is true. It might be a late one, though. Ty and I have a date with *The Game of Life*."

I shake a finger at her. "All that lies that way is misery."

She smiles. "I remember."

I'm hit with this overwhelming need to kiss her. I stumble

to my feet and run a hand in my hair. "We'd better get going. I'll give Alec a chance to cool down."

Jenna nods. "I'll call you later."

"Please," I say, and Gabby and I ascend the stairs. When we get out to her car, she squeals.

"You two are so cute!"

I roll my eyes. "Yeah. Our sexual frustration is super adorable."

Gabby starts the car, but doesn't back out yet. "Jenna is awesome, though. And she smells like coconuts. Can you find out what shampoo she's using? Because that stuff is goooooood."

I groan and whack my head against the headrest. "You are killing me."

Gabby gives me a pitying look. "Are you okay? I mean, this isn't being too stressful, is it? Because if it is—"

"I'm not going to use. I don't even want to right now." And I don't. But god, four years . . .

Gabby sighs. "That's good."

"Yeah, really good." I roll down the window and stick my arm out. Gabby's car technically has air conditioning, in that the little light comes on and Gabby swears the air that comes out is incrementally cooler than the heat outside. But I don't think even she believes it.

"So what are you going to do now?" she asks.

I'm struck with a sudden idea. "I'm going to go to the hardware store and figure out how to rig a cello case so it never closes again. Want to come?"

Gabby looks skeptical. "You. Are going to the hardware store."

"Are you going to help, or just mock?"

"I'm definitely coming with," she says. "Because I am not going to miss Felix Mays trying to *build* something."

"Good call. I'll be right back."

I run back inside the studio to grab my old cello case, and see Jenna and Ty lounging on the couch while Jenna catches up to him in *Angry Birds*. I wish more than anything I could join them, but instead I load the case into Gabby's car. We wander cluelessly around Home Depot until two sixty-year-old gay men take pity on us, point out which brackets and bolts to buy, and then drill the holes and install the hardware in the parking lot with tools from the utility bed of their pickup truck.

Permanently open, the case barely fits across Gabby's backseat, and only if we move the front seats all the way forward. "Okay," Gabby says. "I have to get to work. Are you going back to Dad's?"

"I've got to hit a meeting," I say. "But yeah. Eventually."

Gabby squeezes my arm and then drives me back to get my car. But before I do anything else, I have to talk to Alec.

I text Alec and tell him I want to talk. He texts back that he's at the studio and he'll be there for the next several hours, so after I go by the clinic to get tested and pick up my prescription for the next two days, and then pick up the spare cello case from my dad's, I drive back.

I find Alec sitting on the couch with his guitar, playing a riff of "Fly Me to the Moon." He plays so slowly the song feels melancholy, and I sort of feel bad for him.

But not bad enough not to say what needs to be said.

"Hey," I say.

Alec stops playing and gives me a hard look. Or maybe that's just his face. "Hey." He says nothing else, just waits for me to speak.

"I'm here to ask you to cut us some slack," I say. "We're doing the best we can under the circumstances. Especially Jenna."

"The best you can."

"Yeah," I say. "And we're following your rules, so if you could please just get off our backs, that would be great."

Alec sighs and plays another chord, but doesn't continue.

The notes hang in the air, with no bridge to connect them. "Felix," he says, "you're a damn good cellist."

"Thanks. But that's not really—"

"And that's why you're still a part of the band. We don't have time to replace you, sure as hell not with someone who's as good as you are."

I'm not sure what to say to that. I'm sure Jenna would take offense to the idea he can just decide to kick me out of the band without consulting her, but the fact is, he isn't, so I wait to see where he's going with this.

"But this thing with you guys," he says. "I've told Jenna over and over, you just need to do it and get it over with. Break the tension. Having it off so we can all get back to playing the music, okay?"

I shake my head. "That's the thing. It won't be over."

Alec looks exasperated. "And why is that?"

I don't want to lie, and really, there's no reason to. "Because it's not about sex. We care about each other." I close my eyes briefly. It's more than that, but I'm not about to tell Alec the whole truth—definitely not before I've told *her*. "We want to be in each other's lives, and if we spend one night together, we're going to want another. And another. We're not going to stop wanting to be together."

Alec stares at me. "Really."

"Yes," I say. "Really."

"And Jenna wants this too."

"Yes," I say.

Alec rolls his eyes. "She thought she wanted that with me once, too."

I nod. "I know." I want to tell him it's different with me, but I know I'll just sound naive and deluded. And the truth is, I can't know that. Not for sure.

"You've known each other, what? A week?"

Exactly a week, as of today. "Yeah," I say. "But it's true just the same."

Alec sighs. "You're not doing her any favors, you know. This is just going to make everything more difficult."

I try not to squirm. The last thing I want to do is to make Jenna's life harder, but I can't believe it would be *better* if I walked away. Easier, maybe, but some things are worth a little hardship.

I desperately want to be one of those things.

"We're following your rules—" I say, but Alec talks over me.

"Screw the rules. What happens when someone hacks your phone?"

"We thought of that already. We're using burners."

Alec shakes his head. "Sooner or later someone is going to get a picture of you two looking at each other the way you do. There's no way we're getting through four years of this unscathed."

"You're right," I say. "There's no way we're getting through four years of this."

Alec glares at me, but I can taste the truth of it. The last few days have been so intense. It can't last forever. Something is going to break. And I know I'm hoping it's the band while Alec is hoping it's us. Except I need this job, and Jenna loves the band. I know she does, or she wouldn't have put up with Alec's crappy rules for the last year.

"Fine," he says. "I'll cut you some slack. But think about what you're risking here. We're getting enough attention for the next few years to make all of our careers. Don't you want that? Hell, if you care so much about her, do you want to ruin it for her?"

I look at the floor. I don't want to hurt Jenna, but I know what it's like to get everything you're supposed to want and discover it doesn't make you happy.

"I'm not sure," I say.

Alec strums another chord. "Yeah, well. Stay out of the way of those of us who are, will you?"

I nod, and leave him alone with his guitar.

TWENTY

Felix

Later that night, I bring by the adjusted cello case, and Jenna answers the door. She's clearly showered, with her wet hair up in a loose bun, and she's wearing yoga pants and a Yellowcard t-shirt. She's also wearing glasses, though I didn't know she wore contacts. It's nice to see what she looks like when she isn't going out. Another glimpse of the life I wish I was a part of.

"Hey," I say. "I didn't want to interrupt your game, but I brought this by for Ty."

Jenna is looking at me, horrified, and I think for a second I've done something terribly wrong. "If this is a bad time—"

"No!" Jenna says. "No, I just—" She puts a hand on her hair and grimaces. "If I'd known you were coming by, I would have . . ."

My stomach plummets, and all sorts of scenarios fly through my mind, culminating in an image of her and Alec having a heart to heart and getting back together thanks to my intervention. I'm practically waiting for him to come to the door in a towel, when Jenna finishes her sentence.

"I would have put in my contacts at least," she says. "I look like a mess."

I blink at her as I come back to reality. "What?"

Jenna is folding in on herself, and backing away from the door. "You must be wondering what you've been doing with me." She says this like she's joking, but I can tell she means it.

"*Jenna*," I say. "You're beautiful. You're always beautiful. You don't have to dress up for me."

She looks surprised, and I try not to take it personally. But really, how shallow does she think I am?

"I have sisters," I say. "I know what girls look like without makeup."

"Felix!" Ty comes flying by Jenna and throws his arms around me.

I squeeze him back. "Hey, kid. I know how much you liked hanging out in the cello case, so I've got it all set up for you."

Ty's eyes light up as he looks at it.

"You take the brackets off, and it's mine again," I say. "But as long as you don't lock yourself inside, you can keep it until your mom is sick of it taking up space."

Ty lies down in the bottom of the case. "It's like I'm a vampire!"

Jenna smiles at me, but she's fiddling with her glasses self-consciously. I smile at her, and show Ty the holder for my bow. "See? I left the lid on so you can store stuff in here."

Ty cackles in an eerie impression of the Count. "Mom! Can I sleep in here?"

"Sure. What do you say to Felix?"

Ty hops out of the case and throws his arms around me again. "Thank you, Felix."

"You're welcome, kid," I say, and help him carry the case into the entryway.

Ty bounds up to Jenna. "Can Felix stay for game night?"

"I don't want to interrupt family time," I say.

"Felix might have other plans, you know," Jenna says to Ty.

I look at her. Even if I did, I'd drop anything for her. "I don't, actually."

Ty looks at me hopefully, and Jenna gives me a tentative

smile. "You're welcome to stay," she says. "But don't feel like you have to."

"Sure, kid," I say. "I'll play."

Ty cheers and runs back toward the kitchen, and I step in and close the door.

"I thought *The Game of Life* brought you nothing but misery," she says.

"Yeah," I say. "But any time I spend with you does the opposite."

Jenna's smile widens. "You might like it better now, anyway. I made a couple changes." We follow Ty to the kitchen where *The Game of Life* is already spread across the table, along with bowls of popcorn sprinkled with M&Ms.

"You can start at the beginning," Ty says.

"Give him a head start," Jenna says, passing her bowl over to me to share. "We're already halfway in."

"Fine," Ty says. "You can start with a career. Here." He holds out the deck to me.

I draw a card. "My career is . . . Gigolo?"

Jenna tries valiantly to hold in a laugh. She's blacked out the word *banker* with a Sharpie and written in her own addition.

"Seriously?" I ask.

"You'd be great at that," Ty says, and Jenna's laugh slips out. I grin over at her. God, that laugh . . .

"Gee," I say. "Thanks." I sit down next to Ty and select a little car and a tiny blue peg.

Jenna hugs her arms across her chest. "I really am sorry I'm not dressed."

I want to make some comment about never needing to apologize for being undressed, but I don't because of Ty. "You're gorgeous," I say. "Ty, don't you think your mom looks pretty?" I take a small handful of popcorn and M&Ms while he scrutinizes her.

After a long moment, he shrugs. "She's looked prettier."

I shake my head at him. "Clearly I need to teach you some rules about women. Rule number one. If someone asks you if a girl is pretty, you say yes."

Ty looks skeptical. "You shouldn't lie."

"Do you know what a white lie is?" I ask.

He thinks about this. "A lie about something that's white?"

"No," I say. "A white lie is when you don't tell the whole truth, because doing so would hurt people's feelings."

Jenna raises an eyebrow at me. "So you're just telling me I look pretty because that's the rule."

"No," I say. "*I'm* telling you that because it's true. I can't help if the kid is blind."

"I'm not blind," Ty says. "My vision is 20/20. I had it checked."

Jenna shakes her head, but she's smiling.

"Okay," I say. "Let's try this again, now that you know the rule. Doesn't your mom look pretty?"

Ty looks at her for longer than is necessary. "She looks pretty, but she's looked prettier."

"Better," I say through a bite of popcorn. "Ready for the other rules?"

Ty nods solemnly.

"Never admit a woman looks fat, even if she does. And always say she's smart, even if she isn't."

Ty makes a face. "That's not fair. Katelyn from school called me dumb, and what if she does that again this year? Why can't I say that to her?"

"Because you shouldn't be saying that to anyone," Jenna says. She narrows her eyes at me. "How am I supposed to believe you now, when you say I'm pretty, or thin, or smart?"

"Ah, I've neglected rule number four." I lower my voice conspiratorially. "Never tell a girl about the rules."

Jenna picks up my gigolo card and throws it at me.

"Hey!" Ty says. "Don't lose the pieces!"

"Sorry," Jenna says to him. "It's Felix's turn."

"For the record," I say, "you should follow those rules for everyone. No one wants to be told that they're ugly or fat or stupid." Jenna nods her agreement, but Ty's already back to concentrating on the game, switching his peg children around in the car "so they can try out all the seats."

We play for a while, and Ty racks up more children and wealth and Nobel Peace Prizes while Jenna and I starve to death alone in our plastic cars, having inexplicably spent our salaries on tennis camps and hosting charity police events.

I groan as I land on "Buy a High Definition TV, pay $5000," and fork over the very last of my money. "I'd think a gigolo would be a more lucrative career. Like I could at least afford a *TV* for my decrepit fault line house."

Ty gives me a serious look. "Mom says people don't appreciate the arts."

I look at Jenna, and she laughs again.

Ty glances back and forth between us and then stands up from the table. "I'm going to go poop," he says, scooping a book off the couch as he passes it, then looks at me. "I read when I poop, like a gentleman." And then he trots off to the bathroom and leaves us alone.

"I don't know where that kid came from," Jenna says, shaking her head.

I laugh. "That's the first thing I ever said to him. He'd just finished telling me that Mason is a douche. And he very articulately told me that he came from his mom and his biological father."

"That doesn't surprise me."

We smile at each other, and I realize our hands are both resting on the table, inches apart.

I pull mine back, and Jenna hugs hers around herself again.

I clear my throat. "Wherever he came from, I love that kid."

Jenna stares at me. "Really?"

I wish I could snatch the words back. I don't want to come off as creepy, and everyone seems to think I shouldn't want anything to do with Ty. When I hesitate, Jenna frowns. "It was just an expression," she says.

"No!" I say. "I mean, I like the kid. He's smart and hilarious." And tenacious as hell. I'm pretty sure he hasn't given up on the idea of me being his dad. To the contrary, we're probably encouraging him.

"He is." She looks like she wants to say something else, and I cock my head at her.

"What?"

"Nothing," Jenna says. "It's just . . . that's a big part of why things didn't work out with Alec. He's good to Ty, but me having a kid was definitely baggage, you know? Something he'd put up with to be with me, not because he was actually interested in being Ty's father. And I wanted better for Ty." She winces. "Not that I'm saying you need to—"

"I would, though," I say, my heart pounding as I feel the truth of those words, too. "I mean, if we were to work out. I'd want to be a part of his life, too." I smile. "I don't think he'd stand for anything else, do you?"

A slow smile spreads across her face, and she puts her hand back on the table. "No, I don't suppose he would."

I stare at it, and wish for all the world that I could take it in mine. We're talking about a future now that goes far beyond the next four years, and I want to say exactly the right thing.

But Jenna speaks first. "We can't do four years of this."

"I know. I told Alec as much." I gesture to her hair and clothes. "And if you're trying to make me want you less, it isn't working."

Jenna melts into her chair, and I'm glad I'm at least doing something right.

"Also, what did you tell him gigolo means?"

Jenna grins. "Someone who does a *jig*."

I groan. "That poor kid. Someday this misunderstanding is going to destroy him."

"I know. I'm a terrible parent. I just couldn't sit through this game again without spicing it up a little."

"I warned you."

She elbows me. "Which you just *have* to keep reminding me, don't you?"

My skin tingles where her arm hit mine, and I lean back in my chair.

"I'm going to put Ty to bed in a minute," Jenna says. "He's so close to winning, I think we can call it here."

I nod, and scoot back. "I should go."

"No," Jenna says, and then, quieter, "would you stay?"

I'm surprised she asked, and there's no way I can turn her down. "Yeah, of course."

Jenna smiles.

"I talked to Alec," I say. "And he seems to have let go of the cello manager thing. So at least there's that."

"Was he awful about it?"

"No," I say. "I may have told him how much I care about you."

Jenna looks surprised. "How'd he take that?"

I shrug. "I'm pretty sure he thinks we're idiots."

Jenna rolls her eyes. "Yeah, well. It's mutual."

Ty comes barreling out of the bathroom, and Jenna spins around to face him. "It's bedtime," she says, cutting him off before he can leap back into his chair at the table. "Go get ready and then I'll read to you."

Ty's face falls, and then he glances at me. "Can Felix read to me?"

Jenna looks at me.

"Sure," I say. "If you do what your mom says."

Ty races around the house between having a snack and getting into his pjs and brushing his teeth. When he's done, he hands me a well-worn copy of *The Prisoner of Azkaban.*

"Hey," I say. "I've read this one. Who's your favorite character?"

"Hagrid," Ty says.

"Tell him why," Jenna says, putting the pieces of *Life* back into the box.

"Because he's big," Ty says. "So everywhere he goes,

everything smushes him."

I smile. "But I bet he wouldn't fit in a cello case." I open to the chapter he bookmarked and start reading about Dementors and Patronuses and general defense against the Dark Arts. Jenna finishes cleaning up and curls up in the armchair across from us, listening. And I can't help but feel for a moment as though we actually belong together, the three of us—and even if it's only a glimpse, a taste of a potential future I want desperately but am unlikely ever to have, I'm still glad for it.

After Jenna takes Ty up to bed, I stand at the bottom of the stairs, waiting for her. "Are you sure you want me to stay?" I ask when she joins me. "Could be dangerous."

"I'm a grown-ass woman, you know. I can control myself."

I give her a weak smile. "Yeah. But I've had your voice running through my head all day telling me exactly what you want me to do to you . . ."

"Yeah, well," Jenna says. "I've been thinking I might need some more details about that conversation you had with Alec. Something about how much you care about me? I'm guessing you didn't use the words *emotional intimacy.*"

I laugh. "I did not."

"That's good. There's no possible way to explain it to him. I'm not sure there's even a word for what we are."

My head spins, and I feel warm all over. "I think there might be. It's two words, actually."

Jenna raises her eyebrows. "Oh?" She's standing one step above me, and I could reach out right now and wrap my arms around her waist and sweep her into me and kiss her and never let her go.

She gives me one of her trademark coy smiles. "Am I going to have to get it out of you?"

That's a dangerous proposition and I know it.

Jenna takes the last step down. She's so close I can smell that coconut shampoo Gabby was talking about, and all I want to do is reach out and hold her. I hate myself for what I'm about to say.

"I really have to go," I say. "Or I'm going to kiss you."

She looks up at me. "At least tell me what the two words are. Otherwise I'll be up all night wondering."

I doubt that's exactly what she'll be thinking about all night—I already know what's going to be running through my head. And maybe it's because I'm not allowed to touch her, and this verbal intimacy is the only kind we're allowed, but the words fall right out of my mouth. "Soul mates," I say.

She makes this small noise. "You think so?"

"I don't know how else to explain it."

"Soul mates," Jenna says, barely above a whisper, and she reaches for my hand. Her touch sets my whole body tingling, and I swear the lights are growing brighter and the whole world is growing softer around the edges and I reach out and take her other hand.

I'm dizzy, and the room is spinning, and my face dips toward hers before I catch myself. I groan and take a step back, rubbing my forehead. "If we're going to follow the rules, we need to have these conversations over the phone. If we keep doing this, I can't be held responsible for my actions."

Jenna presses her lips together, and then she takes one step closer. I can feel the heat from her body, and it lights a fire in mine. "Honestly," she says, "I've had it with Alec and his stupid rules that only give him what *he* wants." She slides her hand up my arm.

I can't take it anymore. I wrap my arms around her waist, push back a damp tendril of hair that's fallen out of its elastic band, and press my lips against hers. Kissing Jenna feels like coming home after a long time away. It's warm and familiar and wonderful and as natural as breathing.

And then the door opens, and Alec walks in. Jenna and I both turn, but Jenna holds onto me, and we don't step apart. Alec gives us a dark look, and then hangs up his keys. He walks in a wide circle around us and heads up the stairs.

"Aren't you going to say anything?" Jenna asks after him.

Alec doesn't even turn around. "I don't have anything to say I haven't already said." He walks up the stairs, and his boots clomp down the hall above us.

For a second, Jenna and I just stand there, our arms still around each other.

"I should still go," I say. "Because we both know where this is going to lead, and I still can't stand the thought of being with you just once."

"I'm done with the rules," Jenna says.

"Me, too. But unless you're done pretending to be with Alec, unless you're done with the band, what are we going to do? As much as I hate to say it, Alec is right. If we sneak around, we're going to get caught."

Jenna leans against my chest. Having her this close takes my breath away, but I know I'm right. I want to hold on to what I felt at the hotel. I love her and I want to do right by her, not throw everything away on one night.

"What if you stayed here?" Jenna says. "Like, in the guest room, officially. We can tell people our new cellist needed a place to live, and you can sleep in my room at night, and Alec can deal with it."

My heart beats faster. There has to be a catch, some reason this can't work.

"We'd be able to keep this up longer that way," I say. "Don't you think?"

"Definitely," Jenna says.

"Still, though. Probably not four years."

"Probably not. But I've been unhappy this last year, and even before that. I don't *want* to keep going with the five year plan."

I press my forehead to hers. "Maybe we could make it through the tour, and then figure out our exit strategy."

Jenna holds her breath, and for a terrifying minute, I'm sure she's going to say no. That's fast—just a few months, where until today we were looking at years.

"Okay," Jenna says, quietly. "So you'll stay."

Chills run down my body. "God, yes. Please let me stay."

Jenna leans in and kisses me again, but I cut it short.

"You have to tell Alec," I say. "I really do not want to be interrupted when he realizes he has more stuff to say."

She grins and bites her lip. "I'll tell him."

And I follow her up the stairs, stunned, lightheaded, and still unsure that I'm not downstairs dreaming on her couch.

TWENTY-ONE

Felix

I follow Jenna into her bedroom, where she walks across the room and opens the opposite door, leading into Alec's overlarge closet. Jenna's room is dominated by her white, fluffy comforter and a large white dresser with a geometric black tree painted across the front of it. Papers sit haphazardly on the nightstand, a mix of sheet music and scribbled notes and what looks like recipe cards. Draped over her lampshade are a couple macaroni necklaces, the kind I remember making in kindergarten. Her room is all bold contrasts and soft corners and homey lived-in warmth, whereas from what little I can see of Alec's room through the open door, I can tell it's black satin bedding and wallpapered with concert posters.

"Felix is staying the night," Jenna says, and while I can't fully see Alec, he manages to shift angrily.

"Fine," he says. His television switches on. Loudly.

Jenna closes the door again, and locks it from her side.

"Is he trapped in there?" I ask.

"No. He has a key. It's just like a warning thing. I'll unlock it before we go to sleep."

I stand stupidly at the edge of her bed, while Jenna glances around as if scanning for anything embarrassing she might have accidentally left out. The idea of falling asleep here should be thrilling—and it is, so much so that my brain seems to have gotten a swimmer's cramp and is currently drowning in a sea of its own anticipation.

Then I remember I don't have a condom. I have the ones that were dropped in my cello case but those are currently sitting in my car in the summer heat.

"Um," I say. "I don't have a, do you have any—" My mouth turns into taffy and I choke on my own words.

Jenna gives me a weak smile. "I do." She motions toward the nightstand. "In the drawer." She takes a step toward me, and rests her hands lightly on my arms. "You have done this before, right? Because you seemed to know what you were talking about, so I assumed you weren't a virgin."

I look up at the ceiling. "I wasn't this nervous when I was."

Jenna smiles at me like this is the cutest thing she's ever heard, and rocks up onto her toes and kisses me.

Which is exactly what I need. All the passion and longing of the last few days crash down on me, and we kiss like long-lost lovers who've only just found each other again.

Her body presses against mine and I'm riding a high like nothing I've ever felt—certainly not on heroin. Drugs dull my senses, turning me on to a world that's intangibly happy and all-consuming. The feeling of having Jenna in my arms is sharp and real—like I'm a piece of a puzzle that's just snapped into place and all around me the picture is coming together. I lose track of time, feeling for all the world like I could just get lost in this kiss and never want more.

And then she pulls me down on top of her on the bed, and damn if I don't want a whole lot more. She pulls off my shirt and runs her hands up my chest and my whole body is singing, like we're two frequencies vibrating together in a perfect harmony.

Gunshots and screams ring out from Alec's television, and I jump and then glare at the door.

Jenna laughs. "It's better than the sounds that sometimes

come out of there," she says, and I laugh with her. Frankly, most of Los Angeles could be engulfed in riots and bombing and I wouldn't want to be anywhere besides right where I am. Jenna sets her glasses on the nightstand, on top of the pile of papers, and then she lifts off her shirt and pulls me under the covers with her. We both shed our pants and there's just thin layers of cotton between us and I'm lost to everything but the heat of our skin and the chorus of screams and death coming from Alec's side of the wall.

Jenna moans softly and I know she can feel how much I want her, and I'm struck with the need for her to know how much being with her transcends all my past experience. I pull back and run my hand through her hair, which has already fallen out of its loose bun. Jenna looks over at the door to Alec's room again and then gives me an apologetic glance. "I'm sorry about that," she says. "We can take the guest room if you want."

But she misunderstands. I look into her eyes, and like my therapist recommends, I'm honest about my emotions.

"I figured out what that third thing is," I say, my previous fears distant, muted by the feel of her in my arms.

Jenna smiles at me, her expression hopeful. "Yeah? What is it?"

And I can't hold this one back, not anymore. "I love you more than anything."

Jenna makes a soft whimpering sound, and she wraps her legs tight around me. "I love you, too, Felix," she says, and god, I could live off those words, if I could hear them every day for the rest of my life.

And then the sweet harmony overwhelms even Alec's soundtrack, and nothing exists in the world besides me and her. My whole consciousness is drowning in her touch, in the sensation of her fingers dipping below the elastic band of my boxers. I smile into her hair. There's something I've been wanting to do ever since we first met on Hollywood Boulevard. Jenna looks up at me, her expression turning to a question, like she doesn't know what the hell I'm grinning about, like just being here with her like this—god, with her *at all*—isn't enough.

And then my hand slides down the soft skin of her stomach and into her underwear, and her head leans back and she shudders. I think I see a smile pass across her lips just before her mouth opens and she gasps and slides her underwear off and out of my way.

I can take a hint. I slide my other arm behind her, cradling her, kissing her neck while she moans and arches under me, and my whole body is humming in tune with hers. I kiss the tops of her breasts, closing my eyes and focusing on her breathing, the way she gasps and moans, listening carefully and letting her tell me what she likes. Jenna's hands are in my hair, and I'm focused like I am when I'm learning a new piece, but there is no music in this world as sexy as her body taut beneath me and the frantic, desperate crescendo of her voice calling my name. I don't mean to stop, but Jenna rises beneath me, rolling me over onto my back, her breath still ragged. Her knees rest on either side of me, and I stare up at her, awestruck.

Jenna's hair gathers on her shoulders in dark waves. Her breath comes fast as she reaches past my shoulder to the nightstand, opens the drawer, and pulls out a condom. I run my hands up her thighs as she tears open the wrapper, and my eyes blink closed as she rolls it on me and now it's her hands that are lingering, doing things that make my whole body shudder. The whole world fills with light, and then I'm inside her, and her hands are on my shoulders and we're moving together. And I get it, everything I've ever heard about sex but never really understood—even before the drugs, when it was good, sure, but not as life changing as everyone said. It's like some part of my soul has been asleep, waiting all along to be woken up by *her*.

I kiss her, wishing I could tell her everything she is to me, but even if I could utter the words, I don't know what they are. Our rhythm intensifies, and Jenna cries out and collapses on top of me. My hands are in her hair, and I'm still inside her, but her body goes weak, and I kiss her forehead, feeling the beads of sweat in her hairline. She looks up at me.

And a shot of panic stabs me right in the heart.

God. The Suboxone. It clearly doesn't give me the same impotence problems as the heroin, but there were also the times on the drugs when I did manage to get it up and still couldn't finish. I flush at the memories of the girls I was with, some of whom would try for over an hour, and I'd still be hard. My throat closes. If that happens now, god, what am I going to tell her? It would kill me to lie to her, but as she trembles against me, I'm thinking about telling her now, at this minute, about the terrible things I've done and now my heart is racing for an entirely different reason.

Then Jenna smiles, and kisses me, and our passion pulls me under like an enormous wave. It's okay I'm not finished, because neither is she. We're rolling together, and now I'm on top of her, and we're moving again like a tide washed all the way out, and now coming rapidly in. I kiss Jenna's ear, whispering her name, and I feel myself approaching the wall built by heroin, the one I haven't broken through during actual intercourse in years. I squeeze my eyes closed as her body tenses and her breath grows sharp, waiting to slam up against it.

But then we're crashing through together, and the world seems to shatter like it was made out of glass, and we collapse, tangled in each other's arms. We're both breathing hard, and I slip my hand under Jenna's chin and bring her mouth to mine.

When I pull back again, there are tears in her eyes.

A second jolt of panic strikes me. "God," I say. "Are you okay? Did I—"

"I'm fine," she says, shaking her head, even though the tears are leaking down her cheeks now, and I brush them away with my thumbs. "I'm better than fine. I'm so happy, it's like—I don't even know what to do with it." She tries to pull away, but I gather her into my arms, and she seems to change her mind and clings to me, which is something I can never get enough of.

"Me, too," I say. And now I'm the one who wants to turn

196

away, which I hide by burying my face in her hair. I want to tell her things I've never shared with anyone, things that before this moment I would have adamantly denied. "You asked if I've done this before, and yeah, I mean, I've had sex. But I've never—I haven't—I didn't—"

Jenna smiles. "You're not used to talking about it, that's for sure."

I laugh. "I never really understood before what all the fuss was about, you know? I mean, sure, it feels good, marginally better than taking care of yourself, I suppose. And it's not like my body didn't want it. But then after, it always just felt—"

"Empty," Jenna says.

I nod. "Lonely."

Her eyebrows draw together. "And kind of gross."

I laugh. "Yes! God, I've always felt like such an idiot for feeling that way. Especially as a guy. I'm pretty sure I'm supposed to think of casual sex as this perfect beacon, but I was never all that into it." Even before the drugs, which is hard to admit, even to myself.

Jenna looks up, studying me. "I get it."

Clearly she does, but I still can't help but be skeptical. "Really?"

She nods. "All those years, all those guys I was with, the way they treated me." She presses her lips together and shakes her head. "All the time, what I was looking for was this. You. Us. All of it."

My heart aches, and I draw her close again. "Me, too," I say, and I mean it, not just about the sex but about everything—the thing I was missing at Juilliard, the emptiness that pushed me into the arms of heroin herself—I was missing *her*. Our connection. Not that being with her somehow fixes me, but it doesn't feel so bad being broken anymore.

The gunshots have died down, and now there's suggestive moaning coming through Alec's door. And I know this is petty, but I can't help myself. "Can I ask you for something?"

197

"What?"

I bite my lip. "Don't ever write a love song for me and then sing it to Alec."

Jenna is quiet for a moment. "I don't know how I could promise that." She sounds apologetic. "I've always been singing about the story, right? So if you're my story, then every song is about you."

I feel warm all over, and almost like I'm floating. It takes me a minute to respond. "Okay, yeah. Never mind, then."

"Are you sure that's okay?" Jenna looks up at me. "It's the opposite of what you asked for, but—"

"I know. But your kick-ass music and your beautiful voice and your awesome lyrics are somehow all about me. Am I supposed to complain about that?"

Jenna laughs. "When you put it that way." She pauses. "Do you really like my music?"

"I do. It's beautiful, just like you."

She smiles. Her skin is soft and warm against mine, and we stretch out together, making as much contact as possible. She rests her head on my chest, running her hand up and down my side. Lying there with her is as incredible as making love to her, not in the least because now I'm invited to be here every night.

Which brings me to the question of the morning. I take a deep breath. "What are we going to tell Ty? Because if he knows I'm spending the night, he's going to expect a little brother out of the deal."

Jenna laughs. "I'll explain that part to him." Her fingers pause on my hip. "But I'm worried about getting his hopes up, you know? He's kind of obsessed with this idea of you being his dad."

She tenses, like she's afraid how I'm going to react to that. She doesn't need to be. "Why don't you tell him not yet," I say. "Not that it'll never happen, but we're doing this for now, and then after the tour, we'll see."

Jenna nods. "That's the truth, isn't it?"

I press my lips to the top of her head. "I know what I want. But I get not wanting to let Ty place his hopes in us while our situation is still really . . . tricky."

She snuggles up, wrapping her arm tight around me. "I'm sorry I'm putting you through all this."

"You don't need to apologize."

"I do," she says. "My career is built on this web of lies and now you're caught in the middle of it. The web, the lies—it didn't seem so terrible before there was us."

I run my nails gently over her lower back. "The way I see it, I'm the lucky one."

She looks up at me, and now she's the skeptical one. "Really?"

"Yeah," I say, and I struggle to explain it. A heavy weight settles in my chest, and I begin a few sentences I don't know how to end. "I told you I did drugs, right?"

"Yeah."

"Well, when I did, there was some bad stuff that happened. Stuff that made me feel like a terrible person."

Jenna squeezes me. "Same here."

I nod. "And if someone had told me I'd be here with you, and we'd be talking about the possibility of someday being a family, that I'd have even a shot at something like that . . ." My breath catches. "It feels too good to be true."

Jenna buries her face in my neck, and I wrap my arms around her, and hold her close. "I feel exactly the same way," she says.

We squeeze each other tight, and I feel like the whole world is spinning around us, and we're at the center, perfectly still. This goes so far beyond limerence, beyond some high to be chased. We're in love, and it's real, and for this moment, I let myself believe that we can withstand whatever life throws at us.

I want to tell her everything. "When I was in New York, it's like I was chasing a dream that wasn't mine. And then I got lost, because I didn't know where I fit. When I was on drugs, I had someplace to belong, but then I knew I couldn't do that anymore, and I was lost again." It's a partial story. A coward's version, probably. But it's something. It's all I can give her right now, not in the least because I'm realizing that the longer I go without telling her, the more I have to lose.

Jenna shifts so she's lying on top of me, bathed in the soft light of the bedside lamp. "I felt like that, too, after Rachel died. But I had Ty. I still felt lost for a long time, but one day, I was putting him to bed, and I sang to him. And it was like everything changed. I was his mother. I knew where I fit."

"I never would have believed that everything can change like that in an instant," I say. "Until now."

Jenna smiles, and kisses me, and I know.

I'm going to do everything I can to make sure this lasts forever.

TWENTY-TWO

Jenna

I wake up in this content, blissful warmth, my body snuggled up tight against Felix. His arm is around me, and I can hear the steady beat of his heart as we lie there.

There's nothing empty or lost about waking up with him. It's the exact opposite. Last night it was like I was finally found, like the pieces of my heart I didn't even know were broken are knitting themselves back together. I'm happy, purely happy, in this soul-deep way I've never been able to fully capture in any of my dozens of songs about love.

Soul mates. I don't think I ever believed in that concept before, but I do now. There's no other way to explain the connection we had from the very beginning, so intense, and as instinctive as my own heartbeat. No other way to explain how I fell in love so quickly, and so completely. But I did, and I know what I told him last night was true—all that time, maybe all my life, I've been searching for him.

For us.

I stretch out against him, so even our toes are in contact.

Felix stirs, and blinks a few times before his blue eyes settle on me. They crinkle at the sides as he smiles. His blond hair juts up at adorably crazy angles and I want to run my hands through it. Again and again.

He opens his mouth to say something, but Alec's door opens. I hurriedly pull the sheet up higher on my body as Alec emerges from his room and ambles to the bathroom in his black silk boxers. He gives us the barest of dark looks.

"Hey," Felix says.

"Hey," Alec says back. And then he goes into the bathroom and shuts the door.

"Well, I'd give that interaction about a four on the Gabby Scale of Extreme Awkwardness," Felix says, and I laugh.

"Gabby requires her own personal Scale of Awkwardness?"

"She seems to think so." He rolls over to face me. "She's pretty sure everything awkward and embarrassing in the world happens to her, but I don't actually think she has worse luck than anyone else." He smiles. "She just has a funnier way of telling the stories then the rest of us."

I link my fingers with his. "I'd love to get to know her more." Just based on how much I liked her when we first met, that would be true enough. But I know how much Felix loves Gabby, and I could see how much she loves him back. And I want to be part of his life every bit as much as I want him to be part of mine.

"I'd like that too." His lips quirk up. "Even if it'll just give you both more ammunition to mock me with."

"Mmm," I say, leaning over and kissing him. "I think your ego could handle it."

He chuckles and pulls me in tighter, trails his fingers lazily along my side, sending goosebumps all along my skin. "Probably. Especially after last night."

"Yeah? Your ego feeling pretty good?" I tease.

"Everything's feeling good," he says, and I smile. I couldn't agree more. I've never had sex like that before, so full of passion and longing and pure, incredible love. Never has it felt so real, or so right—not to mention just plain *hot*.

I *knew* he'd be good with his fingers.

My body is heating up, and all kinds of ready to try that out again, and more, but suddenly I hear the faucet turn on in the bathroom and that reminds me Alec could come out any minute.

I groan. "We're going to have to get up and deal with him at some point, aren't we?"

"Yeah," Felix says, not sounding much happier about it than I am. "With him up, and Ty probably up soon, we're heading towards way higher than a four on the awkward scale."

As much as I want to bask in the warmth of our little haven in bed together, he's not wrong about the awkward potential.

So we get up, and Felix searches for his clothes and I grab some fresh ones, though without a shower we both make our way downstairs looking walk-of-shame worthy. Ty's watching cartoons like he usually does when he wakes up before me, though he excitedly abandons them to bounce around us and ask Felix millions of questions, like "why aren't you going to have a baby?" and "are you going to sleep over *every* night?" and "do you think Voldemort is scarier than Darth Vader?"

Felix takes all these questions in that amazing stride of his, answering each one and the slew of follow-up questions each one requires, while I make pancakes and eggs with real maple syrup. We eat breakfast together, and then Felix clears the plates and does the dishes, like it's a routine we have.

My heart swells at how good this all feels, how natural.

Ty takes a sip from his cup and sets it down, a little orange juice mustache on his upper lip. "So if you aren't my real dad, what are you?"

Felix looks back at me from the sink and raises an eyebrow.

"Your mom's boyfriend," I say, and Felix grins at me.

But I can see it now, just like I did last night when we were playing *Life*, when Felix was reading to Ty before bed. The three of us, a family. I know it's still only a hope, a possibility, but right now it feels like I'm seeing our future.

A future I want more than anything.

When I arrive at practice that afternoon—our last before our Los Angeles performance the day after tomorrow—Roxie and Leo are already there. They're arguing about whether or not the sharp pointed heels of Leo's boots constitute high heels and therefore turn them into women's shoes. I stay out of it.

Felix, Alec and I all drove separately, and Felix said he had some errands to run, which gave me a chance to make the lemon meringue pie I'm bringing, and also to drop Ty off at my parents. I can only imagine the earful he's going to be giving them about Felix staying over. I don't worry about them keeping a secret, but undoubtedly they're going to be concerned about me essentially moving in with a boyfriend I've only known a week. They trust me now, though. And I know they'll love Felix when they see how good he is to Ty and me.

I'm more worried about sharing the news with Leo and Roxie, who may be understandably concerned about how this might affect the band. Hence, the pie—though I wait for Felix to show up, so we can tell them together.

Felix arrives just as Roxie and Leo have decided to stand hip to hip and compare the heights of their heels.

"See?" Leo says. "Your boots are taller."

"Mine are platforms." Roxie gyrates her hip against his. "It's completely different."

Felix comes down the stairs, looking like he's trying not to laugh.

"Guys," I say. "I need to tell you something. Can you pay attention for five minutes without grinding against each other?" I realize with some consternation that I probably sound like Alec. But really, even Felix and I weren't that bad during band practice.

Though we did plenty of grinding last night. My body flushes all over again with the memory. It's been doing that a lot today.

Leo and Roxie retreat to opposite sides of the room and stand behind their respective instruments.

"Grind against Leo?" Roxie says. "Ew."

204

Felix looks over at me and I shake my head. I'm not sure if they're having a fling and trying to hide it from the rest of us, or they're just completely oblivious, but as Leo ducks his head to tune his guitar, I can see the back of his neck is bright red.

It's now or never, I suppose.

I hold up the pastry box and two forks. "I brought you guys a pie."

"Sweet!" Leo says. "Wait, this one isn't for Felix, is it?"

"No," I say. "For you and Roxie."

Leo takes the pie and digs in with a fork, while Roxie protests and squishes up next to him on the couch to get her share.

"There's something we need to tell you," I say.

Leo raises his eyebrows. "Is this a band meeting?" he asks around a big bite of lemon custard. "Because Alec isn't here yet."

"Alec already knows." I take a deep breath. "Felix and I are dating now."

Roxie and Leo both take another bite of pie, and neither looks even the tiniest bit surprised. I wonder if maybe they aren't getting the magnitude of this.

"We're still keeping up the front for the tour," I say. "So the official story will be that Felix is living in our guest room, because he needed a place to stay until the tour. And after that, we'll see." I pause, letting that note of uncertainty sink in. I can't exactly tell them Felix and I are going to be figuring out an exit strategy at some point after the tour, since I haven't broached that with Alec yet.

My stomach twists at the thought of *that* conversation. But I'm going to need to have it, and soon. Even though he's been a dick lately, he deserves plenty of warning, and a say in the story we're going to tell.

"Right on," Leo says, unconcerned.

I hesitate. "You're okay with this? Really?"

Roxie points at me with her fork. "It was totally obvious you guys were into each other. Alec was right. Just do it and get it over with."

"We're kind of thinking of this as a long-term thing," Felix says. He steals a glance at me, and I grin.

Hell yes, we are.

"Sweet," Leo says. "But Roxie's right. It was totally obvious." He elbows her. "How stupid do they think we are? Like we can't tell when two people are attracted to each other."

"For real," Roxie says. "No one is that oblivious."

I stare at them, about to say "No one? Really?" but as soon as I open my mouth, Alec bursts into the studio.

"All right!" he says, with more enthusiasm than I've heard from him since our last single beat out Shawn Mendes on the pop charts. "Everyone pumped for the show?"

Roxie and Leo both whoop and quickly down a few more bites of pie, and I realize I'm staring at Alec like he's sprouted a second head.

"Let's play!" Alec says.

Felix and I exchange looks. Maybe our luck is finally turning. Maybe Alec's ultimately going to be okay with all this. He can be reasonable, after all, and I know he cares about me and wants me to be happy.

Maybe we can figure out a way for all of us to end up with what we really want.

We start practice, and Alec and I sing a love song to each other, but I look over at Felix and he's smiling.

I'm glad he knows I mean it for him.

TWENTY-THREE

Felix

Two days later, while we're setting up for the concert, Jenna catches me staring out at the stadium of empty seats. There are thousands of them—far more than any place I've ever performed. Jenna walks up behind me and stands a few feet away, which feels odd, though not as awful as it did when I wasn't allowed to touch her at all.

"Nervous?" Jenna asks.

"I never get nervous," I say. "I played Carnegie Hall once, with some people from Juilliard. I wasn't nervous."

"But you are now."

A part of me wishes she couldn't see it, but most of me is glad she can. I don't want to hide anything from her. The irony of that isn't lost on me, but what I said to Gabby was true. Before I tell Jenna everything, I have to be completely sure I'm not going to get high if she rejects me.

I want to be sure right now, but I'm not, which is just as well, because even if there *is* a perfect time to tell her everything, it sure as hell isn't right before we go up on stage. It's only going to get more complicated, though. We drove separately, which gave me the chance to take off early and hit a meeting without having to explain myself, but there's only so long I can go without telling her about the meetings and the meds and the therapy.

Talking to her that first night together, even in such vague terms, about being lost, and the drugs, and the stuff that made me feel like a terrible person—it felt so good, like stretching out after a long, cramped flight. And Jenna's been great about everything I've told her. I'm starting to believe she could actually hear the whole truth and still want me.

We're going to make it. I can feel it.

"I've never performed anything I've practiced so little," I say.

"You've been practicing like crazy."

"And yet, still true."

Jenna lets out a small laugh, and I don't look at her. I don't want anyone getting one of those pictures Alec was talking about, with us looking at each other the way we do.

"You won't be able to see them," Jenna says. "Not really. It'll start to get dark while the warm-up bands are still playing, and by the time we're into our second set, all you'll see are the lights."

"We'll be able to hear them."

"Yeah. But they'll be cheering. Someone with an ego as big as yours has to enjoy that, right?"

I break down and smile at her. She grins back. "That's what I thought."

"It's just different," I say. "In orchestra, everything is scripted down to the second. There's a conductor to glare at you if you're not doing everything absolutely perfect."

Jenna nods. "This isn't like that. But you have the set list. You know what we're playing and when. And the rest of it, you can just follow our lead. Alec and I will work the crowd. You just smile and play."

"The smiling part I can handle."

Jenna hesitates, and then she steps forward and pats me on the shoulder. There are techs in the scaffolding above us working on the lights, and sound people checking the mics on stage, but none of them look askance at us. Jenna pulls her hand back before it looks like anything more than a friendly slap. "If there's one thing I'm sure you can do," she says. "It's play."

I bite back about ten different remarks about how familiar I know she is with the way I like to play.

And then Alec comes bounding across the stage. We haven't hit costumes and makeup yet, so his hair is washed but not styled, as per Allison's instructions. Instead of pulled back and slicked with gel, it rests loosely around his face, which makes him look . . . nicer. Or maybe that's the grin.

I've never seen Alec grin.

"Is everybody ready to rock?" Alec asks, in what I can only assume is his stage voice. Roxie whoops from behind the drum set—literally behind it, where she's kneeling and adjusting the stands.

"Technically," Jenna says, "we still have a lot to do before we're ready."

Alec's smile doesn't slip. He points to his temple. "I'm talking about up *here*. The body achieves what the mind believes."

At this point I'm wondering if Alec has some twin brother I don't know about. One who is happier and far more enthusiastic. And prone to speaking in motivational-poster slogans.

Jenna rolls her eyes, but she's smiling. "I got you that cheesy inspirational-quote-a-day calendar *as a joke*."

Alec laughs. "Yeah, well, just like those big-ass marquee letters in the house, I guess the joke's on you, babe." Then he grabs her by the waist and spins her around, and for such a round gesture it feels unreasonably pointed. At me.

Fortunately I'm spared any further exposure to the new-and-improved Alec when Allison calls me back to wardrobe. I change into my costume, which is just as Jenna described: a tight pair of True Religion jeans and a Henley t-shirt in the same blue as my eyes. I tried them on for Allison yesterday, and I like it.

Alec may be hotter, but that doesn't mean I don't want to look like I can compete.

I'm sat down in a chair and my hair is fawned over by a cosmetologist named Lindley, who styles my hair to look more or less like it usually does, but without the ability to move a single strand out of place. Then she puts makeup on me, and I'm not sure how girls make it look so easy to sit through that. My cheeks twitch and my eyes water and from the look of Leo when she finishes with him, she more or less gave up halfway through.

Jenna's still in makeup, and I'm herded back to the stage where I can either chill in the green room—with Alec—or stand up near the edge of the stage with Leo and Roxie and listen to the warm-up acts. I choose the latter. We're carefully hidden behind the wings, and Roxie and Leo take advantage of this by dancing, grinding against each other so hard that it's a wonder Leo's leather pants don't catch fire.

I try not to listen to the cheers from the crowd, which grow louder as our call time nears. Those people out there are in love with AJ. They're here not just for the music, but to bask in the glow of this couple they idolize—transfixed, as Jenna puts it, by the story.

None of them know it—thank god—but I'm a threat to that story. I'm the opposite of what they want for Jenna. I'm worried about how they'll feel about me replacing *Mason*, but if they knew anything about what was actually going on, they'd drag me off the stage and dismember me before security knew it was happening.

My mind freezes. We haven't played together nearly enough. I might not blend. The crowd might hate me. They might all *know*, the way Alec and Leo and Roxie all did. *Looking at each other the way you do.*

I have a good stage face. I'm a damned good flirt, which is much of what stage presence *is*—you flirt with the room, you smile like you know you've got it, and if you do, then the crowd smiles right along with you.

But I've always been a cocky bastard, so I've never had to get up on stage and pretend to be something I'm not. And even though I got tickets for Gabby and Will and Anna-Marie and her fiancé, Josh, that's only four people in my corner out of thousands. And that's if Anna-Marie isn't still pissed at me for that time she thought I stole her shoes.

Jenna finishes with makeup—hers taking the longest—and joins us. She's in this short skirt that's tight around the waist and flares out over layers of black tulle, and long lace-up boots that go over her knees. Her hair sparkles as if it's been misted with glitter—which, given the various spray bottles Lindley possessed, I don't doubt it has. She looks stunning and sexy and ready to own the stage and everyone out there. She glances at Roxie and Leo and gives me a knowing look. Here in the darkness of the wings, we smile at each other.

It doesn't wipe away my nerves, but it damn well helps.

And then, before I'm even close to ready, Alec comes up from the green room in artfully ripped dark jeans and a black leather vest over a white t-shirt. His hair is loose still, but definitely styled. Phil looks up from the phone that seems permanently affixed to his hand and points us toward the stage. Jenna and Alec take the lead, walking confidently hand-in-hand, and I forget to hate it as my stomach crawls up into my throat. I follow Leo and keep my head up. The sun has set but it isn't completely dark, and even through the lights, I can see the roiling movements of masses of people who are screaming as Jenna and Alec walk to the front of the proscenium, waving and grinning and grabbing their mics.

"How is everybody feeling tonight!" Alec shouts, and the roar is deafening. Leo and Roxie are half waving and half surreptitiously readying their instruments, so I do the same.

"Thank you, Los Angeles!" Jenna shouts. "We're happy to see you, too." She blows the crowd a kiss and then turns and directs one at Alec, and somehow the screams grow louder. I check my mic and run a quick tune check while Jenna and Alec work up the crowd and introduce the local backup musicians who will be filling in on keyboard and guitar while Alec and Jenna are singing to each other and the crowd.

And then Jenna spins around and points right at me. "Let me

introduce you to someone we're thrilled to have with us. Our new cellist, Felix Mays!"

The crowd cheers, louder than for the backup musicians, but naturally not as loud as they did for Alec or Jenna. I smile and wave, and Jenna grins at me. And then she turns around and adopts a coy stance in Alec's direction. "What do you think, babe? Should we give them a show?"

"I don't know," Alec says. "Is that what they're here for?"

The crowd gives their loudest scream yet, and Jenna laughs. "I know what they're really here to see." She leans up on the toes of her tall black boots and kisses Alec. A cheer swells from the crowd, and I smile like I'm supposed to.

It's not as difficult to watch as I thought it would be. It's not real. I woke up with the real Jenna this morning and I'll be falling asleep with her tonight. Stage Jenna is pieces of the girl I love, but more carefully edited and with the volume turned all the way up. Everything from the slant of her lips to the sway of her walk is exaggerated and obviously carefully controlled. She's a natural with the crowd, and they love her. It's a wonder they can hear anything past the first few words she says, what with the cheers and the screams. Maybe they can't, but they love it anyway.

And even though she's bantering with her ex right in front of me, I can't help but love it right along with them.

Then Jenna points to Roxie, who counts off and begins the first song.

I'm not sure if Jenna planned it this way—I'm damn sure *Alec* didn't—but the first song has a cello part I could play in my sleep. It's fast but the range is small, which gives me a chance to adjust before we launch into some of the songs where I need to step it up a bit. Jenna's voice sounds even more beautiful on stage, and she sings with all her heart, and I can tell the audience feels it. They respond to her banter with Alec, yes, but also to the story she's telling.

I can't get enough of that story, because even if Alec is acting the part, I believe her when she says that it's all about her and me.

Near the middle of the set, there's a piece Mason wrote where the cello takes over the melody for the bridge and plays this haunting counterpoint to the harmony of the piano and the bass guitar. It's my favorite part of the show, and when we get there, I forget about the audience, I forget to be nervous, and I play it for Jenna with all the presence of my twelve years of musicianship.

When the song ends, the crowd cheers, and Jenna turns to face the crowd, taps one toe behind her, and gestures to me. "Felix Mays, everyone!" she yells, and the cheering grows.

Jenna waves her hand, motioning for them to cheer louder, higher, and they follow her lead. The roar is deafening. When they don't quiet immediately, Jenna grins at me.

I grin back. We've won them over, for the moment at least.

I set down my bow, stand, and offer my most formal cellist's bow. I've done this a hundred times in front of very different audiences, and I don't at all know how this one will react, but it's the best way I know how to show my appreciation.

The whistles and screams and cheers continue. I stand and wave and try to look through the bright lights at the audience.

Damn, if I couldn't get used to *this*.

I've always loved to perform. I love the energy of a good audience, the feeling of completion after long hours of practice. As we finish the set, I'm proud to be here with Jenna, finishing my first concert as a member of the band.

And then Alec steps up to the edge of the stage and raises his mic. "We have one more song for you tonight—" he waits out the chorus of boos that follow this statement— "but before we go, I've got something to say, and I hope you all will humor me." The crowd goes quiet, waiting, and Alec turns to look at Jenna.

She's smiling, but it's more tentative now, and I realize she doesn't know what he's about to say. Something about that makes my chest tighten.

"Actually," Alec says, winking at the audience. "It's more of a question."

Jenna's eyes widen. My ribs squeeze in on my lungs like a twenty-foot anaconda.

And then out of his pocket, Alec pulls a ring box, and opens it to reveal the biggest diamond I've ever seen outside of a glass case. It's even bigger than the giant rock Josh gave to Anna-Marie on that talk show where they spilled their side of the story about what happened with Shane. Much like Josh did, Alec drops to one knee and gives a dramatic pause, in which the audience gasps. Jenna's face has gone pale and terrified, even as she smiles through it. She gives the crowd a panicked look, and I can tell she's leaning into what she's really feeling while trying to keep her cool in front of her fans.

I want to punch Alec. I envision her slapping his face.

"Jenna Rollins," he says. "Will you marry me?"

The crowd is cheering and screaming and wailing but I can hardly hear them. Alec's words echo in my mind. *Jenna Rollins, will you marry me?*

My throat goes dry, and I stare at Jenna, but she doesn't spare me a single glance.

She can't. I know she can't. This isn't real. It isn't. No more than any of the rest of the show, all of which didn't seem as terrible as I'd feared. I try to keep my face neutral, like maybe I was in on it, like maybe I had a fucking clue Alec was planning to propose on stage to *my* girlfriend without fucking warning her first.

"Oh my god." Jenna takes a deep breath, and presses a trembling hand to her lips, and disappears beneath the cover of Stage Jenna again. "Oh my god, *yes!*"

My throat closes up and sweat beads on my forehead and while that could be due to the hot lights, I'm sure I'm not looking even the least bit happy and I'm praying that every last damn camera in the stadium is capturing only the look on Jenna's face as she pulls Alec to his feet and jumps into his arms. Alec is grinning, and now I have an inkling about why he was so happy before the show. He had a plan. He was going to regain control. And while he can't think for a moment that Jenna is actually going to marry him, the fact that he didn't warn her about this is evidence of how he means it.

It's a warning. A threat. A slap to the face—both to her and to me. A reminder that he's the one the fans want her with. She can't just walk away from him without walking away from all of it.

Will you marry me?

Jenna still hasn't looked at me, and I take a long drink from my water bottle and try not to heave it back up. Leo and Roxie are both casting me worried looks, and I force myself to clap my hands and cheer along with the rest of the crowd. Leo and Roxie follow. And then Alec pulls away from Jenna's embrace.

"We've got one more song for you tonight," he says, smiling with his very best lovable, sweep-her-off-her-feet grin. I want to wrap my hands around his neck.

God, how are we going to get out of this gracefully now?

Jenna is beaming, the picture of joy, and my stomach twists and I can't help but wish she was looking that way for me. I look down at the last song on the set list, and I know Alec must have put it there. It's a ballad where Alec does most of the singing, all about his deep love for her, and how being with her has saved him from a lifetime of misery, and he'll never be the same.

He starts to sing, and Jenna flashes the ring at the crowd and manages to summon some tears, which probably isn't a far reach, and I hate Alec all the more. He sings to the girl I love while I play the backup harmony, and neither of them looks back at me. Not even once. At the end of the song, Jenna leaps into his arms again, and he lifts her off the stage, and my eyes unfocus. I can't see this. I can't watch anymore. The rest of their goodbyes to their audience blur, and then the set is over.

When we get off the stage, Jenna turns and finally looks at me. Stage Jenna has made way for Real Jenna, and the horror on her face is enough to make me want to punch Alec all over again. I shake my head at her, hoping the distress on my face doesn't look like anger.

I'm not mad at her. She had nothing to do with *that*. Alec's power play had its intended effect. I'm a mess and she's a mess and he's had his revenge on us for daring to defy his goddamned rules.

We have to get out of the spotlight before we can figure out where the hell we're going from here. We're funneled off the stage and then on again for the pre-planned encore, and I keep my eyes down, focusing on the music, trying to ignore Alec and Jenna as they preen for the crowd as if they're the happiest couple and they're going to get married and make babies and he's going to be Ty's father when I know that even living in the house with the kid he doesn't have a damn thing to do with his life. After the encore we're off to publicity and I carefully keep both Leo and Roxie—both of whom could kick my ass—positioned between me and Jenna and Alec, her because I'm not sure I'll be able to keep from taking her hand, and him because I really don't want a stint in jail for choking Alec until his face is purple and his tongue is bloated in front of a crowd of cameras and reporters.

We stand behind velvet ropes while lights flash in our faces and Jenna answers a dozen questions about how she feels and if she knew this was coming—the last of which, at least, she can answer honestly. Someone asks me how it felt to be up there as part of the band, and I actually give them a thumbs up like I'm fifteen and smile and say, "great," like my command of the English language is significantly worse than an eight-year-old kid I happen to know.

I turn my phone back on and I see messages from Gabby. For a moment I'd forgotten she was there in the audience, with Will and Anna-Marie and Josh. She saw. She knows what happened, and I'm sure she can imagine what it's doing to me. Every message is some version of *Oh my god, are you okay?*

No. I am not. But I know what she's really asking.

Still clean, I respond, though I imagine it's the next few hours she's concerned with. *Keep your phone on? I'll call if I need you.*

You better, she responds.

While Alec is talking, Jenna looks back at me. I lean past Leo, still keeping him mostly between us. I don't know if I'm supposed to come back to the house—if they're even *going* back to the house or if Alec plans to spend the night in some honeymoon suite filled with champagne and rose petals. I taste bile in the back of my throat.

I'm staying with them. That's the official story. "Do you guys need some time tonight?" I ask. "I can steer clear."

Jenna's eyes widen in panic before snapping back into character. "No, you can come home. If you want to."

Even through the act, I can see her begging me to want to, and I nod. I will. I hope she knows I will.

"All right, folks," Phil calls. "No more questions." And then Jenna and Alec wave to the crowd and kiss in front of the open door of the limousine waiting to take them away. Then they climb in and the door closes and they're gone.

TWENTY-FOUR

Jenna

It took everything in me not to look back at Felix when Alec proposed. I couldn't, or I'd give it all away. I couldn't look back at Felix, I couldn't say *hell no* to Alec, not there on stage in front of all our fans and the world. I couldn't do anything but hold onto the mask, the story, and pretend to be happy, even though I am anything but.

Through the encore and the publicity and the whisking away hand-in-hand with Alec into the limo, I force myself to cling to that mask—the ecstatic, giddy, newly-engaged-and-oh-so-happy-about-it mask the fans want to see, that the story *demands*, now that Alec fucking *proposed on stage*—

Keep it together, I tell myself. Brian, the limo driver, is still watching.

I try to calm my breathing, to settle back into the smooth leather seat and Alec's arm around my shoulders, but all I can see is Felix's torn-up expression. All I can feel is my heart slamming against my ribs, and this twisting in my stomach.

And the desire to leave a massive princess-cut-shaped indent in Alec's face.

I unclench my fist and squeeze Alec's knee, in what hopefully looks to Brian from the rearview mirror like a loving gesture, but is hard enough to make Alec wince.

"Congratulations, you two," Brian says. He's our usual post-show driver in LA, and normally we chat we with him for a bit, catch up on how his kids are doing, or his latest grievance with his mother-in-law.

There's no way I can handle small talk right now, but Alec steps in. "Thanks, Brian. I'm a pretty lucky guy."

He's lucky I have a low predilection for murder, is what he is.

"We both are," I say as sweetly as possible, beaming up at Alec and squeezing his knee harder. "Brian, you mind if we have a little privacy?"

Brian chuckles. "Of course! There's some champagne in the back. You two kids celebrate." He winks at us and then the partition slides up. The second it's locked into place I jump away from Alec like I've been burned.

Because I sure as hell have been.

"What the *fuck* was that?" I growl.

Alec rolls his eyes up to the limo ceiling in this sort of weary "oh, here we go" look that makes me even more furious. "It was a pretty damn romantic proposal, I'd say."

I don't want to hear anything about what Alec thinks is romantic. "You had no right!" I say, my voice creeping into a yell. Alec shoots a pointed look at the partition, which is probably soundproof enough, but I'm rapidly losing my ability to care what Brian hears. "You had no right to do this without talking to me first!"

"Yeah? Is that what we're going with?" Alec's voice is snide, like he's so justified he can't be bothered to get worked up about this. "You had no right to move in with our cellist, but you didn't care what the hell I thought about that."

"That's my personal life. It's different."

"Is it?" Alec's blue eyes are cold as ice. "It affects me, too, doesn't it? You didn't even bother asking me if it was okay if he lives with us."

There's a flicker of guilt, but I'm so mad at him, it's not hard to quash. "It's *my* house, bought and paid for by *me*," I say, even though I hate myself a little for playing that card, petty as it is.

But after what he did . . .

"Do you think I love living in my ex-girlfriend's *closet*? Trust me, that's not exactly the dream," Alec says. "But I do it for the band. For our future. Something you could stand to think about more often."

My body flushes. I have been thinking about the future, but not in the way he means it.

I see Felix's expression again in my mind, angry and gutted, and my heart aches. He had to know my reaction wasn't real. He had to know I had nothing to do with this.

But what if he decides that all this isn't worth it? That having to deal with Alec, and this whole messed-up situation, is too much?

I can feel my eyes burning, and blink away the tears furiously. "So, what, I don't consult you on our roommate situation and you do this . . . as revenge? Because we didn't stick to the damn rules, you go ahead and—"

"Oh my god, Jenna. Seriously. That's what you think of me?" I think the wounded look on his face is sincere—Alec isn't great at faking emotions, ironically—but it doesn't mean it's not true, that this isn't some spiteful way to get back at us.

"I wouldn't have before, but given what you just did—"

"What *I* did?" Alec's eyes flash. "*You're* the one who seems hell-bent on throwing everything away on some guy you just met!"

I should tell him I'm not just throwing everything away, that if I was, I sure as hell would have said no on that stage and been done with all of this. But what comes out of my mouth instead is, "He's not just some guy, Alec. I'm in love with him."

"In *love* with him." He shakes his head, glaring at the ceiling. "God, Jenna, you barely know him." The judgment in his tone knifes me. I know he doesn't understand. I know he doesn't really believe something like this, so soon, is possible. But I know Alec, and there's more than that to his judgment—he's thinking I'm falling back into old patterns, being irresponsible, rushing headlong into self-destruction.

My heart squeezes, but I remember the feel of being in Felix's arms, of how natural and pure and right it feels every time I'm with him, like I've finally found this person I didn't even know I was desperately searching for all along.

What I feel for Felix isn't like the past, not at all. It's a future, one I want with all my heart, for me and for Ty.

Not that I'm going to tell Alec *that*.

"Okay, fine," Alec says, running a hand through his hair. "Sure. You're in love with him. Like you were in love with me."

I'm not even going to get into how different things are with Felix, especially because there's no nice way to say that to Alec. "I *am*," I say firmly. "And he's in love with me. And, god, Alec, did you even think about what that must have been like for Felix, seeing that? Did you even—?"

"Felix?" Alec laughs incredulously. "Felix signed on for this! Felix joined our band knowing he was going to have to watch us pretend to be in love."

My mouth opens and closes helplessly. He's not wrong about that—Felix and I have talked about that, and how difficult it might be. But this is different, somehow, and not just because we were caught completely off-guard by it.

I'm not sure how to put to words what line it crossed beyond just the personal betrayal of Alec throwing me under the bus like that. But my eye catches the glint of the big-ass diamond on my finger, and I feel queasy.

"Look," Alec says, leaning forward. "You guys aren't going to last four years. He admits it. Are you going to deny that? Especially now that you're *in love* with him? Our plan isn't going to work anymore, is it?"

I take a deep breath, the guilt back. I should have brought this up with Alec sooner, sometime in the last day or two. I knew I needed to, but the anxiety of it, of letting him down after all he's done for me . . .

Though if I'd known he was planning a proposal, I might have felt a lot less conflicted.

"No." I look down at my hands, and then away again.

Alec nods. "So we need to escalate the story, get out of it faster. Which means we need to be building to an ending. This will be our engagement tour, and when it's over, we'll figure out what's next—cold feet or something. A story that lets us both get out with what's left of our dignity." He holds his arms open wide. "It's not as good as the other plan, but I'm not the one who decided to abandon it."

The fury from before has settled into a cold pit in my stomach.

"You still should have talked to me about it first," I say.

"Maybe," Alec says. "Would you have agreed?"

We'd needed a new plan, and though I don't love this one, it's hard to say how I would have taken it had Felix and I actually been given the option. But we weren't, and now it's done.

"I guess we'll never know," I say.

He glares at me and then looks out his window, and I look out mine. There's nothing more I want to say, not right now and not to him.

Felix, though . . . I think of the way he asked if he should come home tonight, like he actually thought I might not want him there after what just happened. My heart aches and my hands tremble as they clutch my knees. And I can only hope this connection, this possible future, is still worth it to him after all this.

TWENTY-FIVE

Felix

I sit in my car in the private back lot to the stadium, staring at the barbed wire fence separating it from a junkyard full of bent and twisted cars. Some of the staff are clearing out, though the lot is still crowded with the cars of the techs who will spend the next several hours packing up equipment.

I tighten my hands on the steering wheel. I stare at the fence, my eyes counting metal wire diamonds in groups of one, four, nine, twenty-five.

The muscles in my arms are tight, which is the only reason they're not shaking. The tremor instead travels up to my shoulders, my neck, where all my muscles twitch. There's a scream coming from somewhere in the back of my mind, so loud I can't hear anything else.

I can't get high holding onto the steering wheel. If I don't let go, I can't start the car. I can't drive to my friend Izzy's house in Anaheim for a hit. I got paid today, and I intended to use the money to buy Gabby's couch and start paying my dad back, but I know exactly how much heroin that money would buy and it's enough to get through the pay period—maybe more since I won't need as high a dose.

Not that I'll have a job next week if I shoot up. Walk the

mile, I tell myself. Walk it through to the end.

But I can't put two thoughts together that aren't made out of fear and pain and desperation. This is ridiculous, and I know it. Jenna isn't marrying Alec. Nothing has changed between us. But I'm pissed and scared and confused, and my body knows how to fix it, how to make it all instantly go away, and I've been clean long enough now that I know damn well how good it would feel. Maybe I could even get back to the magic of the first time, when all the weight I didn't even know I'd been carrying lifted off me, like I'd suddenly discovered what should have been obvious before—human beings weren't meant to be tethered to the ground. It became completely unfathomable how I'd forgotten I was meant to fly.

My fingers are aching, but I hold on tighter. I haven't had a craving like this since the first weeks of rehab. My body is screaming at me just to find a damn hit already, and most of my brain agrees. There's only one small part of me that stands between them, holding them back with what little strength I have.

But my body doesn't get to decide what I do, and neither does most of my brain. And unless I'm unlucky enough for a dealer to come knock on my window in the backstage parking lot, it doesn't matter how much most of me wants to get high.

I'm standing in its way.

I try to breathe—to my stomach, the way I was taught by my therapist.

I am not going to get high.

Even if a dealer *did* knock, I don't have cash on me. I never carry cash on me. Forget the job, if I fail a drug test, I will break Jenna's heart, and she's been through enough pain and heartache. I think about Jenna and Ty, about Gabby, about my sister Dana and Ephraim and my parents and the band. I think about Katy, and people I don't even know yet that I might hurt if I throw away fifty-six days of sobriety. The last few have been easier, but I earned most of those the hard way, fending off the wolves with nothing but a stick.

224

It doesn't matter what Alec does, or even Jenna, for that matter. I make my own choices, and I choose not to get high.

I watch the dashboard clock. It takes another thirty minutes before I'm ready to pry my hands off the wheel.

When I get home, I can hear Jenna and Alec yelling before I even open the door. From the sound of it, they've circled through these arguments before and are back for round two, maybe three.

I'm not sure if my presence will help or hinder this conversation, but I open the door. Jenna looks over at me, a mix of anguish and relief on her face. I hate myself for making her sweat it so long. Alec doesn't even glance at me as he continues.

"At least he had the decency to admit to my face that you guys had abandoned the plan," Alec says. He points at me, but keeps his eyes fixed on Jenna.

Jenna takes a deep breath. "Felix," she says.

Alec's face clouds over. He's not thrilled I'm here now, and that Jenna's attention has shifted.

"That was a dick thing to do, Alec," I tell him, trying to keep my voice even.

Alec turns to me, and he shakes his head like a disappointed parent, which must take some nerve. "Like I told Jenna, we need to escalate the story. You guys want out sooner, so we'll get you out sooner."

Jenna stares at him coldly, and I have to admit Alec has a point. Even if he is being a dick about it.

"You should have talked to us about it first," Jenna says, I'm sure not for the first time.

Alec looks at me, like he's expecting me to yell at him. And as much as I still want to punch him, I find I have nothing else to say. Alec must realize we're not going to commend him for his fine tactical decision, because he storms up the stairs and leaves us alone.

I'm glad to see him go.

Jenna wilts against the wall. She's taken off her boots, and she looks so small standing there, barefoot, curled in on herself. "Felix," she says, and I see tears shining in her eyes. "I'm so sorry. I had no idea. I understand if you don't want to be caught up in—"

I cross the room and wrap my arms around her and kiss her before she can say any more. Her body tenses in my arms, and she kisses me back frantically, like she's afraid I have one foot out the door.

I pull back, pushing her still-glittery hair back over her ear. "Does this change anything?"

She looks me in the eyes. "It doesn't for me. Not even a little bit."

I'm ashamed of how much relief I feel. I should have known that. I think I did, but it feels so good to hear her say it. "For me, either."

She lets out a relieved sigh, and I feel a bit better. I'm not the only one who was worried. "Are you sure?"

I wrap my arms around her, and she presses tight against me. "I'm sure. You think I'm going to walk away because of *Alec*?"

She laughs, but it sounds nervous. "I suppose when you put it that way."

I kiss her again, and this time she relaxes in my arms. We're okay, for the moment.

I wish I could make Alec stop harassing us, but I don't know what else I can say to him. After a few minutes, Jenna takes my hand and leads me over to the couch and curls up in my arms. My craving for heroin all but fades away, and as much as I don't want that to be about her, I know it is.

"I had no idea he was going to do that," she says.

"Clearly. And I wish he hadn't, but he did."

She shakes her head. "The look on your face . . ."

I groan. "Did I give the whole thing away?"

"I doubt anyone will be scrutinizing your reaction, and if they do, they'll just figure you have a crush on me."

I smile. "And who doesn't?"

"Leo," Jenna says. "I hope."

"Given the way he was dancing with Roxie, I'd say you're in the clear."

"But it bothered you," Jenna says.

I hold her closer, the layers of tulle in her skirt rustling as she shifts. "What Alec did? Yeah, it bothered me."

"But you know it wasn't real, right? I reacted that way because I was playing the part. And maybe I shouldn't have, but he caught me off guard, and I didn't—"

"I know," I say. "It wasn't that at all."

She looks up at me with concern. "What was it, then?"

"I didn't like Alec doing that to you. I knew you weren't okay with it." But there's more to it than that. And all at once I know what it is. "I was jealous. Not of you kissing him, not the performance. That actually wasn't as hard as I thought it would be. Now that I'm allowed to kiss you, and be here with you, I don't care if you have to act like you're with him for your job."

She rests her head on my shoulder. "But the proposal. That's different."

"Yeah," I say. Jenna is quiet. Waiting for me to finish. And I can't help but wonder if this is going to be the time I say too much, and she panics.

"I wanted to be the one doing that," I say. "I want to be the one who marries you."

Jenna looks up at me, her gray eyes wide. "Yeah?" she says, in this breathless way.

I pull her even closer, until she's practically on my lap. "Yeah."

"I want that, too," she says softly, and then burrows into me, and I could just stay here like this forever, holding her. Knowing she loves me and wants a life with me, too. After a moment, Jenna sighs. "I wish we could get out now. I should have told him no on stage. Then we could be done and it would be his own damn fault."

I don't hate this idea. "But we also wouldn't get to tour. And we'd both be out of a job . . ."

Jenna laughs. "There's that."

"What do you want to do when you're done? Do you want to keep playing?"

"I don't know," she says. "Sometimes I think I want to get out of the industry, but I do love performing, and writing music. I would like to change my sound a little. More indie, I guess. Less processed. And definitely more real. I don't want to lie to the fans anymore."

I smile. "I could see you falling somewhere between Ani DeFranco's 'Not a Pretty Girl' and Kurt Cobain's 'Heart Shaped Box.' "

"I was thinking more like Ben Folds. Me and a piano, you know? Only with more love songs. And this time I can tell the real story." She nudges me. "*Our* story."

I melt until I'm pretty much a puddle. "Think you'll have room for a cellist?"

She smiles. "I can probably find a place for you. But what about you? Do you like playing with a band, or would you rather go back to *classical?*"

The way she says the word sounds skeptical, and I put a hand over my heart. "Are you maligning my true love?"

"Now *I'm* jealous."

I shake my head. "I'm going to make you fall in love with classical, yet."

She looks even more skeptical.

"All right," I say. "I'll prove it to you. Let me play you a song."

I don't particularly want to move right now, but I know this'll be worth it. So I get June out of the car and bring over a chair and position it beside where Jenna is sitting on the couch, her bare legs tucked underneath her skirt. "Okay," I say. "Close your eyes."

Jenna obliges, though I can tell she still has doubts.

"This is how much I love you," I say. And I play "The Swan" by Saint-Saens. It's technically supposed to be a sad song, but I've always loved the sweeping highs and lows, and the cadence has always felt to me like a love song.

And tonight it is.

I watch Jenna as I play, as the creases around her eyes ease, and her whole body sinks down into the cushions of the sofa. Before rehab I was never good at being honest about how I feel, but I've never had that problem with music. I used to say that music was my drug, and in a way it was true. All the things I couldn't say or do or sometimes even think, I could play. I pour my whole heart into the song, hoping she'll be able to feel what I feel for her, even though the words, easier to say to her than to anyone, could never fully suffice.

When I finish, she opens her eyes. Now she's the one who's turned into a puddle. "Okay," she says, and her eyes gleam with unshed tears. "I love that song."

I smile. "I'll make you love more of them. Give me time."

"Done," she says.

And I hope with my whole heart that she will.

TWENTY-SIX

Felix

When I walk into my next appointment with Cecily a few days later, I'm ready for a fight. From the long-suffering look she gives me, she knows it before I even open my mouth.

"I'm living with Jenna now," I say.

Her eyebrows go up. "Jenna. The girl you're not allowed to date?"

"Yeah. We may have changed the rules."

Cecily takes a deep breath, and I see her trying to adjust to this. "How do you feel about that?"

"Great."

She narrows her eyes. I know she can tell by my fake smile and bravado that there's more to it, but I'm not giving anything up.

"Excellent," she says. "How's your attendance at meetings?"

It's my turn to narrow my eyes. Cecily doesn't think this is excellent. She's trying to dodge the fight. Which is fine, except I know she'll sneak back around to the subject sooner or later. "I've missed a few. But I'm still going. And I'm still clean."

"Glad to hear it," Cecily says. "Are the missed meetings because of Jenna?"

They are. Now that I'm living with her, it's harder to get away every day without telling her what's going on—all the more reason I need to. But that night after the show scared me. I have to hang on to my sobriety. I know I do. And she does know about the drugs. She just doesn't know everything. Yet.

"I'm in a band that's about to go on tour. I've had to practice," I say. "Plus I've been spending time with my sister, and now my girlfriend. All good things that are keeping me from using, so I'm going to call it a win."

Today when I left the house I told Jenna I was going to visit Gabby, and I did. I've told Gabby several times since the show that I'm okay, but I think she needed to actually see me to ensure that I was.

"How are you feeling about all of that?" Cecily asks.

"Great. How am I supposed to feel?"

Cecily sits back in her chair. "You seem defensive."

Hell yes, I do. "You seem judgmental."

Cecily raises an eyebrow. "Do you think perhaps you're projecting your own judgment of the situation onto me?"

"I think perhaps you've already told me you think it's a bad idea for me to be in a relationship so soon, so there's no reason to pretend you feel otherwise."

Cecily nods. "And that makes you feel judged."

"It makes me feel frustrated. Because you're supposed to be helping me stay clean, and now I feel like I have to fight you for what I want instead of you helping me figure out how to have what I want and sobriety, too."

Cecily looks surprised at my honesty, and I have to admit I am, too. Maybe I'm getting better at this whole talking about my feelings thing.

I suspect Jenna has no small part in that.

"All right," Cecily says. "Fair point. If you've already decided to live with this woman—"

"Jenna."

"—if you've already decided to live with Jenna, you're right. I'm not going to talk you out of it. So let's move forward from there."

"Thank you."

"How is this affecting your relationship with your family?"

I sigh. "My sister thinks it's awesome."

"Your sister Gabby?"

"Yeah." No one else is allowed to know, but I can't explain that to Cecily. "I haven't told Dana. We're not that close. And I think my parents are both glad to have me off their couches."

Cecily nods. "Do you feel like the emotional energy you're expending on this relationship is going to interfere with your efforts to regain their trust?"

"Regaining their trust means staying clean," I say. "And I'm doing that. I'm also gainfully employed, and performing for real audiences again. We had our first show on Saturday."

"And how was that?" Cecily asks.

From the lack of expectation in her tone, I take it she hasn't put any of the pieces together. She has no idea who Jenna is, much less that she's pretending to be engaged to Alec.

"Good. And also rough. After the show one of the band members did something that pissed me off, and I sat in my car for a long time before I could trust myself to go anywhere without using."

Again, Cecily looks impressed. "So you were triggered and you coped."

"Yeah. Give me a gold star."

"How in control would you say you were during that episode?"

God. "On a scale of one to ten? Like a two. But I didn't use. I didn't take my hands off my steering wheel until I knew I wouldn't."

"Good for you. How would you rate yourself in terms of using the tools available to you to manage the episode?"

I pause. That's a question I haven't thought about. "I probably should have called someone."

"Like a sponsor?" Cecily asks.

I glare. "Like my sister. She was available. I asked her to keep her phone on in case I needed to call, but I didn't. I probably would have been safer if I had."

Cecily nods. Again. She's beginning to remind me of the bobble-head Simpsons figures behind her. "And is Jenna someone you can talk to about these things?"

I'm having to hide so much of this relationship, I decide to tell the truth. "She doesn't know everything about the drugs yet."

Cecily presses her lips together. "She doesn't know you're in recovery."

"She does," I say. "But not the details."

"Are you afraid of how she'll handle knowing the whole truth?"

"Yes. And I'm going to tell her, but I want to be sure I can maintain my sobriety first, even if it ends."

Cecily looks impressed that I brought up the possibility of it ending before she did, which I gather is where the conversation was going. "You think the end of this relationship is a risk to your sobriety."

"Of course it is," I say. "I'm not stupid. But being alone is also a risk to my sobriety. I'm working on it. I'm having a lot more good days. But I'm never going to be able to have anything good in my life if I'm always afraid of taking the risk." My voice breaks, and I didn't realize how strongly I felt about this until I find the words. "Maybe some people can wrap their whole lives in the program for an entire year and feel safe that way, but I just feel empty. I need to be doing something. I need people in my life who I can give something to. Being needed makes me less likely to relapse, and not because I'm dependent on it, but because it makes me feel good about myself, which is something I haven't felt in years."

Cecily smiles like I've won her over, which surprises me, because for once I wasn't trying. "I'm proud of you. It takes courage to take the kinds of risks you're taking, and you seem like you're thinking these things through, and that's good."

"But?"

"But I think you need to have a plan for what you're going to

233

do if it ends," she says. "It's good for you to have people in your life who make you feel better about yourself, but what happens when you don't?"

"I won't use. If I have to lock myself in a closet without a phone until I'm in control again, I will not use."

"Good." Cecily smooths out a wrinkle in her tan suitcoat. "Today's a big day for you."

I smile. "Sixty days."

"Have you gotten your chip yet?"

"No. I'm going straight to a meeting after this."

"A lot of my clients tell me the second thirty days are the hardest. Rehab's over, the intense withdrawals are done, but you're getting back into regular life and it's easy to fall into old patterns."

"It's true. Last time I only made it six weeks." It startles me to realize I'm only two weeks past that now, not because I'm afraid I'm going to relapse, but because of how much more in control I feel.

"What do you think the difference was this time?"

I think about that. Even at six weeks, at four weeks, back in rehab, the difference was palpable. "I think I finally hit the bottom. I heard at a meeting once that rock bottom doesn't exist. You can always go deeper, so the bottom for you is the place you decide to turn around."

"For you it was Katy."

That's true, and I hate it. "Yeah, maybe. But Katy was a person with dreams and goals and an addiction that killed her. It's not fair of me to think of her as a thing that happened to me, as something I needed to happen to get better."

"Maybe she wasn't," Cecily says. "Maybe her death is something that happened to her, and you being there for it is the thing that happened to you that finally convinced you to stop digging and climb back up."

"I still hate myself for it." I'm surprised by how much it's true. All the stuff with Jenna, all the struggle to stay clean, it's buried the feeling a bit, but it's still there.

"Do you think hating yourself is helping you stay sober?"

"Obviously not," I say. "But apparently it's not stopping me, either."

"That's good," Cecily says. "Keep working the steps. They'll help you get closer to forgiveness."

The truth is, I don't want to be forgiven. Katy doesn't get another chance, and I know I don't deserve one. I want to believe in God, in absolution, in forgiveness. But. "I'm not sure I think that's a thing for someone like me."

"Do you think your family would agree with you?"

My heart sinks. "No." My parents are pissed at me, and rightly so, but they haven't given up on me. Gabby forgave me, even after the shit I dragged her through. "But maybe I think they're wrong."

"Maybe that's why you haven't told Jenna everything," Cecily says. "Because deep down, you don't think she could know what you've done and love you."

My mouth goes dry. It's true, but I don't know what to do about it. The idea of losing her feels like it's going to destroy me, but maybe by hanging on, sticking around when I know I'm not good enough for her, I'm just setting us both up to have our hearts broken. "Yeah," I say quietly. "I think you're right."

"What makes you think you're so unlovable?"

I have answers, but I can shoot every one of them down myself, so I don't feel the need to utter them in my own defense. "I don't know."

Cecily eyes me for a moment, but when I don't offer up any more, she nods. "Think about it this week. And we'll talk about it at your next session. We have another before you go on tour?"

"Yes," I say. "While I'm gone, can we meet over the phone?"

Cecily smiles. "Glad you asked. We can absolutely work that out. Get to your meeting, Felix. I'll see you next week."

TWENTY-SEVEN

Felix

Gabby texts me at least twenty times the morning of Anna-Marie's wedding. Do I have the address to the reception center? Do I remember where to park and where to enter so Anna-Marie won't see us arrive? Did Alec and Jenna really agree to this? Because Josh already cancelled on the band they'd originally booked, and if we don't show up, we will have ruined the wedding.

I do my best to reassure her. I even send her a picture of Jenna and Alec all dressed up for the wedding. I'd much rather send one of Jenna and me, but there can't be photographic evidence. I'm glad we're only talking about getting through the tour, because the idea of never taking a picture of us together for the first four years of our relationship is gut-wrenching.

While we're getting ready to go, I check to make sure my new chip is in my pocket. Cecily is right, these last thirty days mean more than the ones in rehab. I could have walked out the door there any time, but I was also surrounded by structures to help me stay clean. Out here, there's nothing between me and a dealer but my own commitment, and it feels pretty damn good to know I can do it.

I follow Jenna into the kitchen and we kiss against the pantry doors. She's wearing the enormous rock Alec gave her a week ago, but I try to focus on the way she feels in my arms, the sensation of her hands in my hair. I'm starting to understand what she means when she says she believes in the story. It's our story, and that matters more than all the lies Alec can tell.

We arrive at the venue and set up—Anna-Marie and Josh are getting married in a pavilion on the beach, and then retreating for a reception in the courtyard of this old ranch house covered in ivy and exposed wood. It's very rustic, and their wedding planner has decorated the place in silver and blue and sparkles that somehow manage to look classy.

It's not until then that I realize I've gone straight from a concert that turned into a proposal to a performance at a wedding. I'd say fate must be trying to tell me something, but really what I wish is that it would just get out of my damn way and let Jenna and me figure it out on our own.

Still, standing in the middle of the wedding decor, I'm hoping this might be some sort of preview of my own future. I've been living with her and Ty (and Alec, I suppose, though he's thankfully been avoiding us) for a week and a half now, and getting to be part of their daily lives is even better than I'd imagined. Eating meals together, playing video games with Ty, working on songs with Jenna, the three of us curled up on the couch watching movies before Ty's bedtime, and then making love to Jenna late into the night—it's the life I never even thought to dream of until mere weeks ago, and yet it feels like the one I've been longing for my whole life.

Though I really could do without the ex-boyfriend living in the closet.

Jenna runs a mic check, and through a window I see Gabby crossing the lawn in her blue maid-of-honor dress, flanked by two girls in the exact same outfit. One of them is black and the other's Hispanic, and I assume they must be Josh's sisters-in-law. They're followed by three men in suits—two dark-haired Puerto Ricans who I presume to be Josh's brothers, and a white guy (his friend Ben, I think?) who's wearing a bright green t-shirt under his suit coat instead of a white shirt and tie.

I can only hope Anna Marie already knows about *that*.

"All right, guys," I say, closing the blinds so no one sees us set up. "We've got forty-five minutes. Tops."

From behind the drum set, Roxie swears. "Get over here and help me with this thing," she says to Leo, and they both squat behind the drum set, followed by crashing and groaning noises.

Jenna shoots me a look, and I smile.

"So," Alec says to me. "Do you know who's going to be here?"

"My sister." And then I realize he means who from the industry. "Oh, I don't know. After we play you could talk to Josh. I bet he could point people out to you."

"You know the guy," he says. "Maybe *you* should talk to him."

"Right." What I actually do is text Gabby and ask *her* to ask him—now, before the wedding, before he's surrounded by guests. *If he's annoyed*, I text, *tell him it's the price for the look on his fiancée's face when she sees AJ is playing her wedding.*

On it, Gabby texts back.

"Damn it, Leo," Roxie shouts. "You stepped on my foot. These boots aren't steel-toed, you know."

"Guys," Jenna says, peeking out through the blinds. "Shut up. It's the bride." We all crowd around the windows and peer through the cracks in the vinyl slats. I've only met Anna-Marie a couple of times, and most of those I was high, but I expected her to be the type to pick a sleek, tight wedding dress. The dress she's wearing is actually more of a princess thing, with lots of fluffy gauze in rosy colors that complement the off-white of the rest of the skirts.

She looks gorgeous, which Anna-Marie always does, and also nervous as hell.

I smile. She's got my sister waiting for her, and her bridesmaids, and then ultimately Josh. I can't help but think about what it would be like to be out there waiting for Jenna. I wonder if I'd be nervous about getting married, about seeing her in her dress, about all the people watching us take this huge step.

The thought doesn't make me nervous now. I want it—that promise of forever with her. I know it's crazy, but a lot of things are crazy about us.

"Okay," Alec says. "Crunch time."

We get our instruments set up and tuned, and then get out of the way of the caterers, who are bringing in what look like foil-wrapped ballpark hot dogs by the dozens.

Is Anna-Marie seriously serving HOT DOGS at her wedding? I text to Gabby.

She doesn't answer, no doubt because the wedding is underway. She has, however, texted me a list of people in film and music who will be attending, and I pass that Alec's way.

We all hide in the kitchen, where the caterers indeed hand us some hot dogs and condiments. Leo makes a series of dick jokes that Roxie alternately giggles and glares at, while Jenna and I lean against the counter and try not to look like we're together. Alec sits next to the stainless-steel sink and Googles my list of professionals on his phone, finding pictures so he can casually recognize them between our sets.

As the reception begins, Gabby ducks into the kitchen with a stack of t-shirts with the hashtag #teamjoshamarie emblazoned across the front.

"Seriously?" Alec says.

"Seriously," Gabby says, and she hands the shirts out to each of us. "Wear them."

Leo sifts through the shirts and pulls one out for himself.

"That's too small for you," Roxie says.

"Says you," he returns.

We decide to hide the shirts when we go out on stage. Gabby uses Alec's mic to announce that she has a surprise for Anna-Marie, and then announces the band. There are some screams and cheers from the crowd, loudest of all from Anna-Marie, who clings to Josh and jumps up and down as Alec and Jenna

239

stride out on stage.

The rest of us follow while Gabby gives us a look of exaggerated annoyance. "Um, guys?" she says. "Aren't you forgetting something?"

Leo busts off his jacket to reveal the Joshamarie shirt, and the rest of us tug ours on over our clothes. The cheers are even louder this time, and we all do a quick tune check and then start to play "Forever for You," which is Anna-Marie's favorite ballad from the new album. Jenna and Alec are both playing their instruments, which means they have to do less staring into each other's eyes, but they still manage to pull off some loving glances that make me at once proud of what a good actress my girlfriend is and annoyed Alec can't use any of his acting skills off-stage to be less of an asshole.

Apparently these shirts are the wedding favors, because guests begin to grab them off the tables and pull them on over their wedding clothes. Josh's friend Ben pulls off his tux coat and his green shirt to replace it with #teamjoshamarie, and kisses a guy with spiky dark hair wearing sneakers with his suit that I assume must be Ben's husband, Wyatt.

Anna-Marie grabs Josh and pulls him to the center of the floor. People gather around the tables circling the room, giving them space to dance. Josh kisses Anna-Marie and guides her around the floor, and I'm glad this song is easy to play, because I'm at once watching them and thinking about what it would be like to dance with Jenna with everybody watching.

I wonder if we'd look as happy as these two do. I'm almost positive we would.

After the ballad we play a set of Anna-Marie's favorite songs, which Josh somehow got out of her without ruining the surprise. Alec takes a few requests from the audience, and a dark-haired girl wearing what looks like a crocheted tube-dress requests Shane Beckstrom's "I'll Take You Back," which Alec wisely ignores. Between songs, Anna-Marie hugs Gabby, and I see her thanking my sister for getting us to play.

240

At least today I've been a decent brother. I could use a few more of those days.

Between sets, we get a chance to mingle. Anna-Marie and Josh are greeting their guests, of which there are literally hundreds, ranging from young Hollywood types, to old rich couples, to actors I recognize from the times I've watched Anna-Marie's strangely addictive soap, to a cluster of people with clothing twenty years out of date that I can only assume came in from Wyoming, and a group I gather from my limited high school Spanish flew in from Puerto Rico.

Gabby comes over and grabs me by the arm, and she and Will find me something to drink that doesn't have alcohol in it. We're standing in the corner talking about the ceremony when I notice Alec has Jenna on his arm and has cornered one of the Hollywood types who's wearing the suit equivalent of skinny jeans and a man bun.

"We've been looking for some soundtrack work," Alec says. "We're really good at writing to story, and can work around themes and plot lines if the money's right."

Damn right, they write to story. Jenna looks a little uncomfortable at this pronouncement, but she covers it with a sip of her champagne.

"Actually," Man Bun says. "Are you available next Saturday? I got a phone call this morning that Randall Wex is in rehab again, and he was supposed to play the VMAs, but his people say he won't be out in time."

The words *rehab again* get my heart going, and I take a drink of my punch and almost wish it was alcoholic.

Alec is probably about to shit his pants, but he covers well. "Hmm," he says, looking to Jenna. "It's right before we leave for tour. Could we do that?"

She smiles. "I think we could squeeze it in."

Man Bun nods and pulls out his phone. He actually says, "I'll have my people call your people," and Alec gives him Phil's phone number.

241

I should be excited about the prospect of playing the VMAs, but I find myself thinking it's just another chance for Alec to wave the engagement in my face. I wonder if I'm going to feel this way every stop on the tour, or if it's just the prospect of watching Jenna and Alec kiss for national TV.

When they finish with Man Bun, Alec sweeps Jenna over to us. "Did you hear that?" he asks.

"Yeah," I say. "The VMAs. You really think they'll call?"

"We can hope." He grabs a new glass of champagne from a passing tray. Then he turns his brilliant, performer-Alec smile on my sister and Will, as if Gabby hasn't already met the all-too-real Alec at practice. "Thanks for giving us this opportunity."

"Sure," Gabby says. "Thanks for playing for me." But she eyes Alec's arm around Jenna's waist, and sounds significantly less excited about it than she used to be. She leans into Will, who kisses her on the top of her head. I have to admit, I haven't taken the time to get to know Will overly well, which is mostly my own selfish embarrassment. I know he can't be fond of me after what I did to Gabby during the two years they've been together, but I need to get over myself and make an effort.

Keeping this huge secret from him hasn't helped—but I can tell he's a good guy, and really great for Gabby. And though neither of them are the type for PDA, it's pretty clear every time the two of them are together how much he loves her.

I'm glad she's had him by her side the last couple years, while I was off campaigning for World's Shittiest Brother. For Will's part, he doesn't seem to hate me for all the pain I've caused her, and in fact has been nothing but cool to me. Even though now he thinks I'm some perv who calls phone sex hotlines when I crash in his living room.

Thanks again for *that*, Gabby.

"Must be pretty cool to see your brother play with a pop band, huh?" Alec says. I'm not sure if he means this because orchestra is boring, or because he's so famous she should be grateful to be associated with us, but Gabby waves a hand dismissively.

"I'm used to it," she says. "Our sister Dana breathes and she gets a professional award. Felix farts and he gets a part in a symphony."

I laugh at that image, and Will grins, but Alec hardly seems to hear her.

"Hey, babe," Alec says to Jenna. "Did you get a chance to show Felix's sister your ring?"

I reach into my pocket and wrap my hand around my sixty-day chip.

Jenna's smile wavers, and she looks at Gabby, who stares back. I'm pretty sure they're communicating one of those endless apology loops with only their eyes.

If Alec notices, he keeps up the act, still smiling at Gabby. "Sorry we didn't get a chance to see you after the show. Felix told us you were there, but it was a hell of a night."

Will looks from Gabby to me, and then to Alec. "Yeah, congratulations," Will says, and he sounds like he means it, but I know he can tell something is off about all this. I already regret making Gabby promise not to tell him. It's not like Will is going to talk to the press, and I don't see him blurting it out over cauliflower pizza at guys' night with Josh and Ben.

"Thanks, man," Alec says, and nudges Jenna.

"Oh, yeah," she finally says. She shifts her champagne to her other hand and holds out her ring.

Alec looks me right in the eyes, and he smiles. I down the rest of my punch, now wishing it was a glass of goddamn vodka.

"It's beautiful," Gabby says, though with how morose her voice sounds, she might as well be complimenting Jenna on her fine choice of burial plots.

"Thanks," Jenna says, no more enthusiastically.

Alec looks around at the exposed beams of the arched ceiling. "What do you think of this place, babe? Maybe we should look into it for our wedding."

Jenna takes her hand off Alec's arm and forces a smile, but

she looks ill. "Excuse me," she says. Then she stalks across the room and out the back exit.

I take one step toward her, but Gabby puts a hand on my arm.

Right. I can't follow her. Everyone would see, and Jenna's made enough of a scene that even if I'm casual about it, people might suspect. Alec gives me one more smile and then goes off to work the crowd some more. No doubt he'll have a wedding venue nailed down by the end of the night.

I catch Leo's eyes across the room, from where he's talking to Macy Mayfield, an actress I'm pretty sure is one of Josh's clients. Macy has her hand on Leo's bicep, and Roxie is standing behind them glaring daggers, but Leo is looking right at me. He cocks his head toward the door where Jenna left, and I nod.

Leo extracts himself from Macy, and I appreciate what a damn good friend he is, even though probably he was just using Macy to make Roxie jealous. "I'll be right back," I say to Gabby and Will, and I make a casual round of the room—accepting compliments from several family members on the music, and dodging the girl in the tube-dress, which is so short it rides up her butt cheeks. She actually licks her lips when she looks at me.

No, thanks.

As I approach the kitchen, I see Jenna and Leo standing down the hall from one of the staging rooms. Jenna is still wearing her #teamjoshamarie t-shirt over her dress, and she's hugging her arms to her chest. She gives me a weak smile, which I return.

"What's Alec's deal?" Leo says as I approach. "Why can't people just admit what they're feeling instead of being douches about it?"

Jenna raises an eyebrow. "Seriously, Leo?"

"What?" Leo is the picture of innocence.

"You and Roxie?"

Leo squirms a bit, and stares at his glass of champagne. "I don't know what you're talking about."

"Dude," Jenna says. "It's obvious to everyone that you want each other."

I lean against the wall next to them and nod.

"No way," Leo says. "Roxie is just like that." He finishes his glass, and then hesitates. "Do you really think she wants me?"

That answers the question of whether they're together and trying to hide it. "Obviously," I say.

Jenna nods.

Leo shrugs. "Whatever. Even if she did, she'd just sleep with me once and drop me. That's how Roxie is."

Jenna shakes her head at him. "Leo, that's how *you* are."

He nods into his empty glass. "Yeah, okay. Good point."

I'm about to say something about him being far less douchey than Alec when the devil himself sticks his head into the hall. "Guys!" he shouts, "we're up for our second set!"

We all exchange weary glances, and head back to the stage to finish the show.

TWENTY-EIGHT

Felix

The next morning, Jenna and I are lounging in bed. Alec has left the house, and Ty spent the night at his grandparents' place, so we have a rare morning to ourselves. There's a strip of sunlight from between the curtains falling across the bed and for some reason it makes me think of Garfunkel, this fat old cat my grandma used to have when I was a kid. He was mean as hell normally, and didn't like people—especially little boys who tried to ride their Power Rangers action figures on him—but he loved lying in this block of sunlight that came in from the narrow window by the front door. He'd lie there, soaking up the light, his tail twitching occasionally, purring away like an arthritic motorbike.

I kind of feel like Garfunkel right now, lazily content, only instead of the sunlight, I'm basking in the feel of Jenna pressed up against me, her skin warm against mine. Jenna seems content enough too, despite the current topic of conversation—Alec.

When we left the wedding yesterday, I stayed to help Gabby clean up, and then hit a meeting, so I missed Jenna chewing out Alec for being a dick. I run my hand through her hair as she tells me about it.

"So then he's like, 'Be smart, *Jenna*. Don't throw everything away, *Jenna.*' God. He makes me hate my own name."

"Jenna," I say, trailing my fingers along her bare shoulder.

She leans close and kisses me, soft at first and then deeper. "Well, when *you* say it—" Her phone rings, and she sighs, reaching to get it off the nightstand. "It's my parents," she says. "Hello?"

I can hear Ty's voice on the other end of the phone, though I can't make out what he's saying.

Jenna looks confused, and then she holds the phone out to me. "He wants to talk to you."

I take the phone, and climb out of bed, stretching and reaching for my boxers and a t-shirt. "Hey, kid."

"Felix!" Ty says. "Nana says that it's the fifteenth."

"Great. Did you call just to tell me that?"

"No," he says, like this is the stupidest thing he's ever heard. "But mom's birthday is the twenty-fifth, and twenty-five minus fifteen is ten, which means I only have ten days to finish—" his voice hushes "—my secret surprise. You said you would help me work on it, right?"

"Yeah," I say, and I hear Jenna groan. I turn toward her. "You're not listening to this, are you?"

"No," she says, tugging a white cotton tank top on above her underwear. "I just remembered I'm supposed to meet Allison about costuming in like fifteen minutes. I'm not going to make it."

I point toward my pants, discarded on the floor. "You can use my phone. I have her number."

"Felix?" Ty says. "Are you listening? This is an emergency."

"Because you need to finish," I say, turning around as Jenna picks up my pants.

"Yes. And I can't get Donald Trump's hair right."

I laugh. "Yeah, okay, kid. We can work on it tonight. How's that? And I'll find a picture for reference, okay?" I prop the phone up with my shoulder while I pull my boxers on.

"I looked at one," Ty says, "but I couldn't get the right color."

"It's tricky," I say. "I'm not sure he can, either." Jenna is quiet behind me, and I turn around, wondering if my phone wasn't in my jeans after all.

Jenna is sitting on the edge of her bed, holding my chip in the center of her palm.

My heart stops as she looks up at me.

She knows what it is. It's got the AA motto right there on the chip, as well as the number of days. I've known I had to tell her. I have to do it now.

A quiet peace settles in my gut. I can do it. I know I can. I'm scared, but I don't want to use.

"Okay, kid, I've got to go," I say. "But I'll see you later."

"Okay," Ty says. "Don't forget about the hair."

We hang up, and I set Jenna's phone on the edge of the bed, and then sit down next to her.

"Is this yours?" she asks.

I run my hands through my hair. "Yeah."

The corners of her eyes wrinkle. "How long have you had it?"

I hold my breath for a moment before answering. "Four days."

Jenna stares at me. This is so far from the response she was expecting. "*What?*"

I reach out and I take the chip from her. "I told you there was stuff in my past, right? Stuff I'm not proud of."

"Sixty-four days. You were on drugs *two months* ago?"

I close my eyes. I've gone out of my way to make it sound like this stuff is in the past, because it is. But not by much. "I had been out of rehab two weeks when we met."

"*Rehab?*" Jenna shifts on the bed, moving farther from me. "You were in *rehab?*"

"Yeah." I try not to focus on the inches she's scooted away from me, on the gap already widening between us. She stares at me like I've turned into someone she doesn't know.

"Oh, god," I say. "I'm telling this all wrong. Look, I didn't want to keep it from you, but I didn't feel like I could tell you until I was sure I could stay sober no matter how you reacted. I get it if you're mad. I'm an addict, but it's different this time, and I'm going to stay clean, I swear. You can drug test me every week if you want to. Every day. I can pass—I meant it when I said this wouldn't be a problem."

Jenna continues to stare at me while I babble, and I realize I spent so much time thinking about whether I was ready to tell her that I didn't spare a thought for what I should say.

"*This* time," Jenna says. She's backed herself all the way against her headboard, like she's scared of me. I reach a hand over and put it on top of hers, and she doesn't move toward me, but she also doesn't pull away.

"Yeah."

"As in, you've been clean before."

I cringe. I know how it looks. There's no way to tell from the outside how different it is this time. "I've been to rehab before. Twice. But this time it was my decision. I *begged* my dad to let me go. I wanted to get clean and I've done the work and I'm not going back." I can taste the truth of that. I'm ready for this. I'm not using again.

She stares at me some more, and I don't know what to say.

"I told you about my history," I say. "I told you I did heroin."

Her whole body is trembling. "Yes. But you didn't tell me you were an addict who was *just* out of rehab. *Again*. I've let you into my home, into my *life*, and I have a kid who thinks you're going to be his father. And, god, sixty-four *days*."

I'm shaking, too. "I know. But I swear, I didn't mean to lie to you. I guess I thought you'd have an idea how bad it was. You can't really do heroin without getting addicted."

"So I should have known," Jenna says. "You tried to tell me, but I was too stupid to get it, is that it?"

"*No.*" God, I should have told her the whole truth before, no matter the cost. "You're right. I didn't tell you, and that's my fault, not yours. But I swear to you, I'm clean now. I have a therapist and I go to meetings almost every day and—"

"You go to *what*? You've been going to meetings and you didn't *tell* me?"

She looks horrified now. Betrayed. And I deserve that. I've done this to her. I have to do the brave thing now, the thing I should have done a long time ago.

I need to be as open and honest with her as she's been with me. "Jenna, I'm so sorry. I should have been more honest with you. But it's not as bad as it sounds. I'm on maintenance drugs—a prescription—and they help me with the cravings, they make it easier to stay clean, and—"

"Maintenance drugs." She keeps repeating each thing I say, like every piece is more unexpected and horrifying than the last. "You're on narcotics."

"Prescription narcotics." My throat closes, and I taste salt. Tears are welling up in my eyes and I don't want to cry because I'm the one who hurt her, but I can't help it. "I'm sorry. But they're legit, I swear. You can talk to my doctor."

"I believe you," Jenna says. "But you've done this before. You're a *heroin addict* and you have no track record except that you relapse. You had been in rehab within *two weeks* of meeting me, and you didn't find that relevant. You're living in my house taking narcotics and you didn't feel the need to tell me about it, even though I left you with my son, even though you knew Mason watched my kid while he was high. You've been sneaking around and going to meetings and all those times we talked about the past, all those times *I told you* things hardly anyone else knows about me, you were holding onto this, knowing I thought the drugs were in the past, knowing I might make different decisions if I knew, and denying me that right. That's what you're telling me, right?"

I grip my chip in my hand, and feel the engraving embedding itself in my palm. "It's different this time. You can ask Gabby. She'll tell you. Before, I wasn't ready. I went for my family, but I wasn't ready to change. But this time I did this for me, because I want to be clean."

Jenna shakes her head at me. Tears are gleaming in her eyes. "And keeping this from me? Didn't you also do that for

250

yourself?"

The whole room seems to melt around me, like it's made out of wax.

I did do that for me. I hid things from her, even though I knew she would be upset if I told her. I thought about me, about what I needed, but I didn't stop to think about what I was doing to her, about how she would feel when I'd withheld this information for so long.

"I'm sorry," I say.

That isn't enough, it doesn't even begin to make up for what I've done, and I know it.

"How can I trust you're going to stay clean?" she asks me. "How am I supposed to trust that you're going to a safe person for Ty to love? Do you know how it'll destroy him if he believes he's finally going to have a father and then you get back on drugs and take that away from him?" Her voice shudders. "How it'll destroy me?"

My throat closes. I want to tell her she's enough, that Ty is enough, that this life we've just begun building is far, far more than enough to keep me away from the needle. But it isn't true, or maybe it is, but this is more true: *I'm* enough. "I know it's scary. But if you'll give me a chance, I swear you won't regret it."

Jenna looks at me for a long moment. Tears are running down my face now, and spilling from her eyes as well. "I want to believe you." She hugs her knees up to her chest. "But I can't."

I hear the sound of a blade dropping, the horrible finality of the ax swinging over my head. I'm crying and she's crying and I'm trying to figure out how we got from where we were minutes ago to here, now, with her looking at me and telling me she can't do this.

"I love you," I say.

She sniffles, and her breath shakes. "I know. I love you, too."

We both sit there for a minute, and I'm grateful at least that she's not screaming at me, that she's not yelling at me to go. Then I hate myself for thinking that, because it's what I deserve.

"I'm sorry I haven't been honest," I say. "But I'll tell you everything now. I'm ready. I did some bad things, but I can tell you, now."

Jenna puts up her hands as if to shield herself from the words. "Stop. I don't want to hear any more."

My blood turns to ice. "What?"

I did this to her. Most of it I did before I met her, and if I'd had a single bit of sense in my head I would never have touched the drugs to begin with. If I was a halfway decent human being I would have gotten clean the first time, or the second. I wouldn't have had to kill a girl before I was motivated to get my act together.

I would have done the decency of telling Jenna the truth, even if it meant I never got to love her at all.

And then she says the thing I've been dreading the most: "You need to leave."

"Jenna—"

"Don't," she says, cutting me off. "I don't even know how to process this. I thought we were going to be a family someday. I was ready to let my son believe you were the father he's been waiting for, and now . . ." She scrubs at the tears on her cheeks.

"I swear, Jenna. I would never hurt Ty."

"How many people did you hurt when you relapsed last time?"

I stare at her, stinging like she's slapped me.

She's right. I'm making her all these promises, but I can't, not really. I think this time is different, but is it? I've been lying, when I'm supposed to be honest. I've torn out the heart of the woman I love, just like I've done to everyone else who's loved me.

I've even been resisting therapy, telling my therapist that what I'm doing is for the best, but is it? The way Jenna is looking at me now—like I'm a dangerous addict, like Mason—I find I can't be sure she's wrong about that. God, there's no way I can know if what she's saying is true, and neither can she. That's the problem.

My body feels like it's breaking apart. "You really want me

to go?"

"No." Her voice breaks. "But I need you to."

I sob, and she sobs, and I want more than anything to wrap my arms around her and hold her through it. "Is this . . . is this it? Am I ever going to see you again?"

She nods. "I'll call you."

I wipe my face. "Sure. Right."

"No," she says. "I will. Let me think about it and then we'll talk. At least once more."

I don't know whether to be happy she's allowing me that, or horrified that the next time I see her may be the end. She looks up at me and I see the stark pain in her eyes, and I know. It's not just how recent it was. It's not just that I'm an addict, or that I've relapsed before.

It's because I lied to her. I did it under the guise of maintaining my sobriety, but I used that as a justification to lie, which is the opposite of recovery. It's the opposite of everything I'm supposed to be.

I put on my jeans.

"I'm sorry," I say. "I thought I was being honest enough, but I wasn't. The truth is, I used to lie about drugs all the time, and now I'm trying to tell the truth, but I suck at it, and I didn't mean to hurt you."

Jenna looks at the door. "Where are you going to go?" she asks. And I know what she means.

"I'm going to Gabby's. I'm not going to use." I find my keys and my phone, and I look at her one more time. Jenna's curled up on the bed, crying, and I know she's not going to make that appointment with Allison.

God. Ty. I'm not going to be there to help him tonight.

"I love you, and I'm sorry," I say. "Please call me."

"I will," she says through her tears.

And then I have to walk out the door, and leave her alone with what I've done to her, and somehow I manage to do it without entirely falling apart.

TWENTY-NINE

Jenna

I lose track of time after Felix leaves, just curled up in a ball of hurt and confusion and loss. I cry so hard I'm not sure how my body is even holding itself together anymore. I cry so long my head throbs like I'm hungover.

I cry and cry, lying in the bed that not so long ago was this perfect, safe haven of Felix and me, and now is empty and cold.

I can still see, through the blur of tears, the indent of his head on the pillow. The wrinkles on the sheets where his body was wrapped around mine.

I cry some more, remembering the look on his face when I told him I needed him to leave.

I cry some more, because I really did need him to.

Sixty-four days.

An addict. Rehab, again and again and again.

Meetings and therapy and maintenance drugs.

So, so many things he kept from me. This whole huge part of his life he lied about—by omission, sure, but it feels like lies all the same. All those times we'd talk and talk and I'd bare my soul to him, this person I felt I could tell everything to, and he was holding all this back, just talking around the edges of it.

The hurt is suffocating. The shame, too.

He thought I knew you couldn't do heroin without getting addicted to it, and maybe I did. I should have seen it coming. I should have known somehow. It's not like he didn't tell me he'd had problems with drugs before; he'd even said once that there was more he couldn't tell me yet. But I'd assumed, like an idiot, that it was years in his past, like my stuff. I'd assumed he'd done shit—maybe even some pretty terrible shit, like god knows I have—but that it wasn't part of his life anymore, not something that could threaten *us*, or Ty, or this future we were all building together. I'd assumed that if it was, he would have told me about it himself. Not let me find out like it's this dirty little secret, like I'm the wife finding another woman's lipstick on a dress-shirt collar.

Or like the friend finding the bank statement that shows her bandmate has been stealing money from her.

I sit up against the headboard, my face in my hands. Remembering now what it was like to confront Mason. Remembering the way he lied and wheedled, and then, when Alec and I wouldn't let him off the hook so easily, how he screamed at us and called me a bitch and Alec shoved him and Mason called him names, and it was like our friend had become this person we didn't even recognize.

Felix isn't like Mason, I know that. Even in this, in the finding out of his secret, he was still Felix. Still the man I love, still the man who loves me.

And in some ways, that makes it so much worse. It's easier to kick someone out of your life if you realize you never really knew them to begin with.

I love Felix, with everything in me. But the lies. The addiction. The lack of a track record of staying clean.

Can I live with this? Can I live with subjecting my son to this? What if I do, and it turns out I was wrong?

There's a deep pit in my stomach that tells me I may already know the answer.

I scrub at my face, helplessly. These thoughts are all too

tangled and raw and I can't work through them by myself. I need to talk to someone. Not Alec, that's for damn sure. Not my parents, either—there's too much baggage from my past, and they can't be objective.

That really leaves . . . Leo or Roxie.

I love both of them, but I've known Leo for longer, and something tells me he'd be better for this kind of thing. He's a weirdo, for sure, but when it comes to serious stuff, he can be surprisingly sane. I pick up my phone and call him, and in this choked, teary voice, ask him if he could come over and talk with me.

"Sure thing, Jen." He doesn't ask any more, which I'm grateful for. I don't want to spill it all over the phone and then have to do it again in person.

He must leave his apartment right away, because he gets to my house in under twenty-five minutes. I've managed to pull on some jeans and a hoodie—I'm so cold, just trembling—but I don't bother trying to make it look like I haven't spent the morning sobbing, because god knows I'm going to start up again as soon as I start talking.

It turns out I don't even make it that long. As soon as I open the door and see Leo standing there, in his "Virginia is for Lovers" t-shirt—with Virginia crossed out and Louisiana written in above it in marker, of course—with this concerned expression on his face, I burst into tears.

"Oh, man, Jenna." He wraps me in a big hug. "Come on. Tell me what's happening."

We go inside and sit on my couch, and I tell him everything. I tell him about how serious Felix and I were, how deeply in love. How clearly I saw this future with him, how much Ty wanted Felix to be his real dad. How much I know Felix wanted all that, too.

And then I tell him about this morning. About the chip and the truth coming out and me telling Felix he needs to leave. How I couldn't handle hearing any more, even though he had more to tell me.

"I'm just—" I draw in a shuddering breath. "It hurts so much, you know? That he kept so much from me. He was going to meetings almost every day, he said, and therapy, and all this stuff I didn't even know was part of his life. Like he'd tell me he needed to run errands or go visit his sister, and god, I don't know, maybe it wasn't a lie, maybe he did visit his sister too, but . . ."

"But he definitely wasn't being honest with you," Leo says.

My throat tightens. "Maybe it's stupid, being mad about that. I mean, meetings and therapy, those are good things, right? It's not like he was running out to shoot up. I have the drug tests to prove it."

"Yeah, but—" Leo starts, but I cut him off, the words spilling out of me.

"Should I even feel this way? Hurt like this? Betrayed like this? He came clean when I confronted him. Mason wouldn't have done that. Mason *didn't* do that."

Leo frowns. "Yeah, I mean, Mason would have probably just lied more, right? Like he would have said the chip was from forever ago or something. But, Jenna . . ." He trails off, and my heart sinks. Because there's part of me desperate for Leo to tell me I'm overreacting. For me to be totally wrong about this, so I can take it all back. Leo sighs. "I think it makes total sense that you feel this way. He's not Mason, but it's a *huge* deal, to be living with someone and not tell them you're an addict, especially if your sobriety is so new. That's . . . that's like a life-changing thing, and you deserved to know."

I tug at frayed threads of a rip in my jeans. "He told me he'd had issues with drugs. He told me had a past, a bad one. And god, Leo, you know I do, too. Drugs, yeah, but more than that." Leo doesn't know as much as Alec, and definitely not as much as Felix, but he knows the gist.

"I've done stupid shit in my past, too. So has Roxie," Leo says, and I nod. I've heard some stories, and I know Leo's done harder drugs in the past than either Alec or I have, though I very much doubt he has as many regrets about his past as I do. "But a few years in the past and sixty days is a big difference," he continues. "And a full-blown addiction, one that he had to go to rehab for, like, multiple times—that's something else entirely. He should have told you."

"Yeah," I say, quietly. "He should have."

I don't know how that would have gone, if he had, sometime back at the beginning—which feels so much longer ago than the two and a half weeks it's actually been. Would I have been more cautious? Would I have let him move in so soon? Would I have fallen so hard?

That last question I know the answer to immediately—yes. I was always going to love Felix.

But that doesn't mean I would have made the exact same choices about it. And while I can't bring myself to regret being with him, maybe it didn't need to go this way for us to be together, ultimately. Maybe it didn't need to end like *this*.

Maybe it wouldn't have needed to end at all. But now . . .

I rub at my forehead, which aches from all the crying, but not nearly as bad as my heart.

"Like, I don't even really know what it means that he's on maintenance drugs," I say, floundering in my thoughts. "I think those are narcotics, too? I mean, he's been living in my house, with my son, and taking drugs, and even if they're prescribed, I just don't . . . I don't know what to think. About any of it."

Leo pauses. "It sounds like he'd tell you, if you wanted to know. It sounds like he wanted to tell you more."

"He did. I know it hurt him that I wouldn't let him tell me, but I couldn't—" My voice breaks. "I couldn't hear any more. I didn't know if I could handle knowing more." I look up at Leo, and feel another tear squeeze its way out. "I still don't know if I can. What if—what if it's all worse than I think? What if—"

I don't say the rest of that thought: What if whatever I hear makes him become like Mason, someone I don't even recognize?

I can't imagine that with Felix, can't imagine he wouldn't still be the man I love, even if he's now the man I can't be with.

But it doesn't mean I'm not afraid of it anyway.

Leo leans back into the couch. "So you think it's really over between you guys?"

There it is, the real question.

A long stretch of silence passes before I can get the words out. "I think it has to be. There's no guarantee he can stay clean, and he's been to rehab before and it hasn't worked. And, god, if we were together and it happened again, if he went back to the drugs . . ." I squeeze my eyes shut. "I can't do that, and even more, I can't do that to Ty."

God, Ty.

My heart had already cracked apart at thinking of how much he wanted Felix in our lives, and how I'm taking that away from him. It feels just like when I took away Rachel years ago in that car accident, only this time I'm doing it on purpose. To protect him, sure, but it doesn't mean it won't devastate him.

But now it hits me that I'm going to actually have to sit him down and tell him this, that I'm going to have to look into my son's eyes and break his heart.

He won't hate Felix for it; I won't let him. But he might hate me.

"Maybe it doesn't have to be all or nothing," Leo says, after a moment. "Like, if it's him not having a track record for staying off the needle which is the real problem—and that's a legit problem, Jenna, I get it—maybe you guys could just take a step back. Cool this off for six months, see if he's still clean by then."

Part of me wants to grasp at this idea, cling to it like a lifering in the middle of the ocean, even though it's one I've thought of already, weighed and set sadly aside.

I grip my knees tightly. "It wouldn't work. The way Felix and I are—I mean, how quickly everything has happened for us, the feelings and us moving in together and seeing this future . . . We can't do halfway. I don't think we'd be able to slow down, not really." I swallow past the thick lump in my throat. "Ty, too. He

259

can't back off on how much he wants Felix to be his dad. And if Felix does start using again . . . I just can't risk it. Not with Ty."

Leo stares down at his hands. "God, I'm sorry, Jen. This sucks so bad. I can't even tell you."

A little smile manages to tug at my lips, despite everything. "You don't need to, Leo. I know."

"You really love him. Even after all this."

I nod. "Yeah, I do."

And then I'm thinking again of the look on Felix's face when I told him to leave, of him apologizing and crying, and god, even though he hurt me, I want to take his hurt away, too. Even though he lied to me, I want to be there for him through this, to support him through an addiction that must be brutal and painful and scary as hell.

But I can't. Even if I could take that risk for myself, I can't take that risk for Ty.

Which means I'm going to have to hurt Felix even more.

"But I still have to end it." The hopelessness threatens to overwhelm me, drown me. "I have to."

Leo puts his arm around me and pulls me in against him. "I get it. But if I were you, I'd still listen to everything he has to say first."

I look at up him. "Really?"

Leo thinks about this for a bit, like he knows what he says is true, but he needs to figure out why. "Because you don't want to break up with him and then spend the rest of your life never knowing the full reason behind it, you know?"

He's right. I know he is.

Even if I don't want to hear all the details, I need to, or I'll always wonder.

I sniffle against Leo's shirt. "You're really good at this, Leo. You're a good friend."

"Yeah, well, that and gator hunting. Two highly prized skills."

"Don't forget playing bass."

He shrugs. "Eh. Don't tell my bosses, but I'm really only

passable at that one."

We don't say much more, and he holds me while I cry again, while I shore myself up for talking to Ty later today. For talking to Felix, when I can bring myself to do so.

And I can't help but think of the story Alec and I were telling, the one I believed was true even if Alec and I weren't the ones in it.

The one I believed was Felix and me, and always would be. Soul mates.

But just because we're that—and something deep in me can't let that go—doesn't mean we get the story, the happy ending. Maybe that's all it ever was, after all—a story, and nothing more.

Without him, I can't see myself ever believing in it again.

THIRTY

Felix

When I leave Jenna's house, I don't go looking for a dealer or cruise by any of my old hangouts. I don't let myself add up how much heroin I could afford with what's in my bank account. Instead I call Gabby, and an hour later I'm crying on her couch—or my couch, I suppose, because I've just given her more than the thing is probably worth plus paid her back for the storage of my cello.

I owe her, and this may be my last chance to do so while I still have a job.

Gabby sits on the floor next to the couch with her hand on my shoulder. "God, Felix. I'm so sorry."

I shake my head. "It's my own fault. I messed it up. I always knew I wasn't good enough for her and so I lied to her and it's all my fault."

Gabby shakes her head. "You love her, Felix. You made a mistake, but you did it for a good reason."

My eyes are streaming and my nose is full of snot and I sound like I have the cold from hell, and I hate myself for it. "No. I did this. I did *all* of this. It's about time karma came back around and bit me in the ass for all the horrible things I've done."

Gabby squeezes my shoulder. "This isn't because of Katy."

I sob. She's right, of course. This isn't because of Katy because Jenna doesn't even *know* about Katy. I would have told her, but she didn't want to know, probably because she can already tell what a terrible person I am and doesn't want to have to hear it.

"Karma isn't a thing," she says. "I know too many bad people who have everything, and too many good people with shitty lives to believe that."

She's right. It isn't karma, just the direct results of my own actions. "I should never have done this," I say. "I should never have taken that job. All I did was hurt her."

Gabby sighs and rests her head on my arm. I kind of hate her for sympathizing, because I don't feel like I deserve it, but at the same time, I crave it.

"I want to believe in something," I say. "I don't know if it's God or what, but I want there to be forgiveness for me, and healing for Jenna, and a second chance for Katy. But it's just wishful thinking. If there is a God, I'm damn well going to hell."

Now Gabby has tears in her eyes, and I hate myself for doing that to her, too.

"I wish I could take it back," I say. "All the pain I've caused. All the people I've hurt. God, Gabby, you're the best sister ever, and all the rest of us do is make you feel like shit."

"That's not true. You're a good brother. You went through a bad patch, but remember back in high school? You always stuck up for me." She pauses. "Even when I was mad at you for hitting on my friends."

I manage to give her a flicker of a smile. "You were mad because it worked."

"I was," Gabby says. "You know I'm going to be here for you, right?"

"I know. But not all the time. You have to tell me if it's too much, and I can lean on someone else."

Gabby nods. "Okay. Not all the time. But every time you really need me."

"I know," I say. And it's true, because she always has been, even when I didn't like the way she went about it.

Especially then.

"Don't do that to me again," Gabby says. "I mean it. Don't go back on the drugs."

"I won't," I say, and even though my heart has turned into this howling pit and I feel like both the couch and I are falling through an endless void, I mean it.

"Do you want to use?"

I do, but that desire is buried beneath the part of me that wants to fight through this, that wants above all to survive.

"A little," I say. "But most of me knows there's nothing in the world so bad that doing heroin can't make it worse."

Gabby squeezes my arm, and she just sits with me while I cry my eyes out.

And even if she can't take the pain away, it helps.

Jenna doesn't text me until the next morning. *Can we talk?* it says.

Yes, please, I answer.

Can I come to you?

My gut twists. I wonder if she wants that because she doesn't want to have to kick me out of her house twice. *Of course,* I answer. *I'm at Gabby's.* I give her the address.

I have the place to myself this morning, because Gabby had a shift at the hospital, and Will went off to a coffee shop to write. I'm not sure if he did that because I'm hanging out in his space, but he didn't seem resentful, which I appreciate, though I make a note to ask Gabby if I ought to go back to Dad's tonight.

Dad doesn't know a thing about Jenna, and I'm not sure I can explain now how such a short relationship can have meant so much.

When Jenna arrives, she's put on heavy eye makeup, but it

doesn't hide that she's been crying.

"Hey," she says.

"Hey." I want to put my arms around her, but instead I let her in to the apartment. She takes my couch, and I sit in a chair across from her.

Jenna takes a deep breath, and I brace for her to tell me it's over. "I talked to Leo," she says. "About everything. I hope that's okay. I didn't know who else I could tell."

I nod. I'm glad she found someone to talk to, at least.

"Leo says that you screwed up, but you're not like Mason, because if you were, you would have just told me the chip was from forever ago, and that would have been it."

"Everything I told you was true."

"I know," Jenna says. "But you left a lot of things out."

"I know. I'm so sorry." I want to ask for another chance, but I get the sense Jenna's already composed what she wants to say, and I doubt anything I say now can sway her. My chest aches, and my ears pound, and I want at once for time to stop right here and to get it over with.

"I want to hear the rest of it," Jenna says. "You said there was more."

That surprises me, and I feel a tiny flicker of hope I immediately want to smother. "There's not really more news. Just the details."

Jenna nods. "I wasn't sure if I wanted to know, but Leo says I need to hear it, or I'm going to break up with you and then never know the full reason why."

The force of those words stuns me, and I pause. "So it's over."

Tears fill her eyes. "Will you please tell me?"

"Yeah. Of course." And even though this conversation now feels like it's post-mortem, I find I still want her to know. I love her, and I want her to know who I am, even if it means she doesn't love me anymore.

"I was miserable at Juilliard," I say. "I told you that before."

Jenna nods.

"I was lost. It was like I'd been on this road forever, and I finally got where I was going, and it wasn't at all where I wanted to be. Everything sucked. School wasn't as exciting as I thought it would be, and I didn't have to work as hard as I thought I would, and I dated a bunch of girls, but I'm not all that into casual sex, and that sucked, too."

Jenna is curled up on the couch with her legs underneath her, listening.

"And then one time," I say, "I went to this party. I'd never done drugs before—I didn't even drink much. But I was so unhappy and someone handed me a pipe and I didn't even know what it was, but I thought, what the hell?"

I rub my forehead. "I didn't find out until later that it was heroin, and when I did, I didn't care. It was like I was lifted out of the pit I was in and suddenly floating through the life I'd always wanted, but didn't know how to have. At first it was cheap and good but pretty soon I started needing more, and then I switched to needles and after that I had to be high all the time."

I keep going, telling her about how I stopped caring about everything else, how I stopped trying at school, but still covered for a full six months in New York before I got arrested and stayed in jail overnight and then sold out everyone I'd ever done drugs with because I was a rich boy afraid of prison. I tell her about getting kicked out of school and telling my parents and going to rehab once, and then twice, and staying clean for six weeks before I relapsed again.

"After that, I was gone for more than a year," I say. "I'd burned all my bridges. My family wouldn't help me anymore. I ended up working at a convenience store for drug money and living in a house where all the cereal had weevils and one of the guys who crashed there liked to piss in the houseplants—which were fake."

I take a deep breath. "And then my dealer ODed, and the house got raided, and I was out of drugs and a place to stay, so

I started buying Fentanyl, and did that for a couple weeks, until I got scared. And when I ran out of druggie friends' couches to crash on, I found a new heroin dealer and started picking up girls to do drugs with just to have a bed to sleep in at night."

Jenna's eyes are closed now, and she's curling in on herself, and I want to stop, but I can't. She needs to know. She deserves to know.

Even if I already know she won't be able to forgive me for this last part. I tell her about Katy, how I picked her up and bought drugs, and we went home to her place. I tell her about waking up next to her dead body, how I called 911 and gave them the wrong name and then had to explain that to the cops. "The worst part is that I shot her up. I put that heroin in her arm, and I've thought a thousand times about whether I did it wrong. I don't think I did, but I can't be sure, because all I was thinking about was getting high."

Jenna's crying now. Tears stream down her cheeks.

"I Googled her later," I say. "I found her obituary." I take a deep breath. "She had a sister."

Jenna's eyes open, and her breath shudders, and I know she's thinking about Rachel. And I hate myself for the things I've done, for the person I am.

"I'm sorry," I say. "I wish I could change it, but I can't. And I know you can't love someone like me, and I'm sorry I didn't tell you everything from the very beginning, so you never would have thought that you could."

Jenna shakes her head. "I do love you."

My breath shakes. "Still?"

"Yeah," she says. "Always."

And for a split second, I hope she's going to say we can work it out. That this isn't as bad as she expected, that I can earn her trust back and she can forgive me.

"But I can't handle all this," she says. "I'm sorry. I know it's hypocritical. God knows I've done a lot of stupid things. I've made just as many mistakes, just as bad mistakes, but—" She winces, and I find myself wanting to comfort her, even though it's me who's getting my heart broken.

I can tell that hers is shattering just as hard.

"It's okay," I say. "I understand."

Jenna shakes her head violently. "I don't think you do. It's just—all that stuff I did, the guys I was with. Rachel and the car accident and—I hated myself *so much*, and I still hate myself— " Her breath catches, and she takes a moment to recover, and I'm struck with the horrible realization that her dark past has weighed on her heavier and wounded her more deeply than I ever knew.

"It wasn't your fault," I say. "What happened to Rachel."

She takes a deep breath and steadies herself. "Maybe. But I made a promise I would take care of Ty now. That I would be there for him, and be his mom, and I can't let anything be more important than that. I'm sorry, but I just can't take the risk."

She looks at me, and we're both crying again, and I wish there was anything I could say or do to fix what I've broken.

"I'm not going back on drugs," I say.

"I wish I could know that for sure."

We both sit there for a moment, staring at Gabby's rug, and I realize that's it. It's over. I'm now Jenna Rollins's ex, and as far as anyone is ever going to know, this never happened at all.

I don't have that picture of us together, and now I never will.

"I'll help you find a new cellist," I say. "I know a lot of musicians in the area, and I'll help you find someone good. There's a lot of people who would jump at the chance."

Jenna watches me for a moment, and then she shakes her head. "I want you to stay in the band."

I stare at her. "What?"

"Will you? I'll be leaving after the tour, anyway."

I shake my head. "No. It's your band. I'm not going to—"

"It's not because of you. I've been unhappy for a long time. Being with you made me realize how much, and I'm leaving no matter what you decide."

I hold my breath. I can't imagine seeing her, listening to her sing to Alec songs she once said would always be about me. I can't imagine going back to being near her and not allowed to touch her, this time because she doesn't trust me to.

But I also can't imagine never seeing her again. That feels like the worst thing of all. "Okay. I'll stay."

"Thank you," Jenna says.

I know I should leave it there, but I can't help myself. "You're going to find someone better than me. And that guy is going to be the luckiest person on Earth."

Jenna's face crumples. "No," she says. "I don't believe in that story anymore."

I gape at her, and I feel like my chair is tipping, and I'm falling into an abyss. "What?"

She stares down at her hands, which I can see are shaking. "I don't believe in the story anymore. I can't."

I didn't think I could possibly feel any worse, that there existed a pain beyond what I'm already drowning in, but . . . "No, please, no. I know I screwed up, but please. Don't let me take the story from you. You're going to find someone who's going to love you like I do, and I'm going to read about it and I'm going to cry, but I'm going to be so happy for you. You deserve that. You can't let me take it away."

"I'm sorry," she says, standing up to go. And even though she's right here in front of me I can't help but think that I've killed her, too. We're both crying, choking on our own tears, but as she moves toward the door, somehow she manages to say, "Ty still wants you to help him. Something about a surprise for me."

I blink at her. "Does he know?"

She nods. "Not the details, but . . . yeah. He knows."

"And he still wants to see me? You'd still let him?"

"Yeah. I don't think he's ever going to forgive me for this. But you can help him with his project if you want."

And now I'm crying for the way I've broken his heart, but at least there's one last thing I can do for them.

I can set the kid straight about who's really to blame.

THIRTY-ONE

Felix

When I show up on Jenna's doorstep that night, I'm pretty sure I look like hell. I haven't shaved in two days, and my face is puffy and my eyes red-ringed. A part of me doesn't know what I'm doing here, much less what I'm still doing in the band, but the rest of me understands.

I'm doing what Jenna asked because I love her, and love means doing what you can even when it rips your heart out. It's not something I would have thought myself capable of a few short weeks ago without risking my sobriety, but while I'm playing it safe and staying away from temptation, I'm not white-knuckling through. As much as it hurts, as much as I wish I didn't have to know this about myself, I'm proud I can give her what she needs.

She's too good for me, but maybe I'm not completely and totally worthless.

Ty answers the door, wearing a Lego Batman t-shirt over flannel pajama pants. "Hey. My mom's upstairs. She says she'll come down if we need her."

I jam my hands in my pockets. "Okay."

Ty is still standing in the doorway, not letting me in, and I wonder if Jenna was wrong about him wanting to see me.

"Are you a douche now?" he asks, his eyes narrowed.

I laugh despite myself. "Yeah. I guess I am."

He looks confused. "Mom says you're not like Mason."

"I'm not. But I used to be, and your mom is worried that someday I will be again, and she's trying to take care of both of you as best she can."

He gives me a look of consternation and backs away from the door. Like, literally, he backs up all the way out of the hall, each step carefully measured. "Did you bring a picture of the hair?"

I wave my phone at him. "We can find all the pictures you need."

Ty continues to back up through the house, only looking over his shoulder to get around the pointed triangular coffee table. He shows me where he's already laid out the pages of the birthday surprise, and points to a panel where he's drawn an angry-looking man with a cloud of eraser smears on top of his head.

"It doesn't matter what I do," he says. "I can't get it right."

"I have a feeling there's a hairdresser somewhere who feels the same way. Maybe several of them." I run an image search and we sit next to each other at the table, debating the various merits of the different hairstyles as if either of us has the artistic ability to render them with nuance.

"You should just say you're sorry," Ty says, still looking at the images on my phone.

"I did. She knows I'm sorry. But this is my fault, not your mom's."

"If you say you're sorry the person is supposed to forgive you."

I hold my breath, trying to think of a way to explain this so it'll make sense to him. "Did you tell your mom that?"

"Yeah. She said it was complicated." He frowns. "Adults always say that."

"Maybe. But does your life seem simple?"

He hesitates for a moment, and I can tell this isn't something he's ever been asked.

I click on a picture where Trump's hair appears to be unaffected by gravity. "We should try this one," I say. "And yeah, it's complicated. But I'm going to try to explain it, and I want you to listen, okay?"

Ty nods solemnly.

"Say you made a mistake," I say. "You were at a shop full of glass cases with lots of fragile things in them, and you forgot, and you ran down one of the aisles. But you couldn't stop in time and you slid into the case on the end and you knocked it over and you shattered everything inside."

Ty looks at me with wide eyes, and I smile grimly. "Would your mom forgive you?"

He thinks about that. "Yes."

"Would she still love you?"

This one is easier for him. "Yes."

"Would she let you in the shop again?"

"Nooooooo," he says.

I nod. "Your mom is going to forgive me for the things I did before I met her—"

"Drugs."

I let out a breath. I hadn't been sure how much Jenna had told him. "Yes, drugs. Which you should never, ever, ever—"

"I know not to do drugs," Ty says. "Everybody knows that."

I smile. "Except us douches."

He picks up an orange pencil to try to approximate the free-floating hair.

"She's going to forgive me for not telling her everything, too," I say. "But sometimes something is broken, and you can't fix it."

"Even with glue?"

The corners of my eyes start to tingle, and I swear if I cry any more my lids are going to permanently seal shut. "Even with glue. Didn't you ever break something that couldn't be fixed?"

Ty's pencil stops on the paper, and his voice wavers. "I had a Ninja Turtle, and his shell fell off. I glued it back on, and

Mom even tried super glue which you're not supposed to touch because it will glue your hand to your head, but she did it anyway for me and she still couldn't fix it and then she said we had to throw it away." He sniffles. "It was a Michelangelo, too."

I'm not sure how much of his tears are for the Ninja Turtle and how much are for the situation between us, but I'm willing to bet it's a mix. "Yeah. It's exactly like that."

Ty's face crumples, and he glares down at Donald Trump.

"It's okay, kid," I say. "You're going to have a dad someday."

"I want you to be my dad."

I nod. "I know. I want that, too. But I'm the one who messed it up. Not your mom."

And I feel like I should give him some substance abuse message now. Just say no, kid. Don't be like me. But he's already told me he knows not to do drugs, and I also know there's nothing some douche could have said to me at that age that would have made any damn difference when nineteen-year-old me was handed that pipe.

"I'm sorry, Ty," I say.

He hands me the orange pencil. "It still doesn't look right. You fix it."

And since I can't fix any other damn thing, I do.

I head from Jenna's house straight to a meeting, because if I don't, I'm just going to curl up on my couch at Gabby's and cry and wish I was high. Maybe I'm going do that anyway—Gabby did buy me a Breakup Tub from Fong's that I'm only halfway through—but it'll still be waiting for me after the meeting.

I go to a meeting in West Hollywood near Gabby's apartment. It's a hardcore NA meeting, always full of former junkies. Some of the meetings I go to are more general—alcoholics, sex and porn addicts, even people recovering from things like being controlling or food addictions. The core attendees of this meeting are a tight group of recovering meth addicts who go bowling together on Saturdays and have their morning coffee together at Joe's down the street.

A couple of them nod at me as I walk in—the bald guy with the Stones tattoos who's the de-facto leader of the social group, and the facilitator, who's a skinny guy in his early thirties who just passed three years of recovery from synthetic opiates.

The room is more somber than usual today, and the guy with the tattoos—Jeff—leans over to me as I sit down in the circle of chairs. "Did you know Ronnie?"

I remember Ronnie, a heavyset guy with a deep laugh who did a lot of heroin in addition to the meth. "Not, like, personally," I say.

Jeff moves over a chair and puts a heavy hand on my shoulder. "He ODed yesterday."

My stomach sinks. Ronnie wasn't a friend or anything—I've always declined invites to coffee mornings and bowling. But there's this thing about hearing about overdoses. Every time, I remember how easily it could have been me.

"I'm sorry," I say.

"Yeah, we all are. Just wanted to give you a heads-up."

That was a good call. The sharing will no doubt be all about that today, and it makes me feel bad that I want to whine about my breakup when these guys have lost one of their own.

I lost someone, too, though. And even if they judge me for it, I have to let that be real. The moment I start trying to avoid it, I'll be headed back to the needle.

The facilitator starts the meeting, and already a couple guys look like they're going to cry. Hell, I probably look like that, too, which may be why Jeff thought I might be friends with Ronnie. We read through the steps, and I listen. The step I'm working on always sticks out to me—right now I'm doing step four, making an accounting of everything I've done. It sucks, but

I'm doing it, making notes on my phone whenever I remember something else.

I've added a lot over the last two days.

When we get to the sharing part of the meeting, the room shifts. Some people slouch in their chairs and cross their arms. These are the non-sharers, people who don't want to be here or aren't comfortable talking to the group. Sometimes also people who usually share, but today are too tired or embarrassed by their latest slip or just have nothing to say.

Some of the sharers lean forward on their elbows or rub their hands together, clearly composing what they're going to say. Different meetings have different customs. Some expect you to go up to the front of the room to speak. Others let people talk from their seat. This meeting is arranged in a circle, and when it's time to share, we go around to the left. A lot of people pass, but most of the regulars talk about Ronnie, and how his overdose is affecting them. It's the opposite of a funeral, where instead of talking about the dead, they each share how much they want to get high to dull the pain, or how knowing he's gone makes them never want to touch the stuff again. A big guy to my right breaks down into tears and says he keeps hearing "Spirit in the Sky" playing from his phone, which was the ring tone he had set to Ronnie, and so all day he's just checking it over and over.

Then it's my turn, and everyone looks at me. I almost pass, because I didn't know Ronnie, but damn it, this is a recovery meeting and not a wake, and I've had a hell of a couple of weeks.

I have things to say.

"I broke up with my girlfriend," I say. "I'm in love with her—like really, crazy in love, but it's over now."

Faces around the room crease in sympathy, and I have to look at the floor to continue. There's a sign in the middle of the room, resting on the tile. *What's said here stays here.*

But I know what I'm about to say is going to follow me around for the rest of my life.

"The first time I went to rehab," I say, "it was because my

family found out I was using. I got kicked out of school, and my parents knew why, and they told me I was going to get treatment, and so I did. The whole time I was counting down the days until I could get out and get back to the drugs and be happy again. And one day I was mouthing off to my therapist, telling her how pointless all of this was, and she pointed out and said, 'there's the door.' I left, and I didn't look back. My parents didn't even know I was out before I found myself a dealer and got back on the needle.

"The second time I went to rehab, I thought I'd hit bottom. I'd sold something so important to me that I thought I'd never be able to part with it. I was ready to admit that drugs were a problem, but I still felt like without them I'd never be happy. Like I was resigning myself to this miserable life because the only joy I had in my life was also killing me."

I take a deep breath, and dare to look up. There's a lot of nodding happening. These guys have been there. They get it.

"By the third time I went to rehab," I say, "I understood that drugs only made me happy for a little while, and then after caused me excruciating pain. They'd destroyed everything I cared about—my ambition, my family, my music. I was ready to accept that even the most boring life was infinitely preferable to going back on drugs.

"And then I met this girl." I press my lips together, and it takes me a second to continue. "And for the first time in my life, I was really happy. Everything with her made me happy—being around her, giving to her, loving her, sex with her—all of it. It was better than drugs, because it was real."

I want the story to end there, but it doesn't. I've known guys who said they've lied to their twelve-step groups because it made them feel powerful, in control. If it stays in this room, then for one hour a week, they can be anything.

But I've always felt like the circle is a place for truth, especially truth that I hate.

"I told her I had a drug past," I say, "but I didn't use the words addiction, or rehab. I didn't tell her I'm on maintenance drugs, or in therapy, or going to meetings. I thought I had good reasons for that, but now I think it was all BS. I lied for so long and now I'm trying to be honest but I suck at it. And when I told her the truth, she said she couldn't trust that I was going to stay clean, and now it's over."

I'm getting a lot of sympathy from the room, now, which is what support groups are for, I suppose, but I still don't want it. "I did this," I say. "It's my fault for using, and for taking two and a half years to be ready to get clean. I did bad things and I have no track record of recovery. Just sixty-five days, which feels like an eternity to me, but really, it's nothing, right? And I get that. I don't blame her."

My eyes are starting to tingle, and I know I better finish up quick.

"But now I know that it doesn't matter if I can't outrun the past. I'm not going back to the drugs. Even if she's gone forever, even if I never feel happiness like that again, even if it takes years to get off Suboxone and feel completely normal again—I'm never going back to the heroin.

"That was fake happiness, and I don't want it. If I learned nothing else from her, I know real happiness exists, and I'm not accepting substitutes anymore, even if it's never mine again. I'm an addict, and I'll always be an addict, but I'm never going to back to where I was."

I shrug. "And I guess that's it," I say, even though I know how stupid it sounds to announce you're done when you could just stop talking instead.

"Thank you for sharing," the moderator says.

I want to leave. I want to walk out of the room to be sure no one says anything to me about what I said. If I have to hear from one person that they know how I feel, or that I'll get over it, or that I should maybe keep the one-year relationship rule because this is clearly what it's for, I'm going to have to sit in my car and grip the steering wheel again.

But I don't leave. I sit through the rest of the sharing. I don't really listen, but I stare at the sign in the middle of the floor.

What's said here stays here.

I know what it means. I'm not going to repeat what anyone else says outside of this room. But what I've said has to travel with me. It has to be with me every moment, forever. I have to remember how I feel now, and that memory has to be enough to keep me from taking the easy way out, every minute of every day, for the rest of my life.

I know I shouldn't be doing this for Jenna, because I have to do it for me. But for the first time I feel like I can do it for Jenna *and* for me, even if Jenna leaves the band and forgets me entirely. I can stay sober for me and her and Ty, and for Gabby and Dana and my parents and Ephraim and Katy. Not for one right reason, but for all of them.

When the meeting is over, I walk out without talking to anyone. And while I don't know where I'm going, I know it isn't back where I've been.

Between Phil and Alec, we somehow end up booking that performance at MTV's Video Music Awards. Playing at the VMAs feels surreal in a totally different way than playing Carnegie Hall did. The New York performance was something I'd imagined my whole life that didn't even come close to the high I got from the bumped-up dose of heroin I did afterward. Playing the VMAs isn't something I ever would have thought to dream of, but any excitement or anxiety I might have had about it feels distant now, muted, like I'm an electric instrument that's been unplugged.

Everything feels a bit that way, as if my mind has cut the cord because it can't stand to be in pain anymore. I said I didn't want any more substitutes for happiness, and I meant it, but I can't help but be glad for this: it does seem that there is actually a limit to how bad a person can feel, at least all at once.

Alec texts me a few days before, saying I should practice because we're not going to have a chance to get the whole band together before we perform. That should make me nervous, but really I'm relieved. I'm not sure I'm ready to see Jenna, to figure out what our relationship is going to look like now that even emotional intimacy is off the table.

And I really don't want to see Alec, because as awful as I'm feeling, I may very well punch him in the face.

I arrive and check in and am ushered back to the band's staging area, where Allison the costumer hands me a wardrobe bag. "This was supposed to be Mason's for the European leg of the tour," she says. "So I hope it fits. But you can't go out on stage at the VMAs wearing jeans and a t-shirt, and I don't care what Jenna says."

I take the bag and retreat into the dressing rooms, where I discover the clothes meant for Mason include a pair of bright green pants, a sparkly and equally bright multi-colored jacket with sides too small to actually button, and a chunky silver cross necklace bigger than my hand. I check the bag twice, but there's no sign of a shirt to go under the jacket, and I'm afraid there isn't meant to be one.

Still, I'm not going to argue. I get dressed and put on my black boots and look at myself in the three-sided mirror.

I look ridiculous.

When I emerge, the rest of the band is there. Roxy's pink hair is slicked down and she's wearing enough sequins to cover Los Angeles like snow, and Leo is wearing a strange tie-dyed tunic under his alligator vest that makes him look like a hippy-medieval Crocodile Dundee, so I gather I'm actually supposed to be looking like this. Jenna's clothes are a bit more her usual style, with the bling cranked up a few notches, and she turns and cringes at me. Her eyes linger on my bare chest.

"Is this how this is supposed to be worn?" I ask. "Seriously?"

"It was funnier when I picked it for Mason," she says.

We give each other agonized looks that have nothing to do with the outfit. Behind her, Roxie is sitting on one end of a couch and Leo has perched himself far on the other end, with his knees together and tilted away from her. Roxie eyes him like he's broken out in a pox.

I'm guessing Jenna's assertion they were into each other has made him self-conscious.

On the other side of the room, Alec is on the phone, probably with Phil, or Phil's assistant. "I don't care what the traffic's like. I need it now."

Roxie gets up and motions for Leo to do the same. "Your damn vest is askew again," she says. "Let me fix it."

Leo crosses his arms, his shoulders hunching. "It's cool. Allison will get it."

Roxie slides around the back of the couch and puts her hands on his shoulders. "You're a ball of tension. Let me massage you." Her hands begin to knead his shoulders, and Leo bends over, his torso lying flat across his thighs, face buried in his knees, and lets out a guttural cry of distress.

We're all staring at him. Roxie's hands are still poised in the air where his shoulders were.

"What are you so stressed about?" Roxie demands. "What's wrong with you?"

Leo lets out another cry. His voice is muffled by his tight pleather pants. "I'm in love with Roxie."

Alec lowers the phone. Jenna raises her eyebrows and glances at me. Roxie just cocks her hip and looks confused.

"Wait," she says. "Like, me, Roxie?"

Leo snaps up and spins around. "Do you *know* another Roxie?" he yells at her.

We all stare at them for one breath, two, three.

And then Roxie leaps over the couch and tackles Leo. She slams him sideways down on the couch with a knee on each side of his thighs, and kisses the hell out of him.

Leo digs his hands into her hair, destroying her carefully-shellacked hairstyle, and within seconds they're hardcore making out.

My whole body is getting hot. Alec is right—it's like being in a limo on prom night, only after my date has broken my heart. I'm happy for Leo and Roxie, but Jenna won't meet my eyes, and I can't handle it anymore.

I raise my hands in the air. "I'm out." I turn to leave the room, meaning to go wait for the rest of them in the hallway.

"Felix, wait," Jenna says.

And I turn around, because the truth is, I would wait forever for her. At this moment, four years feels like nothing at all.

THIRTY-TWO

Jenna

When Felix says he's out, I don't know if he means he's leaving the room, or the band, or our lives. I just know I can't let him go. Not completely. He turns around and looks at me, with that haunted expression he's had since I told him it was over.

I did the right thing, I've told myself, again and again like that might finally convince me. I did the right thing, even if Ty hates me and is heartbroken. Even if I feel like my own heart has been shattered into a thousand pieces and ground into a fine sand. Even though we got the latest drug test results back from Phil—less random this time, because I requested we all be tested—and I know Felix is still clean.

That can't have been easy. God knows I've wanted to drown my sorrows in alcohol these past few days, and my past has left me with an aversion rather than an addiction.

Felix is looking at me, waiting to know what I have to say, and I realize there's nothing I *can* say. I want to tell him I'm sorry, and I want him back. I want to be the good mom I failed to be when I was younger, and be sure I'm protecting my son. If I'm being honest, I also want a guarantee for myself, that if I tell him I made a mistake, he's not going to be back on heroin in a week or a month or a year and break my heart again.

"Please stay," I say. And, even though it's not fair, I know what I'm really asking is for him to not give up on me while I sort this out.

"Okay," Felix says. Roxie and Leo are still making out on the couch, and while I wish they'd chosen a better moment, I suppose that's been coming for a long time.

"Oh my god, could you two stop it for two seconds?"

When I turn around, I expect Alec is talking to Roxie and Leo. But no, he's staring straight at me, looking exasperated. He's hung up the phone on Michael, Phil's assistant, who's bringing Alec his spare guitar, because the one he brought has a stripped tuning peg.

"What?" I ask Alec. Because for once, Felix and I aren't doing anything that should make him angry. In fact, we're doing exactly what he wanted in the first place—staying away from each other. Roxie and Leo are oblivious to everyone else, and are getting frighteningly close to dry humping—or maybe just straight-up humping—right there on the couch in front of us all.

"What do you mean, what?" Alec asks. "If you're going to break up with him, fine. But both of you stop *emoting* at each other. We're here to work." He gives a disgusted glance at Roxie and Leo, but then turns his hard glare back on me.

I gape. "Now you're mad at me for *emoting*?"

Alec rolls his eyes. "You know what I mean. First you're going to live with Felix. Then you've broken up with him, but you want to keep him in the band. Now you two are back to making googly eyes at each other, but you're too chicken shit to do anything about it. God, Jenna, stop jerking him around and decide what you want already."

I flush. I didn't go to Alec for comfort about Felix, because I knew he was too pissed about the situation to be supportive. But if he thinks for one minute he has any right to judge the decisions I'm making, to judge *me* for trying to do what's best for me and for Ty—

"Don't fucking tell me what to do," I say.

Alec scoffs, and I want to grab him by the collar of his sparkly shirt and shove him against the wall. We haven't been together in a year, but Alec has always been my *friend*. I've had it with him making things more difficult when I most need him to be a decent human being.

"Someone needs to tell you what to do," Alec says. "Look at the decisions you make by yourself!"

I steal a look behind me at Felix. He's still here, though he's flattened himself against the wall, like he's trying to stay out of this conversation. I can't blame him. It was selfish of me to ask him to stay in the band, in my life, when probably he'd rather get away. Has he already realized I'm not worth sticking around for, that I'm too messed up, too crazy?

Felix glances at Alec, and then nods at me. There's this confident look on his face, like he knows what I need to do, and he's rooting for me to do it, but he isn't going to do it for me.

Felix, whose heart I've broken, who made a mistake, yes, but who has done everything I asked, and been nothing but respectful since. Felix is still here for me, even after everything.

Maybe Alec is right. Maybe I'm being unfair to him.

But at this moment, it's Alec I need to deal with.

I turn back around, fighting to keep my voice from edging up into hysterics. "I'm done, Alec. I'll play tonight, and I'll sing for the tour, but after that I'm out. So just get off my back before I walk out right now instead. You know damn well you can't sing these songs by yourself."

You'd think Roxie and Leo would take notice of this, but they're too busy gyrating on the couch to hear. I hold my breath. This wasn't how I envisioned breaking this news, but I'm not letting Alec stand by and tell me I'm messing everything up anymore, when the biggest mistake I've made was lying with him to begin with.

"Okay, look," Alec says, his voice steady, like he's trying to calm a wounded animal, which is condescending as hell. "I get it. I know you're not doing four more years. But do this smart, Jenna. What the hell are you in such a hurry for?"

"Because I'm unhappy. You used to care about that, remember? We broke up because neither of us was happy, and we tried to keep the band together, because we both loved that, if not each other. But I'm still unhappy, Alec. You may be fine having one-night stands for years and years, but I'm not."

"Please," Alec says. "I've heard so many stories over the years about what's going to make you happy. You want me, you want a career in music, you want to be able to support Ty, you want Felix, you want out. You're never happy with *any* of it, Jenna, and you need to stop destroying everything in your wake."

An icy wave washes over me. Alec knows about my past, and how hard I've worked to become someone who can take care of Ty, who doesn't just lash out and hurt everyone around her. Is that what I'm doing now? It doesn't feel like it, but I can't be sure.

Either way, it's no longer Alec's business.

I lower my voice. "I'm only staying because I made a commitment, but when the tour is done, it's over. I'm sorry, Alec, but you're not going to change my mind."

Alec throws his hands in the air. "What the hell, *Jenna*? You're in love with Felix, but that's over, even though he didn't do a single thing wrong. You know perfectly well he's not on drugs. We've got the test results. But one little thing goes wrong, and you're out."

"How many times do I have to tell you? That's none. Of. Your. Business."

"Like hell," Alec says. "Now you've decided the band doesn't make you happy either, so you're out, just like you were when we were having problems. The problem isn't me or the band or Felix. The problem is *you*. You're messed up and you need help, but you keep running away instead of just goddamned *dealing* with it."

My eyes are burning, but I'm not going to break down and cry in front of Alec. He's lost all right to know what's really going on in my head, not in the least because he's apparently lost all interest in that a long time ago. God, I thought we were still friends. I thought he still cared about me. And maybe he does, but only as a lost child he's trying to save. Only as this rogue element he's trying to control.

"Maybe you're right," I tell him. "But it doesn't change anything."

Alec glares at me. "I care about you too much to let you ruin your life."

I grit my teeth. "If you want to help, *stop helping*."

Alec shakes his head, undeterred. "I'm not going to let you push me away like everyone else."

"And I'm not giving you a choice." I spin around and fling open the door to march out of the room, not sure at all where I'm going. We've been designated this space by the stage crew, and anywhere else I go I'll just be in the way.

But I'm done dealing with the shit Alec's been giving me. I should have told him off a long time ago.

Before I leave, though, I turn to look at Felix. Alec has stepped into the corner and leans there with one hand on each wall. I meet Felix's eyes.

And as if he was waiting for me to give him permission, he follows me out.

THIRTY-THREE

Felix

I follow Jenna through the arteries behind the stage, glad to see the various techs and wardrobe people have decided not to gather outside our dressing room, even though some must have heard. We move past other dressing rooms and green rooms, past bustling staff and shouting managers and stylists who reek of hairspray with hands dyed by colored mousse. At the end of the hall we come to a room with spare sound equipment, and Jenna collapses onto an amp.

"Are you okay?" I ask.

"No. You?"

I lean against the door frame, where I can block anyone from taking notice of her. I'll dazzle them with the brightness of my outfit alone. "No," I say. I'm still stinging from the things Alec said, that Jenna's never happy, that she bounces from one thing to another.

She was happy with me. I was sure of it. But, as Alec would surely say, she was happy with him once, too.

Jenna lets out a slow breath. And while I don't want to disturb this tenuous peace between us, I need to know.

"Is he right?" I ask. "Was I just one more thing that was supposed to make you happy?"

"No." Her hands clutch her knees tightly over the silver fishnet stockings. "You and me were real. But he may be right that you're one more thing I'm running away from."

"If that's true, it was warranted."

Jenna shrugs, like she's not sure anymore, and while I want to cling to that spark of hope, the possibility she might decide she was wrong, I don't want her to do that just because Alec's shaken her faith in herself. She looks so small and alone and scared.

I can't take it anymore. I squeeze onto the amp beside her and put my arm around her. Jenna leans into my shoulder, and glances down at my bare chest.

"I'm sorry about the outfit," she says.

"I'm sorry I messed everything up."

Jenna shakes her head. "Alec is a dick, but he's got a point. I'm messed up. There's stuff I haven't dealt with and I don't know how."

I wish I knew the perfect thing to say, the thing that would give her the answer and make everything okay between us again. But I don't, so I just squeeze her shoulder. "We're all messed up. Just look at Leo and Roxie."

Jenna laughs and turns into me, leaning her forehead against my jacket. "I'd rather not. God only knows what they're doing by now."

I hold Jenna against me, closing my eyes and breathing her in and savoring the way it feels to hold her, when I wasn't sure I ever would again. And while it doesn't change any of the things that are broken between us, I feel a small ray of hope—like maybe, someday, we'll be able to put this back together.

It's not a promise of anything, but I'm sure as hell going to stick around and see.

Phil looks like he wants to kill us when he finally tracks us all down for our stage call. For such a small man—not much taller or bigger in general than Jenna—he can be downright terrifying, though I'm growing increasingly sure his general intensity is spurred on by his steady diet of Red Bull and antacids. "You're on in ten minutes," he says at Jenna. "Have you even done a sound check?"

"We'll be fine," I tell him. Jenna and Roxie will be using equipment that's already on the stage, and the truth is, if the rest of us sound terrible, it's not going to do any more damage to our career than we've already done. We assemble backstage, and Jenna stares at the floor while Alec alternates between glaring at her and huffing dramatically. Leo and Roxie still haven't stopped sucking face, even though Allison is bustling around them trying to fix what Leo's done to Roxie's hair.

We haven't stepped out on stage yet, and I already know this is going to be the most interesting performance of my life, not the least because I'm about to step out on a stage currently graced by Tina Fey.

Tina calls us on, and we walk out on the stage, all of us projecting a confidence that at least three of us don't currently have. Leo and Roxie are exchanging looks and smiling wider than I've ever seen—from Roxie, at least. I set up June while Jenna and Alec grab the mics and wave to the crowd, who clap and cheer uproariously. Alec has his backup guitar, which must have gotten here while Jenna and I were hiding, and Alec and Jenna hold hands and look as in love as ever, and before I'm even done tuning Roxie is looking at me, waiting for me to finish. I nod at her, and she starts to play.

The number we're doing—"When I Saw You Standing There"—is one of the faster songs on the album, and Roxie, fresh off the high of however far she and Leo got backstage, plays it even faster than normal. Alec turns under the guise of singing in Jenna's direction and tosses Roxie a look, but if Roxie notices, she doesn't slow down. I'm glad for the pace change, and more accustomed to following her now, so I focus on the music and play.

When it's over, Alec puts down his guitar and pulls Jenna into his arms and kisses her. The cheers swell, and I'm sure I'm glaring at them, but I don't frankly care who catches me doing that on camera now.

Tina Fey motions them over for a post-performance interview. Jenna leans giddily against Alec, and I can tell by the way her shoulders slump that she's leaning into how worn out she feels. I can't blame her. The sooner they get this over with and we all get off the stage, the better.

Leo puts his guitar down and Roxie climbs out from behind the drums to stand behind Alec and Jenna, and I follow, positioning myself behind Alec's back so at least most of the cameras will have an obscured view of my reaction to whatever Alec is going to say.

It'll be about ten seconds, I tell myself. You can handle not killing him for ten seconds.

"Tell us," Tina says. "Is there a limit to how cute you two can be? Because I think there are some cats on the internet who want their titles back."

Alec laughs. "I don't think there is. And there's a reason for that." Then he turns to Jenna, kisses the top of her head, and says into the mic, "Do you want to tell them, or should I?"

The stage suddenly seems unstable beneath me.

Jenna covers less well this time than she did at the concert. "What?"

"Aw." He slings an arm around her waist, pulling her close. "Come on. We can't keep it a secret forever."

I ball my fists. If Alec has finally had it enough to announce she's leaving him in front of all of these people, right before we're supposed to go on tour, I swear the minute we get off this stage I really am going to punch him.

Jenna stutters something unintelligible, no doubt having the same thoughts I am. Alec grins at the Tina. "Jenna and I got

290

married last week. We couldn't stand it anymore, so we eloped."

My heart stops. Jenna looks at Alec, eyes wide, and I see her freezing between Stage Jenna who has to take this all in stride and Real Jenna who just told him to stop interfering in her life. It's like they both have a hold of her, and she's glitching, stuck between the two.

Breathe, I tell myself. But I don't breathe. Instead I grab Alec by the shoulders and shove him past Tina Fey in her glittering silver dress, past the stage mics and taped cords, pushing him as hard as I can right off the goddamn stage and into the audience.

The crowd shrieks and then goes eerily quiet as Alec clatters into the first row of chairs and lands with his head in the lap of Kanye West.

I stare in horror as Kanye's chair tips and someone—is that Taylor Swift?—catches his chair, and the rest of the row scoots backward in this synchronous wave to get out of his way.

And then Alec is rolling off of Kanye and staring up at me and shouting something that might be *what the fuck, man?* But my ears are ringing and I can't hear. In fact, maybe the crowd hasn't gone silent. Maybe my mind is just physically unable to process anything beyond the fact that I just shoved Alec off a stage at the VMAs in front of Tina fucking Fey and Kanye fucking West and the entire rest of the music industry. I stand there, seeing security climbing the stage to get to me. I feel as if I've fallen into *Pagliacci*, an opera about a clown who discovers his wife is cheating on him and murders both her and her lover on stage, right in front of the audience, as if it's all part of the show.

I was wrong. There *was* more we could do on this stage to damage our careers, and as the shock fades, I know I should be sorry.

But *damn* if that didn't feel good.

THIRTY-FOUR

Jenna

When Felix pushes Alec off the stage, everything seems to break down, like the world is frozen in slow motion. Felix's face appears on the big screen, looking stunned, like he hardly meant to do that. Other screens focus on Alec, who is cussing Felix out from the audience.

Everyone is going to know, now. We aren't going to be able to stave off the questions through the tour, and unless I want to lie and say I had no idea Felix had feelings for me, or he was just a friend being protective, we're going to have to tell the truth.

I don't want to lie anymore. I never should have agreed to lie in the first place. And as security steps on stage, headed for Felix, I recognize this as my very last moment to come clean on my own terms.

It's not just about controlling the story. It's about being clear what the story was in the first place. Tina Fey—Tina Fey!—is looking as stunned as the rest of us, and I take that opportunity to grab the mic from her hands, and step forward to stand beside Felix.

"Wait!" I yell.

The security guards pause for a fraction of a second, looking at Tina, who holds up her hand, though she does step warily away from us. I glance over my shoulder and find Roxie and Leo staring at me, their eyes wide.

Leo cracks a smile.

I pull myself up to my full height, such as it is, and start to speak.

"That's enough," I say to Alec. I looks around at the room at all the people, fans and industry professionals. "I can't lie to you all anymore. Alec and I broke up a year ago."

There's a gasp, and the whole crowd seems to go still. "I'm sorry," I say, and I mean it, and not just because we got caught. "I didn't want to disappoint my fans, and I didn't want to lie. We were telling a story about love, and you all loved it so much, and I wanted to keep giving it to you, because I believe in that story, but it's not Alec's and mine."

Tina Fey waves at security to back up—no way does she want to be the host that stops *this*. It's going to be the internet's most watched clip for the next month, and I'm going to be an internet meme for the rest of forever.

But I don't care. Because my mind is echoing the words I just said.

I believe in the story. I said it with such confidence, even though just days ago I'd been so sure I could never believe in that story again. But here's Felix, standing by my side because I asked him to, even though I broke up with him, even though I broke his heart as badly as he broke mine. Here's Felix, still willing to hold me, even though I said I can't trust him, can't allow him to be in my son's life.

Here's Felix, still loving me in a way I never believed anyone could.

If that isn't the story, I don't know what is.

And so I point at him, as all the screens in the room change to show the two of us, standing here together. Felix looks like he's about to be run over by a semi, but he stays rooted to the spot. And while that might be out of sheer terror, I'm still glad he hasn't abandoned me. "It's my story with him," I say.

Tina's eyes widen, and she's looking around for something—probably a mic, because she's clearly lost control of this show, but I'm not finished. "I'm sorry I lied, but I can't do it anymore. And Alec—" I look down at where he's sitting on his ass on a collapsed chair that no longer contains Kanye West and I'm half expecting Yeezy himself to come on the stage and take my mic away from me and say that *Beyoncé* has the greatest love story of all time.

"Alec, you're a dick," I say, and the crowd emits another gasp. "You shouldn't have said that. We are *not* married and saying we were was wrong, and so was the fake surprise engagement, so thanks for that. But I have to be real now, and that means admitting that I'm crazy in love with our cellist."

I think it takes until then for Felix to really process what I'm saying. Or maybe it's that he's staring at Kanye—there he is, standing behind Alec, glaring up at Felix with this mad dog look and very possibly his next single is going to be about this. But Felix finally drags his eyes away from Kanye and looks at me.

I just said I love him. I said it in front of the entire world, considering the broadcast and the number of phones that are no doubt live-streaming as we speak. I open my mouth to ask if he can ever forgive me for not trusting him, and for being so scared that I ran away from this thing I want more than anything else in the world.

But I don't get a chance, because Felix closes the distance between us and cups my face in his hands. He holds my gaze for just a moment, and then he kisses me, and Felix Mays and I are making out in front of Tina Fey and Kanye West and everyone else in the entire world but damn it, the only people who matter to me at this moment are me and him.

I wrap my arms around Felix's neck and hang on tight, clinging to him desperately. The mic cord drapes down his back, because I'm still holding it just as tight, but someone must have handed Tina a mic, because she clears her throat, and we break apart and I have no idea if it's been ten seconds or ten minutes.

Oh. I have to finish this. I turn back to the audience. "To my fans, I love you all, and I hope you'll forgive me. But I need to go spend some quality time with my boyfriend. Goodnight, Los Angeles." And then I drop the mic—I see a sound guy wince—and kiss Felix again, and then security finally drags us off the stage and releases us in the wings, where we hold each other like we're never going to let go.

And I never want to, not ever again.

THIRTY-FIVE

Felix

Offstage, everything becomes a blur. I'm still processing what happened, that Jenna said she loves me in front of everyone, that she accepted me back into her story, and god, that means she believes in it—and *us*—again. Roxie is yelling "Oh my god! Oh my god!" over and over, and Leo grabs both Jenna and me by the shoulder and shouts "We're coming with you guys in the divorce!" Phil herds us all out to our cars and I realize I've forgotten my cello, but Phil is talking right in my ear. "I'll get it. You two need to get out of here before you get mobbed by the press. Shit." He mutters a few more obscenities while security lets us out the back of the parking lot, and Jenna and I are only able to say a few words to each other before we both have to drive away.

"Meet me at home?" she asks, her eyes wide. Pleading.

"Of course," I say. And then she's gone, and I have the drive back to Orange to wonder what the hell just happened.

Jenna said she loves me in front of the whole world, but I'm still an addict with barely two months of sobriety. What happened on stage didn't solve the problems, and worry gnaws at me. She didn't think that through, not really. Will she still want me when things calm down again?

I arrive at Jenna's house just as the babysitter is leaving, and Jenna stands in the doorway, watching me approach. I'm afraid she'll have changed her mind, but she pulls me inside and locks the door and holds me up against the wall so tight that I can't breathe. I don't want to. And even though I realize as she presses against my chest that I'm still wearing the ridiculous sparkling shirt and the enormous silver cross, the imprint of which is now going to be emblazoned in my skin, I want to freeze this moment and not have to deal with anything that comes after.

"I'm sorry," Jenna says. "I shouldn't have given up on us like that."

I gently push her back and look down at her. "No, *I'm* sorry. I shouldn't have kept all that from you. It wasn't fair."

Jenna shakes her head. "But you made a good point. You have to put your sobriety first."

I sigh and knock my head back against the wall. "I do. But addiction thrives in secret. Lying to you is never the best thing for my sobriety, even if I'm scared."

Jenna gives me a sad smile and settles into my arms again. "Will you forgive me?"

"There's nothing to forgive. Can you forgive me?"

She nods against my chest, and then seems to realize herself what I'm wearing and moves the silver cross out of the way. Not that I care about that right now. God, I wouldn't care if I was wearing . . . well, there's actually nothing I can think of worse than these crazy green pants and loud gaping shirt. But it doesn't matter. She forgives me. She loves me. She wants to be with me.

"But I still haven't solved everything," she says softly. "Alec's right. I have issues, and I think it has to do with my past, and with Rachel's death. Are you sure you want to deal with that?"

I run a hand through her hair. I'll deal with anything if it means I can be with her. "I'm still an addict. I always will be, and clearly I have a long way to go toward handling sobriety well. Can you put up with that?"

"I can. Unless you go back to the drugs."

"I won't," I say, and I mean it. I'm sure I'll have more bad days, more cravings, even strong ones. I still have to taper down off the Suboxone in a year or so. I'll always be an addict; that's never going away.

But I can deal with it. I've stayed sober this long, and I can keep making that choice, one day at a time.

Still. "But if I ever did, you are obligated to immediately kick me out. For you and for Ty."

Jenna looks up at me. "I'd have to," she says. "And I would. But I believe you won't do that. I still wish I could be sure, but I know I can't, and I don't want to be away from you while I figure it out."

This is the best news I've ever heard, and I squeeze her, and then guide her into the living room where we collapse on the couch. "Are you sure about this? Are you sure you can trust me with Ty?"

Jenna nods. "I think part of me was using that need to protect him as an excuse, when really I was just afraid of getting hurt." She sighs. "Are you sure you want to put up with me?"

"I'm sure," I say, but part of my brain is panicking. I'm scared that tomorrow she'll learn something else I've left out and I'll lose her all over again. I'm worried this is all temporary, when what I want—what I've always wanted—is to commit to her and have that be real and permanent.

I don't want to say what I'm thinking, but I do want to be honest. But how honest is too honest? Am I just going to push her away again?

I take the coward's way. "How sure are you?" I ask.

Jenna squirms. "If you still have doubts, if you need more time—"

"No," I say. "That's not—" And I know then that the only way to communicate what I'm thinking is to just come out and say it. "I mean, do you still think someday you could marry me?"

Jenna whimpers and puts her hand over her mouth. I feel like an idiot asking her this when she just told me she's still scared to be with me, but her whole body turns toward mine. "Would you really want that?" She sounds . . . hopeful.

The idea that she might cracks my heart open all over again. "More than anything. Do you think you could trust me enough to do that?"

Jenna nods. "If you start using again, I really will have to kick you out. But I don't think it could hurt any more just because we're married."

She sounds almost apologetic about that, and I grip her hand in mine. "Okay," I say, and I'm grinning like an idiot, which still doesn't come close to showing how happy this idea makes me.

"We're going to get married," she says. She doesn't add a *someday* to that, and I'm afraid if I point it out, some bubble is going to burst. But I think she notices, because she adds, "Is that crazy?"

"Yes. But I think I made an enemy of Kanye West tonight, so when it comes to crazy, I'm all in."

She squeals again, and squeezes me tight. The surreal feeling hasn't left, and I wonder if I'm like that guy from the end of *Brazil*, charging through fantasies that are all in my head. But no, I'm here with Jenna, and she's real, and I'm real, and being with her is the most important thing I've ever done in my life.

Of course I want to marry her. For her, so she knows I'm in this. For Ty, so he can have the security of knowing I'm really sticking it out. And for me, to create something stable, a place where I'm safe, so I can keep working on recovery.

"I love you," I say.

She smiles, and is about to respond when her phone beeps. She checks it. "It's Phil." She looks up at me with concern. "He wants to know what the plan is."

"Shit. I have no idea."

Jenna's giggle sounds a little delirious, and I get how she feels. "What do you want?" I ask.

She thinks about that. "I want to be with you."

"You've got that locked in. What else?"

Jenna snuggles up next to me, and it's a long moment before she answers. "I want to be honest. Real. Before I was telling a story, but I was guessing at it. Imagining what it might be like. And I believed, but it was still only a story." She looks at me. "Now I have something real to fight for, and I want to sing about that."

"Well, I'm in, and it sounded like Leo and Roxie are, too. Do you want to try to do the tour?"

Jenna looks panicked. "The tour *next week*? I don't think I can—I mean, without Alec I don't see how—"

"We could see if it could be pushed back a couple weeks. Maybe a month?" I shrug. "The venues might drop us, but they're shitting bricks right now anyway—they'd probably rather have some show, even a delayed one, than none at all. We can have Phil pitch keeping us on, and we can do a different show. A real one."

She blinks at me. "And you want to put this together in a month."

I smile. "It's crazy, right? But it's an option."

Jenna stares into space as if she's overwhelmed at the very prospect. "Alec might beat us to it." She glances at her phone again. "But Phil says the preliminary buzz on the internet is that a lot of fans are siding with me."

"I bet they are, after what Alec pulled." I squint up at the huge light-up marquee letters, A and J. "Do you know where to get those? Because I'd like to get some for Alec. Specifically an F and a U."

"Ha," Jenna says. "I thought you were going to want an F for Felix."

"That's definitely not what that F is for."

Jenna laughs, and then grows serious again. "I have some songs I could polish up. Ones that are more gritty and honest, and didn't fit with the AJ sound. But there's not enough to fill a whole concert."

"We could play some classical. We could do some covers.

And we could tell the real story. *Our* story."

Jenna's face lights up. "That would be amazing. Do you think it's possible?"

"Pitch it to Phil," I say. "It doesn't hurt to try."

Jenna looks down at her phone, but she hesitates. "Are you sure?"

"Yes," I say. "Yes, let's do it. Put together a tour-ready show in three weeks? All while spending plenty of family time with Ty and each other? Sounds totally doable." Jenna laughs, but I mean it, and from the way she's smiling, I know she believes me. "The Jenna Rollins Real Love Tour."

We're both laughing at the enormity of this ridiculousness, but it feels good. It feels right. Neither Jenna nor I are people who do things halfway.

We're in this.

"Okay," Jenna says. "I better not pitch this to Phil over text. I need to call him."

"Go right ahead." I glance toward the stairs. It's late, and Ty is no doubt asleep. "Can I do one thing while you call?"

"What's that?"

"Can I tell Ty?" I ask.

"You want to wake him up?"

"Is that awful?"

"No," she says, smiling. "Go ahead." She taps her phone to call.

I make my way up the stairs and into the doorway of Ty's room. The kid is fast asleep in my old cello case, with his hands across his chest like a vampire, and a blanket wrapped around his legs. I kneel next to the cello case and put a hand on his shoulder.

"Ty?"

It takes him a moment to wake up enough to look up at me. He stretches out, pressing the top of his head to the case. "Felix?"

"Hey, kiddo. I'm back."

Ty sits straight up, his eyes wide and his hair sticking in all directions. "Are you going to be my dad again?"

"Yeah. For real this time. Your mom and I are going to get married. Is that okay with you?"

He nods. "And then you'll be my real dad?"

I don't want to get into the details of the differences between stepdads and real dads, and I'm hoping eventually, once I've proven I can stay sober, Jenna might consider letting me adopt him.

"Yeah. If that's okay with you."

He looks skeptical. "I thought you said some broken things couldn't be fixed."

I smile. "It's true. But it turns out your mom and I aren't one of those things."

Ty throws his arms around my neck and squeezes tight. Jenna appears in the doorway, phone still in her hand, and she looks at us and melts. I smile at her and she smiles at me, and I know.

I am exactly where I'm supposed to be.

ACKNOWLEDGMENTS

There are so many people we'd like to thank for helping make this book a reality. First, our families, especially our incredibly supportive husbands Glen and Drew, and our amazing kids. Thanks also to our writing group, Accidental Erotica, for all the feedback, and particularly to Heather, our first genuine superfan.

Thanks to Michelle of Melissa Williams Design for the fabulous cover, and to our agent extraordinaire, Hannah Ekren, for her love and enthusiasm for these books. Thanks to Dantzel Cherry and Amy Carlin for being proofreading goddesses, and thanks to everyone who read and gave us notes throughout the many drafts of this project—your feedback was invaluable and greatly appreciated.

And a special thanks to you, our readers. We hope you love these characters as much as we do.

Janci Patterson got her start writing contemporary and science fiction young adult novels, and couldn't be happier to now be writing adult romance. She has an MA in creative writing, and lives in Utah with her husband and two adorable kids. When she's not writing she can be found surrounded by dolls, games, and her border collie. She has written collaborative novels with several partners, and is honored to be working on this series with Megan.

Megan Walker lives in Utah with her husband, two kids, and two dogs–all of whom are incredibly supportive of the time she spends writing about romance and crazy Hollywood hijinks. She loves making Barbie dioramas and reading trashy gossip magazines (and, okay, lots of other books and magazines, as well.) She's so excited to be collaborating on this series with Janci. Megan has also written several published fantasy and science-fiction stories under the name Megan Grey.

Find Megan and Janci at www.extraseriesbooks.com

Other Books in the Extra Series

The Extra
The Girlfriend Stage
Everything We Are
The Jenna Rollins Real Love Tour
Starving with the Stars
My Faire Lady
You are the Story
Beauty and the Bassist
Su-Lin's Super-Awesome Casual Dating Plan
Exes, Lies, and Videotape

CPSIA information can be obtained
at www.ICGtesting.com
Printed in the USA
FSHW010502011019
62566FS